Broomielaw

Jim Hewitson

To ease the reader's path through *Broomielaw* you will find a list of the principal characters at the end of the book in the section 'Cast of Migrants and Mariners'.

Broomielaw was first published as a kindle book in 2014.

Published in 2017 by
Moira Brown
Broughty Ferry
Dundee. DD5 2HZ
www.publishkindlebooks4u.co.uk

Layout and cover design: Moira Brown, based Dundee, Scotland.

Cover Illustration: © National Maritime Museum, Greenwich, London.

Foreword

In the summer of 2013 my eldest daughter Lindsey with her boys Innes and Andrew and husband Alan, emigrated to Perth in Western Australia. One day they were in Scotland, the next they were ten thousand miles away at the other end of the world.

For me, at that moment, the sheer immensity of the emigration journey made by many thousand Scots under sail during the 19th century suddenly came sharply into focus.

In the 1990s I wrote two companion volumes cataloguing thousands of stories of Scots emigrants to the United States and Australasia. The bravery, resilience and initiative of these people form perhaps the greatest testimonial to the character of the ordinary Scot and provides the inspiration for the plot of this novel.

A journey that could last months through some of the cruellest seas and the harshest on-board conditions imaginable was undertaken by young, single men and women, as well as entire families, seeking a fresh start Down Under, either in Australia or the distinctively Scottish outposts of New Zealand.

The *Broomielaw* characters are all fictitious but the brave Scots I encountered in family histories, letters and academic works, provide the template for the people who populate my novel. While this is a work of fiction I have tried to portray shipboard life as accurately as possible.

Could we modern Caledonians, like those who left for the new lands in huge numbers in the Victorian era, negotiate this epic journey today? My view is that with the exception of a very small percentage of tough, devil-may-care, self confident and self reliant folk, most of us would struggle. It is a test of moral fibre from another age.

Perhaps the most we should either wish or hope for in these complex days is to share for a few hours in their great adventure and marvel at their fortitude.

Jim Hewitson
Papa Westray, Orkney.   (December, 2014)

Part One – Embarking

1 Memento Mori

At the entrance to the city of the dead a shady, down-at-heel individual, dragging his left foot theatrically as if it was chained to an anchor, sought shelter from the rain beneath a clump of silver birch.

Cloaked, leaning heavily on a stick and with the right side of his face covered by an odd, haun-knittet canvas mask, he watched and waited.

He had already noted that Glasgow's Necropolis was surprisingly full of life that dank, autumn afternoon. There was an odd, funereal bustle about the place.

Three separate burials were taking place almost simultaneously, two on the slope of the hill which overlooks the cathedral, at the east end of the town. Here, large family tombs, true mansions of the departed, and tall ornate gravestones of marble, granite and sandstone, decorated with scatterings of angels, draped urns, death's heads and other chilling memento mori, stud the hillside.

Although the Necropolis had only been open for fifteen years these impressive tombs spoke of the new prosperity of the Clyde valley, of a revolution in industry, of merchants, industrialists, ministers, doctors and scholars who had all made their mark in Victoria's Britain – and the wider world around them.

The third burial was being conducted more modestly on the far side of the hill, a location usually reserved for tradesmen, artisans, shopkeepers and their families. There today, at the conclusion of a largely uneventful life of hard graft and only very occasional heartache, an old man of seventy-two summers was being laid to rest within sight of his tailor's business out by the Gallowgate.

The little knot of mourners gathered around his graveside. Chilling West of Scotland rain, unrelenting all day, drummed steadily on the lid of the rough-hewn coffin as one by one family members and acquaintances tossed handfuls of damp earth into the pit and shuffled off, heads bowed. Discretely in the background, two gravediggers, rain dripping from their hats, leaned on their long spades, waiting. The simple rituals completed, in little groups the mourners bent into the rain and headed down the winding paths towards the wrought-iron gates.

'C'mon along folks, hurry along and let's get in out of this damnable rain,' urged the old minister as he pulled his dark cloak around him and ushered the few neighbours who had bothered to put in an appearance away from the burial site. They hurried down the slippery paths, everyone watching their feet.

By the main gate the vanguard of another funeral party was arriving. This burial looked certain to be a solemn, even stately, affair. Carriages hauled by splendid black horses with fine brasses, black leather blinkers and bedecked with black ostrich plumes, rain dripping from their flanks, were beginning to draw up on the gravel enclosure just beyond the gates.

With his head cocked to one side the stranger beneath the birch carefully scrutinised the mourners leaving the tailor's funeral as they exited the main gate, gingerly side-stepping the puddles which had formed on the gravel concourse. One mourner, manifestly alone in the crowd, taller than most of the other men and without a hat despite the rain, approached. He seemed to carry the weight of the world on his broad shoulders. Seeing his target, the strange gatekeeper emerged from his leafy sanctuary and shuffled forward into the path. The mourner, rain running down his face, looked the stranger up and down suspiciously.

'You again… What IS this all about?'

The apparition spoke: 'Aye, you remember me from yesterday, Gilchrist…and this time you must hear my story. It concerns the death of your brother. I came from the other side of the world to tell your father how his eldest son died – but I was too late'.

He jerked his thumb in the direction of the hill behind them. The previous day the mourner had chased this creepy individual away from the door of his father's business. His presence had disturbed nearby shopkeepers and their customers alike. The man, he was sure, was either looking for money or he was deranged.

'Whatever it is you want, this is damned bad timing. I'm here this day to bury my faither and there are family matters still to be dealt with. Did you say your name?'

'I am called Aaron Malise.'

'Well, Aaron Malise. I canna speak now but I have over an hour before the mail coach leaves the Tron for Edinburgh. I have farewells to make, then I can meet with you briefly in the Saltmarket. I pray for your sake that you have something of real import to tell me about'. They made an arrangement.

*   *   *   *   *

Down in the grid of streets beside the river, the city of the living was quiet that Monday afternoon. The smart coffee houses of the merchant district and the street markets seemed abandoned. Even the cramped Shipbank Tavern, off the Saltmarket, with its gloomy, peeling walls, sawdust strewn floor and high windows held only one or two regulars.

Unofficial headquarters for Glasgow's Irish population it was in this drinking establishment that young men from the Emerald Isle seeking a fresh start by the Clyde were offered sage advice and through a network of contacts based in the bar often found jobs and accommodation.

The mourner who, bare-headed, had braved the rain in the Necropolis ran his fingers through his lank mop of hair and stared blankly at the wall opposite. He had buried his father, taken care of business matters and had been anxious to be on the road home to the Borders. But now he was so stunned and incredulous at the turn of events, at the news which had just been placed before him, that he was considering throwing the table at the wall or leaning over and tearing the mask from the stranger who had brought such disturbing despatches.

His twin brother Robert had been brutally murdered, or so this doubtful individual claimed. He felt that old, aching fury rise in his breast. At least, he thought, his father who was sent on a despairing downward spiral by the death of his son en route to Australia four years previously, had been spared this dreadful suggestion.

'So you're saying, Malise, that you were a crew member on the *Arran Dubh* when my brother Robert was beaten to death and thrown o'erboard; that you were a witness to his killing. Tell me exactly when and how this happened, if you know so much…'

Malise didn't hesitate. He had waited so long to share this story with the dead man's family. The masked man, who bent low over the table, spoke in a husky accent with traces of the Mersey and the Irish bogs and looked angrily out at the world through his one red-rimmed good eye. 'I know you'll have been told that your brother died from diphtheria or something of the sort, but I can assure he was beaten to death – I was there, I saw it. It was four years ago, the 15th of January, 1853.'

The mourner shook his head as if trying the clear his thoughts. The dates fitted. The background checked. To have it suggested now that his bold, beloved brother, his protector in the hardest of times, his role model, had lost his life in such sordid circumstances was difficult to take on board. His eyes filled with tears of disbelief – and anger - as Malise resumed his story.

'Aye, beaten he was, and thrown half-dead into that dark ocean. After a game of cards in which your brother carried all the luck there was a dispute; a good deal of rum had been taken; Robert gave a good account of himself, and left a few of them bruised and bleeding but they were six, including the first mate, and they beat him mercilessly. He didn't stand a chance.'

An old flea-ridden mongrel stretched out by the open fire scratched and, paws under his chin, watched the two strangers.

The loss of his brother Robert had been a hammer blow for the entire family. Robert, such a boisterous, popular young man with an adventurous streak, had set off with hope, filled with ideas, a sort of ambassador for the family in a New World. He had the promise of work as a carpenter in Adelaide. Had he settled there and if things had worked well one or more of his brothers, his cousins from Argyll, perhaps even his father, might have joined him in South Australia.

Tragically though, the first news of Robert after the *Arran Dubh* sailed from Leith was of his death somewhere in the Southern Indian Ocean. In a drawer in the cottage at home the mourner had a brief note from the skipper of the emigrant vessel explaining the circumstances of Robert's death and an addendum from the shipping company expressing regret and sympathy. Apparently a sudden illness, a common enough experience on the emigrant ships, had struck him down and he had been dead within a couple of days, or so the letter said. There was even a death certificate signed by the skipper of the vessel. And diphtheria was indeed mentioned as the 'cause of death'.

Three porters from the nearby market, the stench of fish pungently advertising their trade, swept in from the rain to their favourite drinking howff and greeted the proprietor of the Shipbank. Shaking the damp from their rough cloaks, they ordered ale. They were a noisy, rough and ready trio but friendly enough. His brother Robert, who liked nothing better than a good argument, would have been very much home in their company, the mourner mused. Anger again rose in his breast. He gripped the edge of the shoogly wooden bench and made to rise. In a louder, strident tone he hissed: 'Dammit, Malise, if you were there on the day then you were surely airt and pairt o' this terrible deed. What evidence do I have that you speak the truth?'

The men at the bar turned to see what was unfolding in the corner of the drinking shop. However, disappointed that no immediate action seemed in prospect, they picked up their drinks and resumed their conversation.

The masked man reached out and gently pulled at the sleeve of his companion. 'No sir, please calm yourself. You would do well not to draw attention to us.'

As he spoke he reached into his jacket and produced a gold pocket watch carefully folded in a silk handkerchief which he handed without words to the mourner. In his turn the mourner gazed with astonishment on his brother's timepiece; he had never thought to see it again.

'So, you stood by and saw my brother beaten to death?'

'On my life, I assure you I did what I could - myself and one other. It's true that I was there. The watch fell from Robert's waistcoat on to the deck as he was attacked. I picked it up. I had befriended your brother – he seemed a straightforward, honest sort.'

'For all I know you were one of this gang…'

'No. I suffered at their hands for my failure to participate in that dreadful act, as you can clearly see…' The stranger whipped off the loose mask to reveal a hideously scarred visage, tight, almost transparent, russet flesh and a gaping, empty eye socket. One side of his face had been destroyed.

'Good God, man, cover yourself,' hissed the mourner. Again the porters glanced across, this time their attention was held longer by the damaged face.

'I am haunted by the memory of it. Every day I am tormented, afraid to let people witness these devil's scars. And I still see your brother's last despairing stretch for survival as he was swallowed by that cruel ocean.'

For a moment the speaker paused, as if struggling to relive a traumatic life-changing moment which he had never before been called upon to describe. He seemed to be walking through the experience, step-by-step.

'With your brother over the side they turned on me, poured lamp oil over my head and set me alight. The pain that followed was indescribable.' He hung his sadly mutilated head in seeming despair.

'And your leg – you are lame also as a result of the attack?'

'No, that is merely a device I have adopted to persuade others that I am more vulnerable than I really am…'

Malise collected himself sufficiently to explain how another crewman, by the name of Effort Handler, who had joined him in trying to dissuade the thugs from killing the young Scot, was also beaten and kicked. As a result of that assault Handler was left partially deaf. This man now lived in Greenock, Malise added as an afterthought.

'We were saved by the arrival of the night watch. The others insisted to the watch and the skipper that your brother had slipped overboard during a fight after the card game. And that I had sustained my injuries in the course of the scrap. One of your brother's killers was a cousin of the skipper.'

'That certainly explains the letters and the cover up…' Gilchrist rubbed his face as he tried to absorb this flood of information. His jaw ached. He realised had been grinding his teeth throughout this tale of horror.

Malise was now in full spate: 'I spent the last eleven days of the voyage in the ship's hospital and was well warned that I would never see Adelaide if I spoke of what had actually happened. And I believed they were in earnest. I had seen them despatch your brother.'

'But for God's sake man, why did you not report this. You had a duty to tell the authorities about our Robert…even if you feared for your own life.'

For a moment the scarred seaman appeared to be considering his options. He stared into the middle distance. 'I know, I know. A thousand times I've asked myself that question. But fear paralysed me.'

Then, as if anxious to have the entire story out in the open he threw the last of the dark porter in his glass down his throat and launched into his final revelation.

'You should be aware that I have tracked you down for one reason only. After all this time the law will never call these men to answer for their crimes - neither for your brother's murder nor for my mutilation and Handler's deafness.. That is certain. And I want revenge but I can only do so much…I need your help.'

His companion, his heart still pounding furiously at the thought of his brother's slaying asked: 'Yes, I see all that. But how do I fit into this?'

'I have my sights set on three of them here in Scotland but a ship will sail from the Clyde in a few weeks with the other three bastards who killed your brother and disfigured me amongst the crew. That vessel is by chance the *Broomielaw…*'

The mourner shook his head in disbelief. He realised he would be missing that dinner time coach.

2 The Emigration Agent

Oh God, not again, not here. Walter Lumsden's knuckles whitened as he gripped the wooden rim of the lectern and tried to steady himself.

Way out there, rank upon rank, a sea of eager, upturned faces were terribly transformed into a regiment of spume crested waves, greybeards, South Atlantic giants rolling to the front of the hall; he saw again, with a pain which punched into his soul, the neatly sewn little canvas shroud slipping down, down into the watery abyss.

By some sinister process, faces, dark faces began to materialise from the hazy spindrift, broken-toothed, bone-nosed and the eyes, so bloodshot; angry, terrifying eyes. The sharp stench of raw alcohol filled his nostrils. Walter's hand rose to his face and traced the path of a purple-black scar which ran from the corner of his left eye to below his ear. It throbbed painfully.

These waking dreams were happening more regularly now, when the emigration agent was tired, when the demons which peopled his subconscious were freed to swim to the surface; and tonight he was weary beyond endurance. Nevertheless, swaying as if mesmerised he found, as he had done before, that he could talk himself out of this odd reverie, back to the real world - if he could just keep talking....

As speedily as it had burst upon him, the waking nightmare began to evaporate, as if someone had poured oil on the waters of despair ... the camphor odour of Sunday suits and varnished woodwork, the gas jets hissing inside their engraved globes along the wall, the rasping, smoker's cough from the back of the hall, but most of all the rough tones of his own voice, dragged him back. Monday night – Haddington Burgh Hall. His breathing became less laboured.

The doctor had mentioned overwork. If he only knew... if only it was as simple as that. Certainly Walter had thrown himself passionately into the recruiting drive, hoping that by pushing himself mercilessly to the point of exhaustion, he might somehow forget.

In a strange, detached way, he listened to himself: '... And with suitable irrigation that sort of acreage should produce a worthwhile annual crop. If anyone wants to look over the figures in more detail, I've pinned them to the blackboard. We'll talk about the kind of acreage you'll need for sheep, next time.'

He flicked through his notes, concentrated on clearing his head and finally looked up. 'Well, ladies and gentlemen. That's us for tonight; unless there are any questions? I hope I've convinced you, despite what young Miss McCutcheon there may have heard, the summer sun in South Australia won't actually make your blood boil. Mind you, dealing with some of the government officers in Adelaide might have the same effect!'

The rosy-cheeked lass in the front row hid her face coyly in her hands and the rest of the audience visibly relaxed, as if the school bell had just been rung. No-one seemed to have noticed minutes earlier when the colour drained from Walter's face. He was relieved but looked again at the five empty seats with the name tabs in the second row. Where were the Gilchrists?

'Now, remember, folks. By next week I'll need sight of your signed testimonials and references. Only a few weeks to go. No slacking or I'll set a pack of dingos on your tail.'

Ritual handshakes, pressing of flesh, were next on the agenda before he could finally get the head down for a few hours desperately needed sleep. For Walter this physical contact was one of the most unsettling aspects of the emigration agent's job. Sometimes, as he felt the sinewy grasp of a farm labourer or the gentler handshake of a grocer, teacher or bank clerk, he found he was compelled to look these honest folk straight in the face. Sometimes he sensed their anxious eyes reaching into his soul, searching. Once again this testing time had arrived.

But there were consolations. Tonight the talk had focused on climate and agriculture and Walter felt it had gone well. These were practical people with no time for frivolities. Some of the men from this particular group of prospective emigrants, mostly office workers who couldn't tell the difference between a heifer and a hayrick, had signed up for special courses offered in Edinburgh and Glasgow, everything for the settler from carpentry to basic veterinary medicine, sheep handling to grasshopper control. They would do well in their new home, he was sure. They must do well. He wanted desperately to be sure of that.

Taking off his wire-rimmed reading glasses and walking down the centre aisle Walter tugged at his stiff collar and smiled as enthusiastically as he could, to the right, to the left, in the direction of the family groups and eager young couples. Sometimes he felt he might cave in under the responsibility of what he had taken on. Two boys, the oldest no more than ten, having sat quietly for an hour, were on their feet and jostling each other playfully.

'Come along you two – John, Calum. Behave yourselves or Mr Lumsden will put your names in his wee black book and you'll be swabbing the decks on the *Broomielaw*.'

The boys looked anxiously at the agent for reassurance then quickly at their mother. Her grin eased the tension.

'Ach, they're fine, Mrs Shaw. High spirits – no bad thing in young sailors.'

Walter patted them on the head in turn as the rest of the crowd began to shuffle towards the exit.

'How far is Australia fae here, Mr Lumsden?' It was the older boy.

'It's ages, isn't it Mr Lumsden, further than Edinburgh.' The younger brother puffed out his chest confidently. They both looked up at Walter awaiting his words of wisdom. They were not disappointed.

'Aye, boys – a thousand times further than Edinburgh.' The older lad let out a long, low whistle and they stared wide-eyed at each other as the emigration agent moved on. Dear God, they could have been Euan and Tom, he thought; the same cheeky grins, the tousled hair that defied all combing. He reached the back of the hall but was once again far removed in time and space, returning to the clapboard homestead beside the Hunter River, two years ago. Could it really have been so long?

At the bottom left-hand corner of the notice board by the stairs was the company poster with an illustration of the *Broomielaw* under full sail, dipping splendidly into the swell. The pen and ink drawing was surmounted by the legend in elegant script:

> *Bound for South Australia and Otago – Broomielaw – A Fast New Clipper of the Clutha Immigration Society, 501 tons register, skipper Silas Ratter, First Mate Jack Zurich. Sailing December 1 – Without Fail!*

In smaller print below, the sailing time, available accommodation, catering arrangements and cargo limitations were detailed and at the foot of the advertisement was Walter's spidery signature and an office address in Glasgow's Ingram Street.

The *Broomielaw* was a big, relatively comfortable ship by the standards of the day, built in Aberdeen by the most skilled shipwrights in the North and making only her third run to the other side of the world. She cut a striking sight with her black hull and broad white band around the superstructure. Since Walter had begun his recruitment for the expedition four months previously there had been plenty of interest in sailing with her. Emigration fever was in the air throughout Scotland and the voyage of the *Broomielaw* would probably be the largest single-ship emigration group to leave the Clyde that season. At most there would be a score of cabin passengers, the remainder being assisted emigrants in steerage.

Walter felt physically shattered but comforted himself again with the knowledge that the first phase of his task was almost complete. If only he could be sure he had not overlooked any obstacles, half-submerged reefs which lay in wait, threatening the expedition.

The Clutha Society had a lot to prove after the previous year's disastrous voyage of the *Pomeranian*. There had been food shortages, all sorts of mysterious equipment failures, thirteen deaths from measles among the children, allegations that the skipper had 'dallied' with a widow woman and as a result of horseplay while crossing the Equator, a young woman had drowned. Generally the passage had seriously dented the company's credibility out in the country. Since then they had lost business to the Leith-based Southern Cross Shipping – their principal rivals on the Adelaide run.

Walter knew that much of the responsibility for retrieving their reputation rested with him. He could still scarcely believe that he had been selected as a fully-fledged agent. He had been so nervous that day of the interview he had almost walked out of the Clutha offices in Princes Street, Dunedin. But the company managers had obviously been impressed and the money they were offering for the eighteen-month contract would set him up for a new start.

However, he remained ill at ease. The Clutha Society was notorious for penny-pinching and to get the best skippers you had to pay top rates. He was uncomfortable that crew selection lay entirely in the hands of Silas Ratter. Stories doing the rounds did not inspire confidence. Ratter had been promoted above his abilities, it was hinted.

The man liked a drink and was, by all accounts, a rough example of the old seafaring school. He hadn't touched a drop in two years the Clutha representatives in the West of Scotland had assured Walter.

The emigration agent pulled his jacket closer around him as a gust of sharp air scurried up the flight of stone steps from the street. His landlady had told him that afternoon that he looked as if he had been put through a wringer; the truth was he felt someone was still turning the handle. He glanced briefly at his reflection in the door opposite. He did look worn out, haggard even, more like a man of 60 than 40. And for the first time he noticed how shabby his suit had become. For the past three months he had scarcely had it off his back.

His straggly fair hair, thinning a little on the crown, his bushy eyebrows and clipped moustache – 'rats' tails' Lizzie had called them – all needed attention. Large, pale blue eyes with their peculiar gleam were Walter's most noticeable feature, windows to his soul, yet betraying no clue to his inner torment. He smiled and pumped the hands of the first departures – 'Good night Mr Sinclair, Mrs Sinclair. We'll sort out Jessie's accommodation before the next meeting, don't worry. Have a safe journey back to Dunbar.'

'I know you'll do your best for us, Mr Lumsden. We put our trust in the Lord, but if it disnae sound too blasphemous, you are not far behind.'

Mrs Sinclair, heading out to Otago with her husband, was a severe, matronly, devout lady with a long nose which gave her a slightly superior air. She was quietly intimidating and spoke of trust without a smile. She was, Walter realised, simply spelling out his obligations. But it unsettled him – again.

The Sinclairs – cabin passengers - were taking their servant girl, a lass with dimpled, laughing features in such sharp contrast with her mistress. But the skipper of the *Broomielaw* was insisting she berth with the single, unmarried women aft and the Sinclairs were having none of it. As far as they were concerned Jessie was one of the family. It was just one of a myriad of problems which fell on the lap of the sore-pressed emigration man.

Below, by the light of the twin gas lamps at the door of the hall Walter could see that a light frost was decorating the cobbles. As the would-be emigrants vanished into the night they left a pattern of footprints on the pavement, leading out into the maze of shadowy lanes and alleys around the hall.

A wee, unexpectedly early touch of Scottish winter did no harm to the cause. Not at all. It might be just enough to tip the balance for the last of waverers, thought Walter. They had to make that final commitment by next week's meeting. Despite his moments of distress, it had been a good night's work. Sixty or so folk, fifteen families with perhaps another dozen ready to sign for the December sailing to South Australia and on to Port Chalmers on New Zealand's South Island. But what had happened to the Gilchrists, he wondered.

3 Home Comforts

The handshakes continued. Some brief and to the point, others lingering affairs. By now Walter could have recognised most of these people by their handshake alone. He had come to know each clammy paw, the chill, dry palm, the bony fingers, the nervous trembling grip or the confident Masonic grasp. Long since, he had come to accept this ritual as an important part of the process, sort of expected here in Haddington just as much as it had been in Inverness or Glasgow. After an evening discussing the pitfalls and precautions of the great adventure, the new life, the families and in particular the senior males, appeared to have this need to seek reassurance and commitment through the clasping of hands.

This was a necessary evil for Walter. But sometimes they stood intimidatingly close. He needed that body space in case the questions started to drift – as they often did – towards his own settler experiences. The fear was they might penetrate the mask which screened his grief. He had become adept at steering the conversation back to generalisations. During his six months in Scotland, despite a number of opportunities, he had kept clear of Stirling. He had only an elderly aunt in his home town now but he could not bear to face her on familiar streets. And the questions. There were always questions.

Having said his official farewells at the door, taken the splendidly illustrated emigrant maps by Johnstons of Edinburgh down from the easel on the platform, rolled, tied them neatly and gathered together his papers, Walter spoke in the passing to the hall caretaker. This man was still swithering about joining the expedition. As he began to speak Walter realised that there was scarcely a moment in the day when he wasn't recruiting. 'Six days left, Samuel, then you'll have to sign on the line.' It quickly became clear that the caretaker's decision had already been taken.

'I fear we won't be joining the *Broomielaw*, Mr Lumsden. I've talked a lot wi' Jean but, as I telt ye, her brother was on the *Bannockburn*.' Walter put down his papers. It was worth one more effort to try to persuade the superstitious hall keeper to join the voyage.

'No-one really knows what happened to the *Bannockburn*, Samuel. There was talk of her being top heavy.'

'Aye, maybe so, Mr Lumsden. But the *Broomielaw* is scheduled to leave the Clyde on the first day of December; that's the same date the *Bannockburn* left last year. And I have a bad feeling aboot it.'

Walter found himself becoming exasperated. Probably just the crushing tiredness, he reflected.

'But I've explained to you before, Samuel, the *Broomielaw* is possibly the fastest and certainly the most comfortable ship operating out of the Clyde these days. There's no reason in the world to expect a troubled passage. If you've really set your mind on emigrating then you could do no better.'

'Nae offence, Mr Lumsden, but we're no' ones for tempting fate. Not only that Elspeth has heard stories aboot armies of cockroaches taking over some ships. She terrified o' thae beasties. She was greetin' at the thocht o' it.'

Walter shook his head in resignation and left the caretaker to lock up, heading out into the night through deserted streets, past shuttered shops and the Mercat Cross to his lodgings by St Mary's. Haddington had a splendid air of history and quiet permanence about it. Yet it was small enough to feel you could belong. That was the biggest problem with Australia, trying to convey its sheer enormity and its empty spaces. New Zealand on the other hand, although equally impressive, was of a more manageable scale, like Scotland in so many ways.

*   *   *   *   *

The fresh air had revitalised Walter a little and, as he'd requested, his landlady had organised a pot of tea, bread and cold meat, laid out for him in the drawing room. Walter sat in a golden pool of dancing firelight and read by the soft glow of an oil lamp which Mrs Bonthrone had set at his elbow.

The emigration agent ate slowly, methodically, chewing carefully, stopping every few minutes to pick up the folded copy of the Scotsman newspaper, which he had balanced against the milk jug, to turn a page - continued expansion of the rail network, the appointment of the First Secretary of State for troubled India, growing anxiety over safety in Scottish collieries. He lingered for a moment over the story of a wee lass in Perth jailed for six months for concealing her pregnancy. For a moment he wondered what had become of the baby. Children were now a part of someone else's world.

With the landlady scurrying backwards and forwards from the kitchen and busying herself among the dark furniture, straightening antimacassars and generally fussing, Walter now scanned with professional interest the sailings list, clippers, barques, brigs and schooners, an armada of vessels from Greenock, Leith, Dundee and Aberdeen, offering passage to North America and the new lands in the Antipodes.

The volume of emigrants bidding Britain farewell that autumn was remarkable. At the last count there were thirty emigration agents like Walter operating around Scotland – each with their own special sales pitch. He had encountered a few of them on his travels and generally thought them a shifty bunch. Each was trying to entice people to the colonies with offers of unlimited opportunity; the competition to take them to the promised lands was fierce.

Walter had settled comfortably into the sofa and closed his eyes luxuriously, feeling the warmth on his cheeks as the coal fire did its work.

'As I was saying this morning, I had a letter from my sister in Port Adelaide, Mr Lumsden. You remember, she travelled with the *Oceania*.'

The landlady was a buxom widow of about 55 years who had made it clear four months previously on Walter's first visit that a stone pig was not all she had been prepared to warm the bed with. She stood behind the emigration agent and bent forward, her enormous fleshy bosom resting against his head. She gently massaged his temple with her forefingers. A button on her dress pinged his ear lobe and she apologised.

'My, my, yer tense tonight Mr Lumsden. Aye, as I was saying…Mima says she's finding Adelaide too warm and they're talking of moving on to New Zealand.'

Her fingers worked in a circular motion and it was as if a gentle, radiating warmth flowed from the fingertips into his scalp. For a moment Walter remembered the burning heat of summer in New South Wales, there in the rough fields which they had carved out of the land, there beside the Hunter River. He and Lizzie would never have let the weather beat them. Never. Yes, if heat had been their only problem…

'We could try again if you've a mind tae, Mr Lumsden. You were maybe a wee bit o'er tired yon last time. You know, with a' the worries ye have. I have a few tricks in my satchel to tease tired flesh into life.'

Walter didn't doubt it for a moment. 'No, thank you, I don't think so Mrs Bonthrone, I mean Esther. No, it truly has been an exhausting day.' The landlady sighed a sigh of resignation and, Walter thought, of disappointment also. He made his apologies again and was off down the creaking corridor in the direction of his room wondering why Mrs Bonthrone hadn't re-married. Apart from her other talents, she was a marvellous cook.

Having arranged to be called early so that he could catch the first Edinburgh train Walter seated himself on his bed and spread his papers, travel warrants, family profiles and sketches of the on board accommodation across the quilt and looked around. Although Mrs Bonthrone had no full-time residents, the house had a comfortable, lived-in feel. He smiled as he noted the outline of the stone bedwarmer already in place between the sheets. Walter had almost forgotten what it was like to be somewhere that felt like home and to be fussed over just a little.

A month or so, thirty-five days to be exact, and the *Broomielaw* would be catching a breeze at the Tail of the Bank, saying farewell to the Clyde, heading out past Arran for the Atlantic and the first leg of the incredible journey to Australia and New Zealand. Walter had a firm commitment from over 200 people across the country and with just fifty berths to fill he was unlikely to have to offer last minute incentives to waverers. And when the clipper sailed Walter would be among his emigrants, leaving the Clyde for the second time. This long contract would surely allow him to buy that land on the Clutha and – God willing – some peace of mind.

But what had happened to the Gilchrists? James and Maggie had been among the first folk in the Lothians to approach him, choked at first, like the rest, with doubt and wonder at the prospect of setting in motion such a great upheaval in their lives, but with that familiar excitement already dancing in their eyes. Walter had taken to them immediately, from the moment they had appeared, standing nervously at the rear of his introductory Haddington meeting, sporting their best togs and trying hard to absorb the tidal wave of facts and figures.

Well, at least to Maggie and her girls. James, the brawny shepherd said little. He was clearly a moody individual, but seemed honest and that was surely enough. It was Maggie Gilchrist, the fresh-faced wife and mother with her bright, intelligent smile, auburn curls, high cheekbones and a memorable, ringing laugh, who clearly ran the show. An attractive woman of thirty-five or so, she could giggle like an adolescent with her three bonny daughters, yet gave the distinct impression of wordly wisdom. Lumsden sensed there was a tough streak in the woman, lying just beneath the surface.

He could never forget the way she had glared at a poor clerk who had mistakingly planked himself down in their seats. What a glare! What a woman! Walter also guessed, by the way her daughters, two already in their teens, fussed over her, that she was pregnant again. This realisation had provoked the strangest of emotions in Walter. It was a kind of chilly dismay.

But where were they? Their absence tonight had perplexed and worried him. Perhaps they had decided, after all, to take passage on the *Corinth* in the spring rather than join the *Broomielaw*. Walter wanted every last piece of the jigsaw to fit correctly, all the faces to be where they should be, where he wanted them to be. So before he climbed into bed he sat at the walnut writing desk, thought for a moment as he watched the snow pile up on the window ledge, then scratched a few sentences, addressing the letter to Gilchrist, c/o Sweetshaws Farm Cottages, Ferniecleugh, by Garvald.

Walter breathed more easily after appending his signature. He couldn't let the Gilchrists slip out of his grasp – not at this late stage in the proceedings. It was a woman's face that crowded his thoughts as he sank off into a dark, dreamless sleep. It was his darling Lizzie, surely. Ah, but those high cheekbones…

4 The Theatre Fire

Glasgow's popular palace of fun, the Adelphi music hall, was well alight and Napoleon had stopped breathing. Tongues of flame were sneaking across the stage towards the little emperor huddled in his greatcoat beneath a collapsed backboard depicting a devastated farmyard on the battlefield of Waterloo.

From offstage, having ushered the rest of his company to the stage door, out of the turmoil and confusion behind the scenes, a great hulk of a man bounced across the boards and vaulted the imitation cannon. The front end of Napoleon's off-white horse, dodging falling debris and galloping offstage tried to intercept the big man:

'The roof's coming down, Hamish. Forget the tin man. Run for your life!'

Oblivious to the warning and the blast of heat from the igniting curtain, one arm shielding his face, the big man threw off a cautionary hoof which had been laid on his shoulder, dived forward and began to drag toppled scenery to one side. Beneath the pile of canvas and wood, flame licked around Napoleon's sad, waxy face.

Hamish Mhor McGrimmen ignored a final burst of sidestage advice from the half-horse as he worked to free the emperor, trying to assess the damage as he went. Hamish was certain that the beam across Nappy's chest had done untold damage, his respiratory mechanism would be scrap metal and the automaton's left arm was bent up behind his back in a most distressing manner.

As he worked he tried to shut out the cries and the curses of stragglers among the audience who were scrambling over each other in their haste to escape the fume-filled auditorium. How cruel it would be if the company was devastated on the eve of their departure on the Broomielaw for a new life in Australia, he thought.

Outside in Cochrane Street a light drizzle had begun to drift in from the river and a vast, noisy throng – a mix of wild-eyed escapees from the theatre, patting each other on the back, and excited passers-by, had gathered, spilling off the pavements, jostling and shouting at each other and blocking the thoroughfare. There were smartly dressed diners from restaurants along the way, buxom washer wives, tramps, carters, courting couples and gangs of snotty-nosed weans sizing up the onlookers in preparation for dipping their pockets. The street kids knew that such a crowd-drawing catastrophe could be as profitable as a week patrolling the stalls at Paddy's Market.

Scarlet-collared police officers tried in vain to control the multitude, pushing at the throng with their truncheons and staring meanly at the front rankers who refused to budge.

The engine men were already on the scene, running out their hoses from two water carts which, dragged by huge black Clydesdale horses, had clattered over the cobbles and on to the scene, parting the onlookers like a bow wave as they drew to a halt immediately in front of the Adelphi. Those who had chased after the carts to the scene along Argyle Street helped swell the crowds to numbers more associated with public hangings down the Saltmarket.

Fires were commonplace in the great industrial city of Glasgow in the mid-1800s but the threatened destruction of a theatre was something different. Somehow there was a feeling among the throng that unlike the tinderbox tenements crowding in around the filthy vennels, these vast public buildings of clean, grey sandstone with their tall columns and elegant porticos, should be immune to such infernos.

At first only a misty vapour issued from the front of the Adelphi, caressing the elegant, stiff-robed statues of the Muses ranged along the first floor parapet as it went, drifting off across the soot-stained rooftops on the light north-westerly breeze. But as the reek of burning wood floated across the scene and the smoke became denser, spiralling up into the evening sky, the first lurid jet of flame appeared at the windows. As glass cracked behind them the Muses stared their cold marble stare. Below, the crowd gasped and pointed – and the pump men redoubled their efforts.

'He'll be okay, Conchita, don't you fret so. Hamish knows how to look after himself. He's as anxious to be on that boat as everyone else. He won't take any unreasonable risks.'

The strangest couple in Glasgow – a little lady, no more than three feet in height and a thin, scaly individual with crocodile patches beneath both eyes, more like an amphibian than a man, pushed their way to the front of crowd. The tiny woman, dressed in a dark Spanish gown, mantilla and shiny black dance shoes, looked up at her tall companion.

'Lift me up, Eales. Up there. So that I can see what's happening.' She pointed to his shoulder.

Obediently he swung her up in a wide arc as if she weighed no more than a feather. Having reached her bony vantage point she surveyed the activity, the bobbing heads, the hoses snaking into the building and the exertions of the engine men as they worked the pumps. Water sprayed from dozens of faulty hose joints and pin prick punctures and flowed around the feet of firefighters and onlookers. It was as if a Spring tide was spilling along Cochrane Street.

'He wouldn't do anything daft, would he, Eales?'

'You know Hamish as well as I do, Conchita, he wouldn't take on a job he didn't think he could finish it.' She sighed and bit her lip nervously. Conchita was not reassured.

'That damned automaton. Sometimes I wonder if Hamish cares more for that collection of nuts and bolts than he does for us,' she muttered beneath her breath.

Inside the theatre Hamish had reached his goal. He laid hands on his emperor. With muscles like the craggy rocks of Lochaber and wild straggle of ginger hair on top of a frame nearer seven feet than six, the West Highlander looked like a man made for such dangerous moments. He reached in and grabbed the emperor.

Wasn't he, Hamish, the Samson, the legendary figure, who in 1850 held up the lintel of the collapsing kirk at Kinlochewe on his back, carrying that unimaginable weight for four minutes to allow scores of worshippers to escape after the building was struck by lightning. Truth to tell, he was the same terrified man who had actually set off to abandon the old folk and the wee ones to ensure his own escape, to save his own hide, only to find that fate saw the lintel sag just as he passed beneath. How destiny can shape heroes. How small the margin between glory and disgrace.

By now, inside the theatre, burning debris was falling all around, strips of flaming curtain material danced crazily in front of him in the back draft, like the crimson and gold sails of some Norse funeral longship. For one breath-stopping moment the scenery which had remained upright teetered and looked set to topple on him. Pockets of fire were catching hold independently across the stage; it was time to move.

Finally Hamish was able to hoist the little commander on to his shoulder and stagger to safety, the ferocity of the blaze had scorched his hands and he knew for certain that he had lost his pride and joy, his bushy ginger eyebrows.

*   *   *   *   *

Newspapers in the city the following morning graphically recorded the destruction of the Adelphi. By some miracle no-one had been killed but a score of theatregoers and performers were in hospital. The fire had started offstage while Hamish's Circus Caledonia were in the midst of their 'Battles that Changed History' set, some of the pyrotechnics used to give authenticity to the battle scene having set fire to a backdrop.

While the journals carried many stories of bravery, casualty lists and eyewitness reports from theatre-goers, the rescue of the little emperor went unreported. In their lodgings in London Road, after inspecting the automaton, Hamish came to the conclusion that Napoleon was one member of the Circus Caledonia who would not be making the great journey to the other side of the world.

5 Hauling in the Catch

Earlier on the day of the Adelphi fire, eighty miles away, among the hills of Argyllshire, Elijah Shade stood by a bay window and watched the deep, metallic grey waters of Loch Fyne shimmer in the last slanting rays of the surprisingly warm October sunshine.

Above the meadow a hawk hovered in the afternoon air, almost motionless, silhouetted against the shoulder of the mountain, its quarry finally, irrevocably, targeted. Clouds had cleared from the summits away to the east.

It was sobering, even at this stage in the game, reflected Shade, to think that once events ran their course he would probably never be able to return to this ancient land. Such scenes would be lost to him forever. Aye, a loss, but the reward, ah, the reward. He tugged thoughtfully at his ear lobe.

Shade's bulk filled the frame of the window and for a man with hands like bear's paws, he sipped with a strange delicacy at a dainty square-based Prussian tea cup. Leaning his considerable weight against the window jamb, he strained to watch through the trees as a russet-sailed herring boat approached the jetty below, its day's work complete. His own 'fishing' expedition in these waters, he reminded himself, dabbing at his mouth with the embroidered napkin and returning his cup to the table, was fast nearing completion.

Braeside was the finest mansion in Tarbert, eight or nine rooms he guessed, a stable block and sloping lawns at the end of a steep gravel driveway, all set above a fold of the hills directly behind the town. It afforded spectacular views away to the south, towards the Sound of Bute and the Clyde estuary with the intimidating vastness of the ocean beckoning deceitfully beyond.

Shade had targeted Braeside soon after his arrival when he discovered that the occupant was Mrs Constance Meek, lonely soul, generous benefactor of the kirk of St James, widow of Malcolm Meek, stonemason and quarry master. Over forty years, from the vast quarry at Crarae, Malcolm Meek had supplied thousands of tons of grey, dignified stone for the public buildings, banks, offices and theatres which were helping to transform Glasgow into one of Queen Victoria's great industrial cities.

Mr Meek had been dead these three years and living with only her maid, housekeeper and West Highland terrier, the widow regarded a visit from a representative of the kirk as the perfect excuse to look out her best china. Word in the town was that when she sold the stone business on her husband's death Mrs Meek had converted most of her capital into jewellery. That evening the visitor had seen the evidence for himself. The jewel box, with its cargo of riches, lay in the centre of the table.

Now Shade was running his fingers through his grey beard and eyeing a display of porcelain figurines in an open-fronted display cabinet. In particular he admired the beautiful depiction of the dancing water nymph, frozen in mid-step, her diaphanous shift draped revealingly around her beautifully crafted body. Discretely Shade ran his forefinger down her delicate spine and over her tiny lilywhite buttocks.

'You'll have a top up, Rev. Shade. There's still some tea in the pot. And another wee scone?'

Shade turned quickly, patted his ample gut and shook his head.

'No, I won't Mistress Meek. Still a couple of calls to make this evening then I'll have to look in on Mr Morrison. He's none too great, I fear. Very confused.'

Beneath the table the terrier scuffled annoyingly and persistently at his shoe laces. Shade directed a well-placed but subtle kick at the animal's ribs. It squealed and sprinted for sanctuary beneath the long sideboard.

'Naughty boy, don't you go annoying Mr Shade, Lachie. I've had so little chance to chat with you like this Rev. since you arrived at St James's. You always seem so busy with your visiting.'

The widow Meek took his cup and walked to the ornate fireplace with its carved classical themes, the most stunning – Neptune bursting from the waves, a huge, ugly fish impaled on his trident. Shade liked that powerful piece of work.

Mrs Meek hauled on the scarlet bell pull. Somewhere at the back of the house there was a distant jangle.

'Just to come back for a minute to our arrangement, Mrs Meek...' Shade halted in mid-sentence as the maid arrived and slowly, delicately and deliberately, obviously aware that she was being watched, collected the cups, saucers and the plate of home bakes on her silver tray before dipping politely and heading for the drawing room door. As she left she discharged a coy smile in the direction of the house guest.

'That's a fine efficient lass you have there, Mrs Meek. She fairly brightens up this grey October eve.'

Constance Meek carefully scooped a forgotten crumb from the corner of her walnut dining room table into her napkin.

'Yes, Anne Dagger has been the best maid I've had since Malcolm died – a fine, respectable girl.'

She turned to look lovingly at the portrait of her husband which hung above the crackling fire. Shade frankly thought he looked a hard bastard with eyes like cold granite, as rugged as the stone he'd quarried.

'But I'll have to start looking for a replacement,' continued Mistress Meek. 'She's handed in her notice. Off on some adventure or other. You know what young folk are like these days.' Elijah Shade could just imagine the sort of adventures in which young Miss Dagger would become involved. But oh, that slim, elegant neck – soft as swan's down, smooth as ice.

But for the moment there were more important matters to confirm, Shade reminded himself.

'I would guess that I should be able to get the final valuation by early December – my contact, the gentleman from London I mentioned, comes north soon. And rest assured, your decision to bequeath the jewels to the kirk will remain a secret between ourselves. Meantime I will seek this provisional valuation in Glasgow. It is an extraordinarily generous gesture you are making, Mrs Meek.'

'It is you I have to thank again, Mr Shade. First of all for suggesting the bequest and the valuation and secondly for being such a pillar of strength during the Rev. Morrison's unfortunate incapacity; I know the entire Kirk Session is grateful to you.'

Shade's gaze ranged around the drawing room. Some better than average Highland landscapes, a few pieces of silver plate which in different circumstances...a Chinese vase. Alas, none of this would fit into his carpet bag.

'Yes, the Lord certainly works in wonderful and mysterious ways, Mistress Meek, landing me at the door of St James's precisely at their greatest time of need. I was a ship lost in a storm. But now I've come safe to port.'

'Providential, that's what it was, Mr Shade.' The widow raised her eyes heavenwards. Shade had to agree. The local Presbytery had been at their wits end trying to find an assistant for the aged and ailing Morrison and his brandy-ravaged liver. There were only too happy to find the Rev. Elijah Shade in the community. Shade's explanation of how he just happened to be visiting the archaeological sites of Argyll, was staying in the Imperial Hotel and had been ordained into the Presbytery of New

South Wales the previous year but was currently without a charge, was cheerfully, eagerly accepted. They saw him quite literally as a Godsend.

This last flash of improvisation about his Antipodean ordination had given sufficient breathing space. His plan would be completed before any exchange of letters with church officials in the colony, which took fully six months, could be organised. It was ample time.

Now that Mrs Meek had agreed to part temporarily, or so she thought, with most of her impressive collections of rings, pendants, bracelets and earrings, his carefully constructed confidence trick was nearing its conclusion. Mrs Meek walked with her guest to the front door.

'Forty-eight hours at most. That's all the time I'll need in Glasgow. Pity the jeweller couldn't have come up here with the coach but, as you can imagine, he's a busy man. I'll have your jewels valued and back here before you know it.'

'The world would a better, more benevolent place Mr Shade, if there were more folk like yourself around prepared to give of their time and energy to help others.'

Shade coughed. Not from embarrassment but as if he was trying to stifle a giggle. 'Kind, so very kind of you to say so, ma'am.'

Five minutes later Shade sauntered along the waterfront towards the manse where he knew old Morrison would still be abed, groaning and complaining, the saliva trickling from the corner of his mouth, the bedclothes soiled as likely as not. It would be a pleasure to leave that sack of misery behind him in Argyll, thought Shade.

He noted with satisfaction as he reached the harbour front that his wish list of 'donors' was now complete. The McLintock sisters, old Mrs Topham down at Furnace, Miss Bathgate, the spinster proprietrix of the Imperial Hotel and now the crowning glory, Mrs Meek, her Ali Baba box filled to overflowing with sparkling delights. Every one of them sworn to secrecy – a clutch of little conspiracies in which the women seemed to take delight. In a little while they would be smiling on the other side of their faces, Shade mused.

He doffed his hat to the fishermen who were heading with quiet determination for the back bar of the Imperial.

To complete his perfect day Shade had also received, that morning, the registered packet from Leith. An envelope stuffed with high denomination bank notes – the first instalment of his fee for forthcoming *maritime duties*; that was how the strictly verbal contract had been described. He chuckled to himself. A few months from now he would be collecting the balance in Adelaide and heading for the United States with a new name, to disappear for ever.

As he pushed the manse door shut to be met by the familiar choking mustiness, a combination of stale urine and inches of dust, a croaky voice issued from the bedroom at the top of the stairs.

'That you, Shade? A glass of water, if you please... I was wondering where you had got to.'

Let the auld bugger wait, thought Shade, pouring himself a port in the drawing room and reflecting how his sessions of spiritual guidance with the younger matrons around the town would soon have to come to a dignified conclusion. He also wondered how he could get his hands and other pieces of his anatomy on Anne Dagger before they went their separate ways.

6 The Wanderers

Days of freakishly warm rain had made the two-mile trek towards the head of the valley, beneath the sombre shoulder of Ward Hill, wearisome. Each step was a muddy trial that morning for shepherd James Gilchrist of the farm of Sweetshaws. Like his wandering sheep, his thoughts were running away from him.

He still found the situation infuriating and incomprehensible: How could Brocklebank refuse to free him from his contract so late in the day? As he walked his heart thudded against his breastbone and he found his fists were tightly clenched.

Months ago when emigration had been first mentioned the estate factor had promised, guaranteed, in fact, that the shepherd would be released from his employment in the autumn. And yes, of course they could still go in the spring, but crucially, not on the *Broomielaw*.

Gilchrist had pleaded, cajoled even threatened but it had been to no avail.

Following the sheep trail which tracked the burn, the heavily-built young man trudged onwards, eyes always on the hoof prints danced on through the glaur, up the glen. He tugged at the collar of his shirt. For October it was so clammy, warm even. It was almost unheard of. A bad omen, that's what it was.

As he climbed, the track beside the Ward Water seemed cloaked in a grey, sombre light; the shepherd had counted the bulk of the flock sheltering among the copse of alder trees by the old steading of Dukeston. However, several were still unaccounted for. He cursed under his breath, again and again. Gilchrist was furious – and frustrated - in equal measure.

A few paces ahead his Border collie Gip picked her way effortlessly along the bank leaping from stone to tussock, avoiding the deepest of the puddles. James followed. Every so often the dog would turn anxiously to regard her master, as if sensing his ill temper.

Almost all the arrangements for them to join the *Broomielaw* had been in place. Ironically, that very week James had lodged a copy of their last will and testament with McGloags, the solicitors in Haddington. He had even booked the coach to take their baggage and boxes to the station. They had all been to the doctor for a final check and Maggie's worries about Hilda, a thin, delicate child, evaporated when Dr Swanson pinched the girl playfully on the cheek and smilingly announced: 'She'll stand the voyage alright.'

Brocklebank, the estate factor, a scrawny weed of a man, had looked so self-satisfied as he broke the news at that morning's breakfast-time interview. He left James speechless. The shepherd knew he lacked the eloquence to deal with such a stressful moment. Words did not come easily. Responses would be stilted. Normally Maggie did his talking. He could have physically threatened the factor but the wee man held all the big cards. Brocklebank warned that he would withhold his severance money and through his Lordship's contacts in the Antipodes he would make sure that he never found employment as a shepherd in their new home if the family simply took off.

'Believe me Gilchrist, if there was any other way... but with auld Renfrew taken bad with his chest, I'll never get an experienced hill shepherd at such short notice. In any case, his Lordship has made up his mind that you must stay. No, I have to hold you to our original agreement. You can leave in the summer after the lambing, if you're still so minded.'

But they had to be on that ship, James Gilchrist told himself. Since the day of his father's funeral the *Broomielaw* simply had to be the means of transport to their new home. There was no alternative. He owed it his brother. His dear brother. In the pocket of his waistcoat he fingered the note which Aaron Malise had left him - a note which contained the names of the three remaining seamen responsible for his brother's death. Nothing could stand in his way. Beyond the quest for revenge lay the nebulous prospect of a new life in New Zealand. Whatever, this voyage was their destiny, he told himself.

Lost in these unsettling reflections, fed by his simmering anger, Gilchrist was suddenly aware of movement in the lee of the roofless croft up ahead. He peered through the strange light. Hoof prints he had been tracking certainly led that way. He veered away from the burn and pressed on up the slope, bending into the strengthening breeze. The rainclouds above the hill parted momentarily and weak, apologetic sunshine spilled across the floor of the valley; the sheep were there right enough, half-a-dozen ewes, tucked in against the half-collapsed dyke of an abandoned vegetable garden.

They scarcely noted the shepherd's progress but through the tumbled stones watched every dart and twist Gip made as she neared her quarry, circling in preparation for driving them back down the valley, back to the security of the flock and more familiar surroundings.

Just then a tall figure appeared round the end of the house. Ignoring the chill breeze which was rolling down over the bracken, May Gilchrist hauled off her dampened tammy and waved it enthusiastically in her father's direction.

'They're all here, faither. Auld Kirstie led them away.'

She bent and threw her arms round the neck of an old ewe who nibbled the grass slightly apart from the little flock. The sheep stood her ground, completely untroubled by this display of affection. It seemed that even Gilchrist's skills with the sheep were being overtaken by what he called his 'regiment of women'.

May was a natural with the animals. She would make a farmer a fine wife, thought Gilchrist. She wasn't his child but he was proud of this girl he now called his daughter. She would do away fine in New Zealand no matter what the journey ahead might bring. He felt reassured by that, but eating away at him was the stark reality that Brocklebank had thrown all his careful planning, his quest to avenge his beloved brother and his belated acceptance of a new life in the Antipodes, into jeopardy.

Gilchrist pushed open the creaking gate which lay half off its hinges and entered the garden, a place where flowers once flourished but which had been left to the docks and the dandelions.

'Aye, she's a pure devil for wandering that one. A mind o' her own and no mistake,' said the shepherd. As Gip lay on duty beyond the gate Gilchrist and his daughter ca'd the flock out on to the hill slope. Just then, in the corner of the enclosure he spotted another ewe, a youngster this time, frantically trying to get to her feet, in an effort to scramble off after the flock. But she collapsed in a heap.

She must have been trapped, Gilchrist realised, among the rusty, weed-covered agricultural equipment which lay scattered around the yard and it was immediately obvious that in the frenzy to pull herself clear she had hurt her front legs. Up close the injuries were clearly severe, both legs were broken, ligaments probably torn asunder, bone protruded in several places. Her breathing was laboured and she had a wild, pained look in her eyes.

Gilchrist knew immediately what he had to do – there was no betterment for her. He fumbled for the blade in his pooch then shouted across to his daughter: 'May, take the dog and run the sheep down to the burn. I'll follow you once I've done what's needed here.' The girl and the collie disappeared over the lea. He returned the blade to his pooch.

This was a tough duty which a hill shepherd occasionally had to perform. But today Gilchrist left the blade in his pocket. His heart was thumping in his chest. His head was aching. The unspeakable fury he had felt on staring into Brocklebank's smug, pock-marked face roared inside him again. He clenched his teeth and lifted a boulder from the dyke. The ewe lay peacefully now almost as if she knew the struggle was over. Angrily, violently, he brought the stone down on her skull, once, twice three times. As his fury slowly dissipated he gasped for air, not realising that he had been holding his breath throughout the execution. As the animal's muscle spasms subsided he swung the corpse across his broad shoulders and walked off to join his daughter by the burn.

Was he capable dealing out justice on behalf of his brother? He had never doubted it for a moment.

7 The Ultimatum

By the time he had returned from the hill two hours later Gilchrist had unsuccessfully run around his mind a hundred ways of trying to force Brocklebank into a change of mind. Now he had to find a form of words to break the news to Maggie and to the old battleaxe, her aunt. As he splashed across the yard he had still no idea how to broach the subject.

May headed off round the back of the steading to feed the chickens. Flora was over at Crosskirk where she worked as a kitchen maid and Hilda would be perched like a little bird on the front bench of the single classroom school at the foot of the brae.

Maggie's Aunt Agnes, now in her seventy-second year, was seated by the fire which burned brightly to combat the early edge of winter in the Border hills. She lifted the poker occasionally to stir the coals into new life. Maggie had been baking and was stacking drop scones on a china plate on the table. The room was stone-flagged and sparsely furnished, the main feature being the table at which Maggie worked. Walls and fireside were whitewashed and the light from the fire highlighted the crockery which lay unpacked on the dresser. The window was crowded with flowerpots, fuchsias and geraniums.

At the outer door James Gilchrist kicked off his boots and walked to the fire where he crouched and pushed back the iron frame from which the kettle hung.

'There's a ewe in the shed needing butched. I brocht her down fae the hill.' There no response from the two women.

Gilchrist thrust his hands towards the warmth of the coals in the grate. The kettle whistled gently and as if on cue James simply blurted out the whole sad story of that morning's interview, drawing to a halt with: 'So that's it. I'm still racking my brains but can find no solution. Ah'll have tae contact Mr Lumsden.'

The clunky ticking of the old wall clock, an occasional crackling from the grate and the wind sighing down the passageway between the house and the outbuildings were, for what seemed an eternity, the only sounds in the cosy kitchen.

Over the weeks and months after that first public meeting, it was Maggie who began to devour Lumsden's literature, who spent an hour or two in the library each market day and when, after his father's death, James began to show a sudden grim determination to make the break from Scotland, she had been quietly delighted.

Gradually it seemed to Maggie that at last they had both become convinced that the voyage south was the Gilchrist destiny. In the small hours which God intended for sleep Maggie would be found by the fireside rustling papers and studying the emigration pamphlets.

James Gilchrist was only too aware that since the day she arrived at Ferniecleugh, from the feeing market at Kelso, clutching baby May to her breast, Maggie had never really settled. Theirs was a strange relationship. Even after their courtship and eventual marriage she had been unwilling, or unable, to strike up a real friendship with any of the neighbours in the row of humble farm cottages.

Instinctively these women seemed to sense that Maggie was different. Gossip fuelled stories of her earlier life and her time in Edinburgh. The truth is that most of the countryfolk couldn't even begin to imagine the harsh realities of Maggie's sojourn in the capital. For her part the wife of Sweetshaws, seeing the women forever carrying buckets of water, feeding the hens or the pigs, black-leading the grate, rubbing, scrubbing, baking and mending, had swiftly decided that this would not be the life for her girls. She wanted more for them, much more. And she made sure James knew.

Her sister-in-law Elspeth, James's little sister, had settled well enough in Otago on New Zealand's South Island but since the loss of her husband, needed family around her. It was their duty to meet that need and an unstoppable urge to escape began to overtake Maggie. In those early days Gilchrist was privately

33

convinced that the emigration man had somehow bewitched his wife but when events had moved in such an unexpected direction after the funeral in Glasgow he had joined in the planning with undisguised interest.

Now Maggie's silence, as she selected vegetables one by one from the basket at her feet and laid them neatly on the chopping board, unnerved him. Auld Agnes, who usually liked to chip in with her halfpenny's worth, sat straight-backed, silent and seemingly busy with her sewing, humming gently to herself. Clearly she thought it a time to keep her counsel to herself – the pot was boiling well enough.

Rather than be left behind with her cousins in Melrose, she had agreed to travel. Her verdict had been that if they were determined to be killed, cooked and eaten on this Antipodean adventure she might as well be with them. The way the old biddy always seemed to get her own way, it might be the savages who would end up on the menu, James Gilchrist had often reflected.

'Well, say something for God's sake, wife.' Gilchrist was exasperated. The wind threw a another shower at the kitchen window and Maggie began to slice the carrots with more vigour, the clicking knife answering the call of the big, hissing kettle at the back of the fire.

'Will ye no' speak, woman?'

Maggie, the soup forgotten, wiped her hands on her pinny and turned to face her husband who stood with his back to the fire trying to look steely and determined. For a moment she remained, one hand on her hip, staring at the flagstones at her feet, as if composing herself. Her first sentence was delivered with the knife waved in front of her like a sword. She was a formidable specimen of womanhood when under full sail. Her expressive lips quivered, her eyes narrowed as she spoke and she held herself with all the confidence of a Trojan princess.

'I have not come this far James Gilchrist to give up so easily. It's taken us months to convince the children that our future lies in New Zealand – and longer to convince ourselves.' Gilchrist frowned. 'And James, have you given any thought to your sister Elspeth. She needs us.'

Maggie reached for her cloak which hung behind the kitchen door. Agnes watched this cameo with fascination.

'Agnes, would you see to the soup. Do nothing, James. Touch nothing. Don't write a letter and most of all don't mention this to the girls. I'm off down to Ferniecleugh. They will not treat us like this.'

And so she left for the big house on the hill beyond the Kelso Road. She hurried down the track with that determined stride which James had so admired from the first day he had clapped eyes on her. He remembered then thinking this was surely one lass who knew where she was going. Long ago he had realised as a result of the life he shared with Maggie that strength was not only to be found in muscle and brawn. The presence of Maggie with the bit between her teeth was something to behold. She was dogged and determined, a woman who insisted on justice for herself and her family.

Gilchrist sank into his fireside chair. The hike to the top of Ward Water had taken more out of him than he imagined. He stretched his legs towards the stove. Beside him on the fireside chest lay the small battered brown suitcase with his father's initials embossed on the lid. He had brought it back from Glasgow and the case now held their emigration correspondence.

This included the last letter from Elspeth, received just ten days ago. For three years now she had been pleading with them to come south – with more urgency since her husband's accident – and in this latest despatch she had written of her joy at the prospect of their arrival in Southern Otago. He opened the case lid and picked the despatch from the top of the pile.

Agnes rose wearily to the fireplace and emptied the remaining vegetables from the table into the pot.

Elspeth would take any hint of a delay badly. But what was to be done. Long since Gilchrist had decided that she would never learn of his brother's desperate fate on board the *Arran Dubh*. She had had enough trouble in her life. He would settle any scores.

May burst into the kitchen, a charge of energy on a weary scene. She was carrying a bundle of firewood which she dropped with a crash beside the hearth.

'That's the chickens fed and the rain's gone off, Agnes, just as you said it would.'

The old lady was measuring a spoonful from a bottle of patent medicine. She nodded to May and gulped, holding the bottle up to the light to determine how much of the precious liquid remained.

Gilchrist was oblivious to the kitchen goings-on; he was lost again in Elspeth's letter from the Clutha river. Could it really be two years since his brother-in-law, big, brash, Alec, who looked as tall, straight and invincible as the trees he felled, was killed when a huge kauri tumbled on his forestry crew?

He read: 'Margaret, you will think me so long in writing. But I have much to do in caring for the children. Our Gordon is quite the young man now. Such a sadness came into our lives immediately after the accident but the arrival of you both and the girls will surely make Christmas, 1858 an altogether happier time.' She wrote of their day-to-day life, of the shock of an earthquake followed by a storm of wind and rain and the rapid harvest which followed.

'We had 15 acres of wheat last year, it was £6 a bushel; we considered that a rise. We have nothing to boast of but we feel a little easier now in our circumstance. Once here James will settle, have no fear. It is natural that he is apprehensive about such a change, but there is much work for the competent shepherd.'

The letter continued: 'There is, unfortunately, no further word of Davie (Alec's brother had vanished the previous year on a survey expedition in the uncharted Fjord country of South Island). We are counting the days until you are here. Please write dear sister.'

Gilchrist rose and wandered through to the back store where in a corner half-a-dozen packing cases were stacked reaching towards the low ceiling. The girls had carefully stencilled the destination – *Motherwell Mains, Southern Otago* – boxes which also carried the instruction '*Wanted on Voyage.*' They would be placed so they could be more easily accessed. Their free allocation of 20 cubic feet on the *Broomielaw* could have been filled twice over, he thought.

One box, with pieces of Maggie's sewing machine which James had dismantled the previous evening for packing, still lay open. It was the only substantial piece of household furniture they had planned to take to New Zealand. The rest was scheduled to go at next week's roup which had been advertised over half of Haddingtonshire. Piece by piece he lifted the carefully wrapped machine parts from the box, suddenly conscious that he was under Agnes's cold gaze from the storeroom door.

'See you mind oan whit Maggie telt ye, Gilchrist. Say nothing…and touch nothing. There is absolutely no needcessity to interfere wi' any o' that. She'll be back soon enough once she's done what has to be done.'

The old witch – he had to get out of there before he took the hammer to her instead of the packing cases. She had always made it clear she thought him weak-willed and feckless. If she only knew what he was now planning. She'd surely be impressed. However, he hadn't appreciated that when he took Maggie on he would also be taking Agnes for life. She was the only one of Maggie's immediate relatives who took any interest in her welfare after she was expelled from the family home. To Maggie she was a kind of saint. But this particular day he could have happily drowned her in the broth she was preparing.

He left Agnes and May in the midst of a renewed discussion about the weather and headed back towards the hill, his hill. What was the point of Maggie speaking to Brocklebank. He was a hard man, and not easily swayed, even by a pretty face. They would have to leave without their references or the blessing of the big house.

Gilchrist whistled on Gip who came sprinting across the field to his heel. At least there was still one female around Sweetshaws who jumped to his command, he thought.

8 Facing Daddy Long Legs

'Well, Mistress Gilchrist, this IS a grand surprise. Sit yourself down, please.' Brocklebank the factor patted the padded cushion of an old upright chair beside his desk. Dust rose in a tiny storm.

Maggie had never been in the factor's office. It was an untidy, cramped little box at the far end of the stable block. In the courtyard and around the big house there was a bustle as preparations were being made for the return of his lordship and his family from London for Christmas. Beyond the curtained window the yard was filled with comings and goings and noisy chatter.

This year the Gilchrist family would not be among the throng of tenants at the Christmas party. Maggie was determined beyond certainty that they would be on board the *Broomielaw* in just over four weeks. She could not let a worm like Brocklebank stand in their way. One way or another she would secure James's release from his contract and get those recommendations and references from Sir Robert, so vital in securing land and credit in the Antipodes.

'If this is about James's contract, Margaret – there is really nothing I can do. He must work through beyond next year's lambing. I realise it is a bittie inconvenient for you, but there it is.' He shuffled some papers on the desk in front of him and coughed.

'Inconvenient!' Maggie looked as if she might explode.

Brocklebank was a thin, emaciated character, with a cruel, tight mouth and stick-like arms and legs which cracked as he moved. The kids around the Ferniecleugh estate knew him as Daddy Long Legs. He was a most unattractive character but an individual who knew precisely how much he could squeeze out of life. He was as tight with Sir Robert's money as he was with his own.

'You'll understand that I'm as upset about this as you are.'

He sat behind his desk twisting a quill pen between his spindly fingers. Insincerity oozed out of his every pore.

The factor reminded her so much of the sort of drink-inflamed and foul-breathed toads who used to visit Mrs Stockan's house in Flesher's Wynd, below St Giles during Maggie's time there. Advocates, shopkeepers, town guards and yes, even men of the cloth – all of them scum, womenhaters. Maggie had heard other girls at Mrs Stockan's talk of the occasional gentle soul who had sought comfort in the girls' bunks and their bodies but Maggie had never met such an individual. Not a one.

During those 14 terrible months in Edinburgh Maggie had pledged quietly to herself that men, men just like Brocklebank, would pay for the degradation which she had been forced into in order to feed herself and her baby daughter.

'There is no question. We will be on that boat, Mr Brocklebank.'

'So you say, mistress, so you say.'

There was ill-disguised contempt in his voice but Brocklebank greedily eyed Maggie, searching, exploring every inch of her from his thin, protruding eyebrows. This confidence, this haughty pride, so rare in women from the farms, made his groin tighten. She was different and no mistake.

'I have here what we can spare from our savings - £10. It was supposed to cushion our arrival in Otago, but you can have it...' She took the money from the satchel she had strung across her chest and pushed it across the desk towards the factor.

'Now, Margaret. Come, come. That's tantamount tae bribery. I canna' tak' your money.'

He was looking intently at her, gazing at the strap of the bag, where it crossed her chest, accentuating the rise and fall of her breasts. Maggie looked in control, but clearly she was uneasy, a nerve on her forehead twitching. She was excited and Brocklebank seemed to sense it. It was quite clear that his resolve was stiffened merely at the thought of her discomfort. His gaze shifted to her neck. How soft it looked beneath those auburn curls, especially where the black velvet band encircled her neck.

Maggie dismissed this reverse and pressed on trying to ignore the fact that she was surprisingly ill at ease under the lecherous gaze of the man who, for that moment, held her family's destiny in his hands.

'If money is not acceptable to you because of your moral principles – I called in at Carsfern on my way here. Young Alastair Milne may be inexperienced but everyone says he will be the best shepherd in the shire before he's twenty. Surely he would be capable of filling James's shoes; and to get a start at Ferniecleugh he says he would work half wages during the first year.'

'Oh, does he now?'

Brocklebank ran his bony fingers across the desk to where Maggie's hand, still clutching their savings, rested. She drew away from his threatened caress and rested her hands in her lap.

'My, my. You have been busy, Margaret. What a fortunate man Gilchrist is to have you to fight his battles. I've always admired you at the barn dances and the Christmas parties. You know that, don't you? You're the sort of woman who needs to be treated well. Perhaps I could take Milne on. I'm sure his lordship would approve.'

Maggie waited. There was going to be a price to be paid.

'His family are model tenants – unlike some I might care to mention who are off to the Colonies at the drop of a hat.'

He looked at her thoughtfully, pulling at his long fingers as if trying to stretch them. 'But I would need some added incentive, if you get my drift. You have the look of a woman who knows how to barter.'

Brocklebank laughed a thin, weasely laugh, just as the four-faced clock high above the stable buildings sounded midday. Maggie counted the tinny chimes up to twelve. She had been prepared for anything, even this.

'You can see for yourself Brocklebank that I am pregnant.'

'Aye, aye that's a damned inconvenience. I had a mind tae bend ye o'er this desk, Mistress Gilchrist. But I'm sure you ken fine what pleasures a man in these, what shall we say, unfortunate circumstances. Call it a wee leaving present if you will. Your rosebud lips are my delight, Mistress.'

He winked an evil wink and made to unbutton his rough trousers. Maggie stood up sending the chair tumbling backwards. She backed towards the door and watched the scraggy man pawing at his groin. The factor was repulsive and his reputation was clearly justified yet, she reminded herself, only he held the key to their future.

'If this has to be, Brocklebank, then it will not be until the last possible moment. Not here, not now. I'll send you a note and we'll meet, but meantime James must have a letter confirming that he is freed from his contract and those references in duplicate from Sir Robert.'

The factor followed her to the door, dark eyes gleaming. It was humid outside and rain was falling again. The grey, lowering sky promised a heavier burden to bear. Watching Maggie hurry off across the cobblestones, anticipating the spoils he had roughly pondered in his bachelor bed, Brocklebank shouted after the figure who hurried into the shadow of an archway. 'Aye, aye, he'll have his letter. But mind on our arrangement.'

Two servant girls who had been polishing brass at the back door of the big house looked at each other and giggled, trying to guess the nature of the discussion just completed in the factor's office. Under the lecherous Brocklebank's gaze they scurried inside. Both lasses had full, ripe lips and knew the factor's office and his preferences well enough.

9 The Pit Blast

The rain had stopped. It was going to be a fine drying day. Having heated a pot of porridge on the stove for her older boys' breakfast and waved Torrance off to school, Belle Macaulay, clothes basket under her arm made her way to the wash-house behind their terraced house.

Wooden pegs clenched between her teeth Belle had draped the first shirt on the line when from the direction of the pit came the sound dreaded by every miner's wife, a muffled blast which for a second set the ground beneath her feet a-quivering. The morning shift, with her Innes, amongst them, had just begun work. She spat out the pegs, dropped her washing on the ground and shielded her eyes against the watery, wintry sun. Dark flame-tinted smoke was licking around the winding gear at the pithead only a mile away across the shallow valley.

By the time she had hitched up her skirt and stumbled into the house, her two eldest sons, Hugh and Guthrie, had abandoned plans for food and sleep and were getting their working clothes on again, alert on the instant. They had just completed a night shift at the Fraser Castle. Already Belle could hear anxious shouts along the Cowgate.

Pulling on his shirt and banging his feet into his boots Hugh watched his mother slowly and deliberately reaching for her shawl. She was hurrying – and yet she wasn't. Twenty years previously she had made that long walk to the pithead at Glenburn Number 2 in Ayrshire where her father and brother were lost, crushed, the life squeezed out of them beneath thousands of tons of sodden moss when a seam was driven too near to the surface. Their bodies were never recovered.

'I'll run on ahead wi' Guthrie, mother. They'll be getting rescue teams together. We'll look for you over at the pithead. Mind and wrap up warm. And dinna' worry. Faither's a survivor,' said Hugh reassuringly.

It was true enough. Innes had walked out of the pit after two previous rockfalls with only a crushed thumb to testify to his brush with death. But there were never any guarantees in that dark underworld. They all knew, although it was never said, that an explosion was an altogether more sinister event.

Outside in the street the Macaulay boys, the studs of their boots sparking on the worn cobbles, dived into the stream of folk now silently, nervously trotting towards the colliery. The boys broke into a run. Between the chimney pots on the brae they could see that an ominous plume of grey smoke was now pouring from the shaft.

Twenty minutes later at the pithead Belle joined a crowd of ashen-face women. Dark shawls drawn hastily over their heads, quietly consoling and reassuring each other, respectfully seeking out information from officials by the gate; any snippet of news which might give them hope or a clue to the fate of their loved ones. There was an unspoken code of conduct in such desperate situations and the women, despite the terror which gripped them, followed it stoically, and to the letter.

Soon they were joined by their children who had been in the playground awaiting the start of school when the underground blast rocked the village.

Young Torrance, a twelve-year-old but sturdy and straight like his father, clutching his school books, was suddenly at his mother's side. Without speaking she grasped his hand and squeezed it tight.

'Is there no word, ma'? I could go and ask if I can help,' said the boy, standing on tiptoe to see more easily across the bustle of the yard which surrounded the pithead. 'I could carry water, or help with the injured.'

'There's help enough down there for the moment, Torry. Your faither would want you here by me. Hugh and Guthrie will make sure the family play their part.'

She gripped his hand even tighter and the boy resigned himself to the role of comforter rather than rescuer. It always seemed to be like this for the youngest in the family, he thought.

At this stage there was little emotion amongst the crowd which was now several hundred strong. Standing quietly exchanging a few words Belle and her son watched the comings and goings. At their feet, their neighbour Mrs Macdonald's kiddies played beside a puddle, launching their twig boats into a rainwater ocean.

Information was scant but Belle had seen Duff, the mine manager, lead a hastily gathered rescue party to the main shaft. Men who had only just finished a long night at the coal face, including her two sons, were among the first volunteers. With a raft of emotions, pride, fear and helplessness among them, she saw her boys at the head of the stern-faced team, bunnets reversed, clad again in the rough overalls which they had hung on their pegs only an hour before. Belle hoped the Lord, from whom she had drifted away in recent years, would protect them.

Soon miners who had been working in other parts of the pit started to appear on the surface, grimy-faced, anxious. Some stopped only long enough to speak to their families and take a long draught of water before rejoining the search for their missing colleagues.

As the morning progressed rescue teams began to arrive from surrounding collieries and from the huge Lanarkshire pits, strangers to the village, but, as always, comrades in such a crisis. Police officers were there in numbers also and smartly-dressed representatives of the Glasgow and Edinburgh newspapers appeared on the fringes of the crowd before gathering at the steps leading up to the pit manager's office.

The morning of promise was no more. A thin rain coated the village and the valley in dismal grey. A minister, clasping his Bible in one hand and pushing his thin white hair back from his brow with the other, edged his way through the throng, stopping here and there to comfort a distraught spouse.

Every so often there was a flurry of activity as soot-stained men, almost collapsing with exhaustion and coughing and hacking as they cleared the foul air from their tortured lungs, emerged from below. On some occasions they returned with survivors and on others they carried a blanketed body on a board. These were laid out in the colliery carpenter's shop which had been transformed into a makeshift mortuary.

A pattern began to develop. There would be a choked scream and a rush of women to comfort someone in the crowd who had been gently told by a pit deputy that their husband, son, brother or father had been recovered, dead.

Mrs Swift, another of the Macaulays neighbours from the Cowgate and a woman who knew everything that was worth knowing in the little mining community came shuffling over to speak to Belle and her boy, nodding seriously to acquaintances as she threaded her way towards them.

'You must na' lose hope Belle. They're saying that maybe as many as four dozen men are shut off at the Number 4 Heading. Your Innes and my Tam must be among them. All the other roadways have been cleared.'

Over the hum of activity around the pithead the chimes of the burgh hall clock rang out over the houses. Belle could scarcely believe it but she had been standing outside the yard for six hours. Without warning the sun burst from a bank of clouds illuminating the grim scene and at the same moment there was an excited shout from the steps of the manager's office.

10 Entombed

Innes Macaulay was seated with his back to the damp, rough-hewn wall near Number 4 Heading. His head had dropped forward on to his chest and he seemed to be consumed by a troubled, exhausted, painful, yet apparently merciful slumber. He shivered involuntarily from time to time.

His tormented mind was being visited by two very different but equally disturbing images. The first was of a beggar crouched in a doorway, Glasgow's High Street, Innes thought. The man tapped the paving in front of him with a thin stick. Around his neck he wore a board with the message: 'Dear friend, I am Blind and Friendless'.

Then there was a rock tower – a huge pinnacle which reminded Innes of illustrations of the rock stacks in Orkney. But this storm-tossed sentinel had a jet black sheen as if made from coal. It was badly eroded, precarious and crooked near the summit, looking for all the world like a beckoning finger

Beside him in the darkness of the cursed pit, weary bodies were huddling together for warmth, clinging to the rocky walls of the roadway and away from the rising water in the centre of the tunnel. The oversman splashed along the passage pushing his oil lamp into the faces of his crew strung out along the walls.

'That's the spirit boys. It canna' be long now. Keep yer pecker up. We'll be rescued for sure.'

However, he noticed the eyes of the 42 miners from this section of the morning shift at the Fraser Castle colliery were duller now and through the coal dust they carried a strange, hunted expression, like a deer cornered by the hounds. The oversman whispered a few more words of encouragement and moved off into the sepulchral midnight.

Innes reached down scraping his fingers across the floor of the passageway until, with a start, he came in contact with the chill tide rising at his feet. It was only six hours since the explosion but for the entombed men it had already seemed like a lifetime. Imagination played strange tricks. Were these dank walls actually closing in, compressing their sanctuary? There were moments when Innes felt it to be true. In this dark hole in the ground it was easy to forget that only a few yards above them was a world of sunshine, waving grass and loved ones. Wasn't there?

As they waited each man explored his stream of memories all of which included warm moments and companionship – keeping the dread of being buried alive at bay, at least temporarily. Some prayed, but most explored images of their loved ones. And there were tears in some eyes. Also in the past hour each breath had become more laboured and difficult. And this was no flight of the imagination. Oxygen was slowly disappearing from their subterranean prison.

Innes Macaulay had known from the moment he caught the angry blast of the fire damp explosion that he had lost his sight. Three of his workmates, only a few yards in front of him, had caught the full force of the blast. They had been laid gently side by side in a dry inshot, caps covering their faces. They had lost so much more, thought Innes, when he learned of their fate.

For the first hour following the blast, after caring as best they could for the injured, the miners organised themselves into teams to dig and scrabble with shovels and bare hands at the great mound of coal and rock brought down by the explosion and which now blocked their way to the blessed daylight.

Another body had been uncovered as they worked and as the air became heavier and more precious the oversman had ordered the weary miners to rest.

Somewhere along the roadway, out of the thick cloud of darkness a squeaky, almost timid, voice had begun to sing – 'Guid me O thou Great Jehovah…' The anonymous comforter struggled through the first couple of lines of the hymn, the sultry blackness seeming to swallow the words almost before they were uttered.

Innes surfaced into consciousness and gasped, his face a tight mask of pain. Strange how at first the only discomfort had been in his shattered arm. In his half-conscious state he had also been helping Belle, his lovely, precious Belle, to finish final packing and then inexplicably, when the cairt arrived, she and the boys had gone off without him. They hadn't even turned to wave. He shivered and shook himself.

His right arm, smashed when he was thrown head over heels into the heavy, wooden coal buggy, was surely broken.

But oh, his face. Panic and fear welled up inside again. Blind, he was blind! Macaulay was about to cry out again when a strong, reassuring arm was laid upon his good shoulder. 'Now, haud on there, Macaulay,' came the cool, unruffled tones of Tam Swift, workmate and neighbour in the Cowgate. 'You don't want to be spoiling the wee buffer's party piece.'

Right enough, the singer along the passageway was growing in confidence with every line, getting into his stride, and the strains of the hymn were being taken up by the entombed miners, one by one along the roadway. The refrain seemed to grow and gather strength. The men sang of their Strong Deliverer. The swelling sound swamped the dark passageway with unexpected hope, reaffirming their spirit of togetherness, a camaraderie which was almost tangible in that sombre vault.

'Are ye no' hurt, Tam? Innes groaned. 'You were so close tae the blast. You must have taken a real belt, man.'

'Listen tae that voice, wid ye; is that no' just splendid? Tam's voice was barely a whisper. Calmer now Macaulay was able to respond: 'Aye, but my eyes, Tam, how will Belle and the boys manage wi' me sightless?'

'You have to come through this. There's a ship waiting for you and yours at the docks in Glasgow and beyond that a new life in Australia. Remember that farrier's business. It's a' you've talked about this past year. You were going to take youself out of the darkness and into the light, remember?' The soothing voice seemed to be coming from a distance yet it wrapped Innes in comfort.

Over the final verse of the hymn a new sound – a faraway scuffling, the distant chipping sound of metal on stone away to the left where the massive rock fall had sealed them in.

'Listen to that Macaulay. Do ye no' hear. They're coming for you, by God. Did ah no' tell you they would come.'

'They're coming US, Tam, for US!'

To his astonishment Innes Macaulay found himself singing as lustily as his neighbours. Ignoring the fierce tightness around his mouth and the fact that his throat felt parched and dusty, he croaked a few lines. He wanted so much to cry but his eyes and face felt tight, fused into immobility. The sound of digging was perceptibly closer now and was that a cheerful shout of encouragement from beyond the wall of their tomb? Tam Swift seemed to have moved off down the tunnel.

In the yard above the news spread rapidly. A grimy, bare-headed overman sprang halfway up the stairs outside the manager's office and faced the anxious throng below. 'They've broken through at Number 4 Heading! And the boys are singing!

11 The Big Decision

Twenty-two men died in the Fraser Castle Pit Disaster in October, 1857. It would have been three times that many if the rescue teams had taken half-an-hour longer to reach the men at Number 4 Heading in their almost airless vault.

Innes's recovery from his burns and clean break of his right arm had astonished the doctors. He was a genial if sometimes awkward patient, refusing to stay put in his bed in the cottage hospital's west wing. However, his rebellious streak did seem to have a positive effect on the other casualties, jolting them out of self-pity and coaxing them towards the world waiting beyond the hospital doors. He soon got to know the layout of the ward and shuffled his way from bed to bed, chatting with his mates. He teased the nurses mercilessly.

Belle and the boys organised a visiting rota which allowed everyone to get on with their daily duties. Mother went down into town in the evening to sit by Innes's bed and bring him up-to-date on all the latest gossip while Torry went along after school. Hugh and Guthrie called by during the day after snatching a couple of hours sleep. The colliery had been back in production within a week of the blast.

The visiting rota also gave Belle the chance to take up all the arrangements for the voyage and travel into Glasgow on a couple of afternoons to see the agent in his office in Ingram Street. He had been very sympathetic and said he would understand completely if the family decided to cancel or postpone their emigration plans.

'He'll no' hear a word o' it, Mr Lumsden. As soon as he'd got his strength back he was telling the boys how they would operate the business in South Australia. He seems to have it a' planned out.'

'Do you know, Mrs Macaulay, Belle. Only a few days ago I was reading of the terrible conditions in the pits. Your man seems to be a real battler. And that sort of determination is infectious. He'll be a delight to have on board the *Broomielaw*.'

'The boys and I will make sure he's no extra trouble on board ship, Mr Lumsden. He's a tough tyke is our Innes.'

However, it had been a sore time for everyone. Beyond the lace curtains of the treatment room lay the beautiful winding valley of the Fraser where Innes had fished on long summer evenings at his shift's end. He knew he would never see those haunts again. However, he swore he would not allow those precious images to grow dim. He would colour them anew every day, he told himself.

The day the bandages came off Belle sat holding her husband's hand, squeezing gently. They had been well warned that there was little or no chance of him recovering even partial vision but as the nurse gently unwound the bandages, Belle had not been prepared for the mask of scarred and livid flesh which her husband's face had become.

Innes sensed her hands tighten and heard her shallow gasp.

'I fear I'm no sae bonny now, lass. Is it that bad? You can tell me. Efter a', I'm the only one who'll no' have tae look at this ugly mug.' He smiled, but it was a grimace as flesh stretched tight across his cheekbones.

The doctor, a young, enthusiastic Fifer had been standing by the door. He stepped forward and examined Innes's face, turning his patient's head carefully towards the light, Large patches of skin on his brow and cheek were translucent yellow and red, marbled and mottled. His eyebrows had gone and his hair had been seared off, except for a patch on the back of his head.

And then there were his empty eyes. Belle sobbed again. The doctor gently and reassuringly reached over to squeeze her shoulder.

'He really has made a remarkable recovery, Mrs Macaulay. Mind you I would still advise against the sea trip before next year, but from what Innes says, your minds are set on it.' Innes reached out, seeking to grasp the young man's hand.

'Belle and I thank you for your concern Mr Stuart; you've worked wonders. But if there ever was a time for a fresh start, then this is surely it. You understand?'

A week later Innes Macaulay went home, sitting straight-backed on the bench seat of the cairt behind old Sally, the Clydesdale horse, Belle on one side and Alec Johnson, the tattie merchant on the other. Alec, an old pal, had offered to take him home to the Cowgate.

The strange dream of the blind beggar was fading. Innes now seemed to recall that he had passed such a sad specimen of mankind in the Saltmarket on his last visit to Mr Lumsden's office before the explosion. That would explain it, he reassured himself. But the pinnacle of black rock continued to haunt him like of a memory of someone else's life which had invaded his subconscious.

As they negotiated the bend at the foot of the hospital brae and entered the High Street, Innes took in great draughts of fresh air and put his arm around his wife. He had been unable to attend any of the funerals of his comrades from the pit and was already asking Belle to take him to the cemetery in order that he could pay his final respects.

'Tell me again about Tam, Belle, How do they say he died?'

Apart altogether from being overcome by grief, Innes had appeared quite taken aback and confused when he learned how his neighbour had been killed stone dead along with two other workmates in the blast. When he first heard the sad details his immediate reaction had been: 'That just cannot be, Belle. He was speaking...' Whatever Innes had thought to say he then opted for silence, keeping his counsel to himself. However, when the oversman who had been at the Number Four Heading with him visited the hospital Innes insisted that he recount every last detail of the tragedy.

At the front door of the terraced house a group of neighbours had gathered to welcome Innes home. Politely he shook hands and thanked them for their consideration. He hugged Mrs Swift with a special warmth and wanted so much to tell her about his comforter in the darkness. But how could he, Innes realised, with a new dismay. Belle took his arm and guided him up the well scrubbed steps and in to the house.

'You must say now if you feel this voyage to Australia will be too much for you, Innes. You always were a stubborn beggar.' He gently squeezed her hand in response. The boys were also there to greet him. Torry had even been permitted half-an-hour off school. After the fuss died down, the tea had been poured and Innes settled in his old brown fireside armchair he called Belle across to his side.

'Is this battered auld face still worth a cheeper?'

Lovingly Belle leaned forward and kissed him on the forehead, marvelling at the glassy warmth of the scar tissue.

'You asked me if I felt up to the journey to Australia. I'm ready for this, Belle, with all my heart and soul, I am ready. It is God's will and our purpose that we should go. I've never been more certain.'

Belle knelt on the floor beside her husband and wrapped her arms around him.

'Tell me, my love. What was it like down there in that tunnel? What exactly happened?' she asked, snuggling against his shoulder. 'You've said next to nothing.'

Remembering the words of comfort, the companionship of those terrible hours, Innes replied simply: 'Believe me, Belle, there is a story to be told. But it will wait for another day. Suffice to say, at my moment of greatest despair, I was not alone. I had a guide and comforter and somehow, I feel he's here still.

'For now, there's a ship waiting at the dock in Glasgow and we must soon be on her.'

12 The Highest Tide

Beneath grey, sombre evening skies the tidal flats stretched as far as the eye could see, reaching out to touch the distant waters of the Clyde. Near the shore small boats heeled over in the grey mud. Here and there were gentle undulations on this seemingly endless plain; shallow mounds surrounded by rivulets which snaked almost imperceptibly downwards to the river.

The monotony was broken by the occasional glacial erratic, large rocks dragged across the estuary and deposited by the retreating ice sheet ten thousand years before, a snagging danger for generations of fishing boats. Indeed, the skeleton of a small steam trawler, rusted and stark against the evening sky, lay on the edge of one of the sandbanks. It was fully low tide and a sliver of crescent moon could just be seen between the rolling battlements of cloud.

Two men trudged across this alien landscape towards the wreck, skirting the water courses, one pushing himself along in a determined manner with the aid of a hefty blackthorn stick, the other, a younger man, casting nervous glances around him.

'Tell me again... you overheard some discussion in the wine shop about how the proceeds from the Ayr mail coach robbery had been hidden out here, Walker? Is that the way of it? The younger man splashed through a shallow pool of water. 'That was some stroke of luck, eh?'

His companion adjusted the strange sackcloth mask which he wore as he spoke: 'They were unaware of my presence in the snug. They planned to return for their haul at the end of this week. That's why we have to act quickly.'

Together they stood finally in the shadow of the stricken vessel which lay half buried, with the sand creeping up her superstructure and with anything of value already stripped from her interior. A weak, pale yellow sun was sinking behind Kintyre, its last attempt at illumination before the close of day.

'A tin chest, you said? That's what we're looking for, eh?'

The younger man scrambled inside the metal ribs of the boat, lifting a hatch cover and pushing piping to one side as he went.

'Aye, they said it would take them both to carry,' shouted his companion.

'That's why it was important for me to bring someone else in on this. I suppose you might say you were lucky that we were working next to each other in the tannery.' As he spoke he laid his walking stick to one side on the sand and with surprising agility clambered up into the trawler. In his hand he carried a sturdy chain. He edged up alongside his companion.

The younger man, still with his back to his fellow adventurer spoke: 'No sign back here of anything, Walker. Let's try up nearer the bow.' He rose and prepared to edge forward through the hull.

As he spoke two events took place in the blink of an eye, or at least that was how it seemed to him. There was a clang of metal on metal as the masked man secured one steel ring around a sturdy stay and in the same motion snapped the other cuff around the young man's wrist.

'What the hell! What are you playing at, for God's sake. Get this bloody thing off of me, Walker. I'm warning you, old man...'

Aaron Malise stepped back to admire his handiwork. The handcuffed man pulled frantically at his chain. This man, one of the gang who had mutilated him and killed Robert Gilchrist, would not be going any further this evening.

'There is no tin box, Connelly, you bastard, and my name is not Walker. There was a robbery alright but where the stash is – your guess is as good as mine. No, I have brought you out here for a totally different reason.' So saying he whipped off his mask.

The prisoner gasped then groaned at the sight of the scarred face which now regarded him with such venom.

'So you remember me - *The Arran Dubh,* young Gilchrist? It's all coming back, is it? You've got half-an-hour, I reckon, to reflect on that night, to make peace with your maker before the river comes to take you. I want you to see death come creeping up on you...'

A herring gull landed precariously on one of the trawler's metal ribs. It cocked its head to one side and appeared to be watching and listening to the confrontation that was taking place below. Inexorably, yet in slow time, little by little, the water in the shallow channel beside the wreck was beginning to rise.

'For pity's sake, free me. It was ….. and Rag. They forced us… Please, please….'

Having clambered down to the sand Malise bent to pick up his blackthorn stick and turned again for the shore where lights were already twinkling in the dusk.

He moved off ignoring the pitiful sobs behind him and a few hundred yards nearer the beach, what were now frenzied screams from the captive in the wreck were almost beyond earshot. Dusk cloaked the river by the time Malise climbed up the gently sloping beach to the edge of the Greenock road. Slowly the small boats began to right themselves.

Behind him the water was rushing to fill the channels and cover the mud flats. The Clyde was returning to claim its own, the tide was turning.

13 Circus Caledonia

It wasn't every day that Walter Lumsden's pokey little office in Glasgow's Ingram Street was so colourfully tenanted but the delegation from the Circus Caledonia represented no ordinary emigrants.

Peering over the edge of his desk with those soft, green eyes and a riot of dark, curly hair escaping from beneath her pill box hat was the little lady who was advertised on the billboards around town as 'Undoubtedly the Smallest Flamenco Dancer in Christendom.'

She smiled warmly at Walter who had glanced once again over his notes.

Beautiful, thought Walter. Beautiful, but somehow compressed, as if her wonderful, bubbly personality had been squeezed into a body many sizes to small for her and from which she was desperate to burst free and to lead a full-sized life. Her voice seemed little more than a squeak. It was difficult to guess her age, perhaps thirty, and Walter found himself asking the age-old questions which average, run-of-the-mill members of the male species always seemed to pose privately about such singular people.

Angry with himself, he chased the word 'freak' from his consciousness. After all, he reminded himself, Conchita's was a physical abnormality. If someone could see inside the mind of Walter Lumsden, he reflected, they would surely find that people could be stunted in other, equally distressing, ways.

'It was kind of you to see us at such short notice, Mr Lumsden. We realise you will be very busy with just two weeks until the Broomielaw sails.'

Walter glanced up from the pile of documents which ranged across his battered old desk. Untidy as it was the chaos of papers and ribbon-tied files didn't seem out of place in the shabby, rented third-floor room. He would be glad to see the back of its musty corridors and cold-tiled close.

Towering over Conchita was Hamish, the 'Lochaber Ox' – the man built like the mainmast of a warship but with the most open and sincere smile Walter had ever seen. Hamish seemed very protective of the little lady. Again, Lumsden found himself wondering. Seated on the window ledge behind Hamish, sucking his cheeks and sipping a glass of water was the third member of the delegation, a wiry individual with long, very long, arms. Walter had been amazed to discover on shaking hands with the man they called Eales that he had unusual webbing between his fingers. The rest of Conchita's group – The Celebus Midgets – claimed to be the only Scottish company of miniature clowns.

It was Lumsden's experience that most of these exotically-named performers who crowded the fairgrounds of Central Scotland and were claimed as residents of lost worlds or fantastic kingdoms, usually hailed from a row of miner's cottages in darkest Lanarkshire.

'Now, let's recap, Conchita. First of all your letter of September...' Somehow Walter Lumsden plucked the appropriate single sheet from the landscape of correspondence.

'Correct me if I'm wrong. Your group is off to try your luck in the concert halls of Australia and you've already had several offers of work in Victoria, providing you get there by the end of February?'

'Yes, that's it. Mr Lumsden. That's how things stood last month.' She peered over the edge of the writing bureau.

54

'Please, Conchita, sit up on the desk if you'd be more comfortable.'

She nodded and Hamish lifted the little lady like a feather, depositing her gently on the rim of the desk next to Lumsden. She placed her tiny hat on her lap and shook her hair. 'Thank you, Hamish,' she beamed at the big man.

Lumsden noted with surprise that the strongman's hands were not the big paws he had expected but that he had thin, delicate hands, more like those of a clockmaker or a musician. He also seemed to be recovering from some minor burns to his arms and face.

The emigration agent flicked over a couple of sheets. 'It's true that to meet your schedule you would have to leave on the *Broomielaw* or *The Spirit of Speed.* The Southern Cross company has billed *The Spirit* to depart a day or two after us. That really would be your last opportunity.'

There was silence for a moment. The rumbling of the carts in the street below and the coo-cooing of the scruffy pigeons on the window ledge were the only sounds. Walter leafed quickly through the file of sailing notices and finally scratched his head. 'No, you would be cutting it too fine if you left any later. There really seems to be no alternative. And am I right in thinking we were unable to help you in September?'

'Actually, the problem seems to have resolved itself a little, Mr Lumsden. The rest of our party – including Mr Eales here – have secured berths on the *Spirit of Speed* and we have come here again as a last resort. We know every berth on the *Broomielaw* is taken but only Hamish and I now need accommodation.'

Walter Lumsden spread the passenger manifest in front of him and waved a letter. 'It's true enough, Conchita, we quickly filled the remaining places. But this very morning the Moir family from Lenzie – six of them in all – have cancelled. The man of the house and his eldest son have secured work on the construction of the new Caledonian railway line. It seems you're in luck, and we can squeeze in your regiment of clowns as it happens. The eyes of the little people around the desk lit up.

Conchita's eyes lit up. 'Hamish, Eales, do you hear? We have berths on the *Broomielaw*....we all have berths. The web-fingered man coughed. 'Yes, it does seem fortune smiles on us, truly.'

'Oh, Mr Lumsden, how can we thank you.'

'I think you should be thanking the Moirs, but as a wee starter you might consider what you and your group can contribute to our concert parties!'

They laughed and a whistling kettle on the corner stove demanded a celebratory cup of tea. They would bunk in the single persons' accommodation and while Lumsden reflected that some of the straight-laced matrons on the *Broomielaw* might find these most recent recruits to the expedition rather unsettling initially, he knew from his own experience that there would also be long spells of boredom – and anxiety – when their special skills in entertainment would be worth Hamish's considerable weight in gold.

It was partly on the same basis that, just the day before, he had agreed to a request from the city magistrates to take on board a group of young street musicians who called themselves the Coocaddens Gutter band, who having appeared in court on umpteen occasions for disturbing the peace had pleaded to be allowed to try for a fresh start in Australia. To find room in the fo'castle for this quartet and rid the city of what they saw as a nuisance, the magistrates had been prepared to pay the Clutha Society a tidy incentive.

Having checked Hamish and Conchita's documentation Walter escorted the unusual group down to the street. Conchita was skipping down the steps, hand-in-hand with Eales, surrounded by the Celebus Midgets while Hamish lingered at the rear, clearly anxious to speak with Lumsden. On the half-landing he took the emigration agent by the elbow.

'I have a very special box which I'd like to have access to during the voyage rather than have it placed in the hold, if that's possible, Mr Lumsden. It would mean I could work at sea. It's part of our act, a prop which we hope will form the centrepiece of the show Down Under.'

'Well, as long as you're not trying to smuggle out the Crown jewels,' responded Lumsden.

It was an unusual request. Space was so precious that special privileges could only be offered in exceptional circumstances.

Walter Lumsden looked up at Hamish; it was like gazing up at a craggy mountain. He was big, too big surely to be devious or speak anything but the truth.

'I'll look over the cargo manifest and speak to Ratter – the skipper. There may just be a corner in the aft sail locker where we could squeeze you in. What sort of size would it be?'

They emerged into weak autumn sunshine and Eales screwed up his codfish eyes in the watery light. Passers-by turned to gaze at the strange crew gathered in the closemouth. Accustomed to the glare of public scrutiny the members of *Circus Caledonia* were unmoved. The emigration agent suddenly felt a surge of pride at the thought of having these colourful yet surprisingly modest people among his passengers.

Hamish spoke again. 'You asked about its size, Mr Lumsden. Well, the box would be perhaps six feet, by two, by two. Coffin-shaped, I suppose.'

14 His Master's Voice

The Hall of Doomy had never recovered from being sacked by redcoats after the Forty-Five. The east wing was a ruin where blackbirds and starlings squabbled and ivy clambered; the remainder of the crow-stepped laird's house carried an air of quiet, musty dereliction.

William Bigland, third son of Thomas, laird of the island of Stormay made his way along the wood-panelled second-floor passageway, the dark, varnished boards squeaking beneath his tread. A summons from the old man to his study at the top of the house was a worrying event. In his 21 years William had been in that room too often, and it invariably meant trouble. Passing under the stern gaze of his Bigland ancestors whose portraits inhabited the corridor, he approached the study door.

His father's Irish wolfhound Cormac was stretched across the doorway, his big, sad eyes fixed on William as he approached along the corridor. He budged not an inch but began to emit a low, threatening growl. The third son and the big dog were enemies of old. Did the creature sense that William was well down the pecking order in the Bigland family; that he could be intimidated without fear of reprisal? Certainly William had always felt that the animal rated more highly in the hierarchy of the house than he ever had.

William stared fixedly at the recumbent beast and hissed: 'Move your hellhound's arse out of the way, ye great brute of a…'

As he spoke the door swung open and the vast bulk of the laird filled the entrance. He was a man in his early sixties, heavy jowled with a moth-eaten periwig perched on his domed skull, displaying a style long since abandoned by the gentry in the south.

'Aye, it's you William. Get yourself in here. What were you mumbling about out there?' He wiped the back of his hand across his mouth and ushered his son inside.

'Cormac and I were just discussing the weather, father.'

The laird looked at his son with that familiar, humourless squint, so like his predecessors in the rogue's gallery in the passageway. William was directed to a chair with an imperious sweep of the old man's hand.

On his wide mahogany desk, as always, the old naval commander's cutlass lay unsheathed. He found it kept the more impertinent tenants in line during discussion on their rentals. A spirit of defiance which had been abroad amongst ordinary working people seemed to have reached as far as Stormay. And it wouldn't do. And if that wasn't enough, his own sons were now far from shipshape and compliant.

The Laird of Doomy looked at his youngest son and considered his offspring. Thomas Jnr., heir to the estate, had lost a small fortune the previous month with his trading speculations and at the card table in London and Robert, the second son, seemed to have become a permanent fixture in Edinburgh with his set of dandified friends. Now there was his youngest son William's damned shenanigans.

'This is a serious matter, William,' he said, lowering his portly frame into the armchair. 'More serious than I think you imagine.'

The young man shifted uncomfortably in his seat, his mind accelerating through his spare time activities, cataloguing possible misdemeanours which might merit a session with the Doomy inquisitor.

'If it's about that consignment of port from the French privateer, father; that was just a wee bit of illicit trading, and it was my money I used...'

The laird brought his fist down on the desk, sending quill pen and paper jumping. His face turned the colour of the wild blaeberries which grew on the North Hill of Stormay.

'You know perfectly well it has nothing to do with the port. It's Queenie, you randy pup!'

Queenie, sweet Queenie. William felt the anxiety, the uncertainty lift from his shoulders. There was nothing worse than some alleged crime being sprung out of the blue. But Queenie – he had guessed there might be something said. However, he could handle that.

'You'll have a brandy, lad.' The phrase was so much more of a command than an inquiry. Rising, the laird made his unsteady way to the walnut sideboard, his limp suggesting a war wound – or perhaps a lengthy acquaintance with the agonies of gout.

This was an odd, disturbing change of tack, thought William. The younger sons of the big house were usually kept at a distance. They were given little responsibility and it was always accepted that they would have to make their own way in the world. A drink proffered in the mid-afternoon was a unique, and unsettling, event.

'No, I won't, actually, father. I've some papers to sort out and...'

'You'll be taking a drink. I've a feeling you're going to need it before we're through here.' The glass was pushed into his hand. William sat up, alert now. Something very disturbing was about to take place, he felt sure.

'Look, father, this is simple enough. Swanney found us behind the smithy, Queenie and me. It was just one of those things. You, of all people should understand that.'

He looked across the desk at his father whose sexual adventures on the island over half-a-century had touched almost every family, had earned him the nickname of 'The Parish Bull' and had kept the church solvent through his fines for fornication. Hung-like-a-Hereford was the word from the more active of the serving lasses. The fact that he had virtually no neck and thyroid trouble made his red-rimmed eyes bulge alarmingly added to the bestial image. How often William had thought that a ring in his nose would have added that final touch.

'You've done it, stepped over the line this time, Will. The grieve did not spare me the seedy details – the girl on her back in the hay cairt, skirts up around her waist, drawers around her ankles and you in the saddle, making the wheels shake.'

Christ, I don't need this, thought William. The old bastard's enjoying every minute. The laird's son rose from his seat and made for the door.

'Sit down and finish your drink, boy. I did not give you permission to leave!'

Clearly there was to be no argument. Top of his class at the law school in Edinburgh he may have been, feted by academics, but for the moment he was again the mischievous schoolboy. Sheepishly William regained his seat and sipped at his brandy. His father stood by the window watching the race of windblown water in the South Wick, composing himself, and then turned again. Just below, in the walled garden, a chorus of starlings began chirruping.

'You have given me certain cause for pride over the years with your academic success, William. I see more of myself in you than I do in the other boys. But as my third son you were always destined to find your own fortune. This event only hastens the process. I cannot impart this news gently – the lass between whose legs you found so much pleasure is your sister.'

William felt his jaw drop. He placed the glass on the edge of the desk and shook his head. Queenie – his sister!

For long moments the men looked at each other – the father allowing time for this stunning information to sink in, the son feeling an uncomfortable shiver trace his spine as he remembered the smooth, muscled legs locked around his thighs, the hungry mouth and the declarations of love whispered in heat. His sister, for God's sake.

William was suddenly aware of his father at his shoulder. His glass was being refilled. Returning to his seat, and still awaiting a reaction to this news, the laird opened one of the heavy vellum-bound rent books and flicked slowly through from front to back. Each farm had its own pages and he stopped occasionally to run his stubby finger down the columns of figures. The income from the farms had been much lower in the past few years, hardly enough to sustain the Biglands in the style they desired. One less mouth to feed would be a help.

'You know, of course, that as tradition required I still exercised the right to the bride on her wedding night – right up until twenty years ago. And don't listen to the stories. Most of the women were glad to have someone as considerate and experienced as me to plunder their maidenhead rather than some clumsy farmhand.'

'What are your trying to tell me, father? Queenie was the product of some medieval tryst between you and Regan from Clett?'

Thomas Bigland IV, Laird of Stormay, closed the rent book with a stoury bang.

'That's about the length and breadth of it, William. I should have told you earlier, perhaps, but I thought that you would have had more sense than to put yourself about so close to home.'

How bloody ironic, thought William. The old bugger, who had taken the biblical injunction to go forth and multiply in its most literal sense, preaching at him.

Rising again, the laird crossed the floor, coming to a halt below the portrait of George, his great-grandfather, the brave Jacobite who had built the Hall of Doomy and who had hidden for a year in a sea cave to escape the government troops after Culloden. The laird liked to think he was made of the same stern stuff.

'You know your ancestor there had to go into exile because he picked the wrong side in the Forty-Five.' He pointed up at George, who had been captured for eternity, head held high, sporting the Bigland jowls and splendidly kitted out in full Highland dress on the steps of what looked like a Roman temple, eagle feather in his cap and two hunting dogs asleep at his feet.

'You see, I've been asked to become Lord Lieutenant of the County. It's a great honour but word of your misdemeanour – if we can call it that – is bound to reach the town. I fear you are about to become the latest of the Biglands to be forced into exile, William.'

The Bigland boy was quickly on his feet. 'But, for God's sake, father; the girl is at most my half-sister. It's scarcely a capital offence. Won't you reconsider this. After all, Queenie has a sister in Thurso. Send her away.'

His protest was waved away disdainfully.

'Unless I'm seen to act quickly and with conviction my chance will have gone and you know her Majesty is due in the islands in the spring. You have a comfortable cabin on a clipper leaving the Clyde for South Australia in a week. I've dealt with the emigration agent Lumsden myself. All the arrangements are in place.'

William listened to this life-altering pronouncement with a growing sense of disbelief. He was about to be sent away. He remembered that George the Jacobite had settled in the Carolinas but after the prison colony at Botany Bay began to flourish two of the grandsons had moved there and now operated a shipping agency in Sydney. He was to become a law clerk in that family firm, at the other end of the world.

The interview reached its conclusion and in a dwam William pulled the door of his father's study shut behind him. Cormac yawned at his feet. Without a second thought William put his full weight on the animal's tail, twisting the heel of his boot and then sprinted for the end of the hall – slamming the heavy door at the top of the stair in the pursuing hound's slavery muzzle.

'That'll teach you, ye smelly lump o' sharn!'

Would it be such a bad thing to leave Doomy, the dog, his dementit father, even dreich auld Scotia behind? And truth to tell Queenie was suffocating him. It seemed on closer reflection to be a most fortuitous turn of events. He would, of course, continue to play the martyr but suddenly William Bigland, last official recruit for the voyage of the *Broomielaw,* felt better, much better.

15 Doondie's Wake

Later that same evening as the wind swept in from Fair Isle, Will went looking for Queenie Stout. Her neighbours at the cluster of flagstone-roofed cottage by the east shore said she was with her mother at the tounship of Blaebister. Doondie Maclean was dead and Regan and Queenie were among the island women who had volunteered to sit with the widow during her night-long vigil beside the body.

William took the track south, past the corn mill on the headland. The twinkling lights of Blaebister lay ahead of him, across the marshy ground in the fold of the hill.

Old Doondie, who despite his eighty years had a fresh, optimistic approach to life. Drowned the previous night, he was found face down in the still, dark waters of the mill lade. The boys from Hookin' brought him home on an old door.

It was odd that he should, after all, have met his death by drowning because Doondie was a crofter through and through. He loved the land, felt in tune with all its moods but was suspicious of the sea and ships and the Macleans of Blaebister was one of the few island families not to own a skiff.

'The damned ocean is no' to be trusted,' he had confided in William one afternoon as they stacked sheaves on the hill and watched the little fleet of twenty skiffs scuttle out of the bay for the Stormay Bank with its shoals of cuithes, out there under the hammer head clouds.

William lifted the latch on the door, removed his hat and stepped into the low, cramped flagstone-floored lobby.

'It was guid o' you to come, Maister Will.' A silver-haired, stooped old man, Doondie's elder brother, emerged from the dark, peaty gloom.

William nodded: 'Aye, it's very sad - a seizure o' some sort, Tammo?'

Bending nearer the old man whispered behind his hand: 'Aye, for his wife's sake we're saying that he must have been taken bad, on his evening wander. You ken how stern she's become since takin' up wi' the Free Kirk and forcing him to sign the pledge. Truth to tell Doondie had a cache o' cratur in thae reed beds by the mill. I think he's maybe just had one too many and taken a header into the lade.'

The youngest son of Doomy chewed on a smile. It seemed a fine way to draw a line under a long life but still strange that he should end his days swallowed by the very element he feared most. William asked in a suitably solemn voice if he could view the corpse.

'Of course, away you go through. The women folk are here and tak' this glass to warm ye.' William threw the large measure of whisky over his throat. Manufactured in a still behind the hill the spirit traced a fiery path to his stomach.

The room was chill and silent, bathed in a flickering butter-yellow light from candles which were set at the four corners of the rough-hewn coffin which was resting on two chairs by the south-facing window. Doondie, a man with a story for every occasion, was finally silent. He lay there in his Sunday best. Someone had even combed what remained of his mousy-brown hair.

William edged forward and lightly touched the widow on the shoulder. She turned and smiled up at him, then turned again to her husband.

On the far side of the coffin sat the sisters from Cott, old Mrs Summers from north by and beside her was Queenie's mother, Regan, who was knitting, and Queenie herself. Will smiled across at the girl and her face lit up. Remembering the circumstances, she settled her features again into a more sombre and suitable mask of mourning. However, catching her eye once more Will discretely signalled towards the door and a moment later they were outside in the yard, under a canopy of stars and with moonlight skating across the South Wick.

'Let's walk down the track a piece, Queenie.'

At the foot of the short path a causeway ran out across the Loch of St Ronan to the ruined chapel. A moor hen disturbed from its slumber scuttled across the glassy surface of the loch.

William described the interview with his father and the stunning news of their blood relationship. He waited for a reaction.

The couple stopped beside the wall of the roofless chapel. The wind was rising and reflections of the lights from the big house danced on the water. The expression in the girl's eyes was worth a thousand words. For William there a came a moment of stark comprehension.

'You knew about this, Queenie, didn't you? You've known all along that we shared a father. How could you deceive me in this way? I'm banished to the ends of the earth, and all because of your selfishness.'

There was no shake of the head, no denial, but Queenie's eyes filled with tears and she reached for her lover. William, however, drew back: 'How could you do this?'

Stepping out along the track with the girl stumbling behind him William Bigland felt that, all things being equal, circumstances could scarcely be improved. Having made up his mind to accept the inevitable and go to Australia, he could now leave as the person who had been wronged, who had been deceived and fallen into a trap, instead of the villain of the piece. Yes, it was damned near perfect. He had cast off the shackles of his previous life, completely.

Wiping her eyes and trying to keep pace with the young man Queenie remained silent. She had spoken only occasionally since the day five years previously when her two brothers and a neighbour were drowned within sight of shore on their way back from the fishing at the Stormay Banks. Standing on the sand, waiting to greet them, she had watched their skiff go under on a calm summer's afternoon as if some great hand had dragged the craft to the bottom. The bodies of the boys were never discovered.

The two figures, a distance between them now, left the causeway and clambered up the slope to the greystone buildings of Blaebister. The bond between the young people appeared to have been severed – perhaps forever. But growing within Queenie was the seed of an idea and a calm determination not to give this man up so easily.

16 Driven to Distraction

It was the sort of crazy burst of summer in October which can make winter's long, dark days seem that wee bit more tolerable: ridiculously high temperatures, impossibly blue skies and unseasonably calm conditions.

It was the selfsame balmy conditions which gave Aaron Malise what he considered an inspired idea as he schemed the elimination of his second victim.

During discreet inquiries in the public houses of Port Glasgow and Greenock Malise had discovered that Dougal McKinstrie, an evil wee type in his mid-40s who had served as a topyardsman on the *Arran Dubh,* was now working as a labourer on a lochside estate beyond Inveraray in Argyll, the territory from where his branch of the clan hailed.

Malise boarded the mail coach bound for Kintyre. As they rattled along beside the Gareloch where the sun mica-danced across the miniature waves, Malise ignored his motley companions - a loud, red-faced wool trader from Campbeltown, a coy serving girl and a flirtatious soldier - and reflected on his plans for McKinstrie. For their part the trio were interested and intimidated in equal measure by the strange man in the cloth mask.

Malise had considered the merit of an axe murder, poison, he had even pondered the possibility of another imaginative drowning, perhaps in something like a vat of beer but as they stopped briefly in Arrochar, with the hum of clouds of insects in the roadside bushes, the answer came to him fully formed.

The coach, horses snorting and flicking their tails to keep at bay the winged beasties which had overstayed their autumn welcome, took off for Lochgilphead and Malise allowed himself a smile of satisfaction, dozing for the rest of the journey. From his base in the *King's Arms* he had two days reconnaissance work ahead of him.

The weather held fine, with bright sunshiny days and humid, overcast nights which always brought the threat of thunder and rain. It was truly an Indian summer.

Malise quickly selected his ground for action. Rory's Ha' was a small ruined keep, of indeterminate age, sitting on a lonely rocky point of land which jutted out into the loch a couple of miles along the shore from the estate. It was impressive in its own derelict way with crows spinning above the shattered battlements and trees crowding the roofless interior, but it was seldom visited.

Legend had it that a score of the McKinstrie clansfolk had been burned to death when the keep was torched during a clan feud in the first years of the 17th century. It was an eerie and threatening location.

Malise remembered how on the *Arran Dubh*, McKinstrie was forever boasting of his tough pedigree, his proud clan background, of how he was directly descended from the chieftain who had perished in the destruction of the keep.

Although most of his family had abandoned the district for the dark, satanic workshops and big wages on offer in the industrial slums of Glasgow, the topyardsman had demonstrated a strong affection for the area and for his ancestors. It was no surprise to anyone in the community, Malise learned, that McKinstrie had returned to Inveraray after his years at sea. For the next two days as he stalked his intended victim Malise reflected how happy he would be to put the bastard in direct touch with the grandfathers for whom McKinstrie had expressed so much affection.

Eventually when he was sure he had the right man and that his routine was fixed, Malise moved in. On a quiet back path to the estate, overhung by venerable oaks and sycamores and well away from any other human being, he made his play.

'You say you are studying clan histories yet I tell you, man, you're voice is very familiar.' McKinstrie looked again at the strange masked individual who had barred his way.

'Aye, be that as it may. It's the story of the McKinstries and the burning of Rory's Ha' that I'm interested in. And folk hereabouts tell me you are the last representative of that family in the area.'

'Possibly so... as it happens I can spare an hour this afternoon.'

And so an arrangement was made. After a still, sultry day in which the afternoon sun managed to produce unseasonable warmth, the two men took the lochside track for Rory's Ha'.

The attack when it came was vicious and unexpected. Malise felled his victim from behind with the stout branch he had collected from the ditch. He then dragged the unconscious man through the undergrowth almost to the edge of the rocky shore where he set to work.

As he came too McKinstrie found himself slumped on rough ground at the top of the shore. He was tightly lashed to the sinewy roots of an overturned tree. His wrists ached and he felt as if he had been kicked by a mule. He could also sense blood trickling down his back from the wound on his head. Testing the rope that he held him securely, he groaned.

His captor stood at the water's edge, with his back to him looking out across the still waters of the inlet towards the ruinous keep. The sun was dipping behind the Kintyre hills. Malise turned on hearing the movement behind him. He swatted a solitary midge which had buzzed into his eyes and walked across to stand over his prisoner.

'Aye McKinstrie, you're back with us, I see. It wouldn't do for you to miss all the action. After all you're the principal turn in this wee drama.'

The prisoner moaned again and shook his head as if trying to clear his thoughts.

'I know ye now, man. That voice. You're Malise - fae the *Arran Dubh*. But this is crazy. You must remember what happened. If this is some sort o' revenge you're set on then you've got the wrong man. After Gilchrist went over the side I told them you wouldn't be stupid enough to turn us in. You must surely mind on...'

'Well, my recollection is quite different. I saw you kick Gilchrist about the head and wouldn't I be right in thinking it was you who helpfully went off to find the lamp which provided the oil to leave me looking like this...'

Malise tore off his hood and pushed his scarred visage into that of his prisoner. He then began to test the security of the ropes which held McKinstrie fast to the tree roots. Reaching into his jacket pooch he produced a little jar. He dipped the corner of his jacket into the golden liquid and smeared it across McKinstrie's face. Clearly satisfied he stood back and admired his work. He then gagged the prisoner remembering that the punishment he planned often resulted in insane screams from the tormented victims.

'Sorry I can't stay around to share your big moment but they'll be plenty of friends here shortly to join the fun...'

As Malise clambered up the bank and into the wood, the first of the evening midgies, attracted by the heather honey, settled on McKinstrie's eyes, nose and mouth and on the trail of blood running down his neck. The self appointed executioner had read with quiet satisfaction that when this form of punishment was used by the clan chiefs in the 16th century the prisoner usually went mad before eventually dying of shock.

17 The Inquisitive Elder

In the grubby, gloomy back room of the *Elephant & Castle* in Dumbarton's High Street the passengers from the Campbeltown-Glasgow mail coach took a light lunch of bread, broth and fruit while the horses were changed for the final leg of the journey along the Clyde to Glasgow.

In different circumstances the clergyman who had occupied a leather corner seat near the window might have seemed like a favourite, jovial uncle, a thick-set man, with an aura of strength. However, on this winter afternoon he looked out-of-sorts and ill-tempered. In fact, he was nursing a mad impatience to be on the road, or accurately, to be on the open sea.

Shade raised his head as horse hooves clattered on the cobbles in the lane outside. It had been a poor, overcast day and the light was already fast vanishing. Discretely he surveyed his fellow travellers, trying especially to avoid making eye contact with the one remaining passenger who had arrived in the inn a few minutes previously to join the coach party. Shade had recognised him immediately and concentrated on the plate of thick vegetable soup in front of him, supping with studied concentration. But it was too late.

The newcomer who had initially settled to read put aside his book and removed his wire-rimmed spectacles. He threw a greeting across the back room of the inn: 'Well, it's yourself, Mr Shade. A wee weekend trip into Glasgow, is it? A chance to meet up with your brethren at the synod, no doubt?'

Looking as if conversation was absolutely the last thing he wanted just at that particular moment the Shade glared at the speaker: 'Aye, Chisholm, something like that…' He could snap this little man with his like a twig, scuff him away like a bug on his shoulder. Chisholm was an area salesman on the Clyde coast for a firm specialising in surgical appliances; he was an elder in the kirk and the most nosy and wearisome busybody. This was agreed throughout the parish.

However, Shade recalled – with a brief inner sigh of relief - that all such irritations were almost behind him - for ever.

Moments later as the company stood in the half-light in the doorway of the Inn and prepared to re-board the coach, Shade clambered with surprising agility up the side of the coach to check that his baggage was secure.

'That's a powerful lot of luggage for a weekend trip, Reverend, if you don't mind me saying so.' Chisholm, who saw it as his sacred duty to keep the ladies of the community well-supplied with tittle-tattle, was clearly fishing for information.

'I don't think I ever made mention of a weekend trip, Chisholm,' came the response. With growing interest the kirk elder had noted that the minister had three heavy carpetbags stacked on the coach roof.

'Well, I hope you're not running away with the communion silver or the funds for the refurbishment of the bell tower!'

The tight-lipped stare which Shade offered in exchange forced the salesman to abandon any efforts at humour.

'You're due a break, minister. I've been saying that to everyone in the kirk session.'

'That's kind of you, Chisholm.' One question too many, thought Shade, and Chisholm, the elder, would find himself fish fodder in Glasgow docks. He would see to that.

'From all that's been said and from my own observations, you've been hard at it since you arrived here in August. I'm sure the presbytery would look upon your long term connection with Tarbert in a very favourable light.'

As the coach pulled out along the Glasgow Road, Chisholm returned to his book – 'The Perils of Fanny'.

Across the coach Shade chuckled to himself. If this halfwit only knew, thought the minister, tapping a pinch of snuff on to the back of his hand, sniffing vigorously and feeling it bite into his sinuses.

Three months in that God-forsaken clachan by the loch, a hellhole with heather, herring and midges, had been a penance for sure but he was leaving with his gifts, his going-away presents from the spinsters and widows of the parish. He reassured himself by patting the pouch which was safely stowed in the deep inside pocket of his coat.

Everything was in place. There would be no stopping him now. With the Leith money now safely hidden in his luggage, he was finally ready to break any remaining ties; he could look forward to comfortable middle age wherever he ended up, with the opportunity and the money to indulge his little fantasies as he pleased.

Although his brother knew about the jewels he had no idea that Shade was also in the pay of the Southern Cross. Family loyalties only went so far and in any case seafarers – kin or not - were a strange lot. No, he would keep his counsel on his other activities.

The coach clattered through the trees towards Old Kilpatrick. Away to the Southwest the skies were clearing just a little, a band of brightness as the clouds were breaking and thinning promised some welcome late evening sunshine.

'A better day tomorrow, Mr Shade, by the looks o' it.'

'Aye, Chisholm, that's for sure.'

18 The Bengal Merchant

Glasgow's docks were, in the middle years of the century, the busy heart of what was fast becoming the Second City of Victoria's Empire. Warm morning rain slanted across the quays as heavy laden wagons dragged by huge Clydesdale and Shire horses rumbled and rattled over the cobblestones. Casks were being rolled, bales piled and the stevedores splashed through ankle-deep puddles. Along the waterfront lay forty vessels or more.

From her billet at the grimy window of the *Bengal Merchant* public house opposite Victoria Dock Queenie Stout had been watching wagon after wagon arrive, laden with wooden crates, the last of the priceless possessions of the emigrants soon to sail on the clipper ship *Broomielaw*. Stowing of the bulk of the cargo, which was to remain unopened until reaching Adelaide, had been completed in the previous few days.

Excited family groups were also beginning to appear either by coach or on foot, spilling on to the bustling concourse, grasping their hand luggage tightly, wide-eyed, like travellers who had just disembarked in some exotic foreign port. Somehow Queenie felt a great distance between herself and the emigrant throng for whom this day was clearly the culmination of many months, perhaps years, planning. She had catapulted herself into this great adventure.

Bending into the showers the crowds pressed forwards towards the quay with the children pointing excitedly at the tall masts of the brigs, barques and clippers which soared above the wooden sheds. Many groups appeared to include other family members there to see the emigrants off, in what was in so many cases, a final, heart-wrenching farewell.

Across this animated scene the families would advance, between lines of barrels, crates and coils of rope, children jumping puddles while parents ushered them out of the path of the enormous, clomping carthorses and forward to the beckoning doorway beneath a huge, painted hoarding – red on white - which read – BERTH 6 – BROOMIELAW – FOR ADELAIDE & PORT CHALMERS.

One family, she saw, parents and three girls, unusually had a Border collie in tow. The man seemed to lag behind, as if weary after some long, exhausting journey. The collie barked a warning and showed its teeth to a mangy crossbreed skulking amongst the stationary carts.

Next came a fascinating parade – a huge oak of a man wheeling a barrow, a thin individual with fishy eyes who proceeded clumsily as if unaccustomed to walking and a little, well dressed lady, no more than three-feet tall.

The fishy man bent to kiss his tiny companion goodbye and shook hands warmly with the giant before the odd couple moved into the dockside sheds beyond which the *Broomielaw* was berthed. He then turned on his heels and tottered off looking with satisfaction at the grey, lowering skies.

Queenie, while intrigued and excited by all this activity was also afraid. She hadn't removed her soaking bonnet or cloak for fear she might have to run from this drinking den. However, the information she'd been given by her cousin the herring fisherman at Thurso had proved accurate enough. The *Bengal Merchant* was the place to arrange a last-minute, clandestine passage to the Antipodes. The bartender had pointed out Mooney, known to the locals apparently as *The Kelvinhaugh Lad*, who was seated in a corner. Negotiations opened.

After their conversation Ezra Mooney, a crewman on the *Broomielaw*, had left to check the cargo list and establish the best part of the hold to hide away. He told her to sit tight and wait for his return. Now Queenie was terrified over the possibility that Mooney might simply take her grandmother's necklace and ring and leave her here in this sinister establishment to have her throat cut.

Helping a stowaway aboard could get him the lash he had told her when she whispered her plan. But when she produced the jewellery he gestured her to put it back in her satchel. He would see what he could do.

'Once aboard you must stay hidden until the ship is beyond Madeira and then you can give yourself up, young miss,' said Mooney.

She had looked at him aghast.

It was likely, the crewman explained, that at worst she would be set to cooking or cleaning duties for the remainder of the voyage. By then the hold would have become insufferably hot and airless and in any case they would be too far from land to consider putting her ashore before Australia.

Queenie was sipping from a tumbler of water which the crone who was collecting glasses had placed in front of her. For the past five minutes – as she waited for Mooney's return - she had been aware of a dozen pairs of eyes observing her.

In turn Queenie watched the rain streak the windows and listened to the fiddler sheltering in the doorway of the baker's shop next door as he scratched out a series of lively jigs. Somehow the music, although bright and cheery, made her sad. It told of Stormay dances and familiar sights and sounds now left behind her. With all her worldly possessions in the carpet bag at her feet, Queenie was lost in these memories of her island home, images of her William and wonder at the adventure which, she guessed, had already begun.

Her mother, she knew, would be distraught. But Queenie told herself she would write once she got a job in Australia and had sent a first cash instalment to the grey stone-walled croft above the east shore.

She had already astonished herself by the way in which circumstances had forced her out of her shell – just to seek help, guidance or directions from people in the street. William had said that folk south of Thurso were ogres or thieves. She hadn't found it so. Already she had discovered a warmth in ordinary people which surprised her.

'Soor' Queenie they had called her on Stormay because she had found it so difficult to smile since the day her older brothers, Erlend and Peter, had drowned within sight of their front door returning from that long-line fishing expedition north of the island. Somehow, the islanders felt her to have been mentally unhinged by the loss of her kin but, in fact, she excelled at the wee island school.

However, the pleadings of the teacher that she be allowed to attend the Grammar School in the town went unheeded by her parents. It was unthinkable. She was needed to bring money into a poor household which had already been deprived of two wage earners by the cruel sea. Almost as soon as she had closed her school books for the last time she was in service at the Hall as a kitchen maid.

She was shaken from her reverie as the door of the public house was pushed open and a tide wave of dockside and street noises – squeaky cart wheels, yelping hounds, squabbling drunks, the distant scrape of the fiddle - flooded into the dingy lair.

19 The Man in the Top Hat

In from this increasingly murky day, with rain now drumming on the pavements, entered a heavy-set well-dressed man with a grey beard, cut fairly short. A toff in such lowlife surroundings - how strange, thought Queenie. Dressed in a greatcoat, closely fastened around his neck, he wore a top hat which he removed and shook vigorously sending glistening showers of raindrops into the air. He looked set for a night at the opera rather than a refreshment in a spit and sawdust bar.

Waiting for his refreshment to be poured the man glanced over his shoulder in the direction of the docks and then opening his coat extracted his pocket watch from the waistcoat. Nodding with satisfaction he replaced the timepiece and reached inside his coat, producing a canvas pouch. He began to gently finger the contents without untying the draw strings.

In the company of stevedores, carters, beggars, vagabonds and prostitutes – the dubious clientele of the *Bengal Merchant,* this newcomer might as well have been a citizen from the strange lands of Mr Defoe, Lilliput or Brodbogdanog, so out of place was he.

He carried his nip glass to a corner table where he sat down, produced a large black-bound book from his carpet bag and began to study the work intently, taking deliberate sips. He paused at regular intervals, raising his eyes from the text as if he was testing himself on memorised passages.

Such an outlandish customer was certain to attract unwanted attention in here, thought Queenie, but at least, for the moment, it diverted interest from her.

She watched a narrow-eyed, unwashed individual as he moved around the howff. He had a plume of mousy hair, wore a distinctive red and white neckerchief and moved with a determination which suggested the possibility of a rumpus. This troublemaker took a clay pipe from his mouth, halted beside the newcomer's table and hacked noisily on to the sawdust-strewn boards at the stranger's feet.

'There's no way you'd know this chief but it's an auld tradition in this bar that first timers buy a round o' drinks for the company.' He looked malevolently across the tables at his band of cronies and winked. This clearly was rare fun.

The stranger studiously ignored him, gently tugging at his ear lobe before carefully turning another thin, rustling page of his book in which he was apparently so completely absorbed.

'Aye, and failure to purchase drink can result in the confiscation of personal goods.'

The bar fly reached down and made a grab for the bag. Instead he found himself on the receiving end of a swinging right uppercut delivered by the reader from the sitting position yet worthy of the prize-fighters who visited the booths on Glasgow Green. Neckerchief man gasped as his lower teeth punctured his upper lip and he was lifted into the air and propelled backwards by the force of the blow. Landing with a thump on his backside against the wall, a heavy iron bucket used for infrequent swilling of the pub floor was dislodged from its shelf above and fell with a resounding clang on the pub joker's head. He slumped into unconsciousness.

In the melee the stranger's table had been overturned and having set it to rights and tucked the chair underneath he casually returned the whisky glass to the counter, looking around for any other takers.

'It's a rowdy house you're operating here, landlord.'

The barman had deliberately turned his back on the outsider and set to rearranging his stock of grimy tumblers and pewter tankards.

'I think you dropped this, sir.' Using both hands Queenie picked up the heavy Bible which the gentleman had been reading and dusted it off with the back of her glove before handing it over with a polite curtsy. He held her hand overlong.

Up close there was something quite unsettling about the man with his narrow eyes which seemed to fix her on the spot. She remembered the way old Bigland, her father, was wont to look at her in that half-leering, half-affectionate way and she felt uneasy, stepping back immediately.

'God bless you, my girl,' he said with an odd sort of hesitancy. Returning the Bible to the interior of his bag and glancing briefly at the throng of ne'er-do-wells who had gathered around the victim of the fallen bucket and were staring threateningly in their direction, he said: 'If you're prepared to take the advice of a humble clergyman, I would strongly suggest that you find a more civilised place to pass your day. I fear that the Lord will have his work cut out with this bunch of ruffians.' That said he swept out of the door.

A toothless hag who had been smoking a pipe and looked to be wearing a jute sack as a dress, glanced up from her work tending the casualty and waved a fist at the man as he left.

You may be many things, Mister, thought Queenie, but humble clergyman you are not.

Mind you, his advice was surely sound. Queenie would have run from that miserable cesspit of humanity in a moment, followed the strange preacher out into the rain – but she had to wait. It was so close to sailing time and Mooney the deckhand was her only hope.

She thought again of William who by now would surely be unpacking his bags and finding his way around the ship. Would he be thinking of her? Surely he would, she reassured herself. He was upset at their father. That was all. Of course William would forgive her for following him. How pleased he would be to see her, wouldn't he? They would sail off to a new future together and…

Queenie jumped. An ugly, unshaven face was pressed against the glass only a few inches from her shoulder. Mooney grinned through the grimy glass, his whole demeanour suggesting a successfully completed mission. His gap-toothed smirk and gestures calling her outside suggested that, at the last gasp, he had indeed secured her a secret corner for her on the *Broomielaw.*

Heart racing as she left the bar, Queenie saw the battling clergyman in a nearby doorway deep in conversation with a uniformed naval officer. Then they were joking, laughing and exchanging backslaps, as if they hadn't seen each other in years. Together the men began to peer at the contents of what look like a small pouch.

Mooney grabbed her wrist and dragged her off through the rain towards the cargo storage areas: 'Come on, missy, you've a ship tae catch.'

20 The Last Stitch

'Wakey, wakey – rise and shine!'

Sailmaker Louis Cartwright shook his throbbing head as he slowly recovered consciousness. He screwed up his eyes trying to focus on the grotesque face which hovered above him, half concealed by a hemp mask, but his vision was blurred, nothing was clear.

'Well, my old shipmate, pleased to see you back in the land of the living – at least for a wee while. I wouldn't want you to miss this,' chirped the person peering down at him, who then whipped off his mask to reveal a badly scarred face and one empty eye.

Cartwright gradually began to absorb his surroundings. He was lying on his back looking up past this strange apparition into a stand of fir trees which swayed in unison. Above the trees, stars were beginning to appear in a dark blue sky. It must have been a beautiful day, but now it was evening.

He had been in the inn at Dunecht; he remembered that much. And he had fallen in with this oddball and shared an ale or two. After that he had no memory of the day, except that he had felt drowsy, so drowsy.

Now, trying to move, he found his hands were bound to his side and his feet lashed together, but more than that he became aware that he was tightly wrapped in some sort of winding-sheet. Rough against his face as he turned his head from side to side the material felt like canvas or sailcloth – his stock in trade. He sensed that for some reason there were boulders tucked around him inside the sheet.

'I have a train to catch so we will, I fear, have to dispense with all the formalities.'

Cartwright, with a growing sense of dread, turned his head to see that the crazy man now appeared to be, slowly, deliberately, threading a length of twine into a huge sailmaker's needle. Then came the chilling realisation that the cloth that enclosed him, leaving only his face to peer out at a darkening world, was a shroud. The sort of mortcloth used to conduct burials at sea. Over the years he must have manufactured a hundred of those. He was powerless to move his arms and legs.

'I've watched you do this often enough, Cartwright. Sewing poor souls into their shrouds before we sent them into the depths. Lot more to it than I imagined. Quite a skill. Yes indeed.'

The sailmaker peered through the opening in the canvas sack at his tormentor.

'It's you Malise. You were on the *Arran Dubh*. What's going on here? Listen, for God's sake...'

'Well, my friend. What's happening here is that you are paying a debt. This poor, scarred face is your doing, you and the others and there is the small matter of the boy Gilchrist. Very remiss of you to put him over the side without the proper rites, don't you think?'

The voice from the shroud was now filled with dismay.

'Oh, Lord Jesus Christ. You've mistaken me for my brother, Andrew. He was the sailmaker. I was a deck hand and was never part of that gambling school where the boy Gilchrist was killed. This is a terrible mistake.'

This pleading seemed, for a moment, to have an effect. Then Cartwright felt his heart thump inside his chest as Malise bent over him and pinched the soft tip of his nose between thumb and forefinger.

'You'll be keeping me right here, Cartwright. Wouldn't want to cause you unnecessary suffering, then I'll sew you into your bag and tip you over the edge of this quarry; they said at the inn that the water here could be 100 feet deep. With your cargo of rocks you'll stay down there for a long, long time.'

Cartwright started to wail – a pitiful, haunted sound which became an agonised scream as Malise pushed the needle through the soft flesh below the nasal bone, hauling the twine through and then dragging the needle through the canvas, before pulling his handiwork tight.

Then through his pain and anguish Cartwright felt himself being propelled forward on to a slope and he began to roll, slowly at first, over and over, faster and faster before he was dropping, turning and twisting through the air, inside his dark shroud.

Close by, even in his final distress, he thought he heard a scream and then a dull thud as if something had struck the rock face next to him.

High above on the edge of the quarry, Malise had stumbled as he rolled his victim into eternity, the banking had given way and along with a shower of rock fragments and Cartwright's winding sheet he toppled into the black depths, crashing into the quarry wall as he dropped. Below in the gathering gloom startled ducks settled again on their sinister pool.

Amongst the ripples a stout blackthorn thick floated on the inky deep.

21 To the Tail of the Bank

The pilot cutter *Endeavour* took the *Broomielaw* in tow around midday to the sound of splashing ropes and shouted commands ringing along the quayside. Relatives walked to the end of the wharf, waving to the last and to the strains of the pipes drifting away across the city on the afternoon breeze, the great journey began with the short haul to Greenock and Tail of the Bank.

Later that week *The Glasgow Herald* reported in its shipping movements column that the fine new clipper ship *Broomielaw* sailed on schedule with over 250 emigrants, 'a set of fine-looking people', for the Antipodes.

For the first half-hour after boarding there had been a mad scramble by each family group to find their allocated berths and to decide who would sleep where. Right up until sailing time carpenters were still putting the finishing touches to the wooden berths as the emigrants spilled on board.

The sleeping quarters had been dismantled, of course, to give maximum space for the last return shipment of wool from South Australia.

Women in particular seemed to find the berth allocations as the first great challenge of their pioneer lives and once installed were prepared to defend their corner against all comers. Children raced about exploring every dark corner and tagging them as their own hideaway, young folk sized each other up, as young folk do, while the men gruffly introduced themselves and their families to their neighbours in adjacent quarters. Scotland being a small place, mutual connections were quickly made, familiar faces and places remembered. A few families stood apart from the outburst of camaraderie, looking bewildered by such a sudden and intimate sharing.

Eventually after much negotiation and debate, while the crew got on with their duties topside, the emigrants sorted themselves out; folk settled on their bunks. Already they were emotionally drained.

There were only a dozen passenger cabins and the remainder of the party were assisted emigrants, accommodated in a double row of upper and lower bunks that ran almost round the ship on the main deck level. The deck was separated into open compartments holding about 15 people who bunked around a clear space some eight feet by four, their cramped dining room and communal space for the duration of the voyage.

This main deck was divided in turn into three large sections separated by bulkheads which were pierced by pairs of low hatches, to port and starboard. The single men berthed forward in merry confusion, the single women aft and married couples together with children of twelve and under, in between. Apart from the time the families spent on deck they lived, ate and slept in their quarters below.

When bad weather kept the topside hatches closed, ventilation was all but cut off, the only flickering illumination coming from carefully monitored oil lamps.

However, on this bright autumn afternoon the hatches were flung wide and fresh air ran the length of the ship. It was almost as if the *Broomielaw* was straining to be on her way and was taking a few deep breaths in preparation for the challenge which lay ahead.

Walter Lumsden was elated – and relieved. He had never expected for a moment that he would begin to look on these families as his ain folk. It was, after all, just a job.

But as he walked through the hubbub of the steerage, nodding to this individual, smiling to the old folk, patting the kiddies' heads and seeing so many familiar faces settling into their quarters; he did indeed feel a friendship and a bond with these people, way beyond the formal emigration contract. The emigration ships were each a separate little world, a universe in minature.

'Home for all of us for the next few weeks, Mrs Gilchrist.' He nodded to the Gilchrists as he moved along the passageway.

'She's a fine vessel, Mr Lumsden. We'll soon have her looking like our own front room,' came the response from shepherd's wife. Her husband sat staring into space, clapping the collie which lay at his feet. The agent was particularly relieved that this family had somehow managed to sort out their last-minute problems and were able to join the expedition.

Such was the excitement below decks on their leisurely way down the Clyde that few of the passengers took the opportunity of viewing the beautiful scenery for which the river was far-famed; only a handful of folk were up top to watch the craggy bulk of Dumbarton Castle rock slip by.

Almost everyone was too busy getting their area of deck into what they considered to be a habitable state to worry about the scenery. Everything above and below decks was hustle and bustle. Pegs and nails were hammered in around the bunks to hang clothes and provision bags. Much shifting and stowing of boxes had to be completed before the temporary abode was considered shipshape.

It was an important psychological moment, this settling in, because many of these folk from the western part of Argyllshire, Ayrshire, Glasgow and Edinburgh had only been given a fortnight's notice confirming the sailing date; so little time to finally dispose of their house, say their farewells and prepare their families for the adventure.

Slowly the emigrants became accustomed, tuned to the gentle motion of the *Broomielaw* in the water. The more perceptive and well-read knew this could only be a mere softening-up for what lay ahead.

For old Agnes Govan the main task was to find a safe store among the boxes for her collection of patent medicines – Pritchard's camomile, dandelion, rhubarb and ginger pills and her precious quinine wine which, she claimed, cured everything from derangement of the liver, lack of appetite and what the old lady called her 'stressful wind', a complaint which was a source of constant amusement to the wee ones.

The children were warned off. 'There is no needcessity for you girls to be touching this thread box. I've stored my pills there and I'll count them every night.'

In every 'partment' and on every steep companionway there was a buzz of excitement as folk began to get to know the ship which was to be their home for the next ten weeks or more, to learn the mysteries of the cooking depot, the intricacies of the toilet arrangements...and most testingly, they were, slowly, getting to know each other.

Innes Macaulay was seated on his bunk, Belle and the older boys were off exploring. Beside his father Torrance was leaning on the bunks, whittling away with his pocket knife as if he was in the kitchen in the Cowgate, carving his initials on a scrap of wood which he planned to fix to the bulkhead.

The second mate, seeing this tall and seemingly mature lad, wanted him put for'ard among the single men but on salvaging their testimonial from the bottom of their box of papers which stated the ages of the Macaulay boys, the mate relented.

'You're a big one for your age, boy,' was his only observation.

Across the other side of the steerage James Gilchrist looked around him, shook his head wearily and addressing no-one in particular declared: 'Aye, this is just as cramped as I thought it would be. I knew it. We're like bloody ewes in a pen. Just as well we're close to the companionway where we can get a breath of o' fresh air.'

Gilchrist had seated himself at the solid packing case in the centre of the open area with Gip tucked in around his feet. The Gilchrists were, after all, on their way all the way to New Zealand. Gilchrist carefully scrutinised every crewmen who passed along the lower deck. As he did so he glanced at a scrap of paper he held in his hand, the note he had uplifted from behind the bar in the Shipbank Inn, the note from Malise.

The shepherd of Sweetshaws was still puzzled and perplexed about Brocklebank's change of heart. The story about the problem having been solved by young Alastair Milne stepping into the breach just didn't ring true. However, he now had other more pressing matters on his mind. He tucked the note down the side of his bunk. And there was Maggie's fall in the byre….

He turned again and shouted across the corridor: 'You said you were a miner in Lanarkshire, Macaulay, until the accident. Clearly you'll no' be taking up that line in South Australia, eh?'

Gilchrist looked across at the ravaged face of his travelling companion who had risen and was feeling his way hand over hand round the little cubicle with words of encouragement and guidance from his son. Eventually he made it back to the bunk. It wouldn't be long before he knew every knot of wood, every creak and groan of the boards underfoot, every voice, and every distinctive aroma of which there were already many.

'A farrier's business – me and my boys. That's still the plan. I had always thought to get back above ground. It's no life for these yins.' Innes reached for and found Torrance's shoulder and gave it a squeeze. 'More to life than coal dust and night shifts, eh Torry?'

'You're gemme. I'll give you that, Macaulay. How do you reckon you'll adjust to the new life – chasing kangaroos, fighting off bushrangers and the like.'

Innes Macaulay chuckled and turned his head towards the speaker. 'We'll cope. Now Torry, where have those brothers of yours got to?'

Maggie Gilchrist, looking pale and tired, nursing a fierce bruise just below her left eye and wearing a silk scarf loosely tied around her neck, appeared again through the excited family groups. At her side were her aunt, youngest daughter Hilda and Belle Macaulay.

The women declared themselves satisfied with the cooking arrangements. Belle had already found herself elected by popular consent as a mess assistant for their part of the family section, responsible for organising cooking as well as the collection and distribution of food. It was an important duty. And Belle shone with pride.

Down from the deck the two older Gilchrist girls, May and Flora, appeared at their mother's side. They were clearly concerned about her health and helped seat her at the long bench which ran down the centre passageway of the steerage. Her pregnancy, now in its seventh month was now clearly a burden rather than a special joy.

The other occupants in the immediate vicinity of their compartment were two Gaelic-speaking families with the best behaved children Belle Macaulay thought she had ever seen. She wondered, with a slight twinge of anxiety if, after weeks at sea, they would be quite so bidden.

Old Agnes lowered herself wearily into her bunk having checked to see that her precious potions box had not been tampered with. Like her, there were one or two older folk on the *Broomielaw* who had opted for the discomfort, danger and uncertainty of a new life rather than be left behind. But they were few.

The two older Macaulay sons joined the company and once all the introductions had been completed the younger folk returned to their berths. From the single men's division joking, laughter and the tuneful clatter and bang of the Coocaddens Gutter Band filtered through the ship indicating that a leaving party was already under way there.

As for the single women there was talk of forming a ways and means committee after supper to ensure that their quarters remained a model of cleanliness and order during the voyage. Natural leaders began to emerge and shrinking violets had nowhere to hide. It was paradise for some, a little hell, that would take so much getting used to, for others.

A strange calm broken only by a child's cry or a shouted instruction on deck overtook the company by the time the ship dropped anchor off Greenock for the night. Fathers and mothers sat quietly on the sea chests stowed at the foot of their berths.

Inward struggles could be found in every compartment. Across from the Macaulays and Gilchrists a young woman with her little boy asleep in her arms was sitting gazing sorrowfully into the face of the child, while tears stole silently down her pale cheeks. Others looked bewildered, their minds revisiting familiar streams and firesides, perhaps imagining strange new landscapes. The noise of celebration had, for the moment, ceased.

It was as if a sudden realisation had come to the emigrants throughout the ship of the enormity of their undertaking – and all they were leaving behind. However, at this point there were few tears; there would be time enough for weeping.

22 The Ocean Awaits

The following morning Walter Lumsden led the way gingerly up the sloping lee poop ladder, the officer from the Seaman's Mission at his heels. Lumsden knew it would take him a day or two to regain his sea legs. In fact, up until this moment he had not been able to summon up enough courage even to look out over the estuary. Clinging to the mizzen rigging he was relieved to see the Clyde was hardly ruffled. Two young herring gulls, riding the gentle swell in the lee of the ship, bickered over a bedraggled jellyfish.

About a mile away lay *The Spirit of Speed,* swinging gently at anchor, making preparations for her departure within the next forty-eight hours. In effect, they would be racing to the other side of the world.

Although skies were clearing down-river, as if to mark the *Broomielaw's* leaving, *The Spirit of Speed* lay beneath a dark mass of passing cloud. A curtain of rain made the vessel appear as if she was enveloped in a swirling mist. High above the *Broomielaw* gulls wheeled and shrieked, fulmars skimmed and the gentlest of breezes snapped at the ropes and braces as if urging the ship to be up and on her way.

Looming above him as he climbed Walter sensed the bulk of the Rev. Elijah Shade, minister/surgeon for the voyage who was preparing to lead the farewell service from his makeshift pulpit at the top of the companionway. At that moment the stocky clergyman, large black Bible in hand, began pacing the boards, tapping the pages, nervously tugging at his odd, bristly beard and glancing skywards as if seeking divine help. Seeing Lumsden appear with the officer from the Mission Shade suddenly looked calmer and in control, perhaps even relieved. Formal introductions were made.

Off to port the rooftops and chimneys of Greenock and Port Glasgow crowded to the shore. Smoke from a thousand hearths drifted out over the grey river and towering cloudbanks which had wreathed the hill above the Gare Loch and Loch Long to the north seemed to be thinning. Several barques were discharging or loading cargoes at the jetties close by the Custom House. The port had a busy, prosperous air.

It was rather humbling, Lumsden thought, as he joined the minister at the rail, to recall how many emigrant ships had already left the Tail of the Bank for the Americas or the Antipodes with their precious cargoes – the dreams and fears of ordinary people. The Lumsden family had started their journey from exactly this location, three years previously, though for the emigration agent it seemed like several lifetimes.

After the overnight halt all formalities required by the government inspectors had been taken care of, food and freshwater stocks had been checked and re-checked, the carpenters returned to shore and within the hour the pilot boat would guide them towards St George's Channel and the open sea.

The sun peeked through the remaining rain clouds. Lumsden had been sleeping better over the past few nights, better than he had done in months, better than he felt he should have. As always, better than he felt he deserved. Strangely, he awoke in the mornings with a sense of anticipation tinged with fear. Not far beyond the lighthouse at Cloch Point one of his demons lay in wait – the mighty ocean.

Despite all the inevitable last-minute headaches, to see the sun mica-dancing on the water and to feel the clipper under way yesterday – albeit slowly – downriver, had filled him with a quiet elation. He tried not to think of the thousands of cold, wet, dangerous miles which lay ahead and gulped several lungfuls of the brisk estuary air.

'Well, Mr Shade, that shower seems to have cleared over. And for once you'll have a captive audience. I can almost guarantee that no-one will sleep through your sermon today.' He pointed to the throng assembling on the deck below them.

The heavy-set clergyman, strands of grey hair lifting in the breeze, smiled back at the agent, only vaguely acknowledging the quip, then returned again anxiously to his Bible in which he had been marking passages with strips of paper.

A gaggle of girls tittered from their perch on a coil of thick rope; they had been brazenly sizing up the young men around them, particularly the younger sailors.

'You must dine with us one of these evenings, Mr Shade. It would be a chance for you to tell me all about the joys of your last charge in Tarbert.' That invitation, Walter Lumsden admitted to himself, was being issued as much out of curiosity as politeness. As it happened, it was never to be confirmed. Again the minister smiled unconvincingly and nodded. Lumsden felt an odd, unspecific uneasiness in Shade's presence.

After a moment it dawned on him that the reason must be that he was the only emigrant he had not met prior to departure, all their business having been conducted by letter with the skipper Ratter as an intermediary. Yes, that must be it, Lumsden reassured himself, watching with a pride which was as warming as it was unexpected, as the emigrant families, his emigrants, streamed on to the deck which was still slick and glistening from the shower of rain twenty minutes previously.

Walter knew they expected so much of him; pride he felt, certainly, but terror also. Why had he taken this vast burden to himself. Was he simply trying to purge his soul or was it part of some greater design?

As for Elijah Shade, he noted with satisfaction that the skipper was missing from the aft deck. He had not expected his campaign to bear such early fruit but Ratter was clearly already the worse for wear. And now that Shade saw a way out of leading the service of departure, he really did begin to feel the sun was shining on his enterprise. He would have to watch this emigration agent, for sure, but that aside he felt confident. What was it that their father had drummed into the boy and his siblings, time after time: 'The Lord helps those who help themselves.' It had been the only worthwhile piece of homespun philosophy from the superstitious old coot, reflected Shade.

Maggie Gilchrist and her girls appeared. Yes, their arrival on schedule at Glasgow had lifted Walter Lumsden's spirits but her bruised and battered condition had disturbed him.

The emigration agent nodded to the family groups one by one. The Sinclairs from Dunbar, cabin passengers, who had been so worried about the accommodation plans for their serving lass were also among the first on deck. Jessie was now in the same compartment aft as the Gilchrist girls and was cheerful about the arrangement.

Then came the quiet Gaelic-speakers from Argyll, the shipwrights, domestic servants, farmers, masons, gardeners, grooms, butchers, cabmen, labourers and coopers, shoemakers and blacksmiths.

From the hatchway midships the Macaulay family made their entrance with Innes, his arm linked through Belle's and, despite his handicap, confidently leading his flock towards the front of the calm yet expectant crowd.

There was James Gilchrist, Lumsden noted, with his dog at heel, clinging to a stay, gazing back upriver. Just beyond him stood the young man, Bigland was the name, thought the agent. He was the lad from the Northern Isles whose father, the laird, had paid such a ridiculous amount of money to persuade a Renfrewshire farmer to give up his cabin to his son. That was a strange business altogether.

Lumsden realised that he could now name every one of these emigrants, even the wee ones. More than that, he could sense their pooled anxiety and private nightmares. He composed himself.

Shade was joined in looking out over the gathering, by Captain Simmons, the elderly, bespectacled lay preacher from the Mission, also Mr Henderson, the shipping company representative and the young, sturdily-built first mate Jack Zurich, his blue eyes, set beneath heavy eyebrows, ever on the alert, However, the skipper Silas Ratter remained a notable absentee from the huddle of dignitaries at the top of the stairs.

23 A Home Over There

Attendance was not compulsory at these services of departure but eventually almost the entire ship's complement, crew and passengers, stood shoulder to shoulder. On the *Broomielaw,* the white line found on most Irish emigration ships, painted from port to starboard just aft of the main mast, was absent. This line, a demarcation designed to seperate cabin from steerage passengers was thought unnecessary on the more egalitarian Scottish vessels.

Some fathers hoisted their wee ones on to their shoulders, young folk having already forgotten their initial shyness were grouped together and crewmen lodged in the lower rigging. These gatherings were now an established part of the emigration timetable. From the top of the steps which eventually led to her hidey-hole in the for'ard holds, Queenie got herself as comfortable as she could, having scanned the crowds for her William. She couldn't remember seeing so many people in the same place at one time.

But Queenie was puzzled. The apparently gentle and modest clergyman who stood ready to open the service was surely the same man who had almost put the troublemaker through the wall in the *Bengal Merchant* public house, the stranger who had acted in such a surprisingly violent and certainly un-Christian manner.

A brief prayer, then the Second Paraphrase was sung. The hymn *There's a Home Over There* was delivered with impressive gusto even by folk who hadn't darkened the door of the kirk for a decade. The Catholic priest from Our Holy Reedemers's in Gourock was first to offer words of comfort and reassurance to the emigrants then Shade stepped forward, cleared his throat an in an exaggerated, almost theatrical, manner and addressed the throng.

'I'll now ask the Rev. Simmons from the Mission to say a few words to us before we bid farewell to Scotland. With his experience I'm sure he knows what is in all our hearts. Rev. Simmons, if you please…'

Now this was something out of the ordinary. It was expected, demanded even, that the clergyman travelling with the emigrants, the man who would share all the trials and tribulations of the voyage with them, should offer the final words of encouragement. It was clear to everyone that Shade liked to do business differently. No bad thing, thought the younger element amongst the passengers. Older folk found it odd.

The venerable clergyman from the Seamen's Mission in Greenock, standing like some old testament prophet above his flock, did not let the unusual opportunity pass. He told the emigrants they were leaving Scotland, a nation which had been made great by the industry, thrift and honesty of their forefathers.

Perhaps inevitably the attention of the younger folk began to wander.

'You carry a great and important burden as ambassadors of the Scottish nation. And while unimagined opportunities to make your way in life await you in the new lands, be warned. You would be well advised to spend little or nothing on drink and tobacco. These have been the ruin of so many settlers.'

There were some raised eyebrows and dismissive smiles among the younger men at this advice but vigorous nods in agreement this time from the elders. On this contentious, yet still light-hearted, note the service ended with another hymn.

Walter had noted the minister's odd reluctance to preach a sermon. He had also noticed something equally strange when the man came forward to lean on the railing – the heavy, calloused hands, not the smooth hands of an thinker and theologian but such as you might expect to find on a farm labourer or a miner, hands like those possessed by Innes Macaulay, toughened by swinging a pickaxe or a scythe. Walter Lumsden must have pressed more flesh than Victoria herself. He knew his hands.

From the departing launch the company representative Mr Henderson shouted across the widening gap between the vessels: 'God Speed, Mr Zurich. And you Lumsden… Let's make this a voyage to remember.' The little group on the launch then offered three cheers which were returned by the ship's company. Across the now sparkling waters of the Clyde the parting salutes echoed.

Zurich, the first mate, a fresh-faced confident young man in his late twenties with a face which was wind and weather-beaten by the salt spray of four oceans and a well muscled body which spoke of hard days in the Roaring Forties and a willingness to lend a hand aloft when the need arose, accompanied the agent below.

'You've done us proud and no mistake, Mr Lumsden. We have some bonny lasses aboard to brighten the voyage and plenty of fit young men to help with deck duties.'

Walter was ready to make his final head count before the anchor was let go. He already felt confident enough in this young man to ask the question which had troubled him for the past half-hour.

'By the by, Jack – where's your skipper? He seems to be keeping well out of the way.'

'Aye, he's coping with departure in his own style.'

Although he had known him for a few hours Lumsden liked Jack Zurich. His soft English accent and manners suggested a middle-class upbringing. That made his success at one of the world's toughest callings all the more impressive. Often the first mate effectively ran the ship. On 'his deck;' Jack Zurich's word would be law, Lumsden guessed, and his honest, blue eyes and confident style were reassuring. When Walter discovered that Jack had already made more than a dozen voyages to the Antipodes, as well as sailing the world in his youth, the agent felt sure that whatever the elusive skipper was up to, his right-hand man could take them all safely to the Australia shore.

An hour later with a succession of groans the main-yards swung round, blocks creaked and the canvas threshed and eventually filled in the modest breeze. The emigration ship *Broomielaw* slipped her moorings and left the Clyde.

24 Scotia No More

Light, unfavourable winds made for slow progress during those first 48 hours at sea. The agony of leaving was being prolonged and some accepted this better than others. James Gilchrist, for one, had taken to his bed, lying on his bunk staring at the rough boards above and listening to the sea noises against the planks; Gip lay stretched out by his bunk.

Ailsa Craig, the emigrant's outpost, was well behind and soon enough the Mull of Galloway lay dark and fast disappearing against the horizon to the north east. Ahead was the Isle of Man, the Irish Sea and beyond, the broad Atlantic.

As dusk fell and the red and green side and stern lights had been rigged word that Scotland was about to pass from sight found its way through the steerage.

Singly and in little groups folk began to gather at the stern and along the port side of the *Broomielaw*, looking behind them through the gloaming, straining for that final glimpse of the homeland. With dry mouths, damp eyes and aching hearts they clasped the rails, gazing at the horizon, the only sounds being the occasional crack of sail and the hiss of the bow cutting into the waves.

Children wondered about the fuss and continued with their games of hide-and-seek and spinning tops among the rope coils and barrels; the city youngsters were fascinated by strange, exotic creatures – the cow, pigs and chickens, housed in their pens on the main deck, staring out at the world through the wooden slats.

Two of the Gilchrist girls, May and Flora, with their mother, had got in tow with Hugh Macaulay on their way up to the deck. Brother Guthrie was playing cards below, already he was very much part of the lively crowd in the single men's section. Without doubt Hugh was a rough diamond. With his strong forehead and high cheekbones he was ruggedly handsome and a keen talker and May Gilchrist felt her heart beat a little faster at the sight of him.

He was so...well...manly, thought May, compared with the farm boys of the same age she had known around Sweetshaws. He carried himself well but obviously had a fine opinion of himself. She kind of liked that too. May followed the others on to the broad deck of the *Broomielaw*. They passed along the side of the steel deck house behind the mainmast with its row of circular portholes of polished brass.

'Your husband doesn't say much, Mrs Gilchrist,' said the young man. The girls politely edged their way forward through the knots of emigrants and found a vantage point, steering their mother to the gunwale.

'No, Hugh. He's a man of few words. But you mustn't mind him. James is accustomed to being alone on the hill. I think he talks more to that collie of his than he does to us. But he knows that our future lies in Otago; he'll settle to the voyage.'

'Look, look,' said Flora dancing on the spot and pulling her shawl closer around her, 'you can still see the land!'

Hugh had wondered since they first met about Mrs Gilchrist's facial injuries. Was Gilchrist a wife-beater? He thought it unlikely but he felt convinced that she had not come by her injuries by 'a silly stumble in the byre' as she had told concerned inquirers 'tween decks.

At the heart-rending moment when sea, sky and land fused into a distant, formless, dark wall, someone aft began haltingly to sing the first lines of *Auld Lang Syne*. The melody was taken up by the emigrants crowding the rail and from the steerage below came more voices raised in song. Soon it seemed that the whole ship's company were saying their farewells.

All too soon Scotland had been swallowed, completely, by the night.

The anthem of farewell and companionship which must have been sung a thousand times in these waters, resonating above the sound of the slapping sails. Above the creamy wake of the *Broomielaw* the flock of birds fell slowly behind

An' here's a haun, ma trusty freen
An' here's a haun o' mine...

Those on deck found themselves, as they sang, clasping each other by the hand, a consoling, comforting act, each transported at that emotion-charged moment to their own fireside, front door or street, back into the company of familiar but now lost faces.

The folk of the *Broomielaw* were strangers no more to each other. They were about to share in an adventure which would test them all to the limits. Even in the gentle waters of the Irish Sea, they sensed that.

Hugh glanced across at May over her little sister's shoulder. The older girl was close to tears. He smiled, comfortingly, and after a moment, her throat parched with emotion and her palms clammy, she returned his smile, but weakly.

Below decks, as the light faded, Walter Lumsden was completing his paperwork in the hope that correspondence, as planned, might be taken off at Cobh on the south coast of Ireland, the last port-of-call before they ventured out on to the night-glimmering surface of the deep. Removing his wire-rimmed reading glasses he peered through the stern windows at the tilting horizon.

The singing from above which rang through the ship struck an aching chord in his heart. He recalled standing with his own family listening to that same sad old refrain.

What had the preacher from the Seaman's Mission said: 'Give praise unto the Lord who ruleth the waves and commands them. Peace, be still' These waves had taken his darling daughter, even before they had crossed the Equator.

How often this despairing loneliness had crept over him like a sea mist. How often he had told himself that by accepting the Clutha Company's Commission he would earn as much money in eighteen months as he might earn by teaching in eighteen years. He would, he must, purchase that fertile piece of land he'd earmarked in Southern Otago.Walter Lumsden wanted to make a fresh start, more than anything he wanted to begin again, to shed his fears, wipe the slate clean, settle in the new land beside the folk on this ship; so sad they were just at this particular moment of parting from the homeland, yet so full of hope and expectation.

Pacing the wooden floor of his cabin, the emigration agent recalled how the old boy from the Seaman's Mission had also spoken on that afternoon of departure of the need for faith, the need to believe in something, the correctness and natural order of things. But Lumsden again heard that gnawing, persistent voice telling him that he had allowed everything he cared for to be snatched away. Faith needed a starting point and he had none. He didn't know where to begin. No family, no land, no direction, no future.

At this moment even the presence, close by, of Maggie Gilchrist, only a few wooden walls away, brought little comfort, only a sad remembrance of what he had lost. Once more his mind raced towards that dark place where terror and guilt made their home. The apparitions, the ghosts who had made his life a misery were not gone, they had simply been in hiding. He rolled back into his bunk, pushing the unopened bottle of spirits away and pulling the rough blanket over his head.

Walter knew that if he peeked out from beneath his blanket they would be there – at the foot of his bunk – Lizzie, the boys and his wee Sarah. Why wouldn't they let him go? After all this time, why wouldn't they let him go? Beyond the fragile wooden walls the unforgiving ocean waited, dark slumbering. Listening to the creaking, complaining timbers he eventually drifted off into a troubled sleep.

Only very occasionally had Lumsden wondered if he, perhaps, was the one who wouldn't or couldn't let go.

Part Two – Surviving

25 Laying Down the Law

Once the hatch cover had been dragged to one side the emigrants could make out, fifteen feet below in the shaft of morning light, a great wilderness of packing cases and boxes shading into darkness in all directions.

The cavernous hold looked full to capacity, every square foot occupied, but among the packing cases there were unseen sanctuaries, cramped, wooden-walled pockets of open deck. Three days out from Cobh and Jack Zurich was negotiating his first minor insurrection.

Able to store only the barest essentials by their berths, this group had conspired to demand that they be allowed into the cargo space for fresh linen and clean clothes. Rather than put up with a repetition of this for the next three months Jack decided to show them that a fixed 'baggage day' with crew supervision was the only possible way to permit access. A below-decks free-for-all was unthinkable.

He knew that in the past year or two there had been frequent complaints from migrants on various ships that the luggage space had not been opened for the entire voyage. He also knew that the Clutha Society wanted, within reason, to accommodate passenger requests. The public image of the company was at stake.

Ratter, on one of the few occasions the skipper wasn't in the company of his new soul mate, the minister, had let Jack Zurich see a letter with the sailing orders from Dunedin in which they were reminded that a top priority was to be given to passenger comfort, safety and well-being. The company, Jack Zurich knew, wanted a well-ordered, speedy and trouble-free voyage. And they also wanted the world to know about it.

However, Jack was also aware that the previous year when all the baggage hatches were opened simultaneously on the *Pomeranian*, a sudden, unexpected squall had swept in from the east and the troubled vessel had almost foundered. The choice of 'baggage day' had to be made sensibly and overseen very carefully.

Normally, the skipper would have been the one to deal with this crowd of complainers and send them on their way. However, he was still almost invisible in the day-to-day routine of the

Broomielaw. Occasionally in the early evening Ratter might be seen patrolling the aft deck, his manner and his bouquet suggesting that he was the worse for drink.

Skippers did from time to time lock themselves away for days, sometimes weeks, on end during the passage feeling that carrying the responsibility for ship, passengers and crew was enough of a burden without actually sharing in the day-to-day operation of the ship. However, seldom did they withdraw quite so swiftly from shipboard activity as Ratter appeared to have done.

The petty mutineers, who mostly seemed to be quietly accepting Jack Zurich's argument, were led by a persistent, pug-faced Glaswegian who wasn't for hearing any explanations and stood above the hatch laying down his version of the law in a squeaky wee voice, almost an echo of the creaking carts of his beloved Gallowgate.

'You can't expect decent folk to go about like the tinklers,' said the little man drawing himself up to his full five feet, six inches. Aware that support around was ebbing away this sporty bantam made his final, solemn plea: 'We have our rights.'

Jack Zurich decided that it was high time this particular debate was brought to a conclusion. This little Brigton battler had clearly upset some of the more pliable passengers.

'Well, in fact, Mr Doherty, you don't. In the captain's absence on this deck I have his authority. And his word is law. I hope that's understood. What do you want me to do – bring in the Macaulay boys to root around there in the dark as they used to at the Fraser Castle pit. You were advised to bring a supply of clothes to last you a month, and a month it shall be. We can't be opening the baggage hold every second day.'

With much humming and hawing the crowd dispersed.

Below in her nest among the boxes and bags Queenie Stout finally allowed herself to take a deep breath as the hatch cover was replaced. Her claustrophobic hideaway was once again wrapped in the darkness of the tomb, the only specks of daylight spearing from the narrowest of cracks in the hull of the vessel.

Queenie had pleaded in vain with her conspirator for an oil lamp, or even a candle – some comfort in that gloomy hold, to be lit only in the direst emergency because of the fire risk. But the Kelvinhaugh lad was adamant. Far too dangerous, he had warned.

Instead through the dark hours she would cling to the little bible which had belonged to her elder brother Willie and which provided more comfort than she could ever have hoped for.

She had listened intrigued for the past few minutes to the first mate's efforts to keep the peace. If the troublemaker with the high-pitched voice had known that there was a service gantry running the length of the starboard side of the ship giving access through a hatchway to a cramped, between-decks corridor, he might have pressed his case a little more forcefully.

During the day, using this gantry to reach the body of the ship, Queenie had been mingling with the passengers as they went about their daily chores. She comforted herself in the knowledge that she was not conspicuous amongst the scores of single young women who were making the voyage.

The cabin passengers thought she was travelling steerage, the steerage passengers imagined she was with the toffs in their private cabins. It gave her anonymity, at least for a wee while. She was already on nodding terms with some of the girls but studiously avoided being drawn into any long, revealing conversations.

Had Queenie's presence been discovered this early in the voyage it was possible, according to her confederate, that she might be landed on the island of Madeira and abandoned in a strange land, amongst even stranger people. It had been a close call.

At mealtimes and at bedtime Queenie disappeared into the bowels of the ship usually to find that Mooney had left some biscuits, a flask of milk, a piece of pie or perhaps even a pudding from the crew's mess. A priceless piece of fruit was occasionally found. Nights, curled up in her rough nest of blankets, were lonely and frequently terrifying. Cases creaked with the motion of the ship and the scurry of clawed feet confirmed she was not alone in that dark, wooden sepulchre.

Her expeditions into the steerage and around the decks, apart from helping her to keep her sanity, also afforded Queenie the opportunity to make use of the very basic washing and toilet facilities. After a night in the baggage hold, listening to the rats scrambling around and feeling choked by the aroma of the wool which had filled the holds of the *Broomielaw* on the last return from the Antipodes, Queenie always felt she wanted to scrub herself from head to foot. She was sure she smelled like the sheds at the Hall of Doomy after the shearing.

The single water closet in steerage was reserved for the women and the children, the men being expected to use the heads on the lee side of the ship, as did the seamen. A few innocent males, unschooled in the matters of wind direction, were rewarded by being drenched in their own urine...a mistake that was never made twice. On other ships men venturing to these exposed locations in too severe weather conditions, had been lost overboard.

The water closet was an amazing, hand-knitted affair and invariably there was a queue by the door. In the cramped cubicle the flush of sea water came from a tank that was kept filled by hand-operated pump worked on a rota basis by the emigrants. This was almost luxury. By contrast, the closet between the single men's and family divisions was flushed, quite effectively, with a bucket of seawater.

Shortly after the mail boat from Queenstown, or Cobh as the Irish named it, had pulled away from the *Broomielaw,* Queenie had spotted her dear William for the first time, from a distance, chatting animatedly with two young men. All three were watching the departing boat bouncing over the waves, returning towards the Irish coast.

Back in Glasgow she had decided against an early on-board approach to William. She had no clear idea of how he would react. She would pick her time and place, long after there was any likelihood of her being put ashore. How astonished and thrilled he would be to discover the sacrifice she had made for him, living amongst the rats, giving up her home and family, her secure life on Stormay, everything just for him.

'Hello there, I don't think I saw you at the ways and means meeting last night; I'm Flora Gilchrist.'

Perhaps thirteen years old, the girl with the rosy apple complexion and lively, interested eyes had appeared from nowhere at Queenie's side.

'You must come along to our next get-together. Our group has lots of plans. Can you sing or dance, or tell stories, perhaps you can juggle with oranges or recite poetry? You must join us, you must.'

Seeing that Queenie's attention was fixed on the trio of young men by the gunwale, Flora lowered her voice conspiratorially.

'That's the Macaulay boys. I don't know the other smart young gentleman, perhaps he's a cabin passenger. My big sister May has taken a shine to the taller brother, Hugh. He's fine, isn't he? Where's your berth, right at the stern? We're nearer the family section.'

Queenie realised that she had already lingered too long.

'Yes, Yes, Flora – put me down for the concert. I know some conjuring tricks.'

'You can make things appear and disappear,' said Flora wide-eyed. 'That's great, Just wait until the others hear.'

'Yes, I'll see you later – sorry you said your name – oh yes, Flora, wasn't it?'

Without waiting for a reply she advanced across the deck and down the steps out of the bright afternoon sunshine towards her hidey-hole. I must be more careful, she told herself, glancing nervously around.

From the poop deck where he too had watched the mail boat turn for home, Walter Lumsden saw the attractive girl in the faded clothes and rough shawl dive below decks. He thought he could recognise and place most folk in their respective family groups but this lass had him stumped. Perhaps she had been ill when the family came for their interview. Yes, that must be it.

26 Mal de Mer

In the 1850s a long ocean passage still meant the same as it had done in the days of the Phoenicians or the Vikings – months of deprivation and hardship with the ever present likelihood of death from shipwreck, foundering or disease and for most, the absolute certainty of seasickness.

The rolling and pitching of the ship, the swaying lamps and staggering passengers had a stomach-churning, hypnotic effect, when it became impossible to recall what it was like to plant one foot after another on a firm city causeway. Each tumbling wave lifted the emigrants towards the decking overhead then left them suspended as it fell - their stomachs seemingly anxious to remain near the ceiling as their bodies made their descent. A cold sweat rushed to many a brow.

Mal de mer, as the French more delicately styled it, had simply to be endured. Maggie Gilchrist recalled hearing this fatalistic advice at one of the emigration meetings. Cod liver oil, bicarbonate of soda, cold tea - none of those so-called miracle remedies worked.

The message was straightforward – no cure, no salvation. A strange detachment from the world and a rumbling hopelessness were all reported by sufferers. It was a cross, an emigrant's burden which simply had to be borne as bravely as possible.

Easy words, thought Maggie, as she looked around at her family and fellow passengers and their obvious tribulation. Coming so soon after the emotion of the departure, it was indeed difficult to bear. When portholes were flung wide to ventilate the steerage, foul odours seemed only to cling more stubbornly to people and their possessions.

An old man on the other side of the trestle table hauled himself up on to one elbow and spewed noisily and violently into a wooden bucket. He then sank back on to his mattress, a picture of misery.

'Oh God, spare us,' he moaned.

Others who had long since emptied the contents of their stomach and bowels, retched drily and painfully and wished they were somewhere, anywhere, but on board *The Broomielaw.* A stench which seemed to penetrate the very woodwork of the vessel engulfed the steerage compartment.

After the relative calm of the passage to Cobh, the emigrants first taste of the Atlantic swell laid so many low. By the start of the second week the wind was unfavourable and for two full days the vessel could only make way by tacking. The *Broomielaw* herself seemed angered by this manoeuvring as if desperate to be on her way, scudding across the ocean. She pitched and tossed, lurched petulantly to starboard or bucketed to port, often righting herself with a punishing jerk.

Hidden from the heaving ocean behind the portholes, the steerage was a shadowy place of misery, children and adults sharing the distress, dark-eyed, green-gilled, glued to their bunks. The low moans which continued night and day were pitiful. And oh, the smells! A few hardy individuals dragged themselves to the water closet or up on deck feeling the need for a little privacy in their distress. There they hung, woebegone and hollow-eyed, over the deep.

The initial euphoria at being under way to the new land had swiftly evaporated and the thought that the entire voyage might be as wretched filled many with foreboding.

In the midst of this melancholy scene there were uncanny individuals, souls caressed by calm, who seemed born to negotiate the obstacles along the swaying deck, busying themselves in cleaning up after the poor, sick souls and generally keeping spirits up. These remarkable souls saw hope and anticipation in even the most grey, monotonous ocean dawnscape.

One such was Maggie Gilchrist. She pondered briefly why she had been spared the curse of seasickness and could only conclude that it was something to do with her pregnancy; that somehow she was blessed seven months into her pregnancy with natural ballast.

Those dark months in the sordid Edinburgh lodgings had also prepared her better than most for the foul-smelling sick bay which the Broomielaw's steerage had become.

In any case, Maggie hadn't been sleeping well and was happier to be up and about helping the stricken.

Recurring in her brief dreams was a scene where she was dragged by the throat down a ship's gangplank on to the quayside. Choking and coughing she would struggle to rip the hands from her windpipe and try to make out the features of her assailant – but they were fluid, ever-changing. One moment it was her husband, the next it was the stick man, Brocklebank. She had a powerful unsettling sensation in these dreams that the ship eventually sailed without her. She would waken in the confines of her bunk to find she was trembling and her hands would rise to the cruel lesions on her neck and her bruised face. She had never imagined, no never, that bone could be so brittle.

Maggie leaned over her husband with a bowl of soup in her hand. 'You'll take a spot o' broth, James. You must have something in your stomach.'

The shepherd groaned and rolled over to face the bulkhead. Within a couple of days of leaving the Clyde James Gilchrist had become a picture of seeming dejection, like a man whose worst fears had been realised. He withdrew into himself and seldom spoke to his girls or the folk sharing the compartment. Maggie wondered if Innes Macaulay's blind optimism about the new life, so often loudly and cheerfully expressed across the passageway, was driving her husband to distraction.

On the few occasions he ventured on to the deck in these first days James Gilchrist would stand by the mainmast, looking out over the ocean as if he expected something unspeakable to emerge from the deep.

Soon enough even these trips to the open air ceased. Now the Sweetshaws shepherd was – like so many others sick as the proverbial sea dog. Ironically, his precious collie Gip seemed untroubled by the rolling motion of the ship and snuffled happily around the berths and tables. In his hand Gilchrist still rolled the pebble from the Ward Burn, rhythmically. He lay flat out in his bunk gazing blankly at the knotted boards beside him occasionally fishing a scrap of paper from down the side of his mattress and staring at it for long minutes.

'Why, our very own Florence Nightingale!'

Walter Lumsden's tall frame appeared around the bulkhead and he found Maggie kneeling by her husband's bunk.

'I think perhaps it's we who should be looking after you,' he said, offering to help her to her feet. James Gilchrist groaned pitifully in the background.

Maggie Gilchrist did indeed look huge; it could only be a matter of weeks before her fourth child put in an appearance. Pushing a strand of hair back from her eyes Maggie straightened stiffly to face the emigration agent. She stretched painfully, one hand on her back, and smiled.

This man has a kind, yet troubled face, she thought. Maggie prided herself on character assessment – she had had ample opportunity to study men in all their strange moods – and she felt convinced that Lumsden's life had not been without it share of woes.

'It's hard for wee ones, Mr Lumsden'

'Walter, please call me Walter, Mrs Gilchrist – and if I may call you Margaret. We're shipmates after all. Your husband is a fortunate man indeed to be in your care.' He smiled with an innocent warmth which caused Maggie's heart to skip lightly. How odd, she thought.

'As for the children, the skipper tells me that the wind is moving to a more favourable quarter. Their ordeal could be over before dusk.' Not before time, Walter reflected, glancing around. The steerage was beginning to look – and smell – like the dread descriptions he'd read of the Crimean casualty clearing stations.

27 Private Prayer?

Walter Lumsden had been shocked to see the face injury which the shepherd's wife had sustained yet had tried so carefully to conceal his surprise when the family embarked in Glasgow. Like the Macaulay boy he doubted the story of the fall and suspected domestic violence. However, Gilchrist did not have the demeanour of a wife beater. The other factor was that the woman herself, a shining light in the sick bay, seemed untroubled, at least on the surface. It was almost as if whatever ordeal she had suffered had steeled her for the voyage, the new life which lay ahead.

'Let's get some fresh air, Maggie. It's a fine, fresh evening.'

Together they climbed out into the saltspray. It was almost dusk and the *Broomielaw* was now slicing impressively through the waves, sails tightening above them. Her movement in the water had indeed changed in the past half-hour and she progressed south-west with a more confident, rhythmic swing.

Moving towards the stern they passed beyond the deckhouse where the apprentices, the bosun, carpenter and sailmaker were berthed; attached was the makeshift galley where the cook worked and slept. Laughter, the chirpy cheery sound of a button accordion and the lilting words of a sea chanty praising the charms of the girls of Valparaiso issued from the deckhouse as they passed. Now the boys had moved on to the delights of strong drink with the promising opening lines:

> *If whisky was a river and I could swim,*
> *I'd take a jump and dive right in.*

As their eyes became accustomed to the gloom the couple could make out the dim figure up at the wheel upon whose weather-lined face the light from the binnacle, the illuminated compass, played eerily.

'There were a couple of matters which I'd hoped you might help me with, Margaret. I suppose they both come under the general category of passenger welfare. First of all I'm obviously concerned about your husband – apart altogether from his seasickness – James seems very low.'

Maggie looked at the agent. Was this the point when she started to confide in someone, in anyone; where she began to unburden herself? Was this seemingly kind man to be her confessor? How much to tell?

'The truth is Mr Lumsden, sorry Walter, up until the final weeks before we left Sweetshaws my husband was still very cool on the idea of this voyage. You know we missed the late October meeting. Early on, with the slightest encouragement, he would have abandoned all our plans. But the death of his father seemed to bring about a serious and strange alteration in his attitude.'

'Surely that initial reluctance was just natural caution on his part? It's such a big step, taking your family to the other side of the world. There are many here on board, I can assure you, still full of doubt about what they have undertaken,' replied Lumsden.

Maggie ran her hand along the smooth polished teak rail. Their eyes met. Suddenly he looked uncomfortable as if she'd knocked on a door deep within his soul, a door marked 'private'; she quickly turned her glance to the open ocean.

'No, at first he felt I was forcing his hand – and to a certain extent I was. James finds it very difficult to make decisions, even those which directly affect the family, especially those that affect the family.'

'Perhaps you're being a little hard on him?'

'Again, no. If he'd had his way at the outset he'd still be on that damned hill and we would be facing destitution; our girls with no future but to run around at the beck and call of some fat-middle-aged farmer.'

Maggie knew there was much more to it than that. She still puzzled over her husband's 'conversion' to the idea of emigration following his father's funeral in Glasgow. It was bizarre.

A wave exploded against the hull close by the fo'castle and sent a cloud of spray running along the rail. In unison they stepped nimbly back into the shelter of the one of the deckhouses, Lumsden steadying the emigrant wife as she stumbled briefly. The singing from within continued with rough enthusiasm:

For Santa Anna has gained the day, along the Plains of Mexico.

'All the girls and I can do, Mr Lumsden, is to hope and pray that James will come to himself before too long. There is a fine, challenging job awaiting him in Otago.'

From the galley, Mooney, the Kelvinhaugh lad, emerged carrying a plate covered with a rough cloth and a tin mug balanced on top. As he passed the couple, swaying with the movement of the ship he nodded in their direction.

'Evenin' folks, we're making better speed now, eh? Portugal is five hundred miles that-a-way.' He nodded off to port in the direction of the empty, slowly darkening ocean. 'At this rate we'll be off Madeira in no time.' That said he disappeared below decks. One of the cabin passengers must have recovered sufficiently to ask for food, thought Lumsden, watching the seaman go. Mind you, they wouldn't be too impressed being offered their tea in a tin mug.

'Well, Margaret, if you'd like me to speak to James, just say. You'll understand that I feel a heavy responsibility for you all. But to that other matter - have you had any dealings with the Rev. Shade? I've been getting one or two unsettling reports.'

Maggie adjusted to this change of tack. 'Nothing of note, Walter.' Their relationship felt that little bit easier each time she spoke his name.

'He's been helping out at lessons and speaking to the womens' group and the Sabbath school. But you could never say he was an orthodox preacher. He seems especially interested in the welfare of the single women and offers private prayer and meditation in his cabin.'

Lumsden nodded. 'Yes, that what I'd heard. Maybe you could let me know if you hear any whispers among the women in steerage.'

Maggie laughed for the first time she could remember in weeks. 'Why, Mr Lumsden! You're thinking to recruit me as a below-decks spy – how exciting! What exactly has the reverend gentlemen been up to? You must tell me.' This bright, almost mischievous side to Maggie Gilchrist was clearly something new and enervating for the emigration agent who visibly perked up.

Their discussion was interrupted by a seasick passenger who had been keeping a lonely, miserable vigil, hanging on to the rail, just a few yards from them, towards the stern. He suddenly lurched backwards and planked his backside on a hatch cover with a countenance suggesting he had seen a mermaid or a sea serpent, or just possibly a mermaid riding on the back of a sea serpent.

He looked toward them pleading: 'Please, please look to the water. I'm surely having visions. I must be very sick – tell me what you see.'

It was fully dusk now. Both Lumsden and Maggie stepped forward to peer over the port side of the *Broomielaw*. As she cut through the water the ship was putting on a spectacular light show. Phosphorescence ran the length of the hull, translucent lime green foam by the waterline. Maggie gasped. When she was girl, she recalled seeing ball lightning dance a jig in her granny's hearth but this was an equally memorable event. Having reassured the anxious emigrant they moved below decks again. 'They say it binds people – witnessing the sea fire together,' said Lumsden.

Maggie merely smiled.

'But you haven't told me what Mr Shade is supposed to be up to?'

Around them the occupants of the steerage had already begun to revive a little with the ship speeding along. Some had recovered sufficiently to be able to shout jokey remarks across the compartments about the mournful appearance of their fellow travellers – forgetting that their own sad demeanour might have been enough to scare the hind legs off a donkey. James Gilchrist had raised himself to a sitting position and with a sour glance summoned his wife to his side.

As Lumsden turned to go, he whispered: 'Just keep an ear to the gossip around the steerage, Maggie. I'm told Shade has a very strange way of administering the Benediction!'

28 That Damn Frenchie!

Trouble in the unlikely shape of auld Agnes Govan had stalked the steerage ever since she discovered that Leon the sailmaker, the flying-fingered wizard of the button accordion, the cheery chap with the shaved head, was French.

The fact that Glasgow had been his base since 1840 as he sailed the oceans, that he had an interesting accent with traces of Dennistoun and Dieppe and hadn't been born during the Napoleonic conflict, seemed irrelevant to the old lady.

Right enough, from time to time, when he broke a needle or got the sails in a raffle he would betray himself with a well-chosen stream of foul and abusive in purest colloquial French. That was enough for Agnes. Within a few hours of discovering Jontot's pedigree she was questioning the officers of the *Broomielaw* whenever the opportunity arose.

'I see no needcessity to employ Frenchies on a British ship. It's a pure disgrace,' she would declare.

Receiving no sympathy her initial reaction had been to declare that she would not sail another mile in the same ship as 'that damned Frenchie'. Having had the impracticality of this suggestion pointed out to her seemed to make the Sweetshaws battler even more vexed. Finally, one washday as they scrubbed clothes in the wooden tubs under a sky of scudding clouds, with Agnes still muttering about justice, Maggie stopped the old woman in mid-complaint.

'What exactly do you think should happen to Mr Jontot, aunt? Should we make him walk the plank – just for being French?'

'You don't know these folk, girl. One of these days you'll laugh on the other side of your face. You know my Davie, yer uncle, came back from Flanders wi' only half a brain.'

Maggie turned away. The story in the family was that the musket ball had actually rendered Uncle Alec slightly more witty than he had been before he left Scotland. But this was never spoken of. In fact, Agnes's brother-in-law Alec, Davie's younger brother had died at Waterloo from injuries sustained in the same bloody assault which saw Davie take his head wound.

Because of this tragedy there was sympathy, or at least a little understanding, in the vicinity of their compartment over her obsession with the harmless wee Frenchman. The rest of emigrants and the crew, two generations removed from Napoleonic conflict, simply thought her mad.

As for Agnes, seeing she was getting nowhere with Maggie, contented herself over the next few days by warning the youngsters, Torrance Macaulay and her grand-niece Hilda, as well as anyone else on deck who cared to listen, to steer clear of the dark-skinned frog-eater and to watch their purses and their backs. The French were treacherous, not be trusted, and creating myths as she went Agnes also warned darkly that it was widely known that to have a Frenchman on board would surely bring bad luck and that when the moon was full they grew hair on the back of their hands.

If she encountered the sail-maker between decks she would glare menacingly and curse under her breath at the bewildered little man who would scurry off into the darkness.

Her suspicions got a public airing fourteen days out from the Clyde at the first meeting of the debating society. Such occasions were keenly anticipated because the truth was that for long weeks on the emigration voyage boredom was the enemy.

When a vessel had sufficient musicians and weather allowed, a dance or concert was often organised on the poop or quarter deck, fishing parties were arranged while school and religious services provided a focus for the passing days. For the most part the hours, days and weeks were spent simply surviving – eating, cleaning and sleeping, perhaps occasionally swapping life experiences, outlining plans for the future. A few had brought books and the women and girls were advised in the emigration literature that they could spend their time profitably with needlework. Routine – and discipline – were seen as vital.

Male migrants were always encouraged to assist where possible in the running of the ship and while tearing along in the Roaring Forties, the wild open salty wilderness in the Southern Indian Ocean (check), they would help with the *pully-hauly* on ropes and braces to change the slant of the sails or more often they would man the pumps to keep the holds free of water.

*   *   *   *   *

Rather ambitiously for their first evening get-together the debating society had decided that the *Matter of Opinion* should focus on the assertion – Mankind Really is a Brotherhood. Three speakers were selected for each side.

As a debating chamber the family section of the steerage left a little to be desired but as with everything else on board, the emigrants made do. Illuminated by the dancing light of half-a-dozen oil lamps the company gathered at either side of the long, trestle table, seated on boxes or lounging against the bunks, just where the huge main mast sank solidly and impressively through the ship. Around this symbol of strength the company elected a chairman for the evening.

This young man from Edinburgh had clearly had a good education. He indulged in an overlong introductory speech, delivered with one foot on a stool and with a series of theatrical gestures which had the children giggling and provoking grumpy stage whispers of 'Get oan wi' it, lad!' from the back pews.

Innes nudged his eldest boy: 'God help South Australia, Hugh; there goes a premier in the making.'

Those for the motion invoked Robert Burns time and time again in their presentation and 'A Man's a Man for A' That' was given laldy. A brief interjection by Flora Gilchrist who wanted to know why mankind 'couldn't be a Sisterhood' was greeted with much tut-tutting particularly from the older women and muttered comments suggesting that young people should be seen and not heard.

As the evening progressed the pro-Brotherhood lobby received much sympathetic nodding and sporadic applause. Those against made a great play on the bellicose nature of mankind, of his desire to make war and destroy or humiliate his fellow creatures.

'If you ask – it's no natural to be too friendly wi' some folk.' It was Agnes, seated on her bunk sewing, who spoke clearly and confidently but without raising her head from her needlework. The crowd turned towards the speaker. This promised to be an interesting contribution to the debate.

'Tak' yon French tyke, the sail-maker.' She stitched away as she spoke. 'Oh aye, nice as ninepence to your face but what is he up to behind your back. Ye canny trust them. It's as simple as that. Tak' it fae me, you canny trust them.'

Here Agnes was feeding a slumbering suspicion and growing unease amongst the steerage passengers. Within a couple of days of leaving Greenock petty thefts had been reported. Nothing serious, just mementoes, little pieces of cheap, sparkly jewellery, baubles, keepsakes which had been left lying on beds and boxes. They had simply vanished. No prowler had been observed and the culprit or culprits remained at large.

'Tell me, auld yin; if you're saying the sailmaker is a villain then what did he want wi' my false teeth? You'd make better use of them!'

The speaker was a bumptious railway clerk from Cowdenbeath and his response raised the biggest communal laugh since the scourge of seasickness had lifted from the steerage.

With a *humph* and a 'Mark my words, you'll soon be laughing on the other side of your face', Agnes returned to her sewing.

29 Moving Forces

Once the gathering had settled again the chairman caught Walter Lumsden's eye. He had taken up Jack Zurich's invitation to look in on the debate. The first mate and the emigration agent stood in the shadows at the foot of the companionway.

'Perhaps Mr Lumsden, who knows all our innermost thoughts (there was some laughter and applause) might have some observations. He is the only one here, I think, with direct experience of our black brothers in the new lands to the south.

Suddenly it became clear to Lumsden why he had felt so uneasy on the fringes of this debate. This was a topic which scared him and forced him to confront issues which he would rather have pushed to the back of his mind, erase completely – if only that was possible. He should have stayed in his cabin, he realised too late, shifting uncomfortably from one foot to another.

This was a topic – the brotherhood of man - which he had simply refused to address in his quiet moments, never mind in a public forum.

Lumsden considered a strategic withdrawal, a fabricated excuse, something about official duties, but it was too late. Fifty or sixty pairs of eyes were fixed on him. Eager and trusting souls awaiting his opinion. It was a new aspect of an all too familiar nightmare. He took a deep breath and a couple of steps forward, leaning on the trestle table with his fists.

'I'm flattered, but I think you all over-estimate my depth of knowledge on the subject.'

'Ach, get oan wi' man,' came Agnes's croaky voice.

'But if pressed I would have to say the Aborigines and Maoris are certainly different from us.

'Their values and their requirements from life are so much simpler than our own. If there is animosity to the incomers, that's surely understandable, at least to some degree. We have, after all, already turned their world upside down. As to whether they constitute part of the brotherhood of man, I would have to leave that to your judgement. The opportunity to make such an assessment will come soon enough.'

Walter could scarcely credit the words, no, the platitudes, which had issued from his mouth. The murdering bastards; they destroyed my family and here I am defending their corner – just because it's the company line. Forgive me, Lizzie.

For Innes Macaulay, who sat across the table quietly listening to the debate, brotherhood meant something totally different, something personal. Innes had listened carefully to Walter Lumsden. Instinctively, he sensed he was hearing only half the emigration agent's story.

By his side sat Belle, holding his hand tightly and occasionally offering a whispered profile of each speaker.

Nations might be coming together in an international fraternity and workers joining in a common cause but from Innes's perspective the most serious and worrying aspect of life in the middle of the nineteenth century was the great gulf which was opening between ordinary working folk like himself and the owning and managing classes.

Two years previously, as a colliers' leader, he had told a pithead meeting at the Fraser Castle that they had to sell their labour and it was their duty to sell it at the highest available price. That brave speech and a threat of industrial action had persuaded the mine owners to abandon a plan for a shilling reduction on the 15 shilling weekly wage.

Innes's cry had been for as fair day's work for a fair day's pay. He remembered his childhood as a flap boy in Govan, sitting huddled in total darkness three hundred feet down opening ventilation doors to allow coal cars through.

To ringing cheers he had told his workmates – 'We will ask no more and take no less.'

Within a week Innes was to find out that fairness had very little to do with such matters. In the unlikely setting of the Kirk, McGovern, the pit manager, had taken him aside as the congregation was filing out and while smiling and nodding at the passing matrons had hissed at Innes: 'A fine speech that on Tuesday, Macaulay, from what I hear. But understand this, as long as I manage this pit there will be no advancement for either you or your boys.'

Innes was staggered by this threat but when he sought the support of his action committee in exposing McGovern, they backed away; they had had their victory. It would not do to rub the faces of the management in the mire. This was the generally expressed view. Innes felt as if someone had ca'ad the feet from him.

For Innes Macaulay it had been the final straw. That same afternoon he had arranged to travel into Glasgow to hear Walter Lumsden speak at an emigration meeting in the City Halls. Within minutes of listening to the agent he was hooked on the Australian adventure.

It was a strange irony that in his last weeks at the Fraser Castle, the pit should steal his sight away. But now he longed for a society where he would find pure comradeship, less class consciousness and where honest endeavour was rewarded. It seemed such a fanciful, idealistic hope – and yet. They said it was so, in the new lands. It was the fresh start which his own father could only have dreamed of.

From the other side of the steerage Maggie Gilchrist, who had been trying without success to persuade her husband to join in the debate, saw the anguish writ large on Walter Lumsden's face as he turned to leave. They had shared those minutes on deck getting to know each other and in an odd, unsettling moment

Maggie realised that whatever caused this man's pain, she was beginning to feel it also.

As if she didn't have enough crosses to bear, she reflected for a moment. Perhaps Lumsden did indeed carry some heavy, unspecific burden, but could it be as weighty as her own?

From several compartments away came the sound of a child coughing. Within the past half-hour the little girl's mother had noticed a rash of red spots on the forehead and behind the ears of the sickly infant. Shade had been summoned but the mother knew only too well what was afoot. The child had measles, the eighth case to have been reported in the past 24 hours.

The debating society wound down their evening's entertainment with a vote which resulted, as expected, in resounding confirmation of the idea of the brotherhood of man.

Beyond Adelaide and Dunedin these people would be on their own, reflected Walter as he and Jack Zurich headed for the upper deck. The emigrants would soon have first hand experience of the native people in the Colonies. They would have a chance to judge, the emigration agent told himself. But surely their settling experiences would be less harrowing than his own?

People moved off to their bunks, final skirmishes being laid to rest and the steerage began to settle for the night. Lumsden met Hugh and May, hand in hand, on the companionway and close behind, summoned to the child's sickbed came Shade. That wild, flushed, faraway look, his dishevelled appearance and the fact that he came from the general direction of the captain's quarters suggested that reverend gentleman had found a companion to share a bottle.

In fact, he was sober. The reason for Shade's disarray was simply that he had been called to the sick bay while completing a most punishing benediction with an attractive spinster from Ayrshire.

30 Napoleon's Recovery

Deep in the ship, at the end of a long, low passageway Hamish, the Lochaber ox and his French assistant busied themselves.

Jontot had taken to his unexpected duties with relish. He was a sail-maker to trade, had been all his life, but his father was the finest tailor in St. Malo and Jontot had served his apprenticeship under his guiding skills. The Breton was now taking the opportunity to show his more delicate tailoring skills.

A solitary beam of dust-speckled daylight from a half-open hatch lit their labours. From time to time the sound of goats bleating or a collie yapping or the echo of voices and laughter from somewhere far above would penetrate this hidden workshop.

Walter and Jack Zurich had no idea what to expect when they accepted Hamish's invitation to inspect progress. They stooped low to enter the after locker.

'If I didn't know better, we'd be thinking that you two were Radicals at work, hatching up some mutinous plot to take control of the *Broomielaw*.'

Hamish looked up. 'Ah, there you are Mr Lumsden. No, this is an ideal location. Peace and quiet to get on with our work. Come in, come in...and welcome.'

The Highlander was standing, a small wrench in his strong left hand, pondering his task. The bench beside him was littered with nuts, bolts and what looked like small winding mechanisms. Jontot was seated near the hatch, needle in hand.

The Frenchman bit on his lower lip, a study in Gallic concentration, as the needle darted along the collar seam of the Emperor's dark blue greatcoat. It still bore the scorch marks of the *Adelphi* blaze but was in the process of transformation. The sail-maker looked up briefly from his work, nodding to the two arrivals before returning to his sewing.

The coffin-shaped box which had been the source of so much speculation when it was carried aboard at the Victoria docks in Glasgow was now` set on its end in the corner of the locker room, the lid flung wide. Cautiously Walter and Jack moved forward, peering inside where a squat, familiar figure stood to attention.

'There he is, gentlemen – Boney himself, First Consul and Emperor of France. Still a bittie charred and sorry for himself but showing improvement every day – thanks in no small measure to his compatriot Leon here.'

'But the face, Hamish, it's bloody astonishing,' exclaimed Jack Zurich, gently prodding the white cheeks. 'So lifelike.'

'Partly finest bone china and cloth to give it flexibility and make it lifelike, well, read for yourself. Here's the wee man's calling card.'

Hamish reached into the top pocket of his jacket and retrieved a crushed bill poster for the *Circus Caledonia* which he handed to Jack Zurich.

The first mate held it to the light and read aloud:

Constructed in Philadelphia PA, the most wonderful mechanotomical figure in the world – the Emperor, Napoleon Bonaparte – which has attracted the admiration of all Scientific Men in London, Dublin etc. Composed of a new and artifice substance termed "Sarmaknos" this is universally allowed to be the most perfect artificial figure ever brought before the public.

As if to acknowledge the plaudits Napoleon suddenly raised his arm in a smart salute. The action was stiff and creaky, yet impressive for all that. Startled both Walter and Jack Zurich took a step back. Hamish laughed.

'Aye he's a devil is old Nappy. That's just one of his tricks. He's a mechanical marvel. God willing, he'll be saluting, doffing his hat and walking by the time we reach Adelaide.'

'Walking you say – amazing. You half expect him to speak,' said Walter Lumsden.

'Gie us time, Mr Lumsden, gie us time!'

Hamish talked as he worked: 'Mr Wellbeloved, who used to own the *Circus Caledonia* brought Nappy back from the States and this wee chap has provided our bread and butter through hard times ever since. People never seem to tire of seeing him in action.'

Jack Zurich peered into the Emperor's glassy eyes. 'I can understand the fascination. Conchita tells me that you rescued him from destruction in the fire at the Adelphi.'

'We'll, I'd no intention of seeing our livelihood go up in smoke, Jack. In any case, having looked after Nappy for all these years I've a soft spot for him, if truth was told. I think the Emperor is ready for his fitting, Leon.'

'What chance you could have him patrolling the ship by the time we reach Adelaide, Hamish?' asked Walter.

'If I can find someone on board with a bit of experience in clockwork mechanisms, Mr Lumsden, he could be bowling along by the time of the concert party. And walking is not the end of it – he has one or two other party pieces up his sleeve. . .'

31 Pen to Paper

On the forenoon of the 16th day out from Greenock the ship was put in a bustle when a sail was sighted, homeward bound for the Mersey. As the ships closed and a boat was put out from the other vessel, a sudden frenzy of letter writing broke out up and down the length of the *Broomielaw*.

The whole manoeuvre was over so quickly, however, that only letters already written, perhaps a dozen, were gathered together and despatched to the *Wings of the Morning*, a sturdy, sea-weathered vessel of about 500 tons returning with a cargo of wool to her home port of Liverpool. The vessels went their separate ways.

'You had no letters to send, miss?'

The soft voice at her shoulder made Queenie jump.

'Sorry to startle you but everyone else between decks seems to have had a pen in their hand. It was always a clever move to have a letter for home ready for chance meetings such as this.'

It was the first mate who had noticed the girl standing, solitary by the rail, clutching her shawl around her head, watching the day boat re-cross the choppy stretch of water between the sailing ships. Jack Zurich had noticed this attractive, rosy-cheeked lass several times – she was always on her own. And always, at least so it seemed, appearing nervous; slightly ill at ease.

'Well no. All my family are already in Australia.' She in turn had recognised the brave young officer with the kind eyes and strong shoulders. His cheery demeanour among the men working with the sails or standing confidently on the swaying boards beside the helmsman could not have escaped her notice.

Jack produced his clay pipe and tobacco pouch. 'You don't mind?' She nodded for him to proceed. When on Stormay had anyone ever given her such consideration? He carefully filled the bowl and examined the stem of the pipe. Striking his flint, the tobacco seemed reluctant to ignite. Eventually he was puffing triumphantly. Jack watched the smoke being whip away on the breeze.

Queenie decided to seize the moment.

'I wonder how long before we are off Madeira?'

'Very soon, a couple of days if we keep this pace. We're getting a fine run of winds, averaging eight to ten knots, I would guess. Yes, a couple of days. Why do you ask?'

'Oh, I'm told the journey only really begins once we leave Madeira behind; after that we will be far from land for many weeks.'

'Well, that's true enough.'

Queenie smiled at the man who leant back against the stays and puffed contentedly on his pipe. She wondered whether he would be quite so cool and collected when she announced herself as a stowaway. Mooney said she must give herself up long before they reached equatorial waters where suffocating, unbearable conditions in the hold would force her to surrender in any case.

Giving herself up – the idea still caused a shiver of anxiety. Mooney seemed to delight in telling her stories of how not so many years ago stowaways were simply thrown overboard into the dark, fathomless depths of the ocean, fed to the sharks, as he so delicately put it. But there were more civilised times, weren't they, she tried to reassure herself. Queenie had struck up a working relationship with Mooney. He was regular as clockwork with her meals and she in turn agreed to teach him to write and pass on what little she had learned at school about the night sky. Mooney was fascinated by the stars and their constellations.

Jack Zurich whose eyes, Queenie thought, looked as deep and mysterious as the ocean which surrounded them, stood now with his back to the rail: 'I hope you're comfortable enough in the steerage. It's far from perfect, I know. If there's anything special you need...'

Well, well, thought Queenie. This was more than formal politeness. He was taking a special interest. How best to exploit this unexpected turn of events?

'An extra blanket or two would keep out the chill.'

'But we'll soon be stewing in the equatorial heat.'

Queenie glanced upwards towards the scudding clouds as if seeking inspirations in the heavens.

'Thin blood – that was always the problem…runs in the family, you see,' Queenie improvised.

'Right, well, I'll bring them along to your berth after tea.'

Panic!

'Eh, no, I'll be taking a breath of air so we might meet right here again.' This was a risky business but she rather liked this man, no, more than that, and he could have no idea just what a bonus two extra blankets would be in that still cold, dark hold.

Smiling demurely Queenie took her leave. As she made for the for'ard companionway Jack looked quizzical then shrugged. He tapped his pipe two or three times on the rail, watched the ash snatched away by the wind then headed off in search of the emigration agent.

32 In The Captain's Cavern

Madeira was again occupying the thoughts of Jack Zurich and Walter Lumsden only a few minutes later when they went apprehensively to the captain's quarters to seek an interview. The old man hadn't been on deck in two days; he had ignored the meeting with the *Wings of the Morning* and on the rare occasions when he appeared he and Jack were inevitably at loggerheads over the running of the ship.

These very public disputes were the talk of the steerage and the crew's quarters.

Apart from Tully, the steward, the surgeon/preacher Shade had become Ratter's only regular visitor and the oil lamp burned late and glasses clinked seriously most nights in the captain's cabin.

But there was a problem now which had to be brought urgently to the skipper's attention; a sad case and no mistake. On board was a young man travelling alone and far gone with consumption. He coughed miserably in the infirmary. Shade, when finally cornered by Walter Lumsden, had boldly announced that he had discussed the matter with the captain and the plan was to land the youth at Madeira. However, it was not uncommon for vessels to remain becalmed for weeks in the lee of the island.

Why, Jack had wondered, was this damned preacher so enthusiastic about the idea of a Madeira stopover with the potential delay that involved. Purely a medical or humanitarian decision, or something else?

'Aye, enter!' came the gravel-edged growl from the depth of the skipper's quarters.

Jack Zurich pushed open the cabin door and they stepped into the gloomy chamber. The air in his hutch was thick and acrid. It took moments for their eyes to adjust to the half-light but beyond the table, covered with a half-eaten meal, clothes spread about the floor and an overturned chair, they could make out Silas Ratter propped up in his bunk on top of crumpled, ominously stained blankets, an empty bottle of rum on the floor beside him. The room had the aroma of a Finnieston public bar on Friday night.

He looked dreadful. Apart from his dishevelled appearance, his straggly beard was matted and filthy. His face was puffy and had taken on a dangerously purple hue. He stared at them menacingly out of bloodshot and swollen eyes.

Seeing this spectre both Walter and Jack Zurich felt relieved that the skipper did not feel inclined, or was indeed able, to put in more frequent appearances on deck. This apparition would be guaranteed to scare the passengers and destroy the morale of the crew at a stroke,

'Well, speak yer mind Zurich; don't just stand there like a dummy,' growled the skipper, lifting himself on to one elbow.

Ratter peered at them through the gloom.

'I fear this stopover at Madeira, which you've sanctioned, may lose us many precious days, sir.' Jack picked his way through the devastation towards the side of the bunk. Ratter's only response was a grunt swiftly followed by a rattly belch.

'Mr Lumsden will confirm, as you already know, that the company are anxious that this is a speedy trip. And if Madeira…'

'I hear you for God's sake, man. And I read the company orders. Do you think I don't?'

123

Leaning over the edge of the bed Ratter shook the room with a rasping cough and concluded the interlude by hacking impressively on the floor beside his bunk.

'Listen, mister,' he hissed. The surgeon says the lad has to be landed at Madeira and landed at Madeira he shall be. Compassion should be our watchword. Shade is a wise man, well, leastways whenever he takes that damned dog-collar off...and besides it's clear to all that he comes from good stock.'

Ratter chuckled to himself in a vaguely maniacal manner.

Walter stepped forward: 'It's not as simple as that I fear, Mr Ratter. The boy is being sent to New Zealand in the hope that the climate will improve his health. He has family there and is desperate to continue his journey. We have no right to abandon him.'

Displaying an unexpected burst of energy Ratter hauled himself up to a sitting position and thrust his face into Walter's. As he spoke a cloud of noxious vapours filled the agent's nostrils and he felt his stomach heave. That sour alcoholic stench, or one very like it, would live with Walter for the rest of his days.

'Why, it's you Lumsden, our emigration agent. Well, can I remind you that on this vessel my word is law. The surgeon has enough on his plate without looking after a consumptive twenty-four hours a day for the remainder of the voyage. He lands at Madeira should it cost us five or five hundred extra days. Now leave me both of you, your complaining hurts my bloody head.'

That said Ratter slumped back on to his pillow and within seconds was snorting violently. The two men made their retreat and closed the door on that acrid cavern. Outside the door Lumsden looked at Jack Zurich and shrugged. It had not taken the *Broomielaw* long to reach the troubled waters which the agent had hoped so passionately that they might avoid. They hastened to the pure air above.

33 The Curse of Tobacco

For the house-proud matrons on board the *Broomielaw,* the struggle to make their little corner of the emigrant ship as neat and tidy as possible, in truly difficult and claustrophobic conditions, was a sore test.

Tropical downpours afforded opportunities for a strenuous washday but generally clothing became grubby, pernickety husbands soon learned to accept that there might be a speck or two on an un-starched shirt and sore-pressed mothers found that the combination of children and tarry topes was guaranteed to make work.

Obtaining some hot water from the cook was always a cause for great rejoicing and the women would redouble their washing efforts. However, working on the swaying deck had its hazards for the washerwomen.

Once when Belle and Maggie were busy scrubbing and chatting about how they imagined their new homes, the *Broomielaw took* such a lurch into a troughs between the waves that it sent Belle reeling towards the hatchway. Fortunately she pulled herself up short of the dark drop. Maggie recovered from her companion's sudden sprint across the boards in time to see her own tub chasing off in the same direction, spilling clothes and hot water about the deck. The ladies had learned not to grumble about shipboard mishaps and once they recovered their equilibrium they laughed until they were sore at the little act of washday theatre.

Generally speaking the select band of cabin passengers was the only group of emigrants who felt able to put on best clothing. The poop deck was specially reserved as their parade ground. Because there was so much less traffic in this area it was inevitably much cleaner than the main deck which at times could seem like Argyle Street on a busy Saturday,

Other habits and behaviour could combine to make life on board more difficult than need be. On many emigrant ships, availability of alcohol was a problem resulting in drunkenness, rowdy behaviour and pestering of women and girls by the rougher elements in the single men's section.

Control of drink normally rested with the purser who could restrict abuse by forcing people to undergo the sternest of interviews. If successful they were charged an exorbitant price for port or cheap wine and if rejected they left the purser's room empty-handed and feeling like a criminal.

But one other person had access to the stocks of alcohol – the surgeon. And he could supply illicit drink rations to whomsoever he chose. The russet complexion and bleary eyes of the skipper during his infrequent sorties into the sunlight suggested that this arrangement was more than just 'tween decks gossip.

And it seemed that others might have access to drink through the auspices of the surgeon. A man called Rag was one of Shade's chosen few as the Macaulays found out when he asked Innes and the boys to fashion a harpoon at the forge. The sailor had a notion to try his hand at spearing amongst the shoals of fish which accompanied and often seemed to be escorting the *Broomielaw* on her journey towards the Equator.

'Delighted to be able to practice my old trade,' Innes told the sailor as he handed over the skilfully crafted spear. Truth was that Hugh and Guthrie had completed most of the work but were happy to let their father take any credit. For his part Innes had been astonished by how much of his blacksmith's skills could still be summoned up despite his handicap and his years down the pit. He still rued the day he had left the forge for better pay.

For their trouble the Macaulays got a bottle of fiery, sticky rum from Rag and were told that there was 'plenty more where that came from.'

However, Rag would have been stunned to learn that his dark elixir was used by the Macaulay family at night with a sponge to wash down their bodies. 'Capital prevention for vermin,' had been Lumsden's advice to his conscripts on the lecture tour. Truth to tell Innes and his older boys also took the occasional mouthful, but purely for medicinal purposes.

In the third week out of Greenock the ways and means committee, formed eventually by women from both the married section and the single female quarters, addressed an equally contentious problem which had caused much debate among passengers since departure...the curse of smoking. It seemed that almost every man smoked – mostly pipes but also new fangled cigarettes – and the temperance ladies, denied the total abstinence from drink on board which they would have wished because of rules and regulations, turned their attention to the smokers.

Once again old Agnes was in the front line crying down what she described in a long and angry address as this 'filthy continental habit'. She still had her guns trained on the French sailmaker but this controversy kept her on the alert meantime.

At an open meeting she held her audience spellbound and she rounded on the male of the species generally for his weakness and stupidity. This, for Agnes, was an opportunity not to be missed and she was on the offensive from the start. The revolutionary cheers rang out when she declared: 'Wherever you go on that deck you drink in the aroma of what should be the fresh breath of heaven, the beautiful sea breezes, the air is polluted by unthinking and slovenly men.'

The younger women saw Agnes clearly as some sort of champion of the female cause, a wizened Borders Joan of Arc, and some stood up to applaud as Agnes produced a stub of cigarette from the pocket of her jacket, threw it to the deck and ground it, theatrically, into the boards with the heel of her boot.

'And more than that the deck is abominably spattered by these hackers.'

A very elegant lady, one of the cabin passengers, who seemed to enjoy the company of the meaner voyagers, raised her hand and Belle Macaulay who had volunteered to chair the gathering smiled and gestured for her to speak.

'Yes, yes. I wholeheartedly agree with Mistress Govan. It seems to be a necessary consequence of smoking that our paths should be strewn with spittle. For myself, this spattering is enough to sicken one, independent altogether of mal de mer'.

This in turn saw a temporary break in the discussion and hoots of laughter as the ladies debated whether it might be more constructive to throw the men – rather than the cigarettes – over the side.

'Mrs Golucky, sorry, it's Golightly isn't it?' There was more laughter as Agnes, confused over names and faces, got to her feet again. 'Mrs Golightly has the rights o' it. The mess up there would make you boak. There's just no needcessity for it.'

All the while the few men in the company – for there were a few and all non-smokers the ladies assumed – held their counsel and sat quietly absorbing this spectacle of women power in action. The smart young man with the glasses who danced all the Macaulay girls including young Hilda at the last Friday evening get-together, Cuthill was his name someone said, scribbled occasionally on a scrap of paper on his lap. Perhaps he planned to speak, thought Belle initially, but no, he seemed content to merely listen to the cut and thrust of the tobacco debate.

One or two soft voices were raised in support of their menfolk's right to smoke but they were shouted down in this impressive atmosphere of female determination which shook the cross-beams and seemed to run through the steerage.

Smoking was not permitted below decks; the fire risk was enormous. At first they had found it strange that in the midst of such a great expanse of water that a naked flame below decks was seen as such a risk to the safety of the ship. Passengers were tutored to watch the lamps and candles as if their lives depended on their alertness. They often did.

Emigrants also often found it odd that candles, despite the naked flame, were seen as less of a risk than enclosed oil lamps because the candles, often kept in a pannikin of water, tended to dowse themselves when they fell whereas lamps once overset and the fuel spilled were quickly out of control.

With timber walls and mattresses stuffed with straw and with the emigrant accommodation directly above the cargo holds, the risk of a dropped light, leading to catastrophe without hope of rescue, was a very real and terrifying one. Fire-fighting techniques were well practised but very unsophisticated – buckets of sea water drawn by hand having proved by far the simplest and most efficient means of fighting fires at sea over the previous half-century.

Last year aboard the *Breadalbane,* one of the vessels on the Adelaide run, there had been a serious fire which was only eventually defeated by battening down the holds and plugging every opening. The fire had been starved of oxygen. It was supposed that most of the migrant ships which vanished with trace had been consumed by fire rather than any other hazard of the sea. And often, with insufficient small boats on most ships, there were harrowing stories of whole families jumping overboard, hands linked, rather than face separation or death from thirst and starvation in an open boat.

At the meeting the atmosphere was now smouldering.

'All those in favour of a delegation leaving here immediately to convey our anxiety over the smoking habit directly to the captain, raise your hands.' Belle thought it high time the talking stopped. The vote was almost unanimous. Belle, Maggie and two younger women were nominated to form the deputation. Agnes, to her disgust, was left on the sidelines.

34 No Smoke Without Ire

Ratter, look like something recently dragged out of the sea, stood side by side with the Rev. Shade on the poop watching the men working aloft – and ironically enjoying a post-dinner smoke – when the deputation from below decks confronted them. The skipper was sooking on a long, white clay pipe while the minister held a cigar between middle and index finger, sucking on the stubby weed. Beneath his bushy brows he was screwing up his eyes against blown smoke.

Spotting the approach of the delegation on the port companionway Ratter mockingly stood to attention, straightened his collar and finger-combed his straggle of hair.

'My, my Rev. Shade! What have we here? This looks like a mutinous bunch to me. But a prettier bunch of cut-throats I've never seen.'

Ratter chuckled to himself and squinted at the women through his sinister, bloodshot eyes. He slapped his companion across the back. Shade coughed and blew a dense cloud of cigar smoke towards the women which was caught by the breeze and dispersed. Word had clearly filtered up to the skipper about the ways and means meeting.

Yes, remembered Belle, the weasel Rag had been skulking in the background during their deliberations.

An inquisitive crowd of emigrants on the main deck awaited developments as the ways and means delegation ranged themselves in front of the two smokers. Rare sport was promised here.

Ratter puffed on his pipe, one eye half-closed, and spat defiantly on the deck at the women's feet.

Abandoning any preliminaries Ratter got straight to the heart of the matter: 'I'm told you find offence in the harmless pastime of smoking, ladies. Would you deny hard-working men their relaxation?'

Belle had seen too many bullies like Ratter in her life. The women could either confront him now with what they considered to be just demands or back off to suffer for the rest of the voyage. She felt her stomach flutter but she believed wholeheartedly in the correctness of their protest. Plain, even pale in appearance she may have been but Belle Macaulay had an inner fortitude, sufficient to scare off Satan's legions. She had a kind way with her and demanded little from life. But the little she expected Belle made damn sure she got and that was generally for her men folk rather than herself.

'We have no wish to deny anyone the right to smoke. But we ask only that you designate parts of the vessel for smoking and that the filthy habit of spitting, except into the ocean, be outlawed,' said Belle calmly.

'Oh, do you now?'

'We believe we speak for the majority in this matter, Mr Ratter.'

'Tell me, woman. How can you have the arrogance to make these demands when you have never sooked on a pipe or chewed on a cigar?'

Belle held the onlookers spellbound. Would this apparently meek and mild miner's wife from Lanarkshire continue the defiance of the captain? Would the skipper's patience wear thin?

'I have inhaled sufficient smoke from others and slid often enough on the deck to know how poisonous and foul the habit is.'

Ratter was enjoying the battle of wits; that much was clear. 'Well, madam, I'd be more inclined to heed your concerns if I felt you knew what you were talking about.' Ratter turned to Shade and raised his eyebrows. 'Go on, man, give Mrs Macaulay a draw on the evil weed. At least then she'll be able to speak with a bit of authority.'

It seemed that the whole ship was now listening to their head to head. The delegation was ringed on all sides by nosey onlookers who nudged each other and whispered. To be asked to partake of the weed was a development the meeting below decks had anticipated. And Belle was in the firing line.

She remembered Guthrie coming home one evening to the Cowgate looking as a green and goggled-eyed as a toad after sampling a first smoke with his friends. Belle had scolded him mercilessly...but her own moment of truth approached.

Shade inhaled deeply until the cigar tip glowed; he exhaled and pushed the 'gasper' in Belle's direction. She stepped back.

Ratter glowered at the women. 'Take it or leave it; but you'll smoke that before I give any credence to your appeal.' Cupping the bowl of his clay pipe in his hand he stationed himself on a convenient capstan, waiting.

Belle stepped forward and took the cigar, looking round at her companions. She was was sure of one thing – if she backed down now the cause would be lost, the rest of the voyage would have to be undertaken beneath a haze of tobacco smoke...and what was probably worse, a fog of contempt.

Almost without thinking she thrust the cigar into her mouth and sucked. The tobacco was disgustingly soggy between her lips where Shade had rolled his tongue around but she tried to put that thought from her mind as the burning smoke rolled to the back of her throat and crept into her tubes.

Every eye was on her.

If she could just stop herself coughing...but it was too late. Her eyes began to flood painfully and Belle found herself retching and choking as she flung the cigar to the deck and the other women crowded round to comfort her.

Shade stooped to pick up the stub and Ratter slapped his thigh. 'I'll give you this, Mistress Macaulay. You're a game one. That's a powerful Havana, Elijah has there and you took a good draw on it. We'll work something out. You'll have your smoke-free areas but I warn you all I don't want such petitions to become a daily event. This is my ship and I'll run her the way I think fit.'

Belle, now a bit yellow about the gills and feeling distinctly groggy, gathered herself together. Somehow this did not feel like a victory.

'Thank you captain, I believe...' She coughed noisily and Maggie who had been by her side all through the encounter patted her back vigorously. 'As I was trying to say, I believe this action will also cut the risk of fire and that's something we all fear surely whether we are smokers or not'.'

Ratter frowned. 'Aye, well. Maybe so. Off wi' ye now. Leave me alone to finish my pipe in peace. Day was when passengers would never have thought to challenge a skipper on the running of his ship. It's a changing world and no mistake. And no' for the better to my mind.'

The delegation from the ways and means committee and a rather subdued Belle Macaulay went back below to report a small victory to the meeting which had remained in session to await the decision.

Back on the aft deck Shade examined the cigar as a treasure beyond price. He must persuade Belle to seek spiritual solace with him. She was a spirited female, like an unbroken filly, that's what she was, he mused.

35 Dancing with the Dolphins

It was soon apparent to the emigrant families that their adventure would be one of startling contrasts – from the sheer misery of the steerage in rough weather to gold-washed dawns with the wind sighing in the rigging; from the heartache and the helplessness of a sickly child to the joy of new friendships.

The *Broomielaw* was, however, specially blessed in at least one respect. Among the brigade of Highland migrants, folk from Lochaber and Lorne, who made up fully a quarter of the passenger complement were two pipers and there was the bonus of a bowlegged fiddler called Jock Semple from Falkirk who could make the cat gut sing marvellously. To see Jock play and dance merrily on the spot was to witness poetry in motion.

On the emigration voyage anyone with even modest talent whether as a singer or instrumentalist, or even someone who could recite a few lines of Burns, was cherished and given almost celebrity status between decks.

It wasn't long before the Friday afternoon concert or dance had become as much a part of the *Broomielaw's* routine as mealtimes or holystoning, the ritual scrubbing of the deck. A precocious youngster Jeremy Brown, a lad of about seven, was appointed, or more accurately appointed himself, as message boy and would scamper the length of the ship on Friday mornings before school, stopping every few yards to ring his handbell and announce the day's activities.

Unsurprisingly this lively start to the day didn't meet with everyone's approval. 'I'll wrap that bell roon' yer lug, boy' came the grunt from beneath a pile of blankets in the single mens' quarters on occasion.

When weather permitted dances were organised on the quarter deck. It was generally agreed that the first such had been an enjoyable event, if a fairly polite and restrained affair as the folk cautiously got to know each other. Subsequent dances were more lively.

Innes Macaulay was a revelation. A man who at home in Lanarkshire would never have ventured on to the floor at any of the colliery dances was transformed, despite, or perhaps because of, his blindness, into an enthusiastic, Belle would have said over-enthusiastic, dancer. She had the bruises on her toes to prove it.

'I'm truly getting the hang o' this dancing business, Belle,' he told his wife as he paraded her through a *Gay Gordons*. 'Tae hell wi' that slow stuff, the St Bernard's and the like. At this rate I'll be game for an eightsome reel before we cross the line.'

'I don't know if my taes can stand it, Innes,' she said giving him a playful poke in the ribs.

Belle had been told by the doctors that Innes, who had seemed calm and in control since the accident, might suffer a sudden and distressing delayed reaction to his misfortune. As yet there was no sign of such a setback. Admittedly, he did whisper to himself from time to time but she saw no great harm in this as he was otherwise cheerful and interested.

On deck that afternoon they had stood there like young things, hand in hand, as Belle tried to describe the taught white sails crowding the sky, towering away in the beauty of their swelling curves towards the vault of blue. Her word pictures told of the sailors clambering bravely amongst the maze of rigging and out along the yards and how shoals of flying fish burst from the sea, a shower of silver arrows.

A school of dolphin skimmed along beside the *Broomielaw*, dipping and diving between the cream-topped waves and Belle did her best to recreate these images for Innes. She would never say, of course, but Belle took some pleasure in being her husband's eyes. It had, she felt, drawn them even closer together.

That unspoken trust and companionship as husband and wife – and as friends – had deepened.

More discretely Belle also provided Innes with a running commentary during the dances. She detailed the setting for her husband; who was flirting with whom, who was dominating the dance floor and who were the day's wallflowers.

Innes heard the heels click in unison, the boards bouncing as the dancers passed by, dresses swirling, the laboured breathing of the participants as they brushed close by at the end of a *Strip the Willow* and the cheery buzz of conversation which competed with the seaburst all around and the lively melodies from the musicians perched on the aft port ladder.

And then there was that smell of the ocean, the taste of salt on his lips, the aroma of the ropes and rigging, disinfectant and cheap perfume. He had heard it said at the hospital that his other senses might heighten to compensate for his sight loss. Innes did not feel that his had happened and in a way felt cheated - and a little confused. But perhaps through time…

'Our Hugh and the oldest Gilchrist girl seem to have hit it off, Innes,' Belle whispered in his ear as they waltzed.

'She's a bonny lass, with a fine, healthy complexion, beautiful blonde hair, and tall, yes, quite tall. She's called May. Maggie says she spent a lot of time with her father on the hill. They're just opposite us now and she's smiling over.'

'The girl has an honest voice. I know that much,' said Innes. 'But that father o' her's is a strange one. I can scarce get a word out of him now.'

It was true enough. James Gilchrist had become almost completely withdrawn. He was sullen, mournful and very prone to seasickness, sitting for hours on his bunk with his head in his hands. Walter Lumsden's counselling had failed completely and Shade's professional advice had been to get himself up on deck and swallow some fresh air. The surgeon had made it clear that he wasn't prepared to waste time with folk whom he suspected were simply feeling sorry for themselves.

It mattered not. Any guidance was being ignored; the shepherd, after initially taking an inexplicably detailed interest in the crew and all their activities, had not been out of the steerage for a week.

Between each set of dances the younger children took the floor, the wee ones sliding around on their backsides while Hilda Gilchrist and Torrance Macaulay and a couple of the older children mimicked their elders with exaggerated, high dance steps and pulled faces which drew applause from the folk on the sidelines and a disapproving glare from Belle.

It was chillier now, the light was fading and the older folk were beginning to drift in the direction of their compartments. The energetic youngsters still produced their own internal warmth and danced on.

Walter emerged on deck having visited the young consumptive in the makeshift infirmary, four beds behind a canvas screen, aft. The boy was certainly better, more coherent but still pleading to be allowed to go on to Port Chalmers. Being abandoned in Madeira would surely be the end of him. But Ratter, as Lumsden and Jack Zurich had seen for themselves, was adamant.

Innes had been guided back to his seat by Belle who had then gone to fetch two glasses of the most popular drink on board the *Broomielaw* – raspberry vinegar. Walter laid a hand on Innes's shoulder and spoke with a cool, reassuring voice.

'You're showing the youngsters a thing or two about the dancing, eh Innes?'

'Is that you, Bob?' Innes Macaulay whispered.

'No, no – it's Walter Lumsden, Mr Macaulay. I'm pleased to see you out on the dance floor.'

'Oh, it's yourself, Mr Lumsden. Well, yes. It's a fine bit of exercise, but the real truth is that Belle is taking the lead. But don't you tell a soul that. I'd never live it down. You'll be looking forward to getting back to your family, Mr Lumsden?'

The innocent, unexpected question struck Walter Lumsden like a blow in the face. He sat down on the hatch cover.

'Well, no, Innes. I've no immediate family left in the Antipodes. I've got my eye on a piece of ground in New Zealand right enough, but who knows.'

'Is that right? I thought Belle made mention of your family, but since the accident my mind has been playing a few strange tricks; I didna' mean to pry.'

The agent felt once again as if someone had placed a heavy beam across his shoulders. Would it always be like this, he wondered. He did not think he could bear it. As ever a voice inside was urging him – Tell them! Tell them!

'My family died– in New South Wales – Innes, in '54.' The words were out almost before he knew it. They had circled his mind for so long it felt odd to hear them actually spoken. February 14, the day was etched in fire in his thoughts. But it had not been so difficult after all to utter those words, he suddenly realised.

And was it his imagination, but had the mere act of verbalising that heart-rending fact lifted his burden ever so slightly. He also knew instinctively, why he had been able to confide, even at a superficial level, with Innes Macaulay. He did not have to look this man in the eye; there was no-one staring in through the windows of the soul, seeing the reflections of his guilt. It had been the second time in the past 24 hours that he had felt able to unburden himself a little.

Maggie Gilchrist appeared through the throng on the far side of the deck. She had spent half-an-hour trying and failing to persuade her husband to come on deck. She glanced around and seeing Lumsden smiled.

'You must excuse me, Innes. Duty calls,' declared Walter.

'Aye you carry on, lad. I'm just warming up for a final spin roun' the deck. And, by the way, sorry if I seemed a bit nosy.'

The emigration agent gently patted him in the shoulder. 'It's fine Innes, it's fine.'

Belle arrived with the reviving raspberry vinegar. The call to the *Dashing White Sergeant* had Innes on his feet. 'Come oan Belle, let's show thae Highlanders how Lanarkshire folk can dance!'

36 Into the Deep

The previous two or three days had been very hard. In addition to having her own husband's increasingly intense melancholy to cope with Maggie found herself drawn into altogether more sombre events. The first death on an emigrant voyage was always a severe blow to the ship's morale, especially if it was a child, as it often was. The fact that on this occasion it was an accident which took place during the Sabbath school cast a dark shadow over the *Broomielaw* as she sped south.

Beetles, youngest child of a Dumbarton tinsmith, was the very spirit of fun and frolics. When the bagpipes played he would jump and clap his hands gleefully. Known to everyone, crew and emigrants alike, he was in the habit of getting in everyone's way.

However, who could be angry with that cheerful little soul; always with a roguish smile playing around an expressive, freckled face which would explode into a grin at the slightest provocation. He got his nickname of Beetles because he collected, inspected and preserved every insect which crossed his path.

Beetles died after a mysterious choking fit and only in the aftermath of the tragedy was it discovered that he had swallowed a large glass marble.

And within a few hours the sailmaker Jontot was sewing a second tiny shroud. Little Ann Broadfoot, the sickly kiddie in the compartment opposite the Gilchrist and Macaulay family groups had developed a chest infection after contracting measles. In the hours before her death she seemed to be scarcely breathing at all – an angel's breath at most Maggie had said after sitting for hours with the child and her distraught mother – and then Ann was gone.

Jack Zurich, who couldn't persuade the skipper that he was needed on funeral duty, decided that to minimise the anguish, if that was possible, the two kiddies should be committed to the deep together. Once they had forced themselves to accept the absolute necessity for the burial at sea the respective parents were at peace with the arrangement.

But Walter Lumsden for one was gripped with an unspeakable misery which threatened to choke him at the thought of the bleak ceremony in prospect. He knew this was an ordeal which he would have to face sooner or later and equally he realised that he would be expected, as agent and mentor of the expedition, to be out on that windswept quarterdeck for the committal of the bodies to the deep. He was consumed with memories of his own daughter. That whooping cough epidemic which swept their ship had taken away 20 young lives in as many days, including his darling little girl, Sarah. He could still recall those terrible rasping, gasping coughs, a dreadful chorus which signalled so many deaths.

In a quiet corner of the quarterdeck a couple of hours before the service, with the sails slapping above their heads and clouds scudding past, Walter found himself trying to explain this secret agony to Maggie Gilchrist.She had looked surprised when he sought her out. But Maggie waited patiently as he rubbed his brow and tried to compose himself.

'It's difficult to put into words, Maggie. But I can't face this without telling someone about…' His words trailed away on the wind.

'Listen, Walter. I feel privileged to be asked to help. But I'm not a mindreader.'

And so the emigration agent told the story of the whooping cough outbreak and of a daughter snatched away from them. There followed a long moment of contemplation.

'You understand, I think Maggie, that it's more than just memories. All this brings back the futility, the damned waste. When the little ones die out here it's hard to believe that some dark force doesn't rule our world. And we left our little Sarah in the ocean. That cannot be a proper way to say farewell, can it?'

'Surely, this is now a chance for you to say a proper goodbye, Walter.'

The *Broomielaw* dipped her bow as if in agreement, dissecting a cream-topped breaker and drenching the foredeck with spray. They clung to the woodwork and steadied themselves feeling the salt on their lips.

'Perhaps. But it's not only that, Maggie. These folk trusted me, they joined this adventure on my say so and now they must suffer the agony of seeing their own children consigned to the ocean.'

Maggie touched him gently on the arm. Walter realised – although she must have been intensely curious about his background – that she had clearly decided that would not be a wise time to ask about the rest of his family. It must have seemed strange, he realised, that he had never mentioned them to anyone. That touch was merely a consoling gesture but for Lumsden it meant much more.

Apart from the therapeutic caresses of Mrs Bonthrone at Haddington which had been welcome but strangely impersonal, this was the first time in years Walter had allowed anyone to reach out to him either physically or emotionally. Courteous, unwanted handshakes were a necessary part of the commerce of life but this, this was different. For so long the emigration agent had erected a façade of competence and control, an impenetrable mask of seeming assurance. Had this bold lass seen into his heart?

'But Walter, why are you punishing yourself in this way. You can't take the burdens of all the world on your shoulders. These are all intelligent and understanding people. They knew exactly what they are getting into.'

Lumsden listened. Did they really? He thought of Maggie's man, James, lying below staring into space, preoccupied with God knows what. Had he even an inkling of what emigration might mean for the Gilchrists and their girls?

And so, after all, Walter Lumsden, reluctantly, even fearfully, with Maggie standing close by his side, went to the brief funeral service. At four o'clock the ship bell tolled its slow, mournful summons and the emigrants shuffled, heads bowed, buffeted by the Atlantic breeze, out on deck. A thin drizzle shrouded the *Broomielaw*.

As they stood in ranks, awaiting the little corpses, Walter Lumsden could not clear his mind of one chilling detail which Jontot had confided. The final stitch, as the shroud was sealed around the bodies, was traditionally passed through the gristle at the tip of the deceased's nose, tying them into their final place of rest. It was a grotesque image which the emigration agent could not erase, no matter how often he shook himself mentally.

The tiny bodies were finally brought on deck on rough boards which were placed at an opening in the bulwark. The four attendant sailors held the boards level while a psalm was sung and a prayer offered. A stillness was felt throughout the ship. For a few minutes all was silent except for the creaking of the timbers and the snapping of sails high above the funeral party.

'Lord, we commit these little ones to the deep.' Walter Lumsden thought he must be imagining it – the Rev. Shade looked up as if he was waiting for a round of applause. 'The time will yet come when all truths will be revealed and when there shall be no more death neither sorrow nor crying. Lord, take these little ones into thy loving care.'

Shade nodded to the escorts as the wind whipped in from the northeast on the back of this miserable, grey day. The shrouds with their sad cargoes began to slip down the boards towards the ocean. One of the little bundles seemed reluctant to go and had to be gently helped on its way by one of the seaman. Lumsden shut his eyes tightly. He felt Maggie edge even closer. Her comforting presence was all that stopped him from turning and running.

Another verse of Psalm 123 was sung and then a closing prayer was offered but the tinsmith, a strong, quiet man, laden with grief, looked set to collapse. Strong hands helped him withdraw with some dignity to join his inconsolable wife below. The muffled striking of the ship's bell accompanied his departure.

37 At War With the Shark

The ship could not continue in such a mournful progress; there were still too many miles to cover, too many dark nights to negotiate. The following afternoon brought a much needed distraction.

'Shark! Shark on the hook!'

The cry came from the starboard side where a group of deckhands, foremost among them the rascal Rag, were testing Innes's splendid harpoon. The whole company, including Jock the fiddler, ran to the rail and peered down at the dark waters. On a smaller vessel such a wave of humanity rolling to one side of the ship might have capsized her. The *Broomielaw* was made of sturdier stock and eased forward comfortably on the swell.

True enough a shark, steely grey, streamlined evil, yet magnificent, was struggling against the taught line. It was already doomed, but the creature's instincts told it to fight on. To the accompaniment of oohs and aahs from the emigrants, a noose was lowered down the line then slipped over the shark's ferocious snout, past its dark emotionless eyes. The noose was drawn along the predator's back towards the tail fin.

For a moment the shark was still, conserving its energy for the occasional burst of shaking and twisting, as it attempted to tear itself free from the vicious hook upon which it was impaled.

'Hold the line taught. We're almost at the tail.' It was William Bigland's shouted instruction. The laird's son had been watching the crewmen working the long lines and had been caught up in the excitement. Many were the table-sized flatfish he'd helped drag from the bottom of the Stormay Sound as a boy. But this shark fishing felt like real sport and as a nooseman he was a natural.

Drawn from its element, taken from the environment of which it was master, the shark, although still dangerous, was doomed. The crew of a sailing ship, so accustomed to hauling on ropes or spinning a windlass were more than a match for an exhausted shark and he was hauled twenty feet up into the main rigging where briefly he made a fine row.

Finally to cries of 'Stand Back There!' the rope was loosed and thrashing and gasping the shark thumped on to the boards.

The beast had scarcely come to rest on the deck before a burly sailor leapt forward, rammed a handspike into its upper jaw and the rest of the fishing crew set upon the shark like a gang of Spittalfield cut-throats. Mothers kept the wee ones well back and fathers with outstretched arms kept the others at a safe distance.

'Seven foot, ten inches.' Rag's voice rose over the excited babble. Having clubbed the creature mercilessly about the head with belaying pins one of the sailors ran a blade along the length of its stomach and coils of blue-grey intestine slurped and slithered out on to the deck.

'What are they searching for inside the shark, Mr Lumsden?' Torrance and Hilda had arrived wide-eyed beside the emigration agent.

'They're at war with the shark, Hilda. He's their sworn enemy.' Lumsden knew of the seafaring tradition which held that every shark had at one time or another eaten a seaman. The men were in fact looking for evidence of this legend – an undigested hand or foot. It was the stuff of childhood nightmares.

'They'll cut off the tail fin and they'll nail it to the heel of the boom to bring fair winds.'

'Does it really bring fair winds, Mr Lumsden?' asked Torrance earnestly.

'The sailors believe it, Torrance, so who's to say they're wrong.'

What was confusing Walter as he watched this strange ritual of the shark killing unfold was that in the midst of the throng, beaming widely as he watched, was the Rev. Shade. On the voyage back to Britain, Walter recalled that ship's preacher reacting furiously to what he called superstitious nonsense. Damned paganism, he had styled it. Shade seemed to find no such problem as he stood amongst a bloody scene more reminiscent of a slaughterhouse.

Under instruction from the crewmen, William Bigland was now slicing away at the tail, sawing and tearing at the fin until he rose triumphantly to display it to the assembled crowd. The young man who had thought to find his calling in the law courts of Edinburgh was suddenly at home on the ocean and master of one of the most dangerous creatures to find its home in the liquid deep.

As Bigland waved the trophy in the air and cast his gaze around the crowd, he thought, just for a moment, that he recognised a face from his past, from another life far from the deck of the *Broomielaw,* there, at the back of the throng.

'Ridiculous,' he told himself. It couldn't be Queenie. She was thousands of miles away feeding the chickens at Cott. The truth was that he had scarce given a thought to Queenie since leaving Glasgow. He shook his head then led the youngsters on a parade round the deck, the fin held high.

From his position on the after-deck Jack Zurich had watched this bizarre event. Looking at the last light of day beginning to fade in the west and at the tall clouds gathering ominously along the horizon, his sailor's sixth sense could trace a different feel to the wind and to the movement of the *Broomielaw* beneath his feet. He shook his head as he noted the strange elongated cloud formations around the horizon and went below to consult his charts. It would take more than a lucky shark's fin to chase away such a looming tropical storm.

38 Before the Mast

The crew of the clipper Broomielaw (578 tons and built in 1852) was the usual colourful bunch found on most emigrant ships operating out of the Clyde – a core of Scots, some Cockneys and Scousers, Swedes, an American, a Greek and 'Spike' Wallace, the Negro cook, a huge beanpole of a man from Baltimore who seemed to stoop with the breeze and bend almost double to negotiate the low hatchways.

Generally the sailors were friendly to the passengers and there was no indication of the contempt which was reputedly poured on emigrants aboard Irish emigration ships to the United States and Canada where the poor families were often described by crewmen as 'pigs.' In their spare moments some the Broomielaw's crew carved in wood, bone or ivory while others made model ships, like those displayed in the shop windows of a thousand seaports. The atmosphere was generally relaxed.

The Scots had heard all the gruesome stories of conditions on these Irish vessels particularly after the famine as so many headed for the Americas. The *Broomielaw* was no floating paradise but it felt almost homely in comparison.

Jontot the sailmaker was a proud Breton and once he started on the squeezebox with the traditional melodies of the Atlantic coast he was off in a world of his own. He was also popular amongst the children because of his pet - a gentle, furry monkey with big round eyes, a pathetic expression in his sad, flat face and long, long fingers. His name was Erebus and he would sit on Jontot's shoulder, looking glumly out at the world.

The captain's steward, who also looked after the cabin passengers, was a Manxman called Tully, a survivor, or at least so he claimed, of three shipwrecks and the carpenter 'Chippy' Carlsen, a master of his craft, was a big, burly Dane whose reputation for caulking seams to make the ship watertight, was second to none.

David Macgregor, the second mate from Dundee with his pioneering experience in Australia was a figure of interest amongst the emigrants, particularly the adventurous young men who listened fascinated to his tales. Macgregor had been a boundary rider up country in Victoria in the earliest days of settlement and made money at the Ballarat gold diggings. Having fought at the Eureka Stockade in 1854 in defence of what he described as 'working men's freedoms' he liked to show the scar from a bayonet on his shoulder.

Many a long evening Innes and the second mate, sharing their radical leanings, would put the world to rights over a glass of rum.

Then there were the sea apprentices, half-a-dozen young lads learning the tough lessons of a life before the mast – the oldest called Tommy Dungannon was a minister's son and a notoriously rowdy element and the smallest and youngest of the bunch was 'Nipper' Jarvis. The two were inseparable.

Some emigrant ships were described in newspaper articles and commissioner's reports as simply 'hell with the lid off', and despite the captain of the *Broomielaw* now posted absent on a more or less permanent basis the ship was blessed with what seemed a crew of reasonably sensible types.

Together this broth of humanity made a formidable working unit when the cry went up – 'All hands shorten sail!' Teamwork was vital. In the Southern Ocean in particular, working aloft on icy foot-ropes, among snapping, frozen canvas, the men relied on each other for survival. Up there you had to know you were among friends.

Down on the deck they could be washed about like flotsam by the heavy seas, sometimes not knowing whether they were still on board ship or over the side in the ocean, or about to be caught in the safety nets like so many herring. It was reassuring to be able to call the men round about friends as well as shipmates.

By first light the day after the shark hunt, the sky had taken on a forbidding pinky-greyness. A pall of rushing cloud shut out the blessed sun and the crew raced here and there preparing the vessel for the storm. Overnight the wind had increased steadily, gusting up to gale force and sails were shortened at 1 a.m. Now rolling waves extended from one side of the cheerless horizon to the other. It promised to be a bleak Saturday.

By breakfast time, with all normal activities cancelled, the ship was diving bows under, doing ten knots and throwing spray as high as the lower topsail yards. Every so often a sea came tumbling aboard, sweeping the *Broomielaw* fore and aft and woe betide any seaman caught moving about on deck who miscalculated the run of these killer waves. Below sheets of water slid across the passageways.

Since well before dawn Jack Zurich had been out on the poop deck, black cap reversed and clearly ready for the serious side of seagoing. For hours he would be found standing shoulder to shoulder with the helmsman, a cockney called Jimmy Ducks or in the chart house poring over the route. The second mate Macgregor stood by Ducks ready to assist, the faces of both men glancing upwards from time to time at the set of the sails.

During the frequent squalls the two helmsmen, arms aching as they fought the ocean, needed all their ability, experience and strength to keep her to a true course, knowing that the slightest deviation might mean her 'broaching to' or swinging round into the trough of the sea and most likely foundering with all hands. The wheel kicked violently under the force of the turbulent ocean against the rudder.

Disappearing beneath of shower of spray Walter Lumsden, wearing a full set of oilskins for the first time on the journey, clambered up to the afterdeck. He shook the water from his face and nodded to the second mate. They watched the wind and strained to keep a check on the compass.

The emigrants were below, the weather hatches long since battened down. There, in the airless depths of the ship they could only imagine the wild scenes as the crew, hanging on by their eyebrows, shortened sail high above the windblasted deck.

'Walter, you'd be better down there with your troops.' Jack Zurich was genuinely surprised and impressed to see the emigration agent out in the elements. Lumsden swept the water from his jacket and squeezed himself into the corner of the chart house.

'You'll be set on a heading for Madeira,' he asked, wiping the window with his sleeve and staring out into the day which in the space of an hour had become like night.

'That's still the orders from below. Ratter is right on one count, The *Broomielaw* is a fine ship. Given a decent break she'll sail through any storm. Please reassure your emigrants on that score.'

Lumsden looked around him. The little deckhouse was bare expect for the sloping table for the sea charts fixed firmly to the wooden wall, the magnetic compass and the chronometer. All that and Jack's trusty sextant, his guide to the other side of the world.

'Are you a religious man, Jack?'

The first mate sipped thoughtfully at his mug of dark tea and smiled.

'If you mean that in situations like this I occasionally find a prayer coming to my lips, then the answer would have to be 'Yes', Walter.'

'Never had you down as a believer, I must say,' Lumsden responded.

'You can't sail the oceans without being impressed by the majesty and power of whatever, or whoever, created all this.' Jack Zurich swept his hand towards the menace-laden horizon. Within the past few minutes daylight had started to evaporate. It was like an early dusk. Tracking round, white tops now stretched across the salt pastures of the great ocean; the towering clouds still mirrored in the deep.

It was Walter Lumsden's turn to nod. It was indeed difficult to imagine how a vessel made of wood and propelled only by sails and the skills of its mariners, with simple navigation aids and no possibility of rescue if they came into danger, could cross these seas – unless something, someone, was watching over them.

And yet Lumsden had long since abandoned any notion of a protector, far less a creator.

39 The Face of Madness

They were both suddenly aware of a wild figure, arriving in a slow and broken motion almost at the top of the companionway, swaying for a moment as if uncertain how to proceed.

Then in the half-light this apparition, bare-headed and in loose shirt sleeves, came staggering towards Ducks, and stood peering into the steersman's face from no more than a few inches. It was Ratter. And he was drunk as a sailor in port after six months at sea.

Jack Zurich and Walter watched this strange scene unfold through the spray-splashed windows. Words were being exchanged then just as the helmsman, who had been joined by second mate Macgregor at the wheel, looked pleadingly over his shoulder at the chart-house, the *Broomielaw,* was struck by a mighty sea.

The men, having had their attention diverted for the merest moment by the mad antics of the skipper, had the wheel twisted momentarily from their grasp by the force of the waves causing the ship to take a sheer which was almost her last. Feeling the enormous pressure against one side of her rudder, the *Broomielaw* swung up to meet the wind. Together helmsman and the second mate caught and held the great wheel struggling to prevent the *Broomielaw* turning side on – with possibly fatal consequences – to the weather.

Above the cracking of what remained of the sails and the torrents of water which washed across the decks, the skipper, having almost realised his apparently unhinged ambition to send the *Broomielaw* to the bottom, set up a series of unearthly yells and yelps and threw himself at the wheel in a lunatic attempt to prevent the two men from bringing her round. All this drama unfolded in a matter of seconds.

Jack, having bounced from the chart-house, threw himself at Ratter and sent him flying across the boards.

At the same time Walter Lumsden flung all his weight on the lee side of the wheel and between them the three men got the helm of the great vessel up, just in time to save the broaching ship from being overwhelmed.

Jack and the skipper rolled and wrestled on top of the skylight above the passengers' saloon as the others at the wheel continued their struggle to keep her on a straight course. Just as the for'ard watch came running to give further assistance Lumsden managed to separate the skipper and his first mate, pushing Ratter's arm high up his back.

At the top of his voice, looking around wild-eyed but still struggling under Lumsden's firm grip, Ratter shouted: 'Arrest him! He has changed course without my authority.'

In his turn Jack issued clear concise orders: 'Secure our skipper, boys. He's unwell.' It was clear enough. The long drinking bouts had culminated in an attack of the DTs. In his present state he was an appalling danger to the ship and to the hundreds of souls on board.

The two seamen looked briefly at each other and at the grotesque figure of Ratter. Moments later he was taken by strong hands and led off.

As the *Broomielaw* slowly regained her equilibrium and began to cope with the storm, a scene of devastation could be made out on the decks below. A large portion of the bulwark on the port side was gone and pins, planks, boards and other indeterminate pieces of wreckage were floating and dashing from one side of the flooded deck to the other. The biggest loss was the sturdy wooden pig pen which had been washed away into the gloom, the poor creatures squealing in terror, still inside.

It was still a time of great danger for the *Broomielaw* but mercifully the good sails held, the sturdy masts, rigging and running gear bore the tremendous strain and the bravehearts at the wheel kept her directly before wind and sea.

With the deranged skipper safely locked in his quarters Lumsden and Jack Zurich dried themselves off and shared a pannikin of steaming coffee and a couple of biscuits in the cramped charthouse. Serious matters were under discussion.

'Taking command…surely it's quite legitimate in the circumstances, Jack.'

'You're right, of course. Ratter would have had us all at the bottom. But it's still a drastic step in any circumstance, relieving a skipper of his duties.' Jack Zurich poured himself another coffee, as thick and dark as the ocean beyond the wooden walls.

'There were plenty of witnesses to his lunatic behaviour today. What the hell has got into the man?'

Jack Zurich, a quiet, efficient, law-abiding man, a well-respected first mate had been forced to this drastic action simply out of desperation. Some might call it mutiny, others simply common sense. He was doing perhaps what he should have done twenty minutes out of Greenock. Now Ratter had forced his hand.

'I had one other matter I wanted to raise with you, Walter. You'll have heard that the pocket watch stolen from the family quarters has been found in the sailmaker's bunk?'

'I did hear some talk of that, Jack.'

'Because it's a crew matter, I'll now have to deal with Jontot's case but obviously this a completely new game for me and I'd appreciate it, Walter, if you sat in while I questioned the witnesses. Keep me on the right track…'

Walter Lumsden got up to leave. 'Delighted to help. Mind you, I really find it difficult to believe that inoffensive wee man is a sneak thief. Well now, skipper – what's your first executive decision?'

'Already taken, Walter. Our passenger with consumption will get his wish. He's going to New Zealand. There will be no stopover at Madeira and to hell with Shade. He makes my flesh creep.'

Before the emigration agent had the chance to agree there came, over the noise of the angry sea, a series of anguished shouts from the main deck. Both men peered into the half-light of the dismal afternoon. Fingers were pointing into the rigging.

40 Fate Takes A Hand

This selfsame Atlantic storm which saw Silas Ratter wrestling with his crew on the quarterdeck like a man possessed by sea demons, was also destined to convince James Gilchrist that he had God (or at least Providence) on his side in the quest for vengeance on his brother's killers.

As the gale strengthened by the minute the emigrants gathered in their quarters trying to reassure each other in the face of this first real encounter with the angry ocean and helping to soothe those overcome by punishing, soul-destroying sea sickness. Water poured down the companionways and as she bucked and heeled the *Broomielaw* often seemed more under the water than above it.

Up on deck, waves began to run the length of the ship, great drenching lumps of water crashing on to the planking, shaking the vessel to her keel. The crew had moved purposefully to their set tasks, securing the vessel for the storm yet at sea during such moments tragedy is often only a breath away.

As Ratter was being escorted below, still ranting and raving at his charges, a terrible accident had unfolded high in the rigging as the final efforts to reef the sails was made in the face of the ocean blast.

The cry of 'Away Aloft!' had sent the men scurrying up the rigging; a mad scramble in an effort to take in the remainder of the sails. Safety lines had been strung across the deck to help the crew move around but there was always danger up among the masts and the web of rigging.

In the blink of an eye two crewmen, edging out along the foot lines on the main-royal yard, became victims of that storm.

As they prepared to furl the remainder of the sail, a fierce blast struck the men who were busy spacing themselves out along the rope and one soul tumbled forward over the yard, sliding down the remaining unfurled canvas before crashing through the rigging to his death on the deck sixty feet below.

His piercing scream had every head on deck turning towards the nightmare scene. The sailor hurtled on to a hatch cover, his shattered body then slipping slowly on to the deck. It was immediately clear to those arriving at his side that he was beyond help.

Up above a second man having made a despairing grab for his doomed colleague side-slipped off the foot line and hung upside down for agonising seconds, his legs seemingly tangled in the ropes, before he too, slid and fell. He had been stationed further out along the foot line and having struck the gunwale with a sickening thud, his body bounced off the wooden parapet and into the dark sea.

*   *   *   *   *

An hour later as Maggie sat on her bunk and whispered details of the accident circulating in the steerage to her husband, James had only one question – he wanted desperately to know the names of the crew members who had been killed.

'Yes, yes, Maggie. It's terrible accident. I get the picture. But did they say the names of the men who fell? Does anyone know down here know who they were?'

'Folk say one was the young Macdonald boy from Gourock and the other who fell, trying to save him apparently, was Evan Richards, the Welshman.'

'Richards, by God. You say Richards is dead, Maggie; trying to save the boy, was he? How very odd.'

James Gilchrist's recent behaviour had been perplexing. But this response to the death of the crewmen was beyond explanation. He sat staring at the floor, saying nothing more but occasionally shaking his head as if in disbelief.

Maggie was confused. 'What do you mean? I don't think we ever exchanged two words with either of these men, James. What exactly do you find odd about this tragedy? They were working in difficult and dangerous conditions up there. You heard Jack trying to reassure the Sinclairs about the dangers just days ago by telling them that working in the rigging was miles safer than riding a horse.'

In his mind's eye Gilchrist was trying to recreate the scene: Richards' desperate lunge in a vain effort to grab his toppling crewmate. Hands greasy from the drenching rain, the boy must have slipped from his grasp. He tried to imagine Richards' final moments, his dismay as he realised he had also lost his balance on the foot line; the instant of shocking realisation, as he hung upside down, as it became clear he was also about to die. His mates would have been edging along the line towards him – but too late. The rush of air as he tumbled, spinning through the gloom towards the deck below…

Not for the first time Gilchrist wondered about this mission he had set himself – to avenge his brother. All the evidence confirmed that Rag, Doig and Richards – his three targets, were all directly involved in his brother's death. He shook his head again as if to dispel the doubt. The reality was that now there were only two. Richards had been swallowed by the deep.

41 Queenie Dines Out

Twenty-four days out from Greenock and it was almost Christmas.

Queenie Stout had thought long and seriously about the dinner invitation. Clearly the first mate, now acting skipper, had taken a shine to her but her decision to share a meal with Jack Zurich was surely precocious in the extreme.

On the other hand, she thought that soon she might have to give herself up. Her double life between the hold and the deck was becoming increasingly uncomfortable and as the weather grew warmer, the hold was ever more airless and claustrophobic. And the hotter it became the more active the rats seemed. They were daring now, running over her feet as they patrolled the packing cases.

However, it was not only conditions in the hold that caused anxiety. As the equator grew nearer several of the women had been eyeing her with obvious suspicion – this shy, attractive creature with the rosy complexion and flaxen hair who flitted amongst the emigrants. She had even imagined on a couple of occasions that she was being followed. It could only be a matter of time before the game was up.

But she liked Jack Zurich and now that he was acting skipper, she realised, it would be wise to cultivate his friendship before declaring herself. Queenie dragged a brush through her hair and freshened herself up as best she could, arriving at the compact cabin just as Tully was about to serve a plate of broth.

Yes, that had been the other attraction of the invitation – food, real food! She had enough of Mooney's scraps from the galley, the occasional piece of brown and floury apple and undercooked carrot did not fill her with joy. Queenie suspected that the scabby whippet which belonged to the carpenter was getting more of square meal than she ever did.

As they ate Queenie tried as best she could to steer her way around any awkward questions. She talked about anything and everything rather than how she came to be on board the *Broomielaw*. The weather proved a usefully broad ranging topic. They also talked about Jack's background; of his father's grocery shops in and around Portsmouth which should have been his destiny but which he forsook for a life before the mast.

Most of all Queenie wanted to know about Australia. Jack told her of the phenomenal growth of Melbourne following the 1850 Gold Rush, of how its population now numbered over 40,000 with almost every nationality on earth represented. Even the town of Adelaide numbered its population in thousands now rather than hundreds. And she was fascinated by his descriptions of the vast, beautiful, empty countryside, of the native peoples and the strange animals.

From the captain's cabin, through the bulkhead, came the strains of *What a Friend we have in Jesus*. The old man, the skipper, was at his rosewood harmonium. Now that he was confined to quarters he played almost all day, the entire gospel repertoire.

Jack ladled the last of the stew on to Queenie's plate and sat back with quiet admiration to watch her demolish the meal. Her fork flashed up and down, from plate to mouth. This lass clearly loved her grub. She happily accepted the second helpings but almost choked on her last mouthful.

'Do you find steerage comfortable enough? Where exactly are you berthed?

The moment of panic passed. It was a reasonable enough question after all. The senior crewmen seldom had reason to be in the steerage. He was simply being polite.

'Oh, I'm fine with the girls. I've slept in more comfortable places, mind you.'

'You said you were from the North Isles. Just by chance there's a young cabin passenger, a Mr Bigland, from your part of the world. He joined us at the very last minute. I must introduce you, if you haven't yet met.'

Queenie hadn't forgotten about William. She was fairly sure he had seen her at the back of the crowd the day the shark was landed and once, from a distance, she saw him gazing along the length of the steerage in her direction. She had stepped nimbly into the shadows on that occasion. She would pick her moment.

'Yes, that would be nice.' Once again, steering the conversation in less worrying direction she asked: 'They say in the steerage that you've locked up that little Frenchman for the thieving that has been going on.'

'Yes, you might say he's in protective custody. I suppose I shouldn't really speak of it until the hearing but things looks pretty cut and dried. Mr Haldane's pocket watch was found under his pillow. Old Agnes Govan saw him sneaking about in the family quarters and alerted the mate.'

'She's not the most impartial witness from what I've heard said,' smiled Queenie. They both laughed.

Under the subdued light of the oil lamp, in the short silence which followed, Jack Zurich marvelled at the progress of events over the past few days. First of all he was in charge of the ship, albeit by default; it was his first command with all the responsibility that brought with it, and to tell the truth he was in his element. Of course, he had the nagging doubts about his abilities. Until you finally assume a command the old sailors had told him you would never really know if you had the metal to see it through.

At times of doubt all Jack had to do was to remember how as a boy in Portsmouth he would, against parental orders, sneak down to the docks to see the great sailing ships arrive and depart.

From the age of about seven he never doubted that the sea was his calling. Those memories were always enough to steel him for whatever task or trial lay ahead. He quite simply loved the sea. Now he had this pretty lass opposite clinging to his every word. What would his father, the sober Methodist shopkeeper, who thought him a worthless, headstrong tyke, have made of all this?

'What will happen to Monsieur Jontot?' asked Queenie.

'We'll tie him to the end of a rope and run him under the keel. I've found that usually discourages re-offending.' Queenie sat bolt upright.

Jack leaned back on his creaky chair and laughed when he saw the look of shock and disbelief on the girl's face.

'I'm only jesting you, of course. We're a bit more civilised these days with wrongdoers. In any case he's the only skilled sailmaker on board and also the best accordion man on the ship. No, we'll find a suitable punishment.'

Queenie smiled across at her confidante. Now here was a problem. Jontot was innocent; of that she was certain. More than that Queenie was sure she could identify the culprit – but only by betraying her own secret. She needed to think about this.

42 The Not-So Holy Touch

'I'm so pleased you felt able to come along and confide in me, Mistress Macaulay' The Rev. Elijah Shade bowed as deeply as he could manage allowing for his paunch and his over-tight grey frock coat and ushered the pitman's wife into his quarters.

Belle had been in the habit of visiting the minister in Fraser Castle after the pit disaster. Previously she had not been a regular church attender but she found his calm, reassuring words a great comfort and just as importantly the Rev. Simpson had been very positive and encouraging once he learned the Macaulays were determined to press ahead with their emigration plans.

It was all very well joining the agitation for better working conditions and higher wages, as she had done in the aftermath of the disaster, but she felt she owed someone for Innes's life. The events had restored her faith in the religion she had abandoned after the loss of her father and older brother in the Ayrshire coalfield disaster of 1839.

She had been so busy since they sailed from Greenock that she had time only for the Sabbath services and occasionally stopped by the ship school to take part in their brief morning worship, a hymn and a prayer. Shade had been quite insistent, however, that she should join him in private prayer and meditation – 'whenever she felt she had a moment.' Her performance with the anti-smoking delegation had clearly made quite an impression.

And that afternoon, with Innes listening eagerly to stories of the scandals in Lanark town council from Matthew Broadfoot, a former burgess and father of the little girl Ann who died from measles, and with young Torrance on deck happily learning to splice ropes, Belle decided to take the plunge.

However, she quickly guessed that Shade, who sat facing her, might be of a different stamp altogether from her minister in the pit town. He had the fiery face of a Glasgow butcher. Arms folded, he watched her.

Shade had taken off his jacket and now sat in his shirt sleeves. Large dark patches on the fabric of his shirt at the armpits and on his chest indicated that he was perspiring freely. He began flicking through his Bible for the text he was seeking. Belle could see the beads of sweat tracing a path down his neck and into the mat of chest hair which sprouted around his open collar.

He was an ugly individual, that was the honest truth of it, carrying extra weight both on his belly, legs and doughy jowls. But he also gave the impression of muscular strength, despite his blubbery demanour. What Belle noticed above everything else were his huge, hairy hands.

Lord preserve us, the man must be covered from head to toe with hair; how repulsive, thought Belle.

Those were ploughman's or miner's hands. It was odd because during her brief encounter with Ratter, she had noticed that the captain shared the same bushy mits.

It had become progressively hotter in the past few days, the *Broomielaw* now having reached 21 degrees north and it was clear that Shade was suffering for his extra bulk. Most of the passengers contrived to wear as few clothes as was possible, and decent. Belle had felt it necessary to open the two top neck buttons of her dress. Despite this immodesty she felt much more comfortable having loosed her tight collar.

That very morning, with their full co-operation she had cut Torrance and Guthrie's hair to the very scalp for the sake of coolness, cleanliness and comfort. Big brother Hugh, most of whose waking hours were now spent in May Gilchrist's company, had politely declined to be shorn. Torrance taunted his elder brother with: 'Miss Gilchrist wouldn't like it, would she?'

Shade read a couple of passages from the Bible; one about the raising of Lazarus and one which Belle recognised as part of the Easter story. Neither seemed to have any relevance at all to their situation and if she hadn't known better Belle might have thought that the readings had simply been plucked out of thin air.

As soon as she told Shade of her hairdressing skills she realised that it had been a blunder. Belle could have kicked herself. His eyes lit up and after a prayer on the theme of God's manifold ways of expressing his love, the minister asked if she would do him the service of trimming his hair also.

Belle was stunned and nervously tried to extricate herself from this unwanted situation; but her excuses sounded hollow. On the surface it seemed an innocuous enough request but she felt decidedly uncomfortable at the prospect of touching this man. He would hear none of her pleading.

The preacher produced a paid of scissors and a brush from his medical bag and tucking a rough towel around the neck of his shirt, he signalled for Belle to commence. She thought she might run from the cabin but that, she realised, would simply cause embarrassment for all concerned. At sea there was no real escape, in any case. The haircutting exercise was conducted in silence – except that is for the sound of the sea sloshing below the cabin window, the clicking of the scissors and a strange, almost musical, humming, or was it moaning, that seemed to issue from the minister every time Belle's fingers came in contact with his scalp, lightly brushing over his skin.

As she trimmed around his collar and ran her fingers across the back of his neck to lift his hair to the scissors he started to shift in his seat, twisting on his fat hin' end. The moans were now more like groans and Belle hurried to complete this unexpected and unwelcome duty, refusing to admit to herself exactly what might be going on.

When he eventually stood up brushing the clippings from his shoulder and turned to face her, Shade had a wild and decidedly un-Christian look in his eyes.

'I must be off to see to the family's tea, Mr Shade. Lots of hungry mouths to feed, you understand.'

'Aye, aye, hungry mouths to feed indeed. And I have a disciplinary hearing wi' the sail-maker to attend – but first the benediction. Sit down!'

Clearly, there was to be no argument. Shade walked round behind Belle Macaulay and she felt his strong hands on her shoulders, kneading the muscles, but gently. This was like no blessing she'd ever seen or heard.

'You should be privileged to be experiencing the Holy Touch…it will be widely accepted in the Kirk in years to come, a real return to sharing. You are a pioneer, Belle, just like the other ladies. Now may the grace of the Lord be with you Belle Macaulay…don't turn around until I say.'

She sensed him bending towards her and felt, just for a moment, his hot breath on the nape of her neck. Seconds later something muscular, warm and firm pressed into her flesh. She wanted to move but felt anchored to the chair.

Just then there was a clatter of feet in the corridor outside and shouts of 'Land! -Land!' Belle, without further thought, was up and heading for the door.

'Oh, damn it tae hell, woman. We are not finished – not by a long way.' She turned briefly to see in the dim light that Shade's mouth was half-open and he was drooling like a puppy waiting for its dinner.

'Sit down!'

But Belle was not for sitting. She would not be resuming that seat, she had decided, on this side of eternity.

'Did you not hear Mr Shade – Land!' Belle was out of the door and on her way to the deck before the minister had even rearranged his lower clothing.

43 A Glimpse of Land

The Cape Verde Islands – an archipelago some 320 miles off the African coast - was seldom seen from the emigrant ships but the

Broomielaw had been travelling further east due to the unusually light northeast trade winds. Hundreds of eyes gazed with fascination at this unexpected sight.

Even after a few days at sea it was easy to imagine that any dry land had been swallowed up by the vast ocean and that nothing remained except the emigrant ship afloat on an endless expanse of water, like Noah and his beasts. As a result the shouts of land sighted had brought every fit emigrant up on deck.

Belle joined her family at the rail, fastening the buttons around the neck of her dress and taking Innes's hand. Automatically for her husband's benefit, she launched into a description of the scene as it unfolded. She tried to push the uncomfortable memory of her encounter with the Rev. Shade to the back of her mind for the moment, shivering involuntarily at the recollection.

First of all the islands had appeared like large clouds which crowded the horizon but as the ship drew nearer they took on the outline of layered mountains. The *Broomielaw* sailed so close to the largest of these islands that Belle was able to describe in some detail what she was seeing.

'It's a barren mountain, Innes. Like Arthur's Seat in Edinburgh, you remember, but without the beautiful green surroundings.' Innes nodded eagerly.

'There are rocks with large fissures which are gleam in the evening sun and dry, withered grass...no sign of cultivated land. Altogether not a hospitable place, I think.'

Walter Lumsden joined them at the rail, noting that Belle looked flushed and somehow out of sorts.

'Yes, I agree it looks bleak from this direction, folks' he said, ''but the island is both inhabited and cultivated on the opposite side. You can find grape vines and orange trees in abundance beyond those barren hills. It belongs to the Portuguese. They call it San Antonio.'

As the islands disappeared into the gathering darkness, a sort of sombre mood overtook the groups of emigrants filing back to their berths. The stewards for each compartment, including Belle, made for the galley. That evening's meal would soon be on the tables – boiled salted ham, a universal favourite.

Belle was glad that after her brush with Elijah Shade that she had something to occupy her mind for the next couple of hours. Preparing the meal was a Godsend.

And although nothing was said along the steerage but most of the emigrants realised that the Cape Verde Islands were probably the last land they would see before Australia, and their destination could still be weeks, even months away.

44 In the Floating Courtroom

'Very well, let's get on with it. This disciplinary hearing to examine the case of Leon Jontot on various charges of theft is now in session.' Jack Zurich checked around the passengers' saloon to ensure that everyone whose attendance had been requested had turned up.

The last rays of the dying sun slanted through the wide stern ports illuminating the dust motes that spiralled in front of the glass, warming the backs of the panel of 'examiners.' It was more like a prayer meeting than a justice tribunal, Jack reflected, but it would have to do.

As for the 'accused', Jontot sat at one end of the captain's table, drumming his fingers on the scarred wood, as if, without his sail-maker's needle, they had lost their purpose.

'The panel consists of myself in the, well, absence of Mr Ratter, the Rev. Shade, acting as clerk, Mr William Bigland representing the cabin passengers and on behalf of the steerage passengers, David Cossar, Henry Coats, George Dawson and George Scroggie.

One by one the witnesses were called. Mr Haldane, a timid wee soul, whose pocket watch had been taken, identified the timepiece and the bosun confirmed that he and the second mate had found the watch after receiving information from Agnes Govan. At the mention of her name Jack saw the old woman, seated near the rear of the room, straighten in her chair, clearly feeling a surge of satisfaction, although with that cantankerous old beesom it might merely have been a touch of wind, he reflected.

By now almost everyone had heard the tales of her husband's scarred face, of how he woke in the night in terror as once again the cannonballs flew across the fields at Waterloo, and of her fondness for her brother-in-law who never returned from Flanders. She did look as if she was there to see justice done.

As for Jack, as he jotted down some notes, he was remembering his father again. How on their Sunday walks beside the canal on Portsea Island he would talk of his hope for his boy's future and impart obscure, often inappropriate, philosophies of life to Jack. 'Judge not that ye be not judged' was one of his favourites. Well, here Jack was, judge and jury, in a floating courtroom. Odd how fate worked its course, he thought.

'Agnes Govan, would you step forward a moment,' said the first mate gesturing to the back of the room.

Maggie Gilchrist's aunt, stooped and silver-haired, yet possessing a kind of simmering energy, shuffled forward to the seat in front of the table, cursing under her breath at the folk whose legs cluttered the narrow passage between the chairs. Once seated she twisted nervously at the strings of her purse, glancing up occasionally.

'You say you noticed the sail-maker, who has already been identified, sneaking around Mr Haldane's 'partment and that you followed him to the crew's quarters?'

She shot a glance at the panel. 'Aye, the Frenchie was sneaking aboot, true enough. Right suspicious like. I decided to see what he was up to. I saw him pit something beneath his pillow and I reported his behaviour to the second mate. It didna' surprise me at all to find that he had been at the thieving. Take it from me, you just canna' trust these foreign types, particularly the French.'

The old woman scowled at the sail-maker who looked thoroughly deflated, as if his world was collapsing around him. By contrast Agnes was in her element and obviously hadn't considered for a moment that Waterloo took place years before Jontot was born.

'If you ask me they types should not be sailing in British vessels at all. I lost a brother-in-law because o' him and his like. We fought a war to…' Jack sensed the beginnings of murmur of approval from the assembled company.

'Yes, well thank you, Mistress.' Jack Zurich saw the way the wind was blowing. The old dear had more than a few sympathetic ears amongst the crowd and he decided enough was enough.

Agnes returned, as ordered, to her seat, exuding an air of satisfaction with her day's work.

Macgregor, the second mate, then confirmed the discovery of the watch but admitted that a thorough search had been made in Jontot's quarters without any other missing items having been discovered.

From the back of the room Agnes was heard again. 'Stashed, somewhere on this boat, for collection later; that's where they'll be. They're sleekit, thae onion munchers.' She popped a camomile pill in her mouth and sat back, awaiting developments.

'Mistress Govan, we've heard your testimony. I'd be obliged if you would now keep your opinions to yourself unless asked.'

Poor Jontot – when called to give evidence in his turn, he was lost. He kept reverting to a stream of impassioned French despite his years on Clydeside stuttering and stammering as he wrung his hands and explained how he had been in the steerage during evening prayers to return an emigration leaflet to a passenger in Mr Haldane's compartment.

'You've no idea at all how that watch might have come to be in your bunk, Leon?'

'None at all. I cannot understand why Mistress Govan should say I took it. If I just had some of my neighbours from the High Street here today. They would tell you I am an honest man.'

Jack wanted this examination over and done with. The Frenchman was shaking in his shoes – and the evidence, at least as the theft of the watch was concerned, was pretty damning.

'Having waived your right to further question witnesses and unless there are any further queries from the panel,' Jack said, looking quizzically along the line of passenger members, 'there can really be only one outcome in this...'

'Begging your pardon, Mr Zurich, sir.' Heads turned towards the door.

'Begging your pardon, but I couldn't allow Mr Jontot to be blamed for those thefts. He's innocent, you see.'

45 A Surprise Witness

Queenie Stout appeared at the entrance to the saloon and then threaded her way forward towards the table. The witnesses, panel members and onlookers turned to stare, intrigued by this last minute intervention. The place was buzzing with speculation.

When Queenie stepped into the room William Bigland's jaw had dropped into his lap. He sat gawping at the girl from Stormay and his confusion was compounded when passing on the way to the captain's table she smiled sweetly at him as if they were meeting at the farm crossroads and whispered: 'Hello Will, I'd planned to surprise you, but not quite like this.'

She turned to address the panel, suddenly poised and self-assured. William Bigland was spellbound. This surely couldn't be the shy girl from the farm of Hookin'. She looked like Queenie but it was new, assertive female who spoke. A girl no more, but a woman.

'I heard Mistress Govan say that the sail-maker was the thief. Well, I cannot speak about the watch but I know where all the other little nic-nacs have been stowed and I also know that Mr Jontot did not take them.'

The sail-maker's face lit up. He was suddenly alert. The panel members looked at each other, wondering where this was leading. What had seemed a straightforward, lack-lustre business suddenly took on a more interesting, challenging aspect.

Jack Zurich congratulated himself. He had, over the past few days, sensed that there was much more to this lass than at first glance. 'Well, go on Queenie. Tell us what you know about this affair.'

'With your permission, Mr Zurich. The jewellery and personal items were in a corner of the main cargo hold, on the port side of the ship, near the big cases marked *Strachan – Mining Equipment.*'

Shade, who had said little during the previous proceedings, listened with a scowl to this surprise development and asked the question that was now on everyone's lips. 'Are you saying, Missy, admitting that you are the one who has been sneaking around this ship pilfering folk's goods?'

Queenie had thought so long about how to respond to this inevitable question. She drew herself up to her full five foot, one inches.

'First I should say that I'm not a steerage passenger. Despite what I might have led you all to think, since Glasgow I've been living in the forward baggage hold with the rats and coming and going among you; yes, I am a stowaway.'

There were gasps from the emigrants in the saloon who in previous weeks had often passed the time of day between decks or at evening prayers with this pleasant and attractive young woman. How had she kept her secret?

'Yes, I did place the stolen items together in the corner of the hold but I must explain that the actual thief was only paying back what he thought was a debt.'

'Enough of these riddles, woman. It looks as if you're heading for the brig as well as Jontot. Someone took those pieces of jewellery,' Shade hissed.

Queenie had never liked the look of Shade. He was a creepy individual and she responded to his questioning by directing her answer to Jack Zurich.

'No guilt attaches to any person on this vessel, Mr Zurich. No-one is to blame. Mr Jontot's monkey, Erebus, is the culprit!'

Again Jack Zurich had to call for silence as the onlookers leaned towards each other chattering and pointing at Jontot and the newly-revealed stowaway. This was proving to be the best morning's entertainment since leaving Greenock.

As for Agnes she saw her new Waterloo victory being snatched away from her and was first to her feet.

'The girl is deranged. She should be locked up for her own safety. Have you forgotten, you were about to sentence the sail-maker, Zurich.'

'I do think that you're going to have to tell us a little more Queenie, if we're to accept this story of yours, which, you have to admit, is a bit hard to swallow.' Jack wondered what other surprises Queenie had for them.

'If you please, sir. The monkey found his way down into the hold only a day or two out from Greenock and I began to feed him scraps from my dish. For long in that dark hole he was my only companion.' She looked across at Mooney; he knew his secret would be safe.

'The jewels, let's hear about the jewels, Missy!' Shade was finding it difficult to disguise his impatience and contempt. Since failing to complete the 'benediction' with Belle Macaulay two hours previously he had been in a foul mood.

Dramatically Queenie, who had been clasping a shawl to her in a bundle since making her unexpected entrance, opened the garment wide above the table spilling a cache of sparkling brooches, pendants, hair clasps, pins, rings and cufflinks, which jingled out on to the table.

'For God's sake, there's my gnashers,' shouted the gumsy but delighted rail clerk, pointing to the set of false teeth grinning from the centre of the pile. Proceedings were halted by a gale of laughter.

Said Queenie: 'He started bringing little trinkets to the hold. I can only think that he wanted to thank me for feeding him – in the same way our cat at home would present us with a mouse at the back door of the steading each morning.'

As if on cue, Erebus, who had been curled up in a ball at Jontot's feet was up on his springy little legs trying to climb on to the table to retrieve his treasures. The sail-maker held him fast by his leash.

'Anyway, I didn't know what to do. So I simply left them. I was sure they would be discovered when unloading began at Adelaide and they would surely find their way back to their rightful owners.'

Agnes Govan was on her feet trying to rally support for the action against Jontot to continue. The panel members, with the exception of William Bigland, who still appeared struck dumb by the sudden appearance of this girl from his past, conversed excitedly.

By now, word of this unexpected development had spread to the steerage and folk crowded the saloon door with more pushing in from the corridor, straining to hear.

'It seems to me that if the monkey took all these baubles there must be every likelihood that he may also have taken Mr Haldane's watch. Agnes, are you certain that it was Jontot you saw – and not his monkey,' said Jack.

Again this was greeted with hoots of laughter from the throng. Agnes was already making for the door but she turned to shout back over her shoulder: 'I knew there would be no justice here. You younger folk forget too quickly the sacrifices made on your behalf. If I had my way that Frenchman would be thrown to the sharks, guilty or not.' She was jeered and cheered in turn all the way out of the door.

Jack Zurich saw the hearing deteriorating into a free-for-all. 'I think in the circumstances that the case against Leon must be dismissed, at least for the moment. Anyone who wants to lay claim to any of these possessions should see the purser during the afternoon.'

This decision was greeted with cries of derision from the other passengers who were just getting into the mood for further theatre. Jack looked across the table at Queenie who was gathering the valuables together, one by one. Meantime William Bigland had rounded the table and was standing grim-faced, leaning towards the girl and hissing at her through tightly-clenched teeth.

The stand-off was interrupted by Jack Zurich: 'And now I think, perhaps, that you and I should have a chat about your future on this ship, Miss Stout. There needs to be some sort of reckoning. And maybe you'd like to come along also, Mr Bigland. You two seem to know each other.'

46 Sabotage!

Trouble brewing in the fo'castle, Jack Zurich had found over the years had a very distinctive aroma. It was like bread which had been fully baked and was on the verge of igniting. The only question was whether you could reach the oven in time to turn down the heat.

He was still finding difficulty gaining respect. Seamen were notoriously wary of a new skipper, especially one who assumed command mid-voyage, for whatever reason. And the crews were wise to be cautious. Only four years previously on the Australia run a notorious individual called Omar Flood, who had been obliged to take over his ship when the skipper died of food poisoning, immediately imposed a tyrannical regime. Four of the crew died during separate beatings and one badly injured man had been sewn in his blanket and tossed overboard, still groaning.

Macgregor, the *Broomielaw's* second mate, had been among that oppressed crew on that ship and had later testified against Flood.

Often as an apprentice Jack Zurich himself, on sweltering evenings in the tropics or storm-tossed passages around the Horn when the howl of the gales in the rigging was said to drive men mad, had witnessed whispering behind hands; the fo'castle politicians sewing their seeds of despair and revolt. Occasionally the scent of anarchy was also in the air. This was perhaps inevitable in such confined conditions among tough men who liked nothing better than to scrap. The pressures might lead to a deputation, hats doffed, at the master's door. But mutiny was a word never spoken.

However, these were anxious times on board the *Broomielaw*. Since the younger man had stepped into Ratter's shoes there had been murmurings. To add to the confusion Jack Zurich sensed that not only was he having to deal with rebellious elements in the 24-strong crew, but he was also conscious of a hidden, disruptive hand at work.

The latest 'accident' had given him much to think about. With Walter he was on deck examining the dismantled sections of the midships chain pump, an impressive piece of machinery equipped with valves which when operated by several men at a winch, could pump out vast quantities of water from the innards of the ship. During the storm the pump had given up the ghost and now they knew the reason.

'Not much doubt, Walter – at least three of these valves have been loosened on their fittings. It took more than the gale to do this.'

'But that's crazy. Who would do that, put their own life and that of everyone else on this ship at risk?'

It was indeed difficult to imagine a motive or a grudge so deeply held that someone would risk endangering the vessel, its passengers and crew. It was surely the act of someone with a death wish. Yet Jack explored another possibility.

'Actually Walter, if someone was determined to slow this ship in her progress to Australia, sabotaging equipment but having the knowledge of just when to stop before putting themselves in danger; that might explain what is going on.'

From the far end of the quarterdeck their discussion was being observed by a group of three men from the first dog watch, the shorter, two-hour evening watch, which allowed for a rotation of the normal four-hour shifts through the day. They had just signed off and were loitering by the fo'castle hatch.

One hundred feet above them more sail was being piled on as the *Broomielaw* scurried to take advantage of the freshening northeast trade winds. She leapt forward, as if imploring the teams who scrambled amongst the rigging to get on with their task in order not to miss a breath of what was by now a spanking breeze.

The cry went up from the second mate stationed at his vantage point next to the poop deck skylight: 'Foretop men aloft, unfurl the topgallant.' There was no time to reflect on the recent double tragedy. From high above them came the slap of newly-opening canvas.

'If you want the truth, Jack, I don't reckon you need to look further than that scrapper Bostock'. Walter nodded for'ard.

At the centre of the group of seamen was a wiry, red-haired character, a Belfast lad, with a leather cap and as Walter's father might have so eloquently put it – 'with a face like a well-skelpit arse'. He was quite obviously a hardy citizen, a foretop-man who worked the yards at the swaying peak of the main mast making him one of the elite crewmen on the *Broomielaw*. With a large brass ring in his left ear he was for all the world a throwback to the age of the bold buccaneers.

According to ship gossip Matt Bostock also had his day as a prize-fighter in the booths at Glasgow Cross - going by the ring name of *Bostock the Barbarian* - and certainly he sported the cauliflower ears and the redistributed nose to prove it. From the moment Jack Zurich had seen him amongst Ratter's hand-picked crew at Greenock he had sensed that the man could be a troublemaker and would stir the pot given any excuse. But endangering the ship and hundreds of souls was a different level of disorder altogether.

However, Bostock was also a skilled seaman, Jack knew, someone who respected the sea in all its moods. Surely he would not toy with such elemental forces. He felt sure of that. Instinct told Jack Zurich this must be the work of someone unaware that their activity could well be a matter of life or death.

From a deck's length away you couldn't make them out clearly, but Jack knew that the man had fists on him like sledgehammers and clambered around the shrouds and along the yards as if these high, desperately dangerous places were his natural element.

Sabotage aside, the overthrow of Ratter, an individual who came from the same hard school as the foretop-man and who had been seen from time to time in bars along the length of Glasgow's docklands sharing a drink with the fist-fighter, had unquestionably given Bostock an ideal opportunity to indulge in some below-decks skulduggery, Jack realised.

'He's a pretty unsavoury character, that one,' said Walter. 'Wouldn't it be best just to confront him with this before he gets up to any more mischief,' asked the emigration agent, standing back, wrench in hand, to look at the pump and admire his handiwork.

'I may not be an engineer but I tighten a mean screw, do I not?' He sniffed triumphantly. Jack Zurich looked him up and down indulgently. 'You're no engineer, Walter, nor, it seems, are you much of judge of situations. Any excuse and Bostock and his cronies in the fo'castle could make life next to bloody impossible for me, for us. I'm charged with getting this ship to Adelaide and on to Otago in double quick time. Out there somewhere is the *Spirit of Speed*.

He pointed at the spread of the ocean, the whitecaps stretching to the horizon.

The company expects a fast run from us. We must be in Adelaide well in advance of the Southern Cross vessel. We simply must. If those boys chose to make things difficult, it could be another Christmas before we sight Otago Heads. No, we'll just have to keep our wits about us and wait our moment.'

47 The Revolting Crew

The inevitable confrontation did not take long to materialise. Later in the week when everything on the ship, even the now languid sails, seemed to be waiting for something to happen, Matt Bostock, foretop-man and booth fighter, appeared with his cohorts seeking an interview with Jack Zurich.

The gist of their complaint was that crewmen were undergoing undue *hazing*. This was a very vague term but implied that the officers had been pushing them too hard, perhaps unreasonably hard. It was untrue in this case, of course, but it was always a useful theme for mischief-making.

Conditions on British merchant ships were generally humane by the middle years of the century and they all knew it. Elsewhere, on vessels of the American merchant fleet, for example, violence was often the order of the day and it was said that the colt, a knotted length of rope, was still in regular use to impose discipline or goad men to work.

A motley portion of the crew, with Bostock at their head, sidled into the day room and ranged themselves in front of the table. Completing the morning's paperwork Jack Zurich slowly and deliberately raised his head. The men stood with their caps and bunnets in their hands...lined faces, rotten teeth, wild hair; they were not a pretty bunch.

One glance told Jack that apart from Bostock, the rest of the deputation were mostly 'idlers' or daymen, crew members who were too weak or old to stand the night watches. Bostock was on a shaky foot-rope and Jack intended to make the most of it.

'So it seems that I'm pressing you all too severely, Mr Bostock, and you Devers and McNab and Cassells. You, Mr Dewar, has lamp-trimming become such a chore?'

Jack Zurich's head-on approach caused much uncomfortable shuffling amongst the seamen who with muttering and a none-too-subtle dig in the ribs edged their spokesman Matt Bostock forward.

'It wasn't like this when Mr Ratter had the ship; he put his trust in his men.' Jack noted that as Bostock spoke his fists were tightly clenched.

'As I do, Mattie, as I do. I know you and Ratter are cronies – but that, I fear, is now history. You know well enough that conditions have been more testing since the storm. We've all been working harder to get the *Broomielaw* shipshape again. If any here feel you've been singled out for unfair or harsh treatment, step forward.'

There was a silence, an awkward silence.

'Seems that somewhere along the way you boys have got your ropes snagged or perhaps someone has snagged them for you.' Jack deliberately spoke through Bostock as if he was invisible.

The foretop-man was furious. He chewed on his lips and Jack noticed that he was clenching and unclenching those pile-driver mits. Seeing that he had been left isolated in the front line Bostock fired a particularly mean and insolent look at the new master of the *Broomielaw*. This problem was not going to go away. Jack realised he had made an enemy and as long as Bostock bore a grudge there was going to be unrest. There had to be a reckoning, on Bostock's terms, and quickly.

But how to nip this dangerous situation in the bud? Jack looked down at the notices of shipboard activities for the coming week which he had been scanning for approval; suddenly a ready-made solution jumped out at him. The notice ran:

Friday, 7 p.m. – The Boxer's Art Displayed. Four bouts of three rounds each. Can Anyone Match the Skills of Matthew the Barbarian Bostock? All Comers Welcome.

'They tell me, Mattie, that no-one can be found to give you a contest and that you don't plan to fight on Friday night. How would it be if you and I squared up to each other for a round or two?'

Bostock's face lit up. 'It'll be my pleasure, Mr Zurich'.

It was as if all his birthdays had landed on the same day and he's just heard that his brother had left him a Victoria gold mine.

48 And in the Blue Corner!

The idea of a boxing tournament had captured the imagination of the younger folk in particular. Reels and jigs, debates and bible classes, even the occasional unofficial rat hunt were all very well, but a bare-knuckle scraps and the prospect of seeing some blood splashed around promised rare sport.

Thus, come Friday evening, the quarter deck was a busy place.

Disapproving mothers and younger children spent the duration of the tourney below decks but some of the older bairns sneaked away to previously reconnoitred vantage points behind hatchway screen and deck gear. These fist fights, everyone agreed, were not to be missed.

The news that Jack Zurich was to take up Bostock's challenge in the fight of the night had guaranteed the rapt attention of every adult male aboard...and a few of the more outgoing lassies. To the disgust of the Sinclairs, the devout couple from Dunbar, one of the single men who clearly knew what he was about, began taking wagers and was soon doing a useful trade at the top of an aft companionway.

There had been a real scramble for the benches nearest the action, batons of wood supported by barrels, and in the blue corner Agnes Govan sat, knitting needles clacking, having claimed her ringside seat fully forty minutes before the opener. Men hung from the rigging and jammed the foredeck and the Macaulay boys were defending the area nearest Jack Zurich's corner against all comers.

The opening bout was a gut-thumping affair involving Cassells – the overweight storekeeper who carried so many rolls of blubber under his stained simmet that it was whispered ringside that he must have devoured all the emergency stores – and a young Aberdonian from the single men's quarters heading for South Australia. Once the emigrant had dodged inside the storekeeper's windmill action, the result was in no doubt and the bag o' wind was soon deflated.

The big man simply sat down on the deck with a thud, gasping for breath and Jontot, who had volunteered to act as referee for the evening, counted him out. When he started his count – 'Un, deux, trios...' Agnes Govan looked up from her knitting and shouted through the ropes: 'In English, you wee garlic-chowin' twerp, in English!' The arena rocked with laughter.

The second bout paired two evenly-matched twenty-year-olds, and in its way was a classic, something for the purist with impressive jabbing and inside work. Actually, it was all too technical and precise for the throng who were baying for more blood after seeing the storekeeper floored. Eventually Jontot declared it a drawn match to a chorus of boos and catcalls.

The third contest was really just a novelty event, a bit of fun, with two tiny members of the Celebus Midgets sparring theatrically and to roars of approval diving between Jontot's legs and pulling faces behind the referee's back. As a result the excitement and desire for more genuine action had reached a small frenzy by the time the arena was cleared for the main event of the evening.

'Be careful,' said Queenie Stout as Jack Zurich, towel wrapped round his shoulders and eyebrows well greased with goose fat and his 'second', a rather excited Walter Lumsden, elbowed their way forward through the throng to the improvised ring just for'ard of the main mast.

As Jack drew level with Queenie, she pushed a red and gold silk neckerchief towards him. 'I've read that at the court of King Arthur the ladies used to give their favourites a token of good fortune when they fought in a tournament. I suppose you could say you were my champion.'

'Might have been better if you'd given him a lump of pig iron to hide in his fist, Queenie,' said Walter, shoving his charge forward. As Jack wrapped the neckerchief around his wrist he looked back at her, over his shoulder and smiling mouthed a 'Thank you.'

The contestants entered the ring to rollicking applause and the old hand Bostock settled in his corner, on the milking stool, with Dewar, the lamp trimmer, close by his side, just beyond the sagging ropes.Walter Lumsden was concerned: 'Are you sure about this, Zurich. He's a mean-looking bastard. Duck and run, Jack! Duck and run!'

Jack Zurich tied Queenie's token to the ropes in his corner. The new master of the *Broomielaw* clearly had the advantage in height and youth, probably in weight also, but there wasn't a spare inch of fat on Bostock. His muscles remained tuned and toned by years of clambering in the yards and when the ship's bell rang for the first round he came out from his corner like a fiery-topped whirlwind, a man on a mission of destruction.

Blows were thudding in on Jack Zurich from the off. The master reeled in the face of this immediate onslaught, his eyes shut, scarcely knowing what was hitting him and as a result for most of the round he found himself in reverse taking stunning blows to the side of the head and painful jabs to the abdomen. He was conscious all this time of the dull roar from the crowd as he leant into his opponent in an effort to calm the tempest which was assailing him.

As the seconds passed it seemed increasingly unlikely that Jack would last the round. He staggered backwards into the ropes and as he straightened again, took a fierce blow to the nose. For a moment he felt his stomach churn. Then he remembered another fight so many years ago in a games hall. Jeers had rung in his ears that afternoon also but on that occasion, he recalled, they had served to steel him for the fight.

A left, then a right sent him reeling backwards towards his corner. Then he was on one knee. Tasting the salty flavour of blood in his mouth, Jack looked up to see Bostock, living up to his surname, hopping from one foot to the other, fists raised, eyes wild, the sweat gathered in beads on the foretop-man's brow and a thread of saliva lurked at the corner of his mouth.

Bostock went to strike him again but Jontot stepped between them: 'To your corner, Mr Bostock'. His opponent punched the air in frustration. He had lost control. Jack could see that now. The man was back in the booths where fist-fodder had queued up to try their luck and be knocked senseless by Bostock the Barbarian, a man who never expected to lose.

Jack Zurich shook the confusion from his brain. And he tried hard to remember what he had been taught. Only moments before his only plan had been to defend himself desperately to the bell but seeing Bostock lost in this nameless anger against the world and Jack in particular, he straightened up. He saw his moment and stepped forward, erect, under control as he had been instructed by his games master, Mr Simkins. Having let Bostock come at him again he did not give ground this time but hit him once, twice, three times, straight lefts which connected with the Barbarian's battered nose. Immediately blood spurted on to the deck and Bostock fell back against the ropes.

In the same movement he was pushed back into the action by the crowd at the ringside who were revelling in this unexpected turn of events. On this occasion as Bostock instinctively guarded his face and lowered his head, Jack caught him with a powerful left hook which sent the foretop-man to the deck, still blowing frothy scarlet bubbles from his long-suffering nose. Jack Zurich in turn stood back blowing on his skinned knuckles and awaiting developments.

Bostock struggled to raise himself from the boards before slipping back to the prone position. Before Jontot had time to lift the stand-in skipper's arm above his head the crowd swarmed into the arena. Jack helped the fallen fighter to his and planked him on a hatch cover. The anger, the bitterness, had vanished from Bostock's eyes and had been replaced by an odd mixture of dizziness, wonder, and yes, admiration.

49 Upon a Painted Ocean

It was the strangest Christmas and New Year week that any of the emigrants could remember. For days the freshening northeast trades had carried the *Broomielaw* rapidly southwards after a slow start from the Clyde. This was the sort of sailing which Walter had hoped and prayed for; the clipper full-rigged, slicing through the waves, sails taut, the emigrants cheery, chatty and optimistic.

Everything now pointed to the *Broomielaw* having a quick passage to Adelaide. They had seen nothing of the *Spirit of Speed* which would be tracking them somewhere out there on the empty expanse of ocean. It was becoming a matter of great pride, among sailors and emigrants alike that they remained ahead of their rival which had been scheduled to leave Greenock within forty-eight hours of their own departure.

However, two days after Christmas and a few degrees north of the Equator, as Innes Macaulay was finishing whittling a selection of little dollies, toy knives and swords, late Christmas gifts for the wee ones, the ship ran out of luck and into a belt of dead calm, the infamous Doldrums. For days around Hogmanay the *Broomielaw* floated idly in this belt of stillness, a few degrees north of the Equator.

In his log Walter recorded the stark reality:

'We are motionless. The sea is a polished mirror. On all sides a wall of heat and the water, a luminescent blue.'

Upon this oily-surfaced deep, the *Broomielaw* was indeed apparently motionless but was in reality being carried ever-eastward by the Equatorial current. She was Coleridge's painted ship upon a painted ocean, straining as if for a signal to resume the great journey. And a sailing ship deserted by the breeze is easily consumed by a sense of total helplessness.

The crew, pushed on by Jack Zurich, trimmed the sails in an effort to grasp every cat's paw of wind and went about their normal duties as if expecting the breeze to spring up, without warning, at any moment. However, Jack knew only too well that the flat calm could maroon an unlucky ship for weeks in the oppressive heat.

Inevitably day upon day of this exasperating calm, with the boat turning through the points of the compass, began to take its toll on the morale of the crew and passengers alike. Tempers became frayed; everyone was edgy. They now knew why earlier emigrants caught in the heat trap that was the Doldrums had called them the 'impossible days'.

It was impossible to find comfort below decks because of the suffocating heat, it was impossible to find sufficient space in the shadows above on deck and impossible to obtain sufficient cool liquid to quench a desperate drouth. With deck space at greater premium than ever a rota was organised to allow people to sleep up top, in the open or under canvas awnings at night when the heat below became almost unbearable. It was a time when a sort of sea madness sat mockingly on most folk's shoulders.

It was difficult to tell the days apart. Dawn broke and within minutes the sun would be climbing into a sky undisturbed by clouds, the scorching globe seeming to hover over the *Broomielaw* until it dipped again towards the horizon and lengthening shadows signalled the end of the day. The sea was a flat, ornamental lake and not an eyebrow would have been raised to see a swan float serenely by.

By night not the slightest breeze cooled the overheated air or ruffled the circle of the ocean. A canopy of stars powdered the firmament, slowly progressing from east to west. It was perplexing and the voyagers felt as if they were locked, immobile at the core of a spinning, overheated universe.

For most folk it was too hot to eat. The emigrants were bathed in perspiration all day and the clamminess of night brought no sense of relief. A foul stench began to cling to clothing, hair, ropes. It was often too hot to sleep and most managed only a few restless hours on their straw mattresses. It was simply too hot. Silence pervaded the boat broken only by the melancholy striking of the ship's bell.

And there was the uncomfortable, nagging fear, that this torture might never end.

Walter took the opportunity of this delay to re-establish what called his *Acclimatisation Classes* where in groups of 20 or 30 he went over the settler's programme on health, hygiene, agriculture and climate. Four years a teacher in Scotland he knew he was good at his work. If things had worked out he would have been teaching in that little white-painted clapboard schoolhouse beside the Hunter River. He marvelled at how he could now begin to contemplate these aspects of his previous life and loss without automatically lapsing into his self-destructive reveries.

The classes were a facility offered on only a few of the emigrant ships and Walter hoped it might have the additional bonus of taking their minds off the desperate situation.

Inevitably, perhaps, he found the attention of his 'students' constantly wandering in the stifling setting; the sweat-soaked emigrants would look towards the scuttles and listen to the water slopping listlessly against the flank of the clipper as they tried to detect the merest whisper of a breeze.

The sails hung limply from the yards and by day it was impossible to step barefoot on the deck. Seawater, thrown on to the burning planks, would rise in a vapour cloud. Refuse from the galley as well as human and animal waste dumped overboard would float languidly alongside. Twice Jack ordered two of the day boats to be lowered and with the oarsmen leaning into their task the ship was towed a few yards away from putrid stench of discarded waste. Tropical rainstorms bubbled up out of nowhere, the rain lashing down for a couple of hours and every available bucket and pail being requisitioned to gather rainwater for washing and drinking.

The dreamy, unreal atmosphere was accentuated by the behaviour of Silas Ratter behind his locked cabin door. With Shade as his only regular visitor he appeared to have become completely unhinged. In the midst of the silence which lay across the ship like a smoking fog he could be heard ranting and raving, laughing, sometimes crying, and the squeaky notes of his harmonium would sound out through the still, dead air.

To add an even more surreal touch his repertoire had now been extended to include Christmas hymns '*O Little Town of*

Bethlehem' was especially favoured – for some unknown reason particularly after midnight.

With Shade, the minister/surgeon as the only visitor Jack Zurich was sure he had closed up all possible avenues for the supply of drink. And yet Ratter did seem to be three sheets to the wind most of the day. When asked casually about this Shade simply smiled, a disturbing, almost defiant smile.

The meals, school and religious services gave some sort of structure to those stagnant, sluggish days but spirits were inevitably becoming lower by the hour. People had become tense and fractious. There was no enthusiasm for games, dances or even the *Matter of Opinion* which had been a twice weekly diversion for the emigrants.

50 The 'Impossible' Days

Another lost day in the pool of calm drew to a close with a scintillating light show, a sunset to remember, away towards the western horizon, painting the canvas of the deep in vivid liquid hues of red and pink. The *Broomielaw* swung, ever so gently, on this surface of stained glass.

Talking occupied the bulk of the day for the emigrants and crew but conversation too had become slowly exhausted. Walter sought out Maggie Gilchrist who was sketching on the forward deck, making use of the last half-hour of daylight before the nightly ritual of safely extinguishing oil lamps plunged the *Broomielaw's* sleeping quarters into the black vault of night save for the lantern of the night watch high on the deck.

More than ever Walter now felt able to confide little anxieties – at least about the journey – to Maggie. He told himself he had no need to feel guilty not least because it appeared that communication between Maggie and her husband had broken down completely. More than he might care to admit their daily chats filled Walter with a new, unexpected hope, and confidence. He felt elated and encouraged around Maggie and bereft in equal measure in her absence. However, his secret fear was that he was losing his heart to a woman who still treated him solely as an emigration agent and a friend. He wanted more, much more.

For the moment, nevertheless, she made him smile as none had done since Lizzie. With Maggie in his life the world seemed a brighter place, his waking nightmares had all but ceased. He wondered if Lizzie and the little ones were now letting him go, gently showing him the road ahead. It seemed to Walter that a refreshing trust was growing between himself and Maggie but he was still sorely troubled by one perplexing and unsettling mystery – the injuries which the shepherd's wife had carried on their embarkation from the Clyde. The emigration agent had asked her more than once if James had beaten her, but she simply shook her head.

Walter had not pressed his inquiry.

On this spectacularly still evening she was trying to capture the muscular movements of two crewmen working with coils of rope. Maggie's charcoal skipped one last time across the pad as she spoke. With a sigh she gazed out at the fleecy clouds which dappled the evening sky then closed her pad and rolled the charcoal stump between her fingers. 'Not enough light now.' With the sleeve of her dress she wiped the perspiration from her brow.

Unprompted Maggie began to speak of her anxieties over her youngest girl. More often now Hilda – at the dinner table and on deck – would make a point of saying how much she was missing her friends at Sweetshaws, the school, and her animals; everything in fact to do with her former life. Over the dishes one evening, prompted by her mother, she confessed what was troubling her. More than anything she felt left out.

'She told me, Walter, that it was alright for May strolling around the deck with her handsome young man and Flora with her women's group; she wanted to know what she would find to do in Otago.'

Walter watched the darkness begin to reach out across the ocean towards them and felt the wooden rail, exposed for so long to the burning sun, begin to cool slowly beneath his touch.

'This waiting on a favourable wind – any sort of wind – unsettles young and old alike. She'll be fine once we're under way again.'

New Year's Day arrived and the emigrant families did their best to put a cheery face on it, if only as some entertainment for the wee ones. The same unrelenting sun beat down from the heavens, the blue dome of the sky made the head spin but the Sunday school children's party went ahead.

Below the poop the helmsman stood redundant by the idle wheel, staring out around the horizon where sea and sky met in an unbroken circle. Families gathered in the late afternoon for 'fun and games', summoning as much energy as they could, given the circumstances. It was another attempt to escape briefly from the frustrating situation in which the *Broomielaw* party found themselves; for a few moments they were able to cast off the lethargic spell of the Doldrums.

All the children's favourite games were on the programme – team games like passing the apple between your knees, spinning the plate and a variation on the game of tig which the children had fine-tuned themselves and which – much to the annoyance of their parents and the amusement of the crew – they had titled *Sharks and Sailors.*

Belle and Maggie with the other ladies from the family department, as the emigrants now liked to call the central portion of the steerage, had baked a tray of cakes and as an extra special treat, pots of jelly and marmalade were produced. Helping in the kitchen was Queenie who, among a long list of punishment duties for having stowed away, was designated kitchen assistant for the remainder of the voyage

However, she had a guardian angel. Jack Zurich was keeping a close watch to ensure that no-one was pushing the girl unreasonably.

The game of tig was in full swing. 'Ha-ha – you're het. I'm the Shark.' A wee chap, no more than five years old, had sneaked up and tapped a burly, red-faced crewman, a brash Ulsterman, on the leg. He looked down at the tousle-haired youngster, one of the Sinclair children, feigned shock and pulled the sleeve of his shirt down over his hand. 'Bitten off, as I live and breath, cap'n, right down to the wrist'. The children squealed with delight and the lethargic chase resumed.

The little ones were proving that it was possible to negotiate these 'impossible' days. Below decks other, less jovial entertainment was being considered.

51 The White Rat

Since the skipper had been placed in protective custody, the Rev. Elijah Shade had worked to tighten his hold over the disreputable seaman called Dermot Rag, known to everyone as the *White Rat* because of his shock of white hair.

His nickname held good because he was also a clype, a tell-tale, a dense but treacherous individual who made it his business to spread gossip around the fo'castle and steerage. On Shade's behalf, on the promise of ample rum supplies, it was Rag who had stirred Bostock and his cronies to rebellious action.

But the Doldrums were proving a sore trial for Shade. He was frustrated. None of the women had expressed any interesting his prayer sessions and meditation in the past week. The old lady and the girl hardly in her teens who had come forward were unsuitable, risky candidates, in different ways – one to weak to lift a stick and the girl, well, she was simply a chatterbox. He had to be careful, despite his desire to feed his needs. Not for the first time he wondered if his prayers were sounding authentic enough.

It was during a discussion, as the children's party was in full swing up above, that Shade, perspiring freely and feeling like a barrel of butter slowly liquefying, poured another glass of cheap brandy for Rag and suggested a bit of entertainment – which at the same time Shade felt sure – would keep the pot of unrest simmering.

Rag was sitting on his bunk tunelessly humming sea shanties and picking last night's salt pork from his rotten fangs with a knife. The talk ranged over Jack Zurich's deficiencies as skipper and the likelihood of an early escape from this breathless zone and then turned, inevitably, to clash ma' clavers, ship gossip.

'That wee lass with the Sinclair family from Dunbar – Jessie, I think they cry her – is a tidy piece o' female flesh, would you not agree, Rag?'

'Aye, she's that alright, meenister, an' breasts on her like fine floor dumplings, I'll warrant. He hacked on the floor and resumed the exploration of his few remaining blackened teeth with his tongue.

'Mind ye, she's a fiery bitch wi' a tongue like a viper on her. Called me rat-face and scratched me when I gripped her during the dance last week. Noo, ah ask ye, meenister. Do I look like a rat?'

Munro's mind, which he felt had been dulled by the heat of the past days, began to click into motion. Here was a chance for further disruption – and some sport for his own benefit.

'They say she was caught with two apprentices in the water closet. Screaming for more by all accounts.'

Rag's red-rimmed eyes opened wide. 'You don't say. Who'd have thought it! You know, Mr Shade, you're a rum clergyman and no mistake. You've a fine, ordinary touch about ye.'

Shade pressed ahead. 'Be that as it may, man. I've seen the way the lass has been giving you the glad eye. You've obviously made quite an impression with your rough ways.'

Rag's ugly, half-shaven face, cratered with salt-water sores and bearing the ruddy testimony of quarter of a century's hard bevvying, lit up. He was probably forty but looked twice that age.

'You say so, meenister? Given another chance I'd make some impression on the wee slut and no mistake.'

Looking at the inquisitive, beady eyes and the pointed, twitching face Shade could see that Rag's verminous nickname had as much to do with his appearance as it did with his anti-social behaviour. Now all he had to do was to persuade the man to act.

'She seems over-friendly, mind you, wi' that lad from Paisley, Cuthill. He's been paying her a lot of attention. I wouldn't waste any time'.

'But where would…'

'Well, not the water closet, that's for certain. If you take her to the sail store I'll watch out for you by the door. That place is well away from prying eyes.'

For a moment Rag hesitated: 'Aye but she'll go running tae Zurich and I'll find myself in the brig for the duration.'

'No, no man. If she can't be persuaded to keep her mouth shut – and honour is something women cherish above all, it's a known fact that accidents happen regularly on board ship, don't they. She'll slip through one of the hatches, unseen. A tragic accident, just like that poor bugger Richards.

Rag thought for a moment and fingered the sores on his face. 'That seems a bit drastic…but naw, by God, she deserves it.'

181

No more needed to be said. Rag leered and rose from the bunk attempting to rearrange his rough trousers and working jacket. He finger-combed his short-cropped hair and rubbed his forefinger squeakily over his teeth.

'Dinna worry about your appearance, Rag. Those sort o' women are interested no' in the cut of your trousers but what's under them.'

'She'll no be disappointed on that score, I'll warrant, meenister.'

A few minutes later Rag sidled up to Jessie who was watching the children at play. She wasn't pretty, thought Rag, plain in fact, but she heated the blood in his veins. He felt a rough anger build inside at the memory of those talons being dragged across his face. Seeing the White Rat's approach Jessie scowled.

'The minister would like to see you below decks, woman. He says right away and he's no' a man to be kept waiting. You are to follow me.'

Of course, a summons from the minister was not to be ignored but Jessie remained cautious. 'I must tell Mrs Sinclair – she's over there with the children.'

'Look, the minister says he'll keep you only a few minutes.'

52 The Gift

Innes Macaulay was enjoying the children's party. It was a noisy event – and he liked that. With Belle at his side describing the action, the races and the tumbles, the tears and the cheers, he sat on a coil of rope occasionally wiping his brow. Where he wondered, did the wee ones find the energy in this heat.

Suddenly, inexplicably, he was consumed with a dizzy, disconcerting sensation of fear, loathing and pain…a whole range of un-summoned emotions which tore at his soul.

He had wanted to Belle about this strange new 'gift' or curse which he seemed to have acquired since the pit disaster but he could never find the correct words. It was so strange but it was as simple as this – he knew things. Having lost his sight he seemed to have acquired a different sort of vision, an extra sense, a kind of second sight.

At first he had been convinced that it was something to do with his old friend Bob Swift, still close by - Bob, who had encouraged him through the nightmare of the cold, black tomb and the pain of the hospital treatment room. Bob, who had been killed stone dead in that horrendous blast but somehow had managed to stay around to comfort his neighbour from along the Cowgate, even after death.

Often he felt Bob was close by and wondered, as the strange experience began, if he was somehow seeing the world through Bob's free-ranging, post-mortem vision. In the aftermath of the pit blast back home he had known the very moment when old Mr Donald three doors along had died from pneumonia; when Mrs Gibson had lost her baby in childbirth and the instant the wee Taggart boy was run over by the milk cairt he had felt the bones in the boy's leg cracking under the metal rimmed wheel. Somehow, Innes seemed able to share other folk's life-altering experiences.

On board ship he had sensed the coming storm and the tension between the skipper and his crew, experienced a dreadful choking unease at the moment the crewmen fell to their death from the main mast and now he was feeling a similar dread. He was tasting someone else's pain, fear and anxiety. Like a cruel tide it washed over him from nowhere.

Belle noticed that suddenly he had gone very quiet. She took his hand whispering: 'What's troubling you, Innes?'

He was staring ahead out of empty eyes, straining as if trying to catch a glimpse of something off in the distance. But this time the experience was very close and acute. He had tried so hard to focus the sensation, to create an image in his mind of what he was experiencing emotionally. This time a picture was slowly forming. In his mind's eye he could see an ugly, pockmarked face, saliva drooling from a half-open mouth filled with rotten teeth, leering.

Innes jumped to his feet, gripping his wife's arm. 'They must hurry. She's in dreadful trouble. Tell them, Belle. They're down below us. Please tell them to hurry.'

At that moment, as Belle tracked down Jack Zurich, close by, a shrill and unnervingly prolonged scream silenced the youngsters at play.

Having dragged Jessie the last few yards into the sail locker, his hand clamped over her mouth, Rag had thrown her face down among the canvas and with one arm across her upper back the attack began. 'This'll teach you to call me a rat, ya bitch,' he hissed.

At the doorway Shade watched as the attack unfolded. He registered everything, the girl's pleas to be spared, how Rag forced her face into the canvas. The minister stood wide-eyed, leering, noting every twist and groan. Then Jessie lifted her head to one side and let out the piercing screech which rang through the ship.

Immediately Shade was gone, vanished like a spectre in the night, disappearing along the creaking passageway as the clatter of running feet from the opposite direction brought Jack Zurich, Walter and the second mate Macgregor out of the gloom to the door of the sail locker. They burst into the cramped compartment and hauled the White Rat off his prey.

Jack Zurich held him by the throat, forcing him firmly up against the wooden walls of the locker, almost lifting him off his feet, clear of the deck. Rag choked and spluttered.

Walter Lumsden was helping Jessie gently to her feet when Belle arrived.

'Just leave the girl with me, Mr Lumsden.' She stepped forward and took charge of the sobbing female, gently rearranging Jessie's clothing.

'Aye, take her to my cabin, Mrs Macaulay. You'll have some privacy, a bit of peace there. We've some business to deal with here.'

Jack Zurich, still gripping the sailor firmly by the throat, turned to the two women as they left the locker.

'I don't know how Mr Macaulay knew what was happening down here, Belle. God knows what else this beast might have got up to had he been undisturbed. She might well owe her life to your husband.'

Rag tried to cough a protest but Jack simply tightened his choking grip and the White Rat's beady eyes began to bulge in his head.

53 Shade Stumbles

Shade, his bulk almost filling the frame, stood gazing out of the passenger saloon windows, watching the creamy wake of the clipper and the long line which the ship trailed measuring her speed across the great, empty ocean. The winds had returned as quickly as they disappeared, pushing them at last clear of the deathly calms; now they were again making good speed. The Line within 24 hours Jack had promised his charges, piling on sail.

'You understand, Mr Shade, we have to raise this delicate matter. Although it's difficult to get a sensible word out of Rag, lying there hog-tied in the brig, the one thing he is insisting on is that you encouraged him to attack that poor lass.'

For the stand-in skipper Jack Zurich rather too much was happening too fast – first Ratter's eccentric behaviour, the tragic deaths of Richards and young Macdonald, then the revelation that Queenie was a stowaway and now this damned business.

'Rape' – the word hung like a penance in the air. Jack knew that in his lustful assault the simpleton Rag had damaged the important relationship between crew and emigrants, possibly for the remainder of the voyage. The passengers were only too aware how much their lives depended on the motley bunch of seamen. Now that trust was punctured.

Responsibility Jack Zurich was prepared to accept but growing unease among the folk in the steerage disturbed him, sapped his self-confidence. Lumsden had indicated that the women in particular felt let down.

Jack was more than ever convinced that some sort of whispering campaign – or worse - was at work on the *Broomielaw*.

For his part Shade could sense Australia ever nearer and with it the chance to finally cast off his old life. And now he had managed to stow his Tarbert legacy he felt more comfortable.

'Do you hear me, Mr Shade? There are a number of reports suggesting that Rag had been a regular visitor to your cabin during these past two weeks.'

Shade appeared to be lost in his thoughts, far, far away, riding the white-plumed waves with the equatorial dolphins. In fact, he was meditating on how this timber-walled, water-enclosed world was simply a miniature of the community he had left behind in Scotland. Here too there were winners. And there were losers, victims, like Rag and the girl. It was how it always had been, how it always would be. The trick was to make sure you kept ahead of the game and stayed with the winning team.

Feeling he had left a sufficiently long interval between question and answer, that he was responding at a pace of his own choosing, Shade finally turned away from the window and declared: 'My first reaction to this accusation, Zurich, is to laugh. If this was not such a serious matter that is precisely what I would do. The man you have in the brig is a scoundrel, an inveterate liar, and perhaps most significantly for you, young man, he's a troublemaker, a sower of dangerous seeds.'

Jack Zurich sat forward in his chair. He didn't enjoy being lectured. Shade knew that look. People, he was well aware, thought his appearance more in keeping with an innkeeper or a slaughterhouse worker and were often surprised when he took a high moral tone. But the clerical garb had always worked wonders. He resumed his attack.

'What do you take me for, Mr Zurich? Some sort of perverted saboteur? If you want my advice, captain (the tone was vaguely mocking) you should be considering the loyalty or otherwise of your crew rather than firing such absurd allegations at the very people you must look to for support.'

Shade turned again to the sloping stern windows, lowering his bulk on to the cushioned ledge. Facing away from Jack, he allowed a wry smile to play across his florid features.

He felt sure he had successfully diverted attention from his possible involvement with Rag to a topic which, ever since the boxing tournament, he guessed, was a trouble to Zurich – the possibility of an insurrection in the fo'castle. Elijah Shade decided he must retain his iron grip on the proceedings, to remain on the offensive.

'You must know, Zurich, that there is whispering behind hands about your captaincy. Your humiliation of Bostock in the boxing tournament only fuelled that animosity. It's a matter you'll have to deal with sooner or later. And as for Rag's visits to my cabin, he is a confused, solitary individual and he simply came for spiritual guidance. Clearly by accusing me, he has now turned on the person he thought closest to him.'

Jack hesitated for a moment. 'He actually said that you were on hand as the rape took place.'

'Ridiculous!'

'Obviously. I have to accept all you say, Shade. The company clearly trusted you sufficiently to appoint you as surgeon and spiritual adviser for this voyage. Though, it's odd that despite your best counsel he should resort to such violence. But you understand we have to look into the man's allegations. He's liable to be spending a few years in the Adelaide gaol as a result of this sorry business.'

Shade pulled nervously on his ear lobe.

'And I'd appreciate it, Mr Shade, if you would leave the running of this ship to me and I'll let you carry on ministering to the spiritual needs of the passengers.'

This mild rebuke delivered, Jack Zurich tried a new tack.

'I meant to ask...you said you graduated Bachelor of Divinity from Edinburgh, Mr Shade, in the early thirties, wasn't it? Adam Enderby, my cousin who hails from Montrose in Angus, studied for ministry at Edinburgh around that time. Perhaps you knew him?'

'No, the name's not familiar.'

'Well he struck up a friendship with the Professor of Hebrew, Peter Livesey, and they both stayed on occasion with my parents at Portsmouth. Livesey was a real wee character, unforgettable really. You must remember him, a pocket-sized individual with long flowing white hair, like a Biblical prophet.'

Shade raced in unabashed. 'Yes, yes, of course, a real character, a one-off indeed. Not too many like that left around these days. Now, Zurich, if you feel you've explored Rag's ridiculous allegations sufficiently, perhaps I can get along to the evening service?'

He tapped his walking stick on the boards and pointed to the wall chronometer before plodding off for the quarter deck, confident he had seen off this awkward episode. However, Elijah Shade left the saloon unaware that Jack Zurich was perplexed. The reverend gentleman had walked into an ambush. Peter Livesey was Professor of Hebrew but, as everyone within five miles of the Edinburgh University campus was aware, the learned gent was tall as a Scotch Pine - and bald as a coot!

54 Crossing the Line

Queenie was slowly settling into her new surroundings in the single women's quarters. To the Gilchrist lasses she was quite simply a heroine. Although, as part of her punishment for stowing away, she was kept at work on kitchen, cleaning and sweeping duties during daylight, in the three hours after the fires had been carefully extinguished for the night at 7 p.m. and the curfew when the oil lamps were snuffed out, they would swap stories and giggle over gossip. Queenie couldn't remember when she was last so happy. These girls were the cheery sisters Queenie never had.

The first opportunity to talk at length with Will, the youngest son of the House of Doomy, since she had emerged so dramatically from her shadow life, came on the day when the emigrants and the crew celebrated crossing the line.

From Madeira onwards as the *Broomielaw* approached the Line, the Equator, zero degrees latitude, anticipation grew amongst the youngsters in particular who had listened wide-eyed to the stories of initiation ceremonies, fancy dress parades and duckings. The wee ones went running terrified to their mothers from their lessons when told by their big brothers and sisters that Neptune, God of the Sea, would visit them as they crossed the Line.

Most confusing of all for the youngsters was the idea of the Line itself. Although parents tried patiently to explain what this idea meant, most of the children were disappointed to find there was no mysterious and massive rusty chain circling the globe, just the same expanse of ocean, stretching from horizon to horizon, which had surrounded them for weeks.

In fact, the *Broomielaw* stole across the Equator about 11.30 p.m. on a Friday, long after the emigrants were in their bunks. Jack Zurich, under pressure from the crew who were keen to observe tradition, dunk the apprentices and show off a little, agreed that the crossing ceremony could go ahead the following morning, also allowing for an hour or two of celebration.

On a bright morning as Neptune and his colourful cavalcade headed aft on the quarterdeck for Jack Zurich's cabin to demand the expected tot of rum, Queenie and William found themselves side by side in the fascinated throng of passengers on deck. To his own amazement the laird's son had in the past few days become very protective of this girl he had so cheerfully abandoned only a few short weeks before.

Imagine, she had followed him all the way to Glasgow and cunningly concealed herself on the *Broomielaw*: living like a fugitive among the packing cases, sharing a berth with the rats, probably feeding on leftover scraps from the galley, putting up with hunger, loneliness, discomfort - and all for him.

He had spent the first weeks of the voyage doing what came natural to the Bigland men, chasing the lasses, with, it has to be said, only modest success. He had grappled in the dark one evening with a big, busty, dark-haired girl from Montrose, but that, to date, had been the sum total of his sexual adventures on board the *Broomielaw*.

Now, all of a sudden he felt a heavy, inexplicable responsibility for Queenie who had given up everything, just for him. Whether these concerns were prompted by memories of her milky-white thighs or from genuine affection, Bigland had not quite made up his mind.

To a great cheer Neptune and his retinue, kitted out variously as a policeman, barber, doctor, came majestically along the deck to where a large wash-tub had been set up, sloshing-full with cold sea water. Dressed in a tin crown, carrying a fearsome trident Neptune (actually it was the Danish carpenter who had spent the past two days between caulking the deck and fashioning his splendid fork) wore long impressive robes which looked remarkably like the spare set of curtains from the captain's state room.

Reaching his throne on a companionway the Lord of the Sea stumbled over his train and almost took a header into the tub, much to the delight of the crowd. He stroked his long flowing beard made from Manila rope and seated himself regally on his throne. Queenie was delighted with this piece of seaborne theatre and clapped her hands. Spotting May, Flora and Hilda at the other end of the deck she waved enthusiastically. Will, annoyed that he was clearly not getting her full attention, wanted to deal with more serious matters.

'We must think to our future now, Queenie,' he shouted over the babble. 'Australia is no place for a young woman on her own. I maybe spoke a bit rashly that evening by the loch.'

Neptune announced that he was ready to dispense justice to those in the crew who were trespassing on his domain for the first time.

Still smiling, and with one eye on remaining on the ceremony, Queenie's serious tone defied her apparently cheery demeanour.

'Don't be so quick to make plans for us, Will. I did come to Glasgow and join this ship and I did it simply to be near you. But since then I've met some wonderful people who have treated me with nothing but kindness. Kindness such as I'd never experienced before. It has opened my eyes.'

One-by-one the half-dozen apprentices, boys of about 14, were led into the presence of the monarch of the deep who sat frowning and waving his trident. Younger children clasped their mothers' hands ever tighter. There was great anticipation among the watching crowd who could only guess what lay in store for the nervous novices. As the weird baptism continued the sooty, soapy water flowed across the deck and around the feet of the spectators like a dark, frothy tide.

Queenie turned to look at William Bigland. She had loved this man in the little world of Stormay. Or had she? For whatever reason he had told her that beyond the island there was only heartache and selfishness. She had found the opposite.

'We must talk more, Will. But you should know that I am a different Queenie. My eyes are opening and if we are ever to be close again, it will be on my terms.'

After sentence was passed on the equatorial trespassers they were shaved – the barber's blade being a half-inch board about a foot and a half long, three inches wide with a blunt edge. The lather seemed to be composed of salt water, soap and soot from the galley and the shaving brush was the end cut from a five-inch hauling rope, the brush part being long and suitably swabby.

The shaving proceeded to roars of encouragement from the onlookers, the barber occasionally lobbing a sooty mass of bubbles at the audience. At the conclusion of each close shave the victims were unceremoniously tumbled backwards into the tub and held under for a suitable period then released, choking and spluttering.

Tallest and strongest of the apprentices, the boy Dungannon had decided that this adventure was not for him and climbed aloft. He was eventually lowered from his eyrie and after an extra efficient shave was dunked under the water for a few seconds longer than his colleagues.

Will looked at Queenie who was clearly enjoying the spectacle, clapping her hands and cheering as each new candidate stepped forward. He could scarcely believe his ears and the authoritative tone the girl was taking with him. The serving lass from Doomy – giving him orders. It was incredible. Having watched them together he was fairly sure Jack Zurich must have had something to do with her transformation.

'Passengers Next!' went up the cry.

To much screaming and squealing Neptune's henchmen turned their attention to the emigrants and particularly the young men. One puff-eyed seaman squared up to William Bigland and shouted in his face: 'Next for Shaving!' Staring back tight-lipped, fists bunched Bigland hissed slowly – 'I think not'. The men understood each other and the sailor went off in search of a more compliant target.

55 The 'Spirit of Speed'

Night running could be a strange and occasionally terrifying business. Even on star-bright nights danger lurked just over the horizon. The emigrants had been made acutely aware of that only 48 hours out of Greenock. During their second night at sea there had been an incident which so nearly put a premature and possibly tragic end to the voyage. The ship was almost run down by a steamer in the Irish Sea, travelling, so it was claimed, without lights.

As it was, the figurehead on the *Broomielaw*, a kilted Highlander with bright rosy-painted chubby cheeks and shiny red knees and what the Gilchrist girls had immediately decided was a stupid grin, soon stopped smiling. He was broken in the rigging of the other vessel and had to be chopped away. It was a desperately close call.

None of the emigrants, secure in their bunks witnessed this incident but the stories which filtered into the steerage from the crew suggested that the hulls were so close that a sailor on the steamer had been able to jump on to the deck of the *Broomielaw*.Apparently he was met with such a stream of profanity from the officer of the watch that he fled back faster than he had come.

As a result of this near miss, when in the early hours of the first Sunday after New Year, with the ship pushing along at eight knots, the call went up 'Light Astern! Starboard beam, sir!' everyone was immediately at their post. In less than ten minutes the pursuing craft was clearly visible under the starlight.

She was a full-rigged ship carrying all plain sail, precisely the same as the *Broomielaw*. Summoned by one of the apprentices Jack Zurich had immediately identified their shadowy companion as the *Spirit of Speed*, which had followed them out of Greenock and which carried the bulk of the *Circus Caledonia* party. Walter Lumsden who had been up and about in his cabin heard the call and joined Jack on the poop.

'No doubt about it, Walter…the *Spirit of Speed*. Her lines are unmistakeable, and by God, she's travelling!'

Jack found it difficult to conceal his disappointment but he was slowly becoming accustomed, hardened, to these setbacks. Equally, he was determined that no-one – crew or passenger – should sense his deflation. Even he had to admit that even in the half light the sight of the Spirit of Speed tearing along with white spray rising from her prow, or as Jack more poetically described it – 'with a great bone in her teeth', was quite spectacular.

'Do you know the skipper, Jack?'

'I do that - Alec Ritchie from Newburgh in Fife. One of the toughest, most skilful mariners working out of the Clyde. He has a constitution like a whale and an iron will. Gruff and rugged, some say, but a fine seaman out of the old school.'

'You sailed with him?'

'First trip to Australia, as an apprentice. He drives his men and the ship mercilessly … while always demanding as much and more from himself. And he never seems to tire. On that voyage he went without sleep for four days during a storm.'

Jack peered through the gloom at the other vessel. He reminded the helmsman to maintain a steady course as the *Spirit of Speed* drew slowly level.

'They say Ritchie took a short spell ashore as an examiner of masters and mates in Calcutta but he didn't last long. During his time there were no passes – everyone was found to be incompetent. That's the sort of standards he works to.'

'Driven, you might say,' offered Lumsden.

'Hard-driven, indeed. A man who thinks he's in control of every situation. Unfortunately, it's never that straightforward out here. This is no classroom. Each individual has to live – or die – by their wits.'

The two ships passed within a cable's length of each other and in the half-light the distance appeared to be even less. As the *Spirit of Speed's* port light vanished into the distance, the *Broomielaw*'s sails shivered in the back draught from the craft to windward. Then the *Broomielaw* ploughed into the other vessel's lee bow wave. Below, in his bunk, unaware of the passing emigrant ship, Innes Macaulay slept. However, for a few moments, even as he slumbered, he sensed a crushing weight of despair, even dread, passing by. Thankfully it went as quickly as it had arrived. He would not remember this strange experience when he woke.

Despite his disappointment at this episode Jack was determined to keep the mood cheery.

'Don't look so mumpish, Walter. She's caught us on the hop but we're scarce halfway to Australia and I would set the *Broomielaw* against any ship of her size when we reach the Forties. Mark my words, you've not seen the last of *The Spirit of Speed.*' Lumsden relaxed. He was encouraged to hear the confident note struck by the young skipper. He had seemed low, under pressure in the past few days.

'An early breakfast for us, I think, captain. I see Tully has your place set below. Would you mind some company over your porridge?'

Half-an-hour later the two men were finishing their coffee. Jack was listening to the ship, his ship, to all the whispered secrets she conveyed to him, the creaking timbers, the sound of Queenie's broom in the corridor, the occasional moo-ing of the milk cow in her pen directly through the side wall, the shouts of the children as they prepared for breakfast and the splash of the sea all around.

Walter Lumsden looked up from scraping his plate.

'Hmm…Delicious. Are you coping with all that's going on aboard, Jack?'

The younger man smiled. 'Just about. Let's put it this way, Walter. I can't see anyone on this ship who might make a better job of command. Unless you'd like to try your hand…'

Walter in turn grinned and shook his head, pushing his plate to one side.

'Not unless you want to end up in Shanghai instead of Adelaide. In any case, you seem to have taken to the captaincy with ease.'

'Yes, well. I've my own safety to think of as well as everyone else; that tends to concentrate the mind.'

Lumsden shut his journal and laid it on the table. 'That's what I like to see in younger folk – selfless dedication to others and no false sense of modesty.' They both laughed.

'By the by, what do you really make of this Shade character, Walter. He's a rum individual. Seems to me that he and Ratter have some tie-up, but I can't work it out. They must be in cahoots. I can't think how else the company would have accepted his application. We may find Shade is not all he seems.'

'I agree. He's a difficult one to fathom.' Jack told him of the minister's clumsy failure to identify the one distinguishing feature of the learned Professor of Hebrew at Edinburgh but Walter remained cautious.

'Hardly a capital offence that, skipper. But odd, I agree. Distinctly odd.'

After all, as things stood, the agent felt they had no hard evidence of misdemeanours or wrongdoing against Shade. They couldn't come down heavy on him just because he made them feel uncomfortable, appeared to have forgotten details or his university days or had a particular calling to be a spiritual guide and counsellor to the female of the species.

'I think he needs some watching. I wouldn't put it higher than that for the moment,' said Lumsden, pouring himself the last dregs from the coffee pot. 'But he does seem to have cast some sort of spell over the womenfolk.'

'Ah hah, and what about yourself, Lumsden? The quiet, efficient, unflabbable emigration man has, it seems, won the heart of a fair and lonely lady.'

'If you mean Maggie, then I think you'll find…'

'C'mon man, it was clear as day that she and Gilchrist are leading separate lives and she's blossomed since you started taking an interest in her…and her girls.'

'Aye, maybe so, maybe so. But I've another 220 passengers to consider.'

Jack Zurich stood up and straightened his jacket, setting his skipped cap on his head at an angle, not too jaunty, but sufficiently formal to let everyone know who was running the show. Walter glanced up.

'Have you decided, Jack, to let Mrs Sinclair see that villain Rag? I gather she's desperate to instruct him in the error of his ways, bring him back on to the straight and narrow.'

Mrs Sinclair had spent a lot of time with her servant Jessie after the girl's ordeal, comforting her, encouraging her gradually back into the society of the ship and to the classes where prior to the locker incident she had been helping with the wee ones. The girl was putting a brave face on it but every so often, for no apparent reason, sometimes halfway through a conversation, she would burst into tears and race off to her berth where she would bury her face in the rough pillow and weep pitifully.

'Yes, I think it's safe enough for her to make a pastoral visit now. Rag seems to understand that he's already in a heap of trouble. Truth to tell, I reckon that half-an-hour listening to the Sinclair woman might constitute a significant part of any eventual punishment,' Lumsden smiled.

'I've told the mate to make certain Rag is bound and to stay with Mrs Sinclair for the duration of her visit. We can't deny the wretch some Christian comfort. That would be less than charitable and after their close contact Shade appears to want nothing to do with him.'

As the emigration agent left he began to wonder if his interest in, his attraction to Maggie Gilchrist – something that he could deny to the world but never to himself – had become so obvious.

56 The Dark Angel

'Yes, I understand that you have your orders, but Mr Rag has a need to unburden himself and he could scarcely feel free to do that with you hovering at his shoulder. We must have a couple of minutes in private.'

Mrs Sinclair was a formidable specimen of Scottish womanhood. Because of her old-fashioned, sombre style of dress and mannerisms it was whispered amongst the children 'tween decks that she might be a witch. It was understandable. Today, tall and angular, her Quakerish air accentuated by her grey dress and hair the colour of old bone, tied in a bun, she looked down her aquiline nose at the seaman as if she was ready to read the Riot Act. For his part the crewman was perplexed and anxious.

Certainly Rag, a rough brute of a man, seemed to be no threat now, shackled as he was by his ankles and, as per Jack Zurich's instructions with his wrists bound for the duration of the visit. But the young sailor had his orders; he was to remain with Mrs Sinclair at all times. It would not do for Rag to claim another victim.

The prisoner sat with his back to the rough hewn walls of the lock-up staring blankly into space. Occasionally he glanced through the bars at the strange, tall woman debating so earnestly in the corridor with his crewmate then resumed his serious study of the wall opposite.

'Look young man, McGuinness is your name, is it not? I'm happy to take personal responsibility for Rag. I happen to have a few cigarettes here. I don't approve of the habit, you understand, but I know it is one of the pleasures for seamen like yourself, far from port.

McGuinness was clearly tempted and Mrs Sinclair pressed her case.

'Five minutes alone will be quite sufficient for this wretch to repent his sins against our poor Jessie. What, I ask you, could happen to me in that short space of time. And remember, I have a voice on me...'

As she'd hoped the tobacco clinched it. What damage, indeed could a hog-tied sailor do? The gaoler turned the big, iron key in the mortis lock. The low metal gate creaked open and they stepped inside.

'Five minutes no more, mistress. The door will remain open and I'll just be through by; should he try anything just shout. Here, Rag, stir yourself. You have a visitor.'

Rag groaned as McGuinness landed a kick on his shin.

'I don't want to see anyone…especially anyone that's going to preach at me. You see what ministers are worth – that treacherous bastard Shade.'

With a warning to Rag about his language in front of the lady, the gaoler left. As he disappeared into the passageway Mrs Sinclair hovered over Rag, dark, and yes, sinister. For just the briefest moment the phrase 'dark and...something angel' came into Rag's mind. For the life of him he could not remember what that second adjective might be. He shook his head, cleared the image from his mind and looked up at the woman.

'I think we should begin with a brief prayer, Mr Rag before we proceed to the business that brings me here.'

From the right sleeve of her dress, from under the ruffle trim, she drew a silk handkerchief. She opened her Bible at the Psalms and at a stanza on forgiveness. The place had been marked by one of her husband's razor sharp leather-working blades.

She began to read. On the deck above evening strolling had commenced.

'Dark and avenging angel' – that was it, thought Rag, with a shiver.

*   *   *   *   *

Since crossing the equator the wind had doggedly refused to turn fully in the *Broomielaw's* favour and the vessel rolled spectacularly, often lying so much to one side that it became awkward if not impossible to eat, sleep or walk. And it wasn't just the dishes which sailed through the air. The children had enormous fun watching sedate strollers suddenly and comically driven to an involuntary run across the decks. Their embarrassment and efforts to stay on an even keel provided the best entertainment for days.

Sleepers were kept awake, expecting at any moment to be roll from their bunks and on to the wooden deck. Across from the Gilchrist/Macaulay den the little baby belonging to the Fowler

197

family had been pitched right out of his mother's arms but being such a bouncy young fellow he was unhurt, although he sat wide-eyed with astonishment, the centre of attention after his flight.

And in these conditions, the misery of those prone to seasickness was endless.

That evening Walter and Maggie sat together at the top of the aft starboard companionway listening to the piper go through his repertoire of tunes – a weekly ritual which had been established since leaving Greenock and in which he was encouraged by passengers and crew alike. Usually he tried to keep the tempo bouncy and upbeat; pibrochs were discouraged.

As ever Maggie had her sketch pad and charcoal and in the rapidly fading light, with sweeping strokes, she sketched the piper,, his feet firmly planted on the swaying deck, his back against the mast, his cheeks puffed beyond reason, head nodding and foot tapping in time to the piece and his long, golden hair streaming in the breeze.

The increasingly familiar southern constellations climbed above the horizon reminding folk again of the new world that awaited them. For all the emigrants as the skies darkened, these were moments of great nostalgia, moments when the realisation that a vast expanse of sea now separated them from familiar faces and places, was at its most acute. A few cried openly. Others, as the notes of the pipes drifted away across the white-capped waves, simply remembered.

One old man sat shaking his head ruefully, his weary, lined face reflecting the memories which clearly were chasing across his mind's eye. Maggie switched her attention briefly to the new subject and dashed off the quick outline of the old man wrapped up in his memories.

Now, whenever they had a moment together, the emigration agent tried to get the conversation round to New Zealand, Walter offering all sorts of advice about how best Maggie could cope with her difficult circumstances and her morose spouse.

'You see Walter, as I've said before, it's a sad story. My sister is a widow now after the forestry accident and her younger brother vanished last year with a survey team in the back country of Otago, she's had a hard time.

Maggie glanced again at her windblown subject as she spoke and with the charcoal stick tried again to capture the piper's careless straggle of hair.

As ever Walter tried to be reassuring. 'It does sound as if things might be difficult to begin with but your sister will be so happy to see you all and I hear that experienced shepherds are thin on the ground. I feel sure James will be in demand and the girls and will find work quickly. The big, new farms are crying out for domestic help.'

It was unspoken as yet but both had considered the possibility that Walter might just have some part to play in their new life. Every time they spoke the discussion seemed to hold this implicit possibility.

'And that's a trio of smart lasses you have there. And that other wee one will be joining them before too long, I reckon.'

With a grin Maggie patted the firm bump on which she rested her sketch pad. 'Yes, this one's got a kick like a horse. It must be a boy.'

It was the screams of two teenage girls by the main mast which signalled the appearance of the spectre at Walter and Maggie's discussion. The tall, gaunt figure of Emma Sinclair arrived on deck, right arm held straight out in front of her, tears streaming down her ashen face. She walked purposefully to the rail, opened her bloodstained and tightly clenched right fist and dropped Rag's neatly pared testicles to the fishes.

57 Battle Scars

The woman then slumped to her knees, her long black dress cascading around her. Eyes fixed on the deck boards she was praying for a blessing on her actions as the emigrants gathered around her. In her left hand she still grasped the tanner's blade. She lifted her head and surveyed the faces in the encircling crowd with wild, wandering eyes.

'Vengeance is mine saith the Lord and I – Emma Sinclair – I am his sword.'

She addressed no-one in particular but made sure that everyone understood on whose authority she had conducted the castration of the rapist Rag. Then she was at the centre of a whirlwind, all around her, babble and confusion. People ran below decks. Others fired questions at her with such rapidity it was as if they were speaking in tongues. Her husband arrived and assisted the distraught woman to her feet.

'An eye for an eye, a tooth for a tooth. So the Bible instructs us, does it not, Kennedy?' she muttered, staring at her bloodstained hands as if they belonged to someone else. Her husband shook his head in despair.

Even now, in shock and beginning to shake violently, the woman who had based her life on the fundamentals of the 'Good Book', was able to justify her dreadful, violent act. In her mind's eye as she was led away she relived every second of what she called her cleansing act and felt fulfilled.

The smooth sheen of the silk scarf pulled tight around Rag's mouth to dull his complaints; the scrambling in the front of his breeches as she knelt on his chest; that look of abject, disbelieving terror in his eyes; the gentle hiss of flesh separating from flesh, the tanner's knife making short work of the seaman's scrotum. It had been over in seconds. It had been almost merciful, she thought.

A chaotic scene was unfolding below where Jack Zurich had been summoned and was doing his best, awaiting Shade, to stem the flow of blood from the neutered prisoner who, only partly conscious, in a dark pool on the floor of the brig. When Rag's custodian arrived he had found Mrs Sinclair's silk scarf on the boards beside Rag where she had dropped it. Yet the prisoner had still been unable to cry for assistance in his stunned agony. His penis had been roughly jammed in his mouth.

*   *   *   *   *

'What could have possessed that poor woman to act as she did, Maggie?' Walter and Maggie had run into each other just outside the cabin passengers' dining area. The frenzy throughout the ship in the immediate aftermath of the assault on Rag had subsided.

Jack Zurich had managed to calm the tense atmosphere by announcing that he would hear evidence in the morning. Meantime Mrs Sinclair had been locked in the state room still protesting the correctness of her action.

'She's clearly disturbed. Her husband is distraught. But you see how they treat Jessie, like a daughter. Whatever its nature, it's a powerful force that persuades a person to act in such a manner.' Walter continued trying to rationalise the deed and felt a degree of confusion over Maggie's puzzling silence.

'People sometimes react to situations with totally unexpected directness,' was all Maggie was prepared to offer. Actually, she could understand only too well what had motivated Mrs Sinclair. Oh yes, she could.

Walter pulled open the door to the cabin passengers' dining section. The room was empty. Pleased to have drawn his companion into discussion he pointed to a table. 'Come and sit for a moment, Maggie.'

'It's true enough what you say, people are unpredictable and the sea, of course, can have a strange effect. It can alter personality. I've seen it happen. After all, the ocean is the cradle and the grave, it is also a great mystery and sometimes out here all inhibitions are stripped away.'

Maggie's back ached. She stretched and without thinking pushing her chest forward. She always found this eased the discomfort and chuckled when she saw Walter raise his eyebrows at her ample bosom.

'Enough milk there to feed the Sunday school, eh Walter?'

The emigration agent coughed nervously. Just occasionally he found Maggie's straight talking odd – and strangely exciting.

'Not but seriously, if we are honest with ourselves, Walter, we all do things we might come to regret later. It's the response of the moment. Like Mrs Sinclair we have a lifetime to reflect on our misdeeds and our mistakes.'

Walter nodded. 'Aye, unlike Rag. He's lost so much blood Shade doubts if he'll see the night out.'

Maggie raised her hand towards his face and to the glossy track which ran from his eye to his chin.

'Your scar, Walter. Where did you come by such a wound….in Australia? She traced the sealed wound. 'Or perhaps you were a pirate?'

'It seems to me, Maggie Gilchrist, that we both have stories to tell about disfiguring facial injuries. Perhaps one of these days we can confide in each other. It may be important – for us.'

Maggie stood up straightening her back with a groan. Her bump was becoming increasingly unmanageable. She had almost forgotten what it was like to be agile and be able to move about without a performance of peching and panting.

The traces of the bruising and angry marks around her neck and face which she had carried on embarkation had all but disappeared in the intervening weeks.

'You must never ask me about those injuries, Walter, never.' There was a sombreness about the way in which she delivered this remark that set the emigration man back on his heels. He looked into her hazel eyes. What did he really know about this woman? Little enough, except that she was beautiful, confident. With Maggie, for the first time in the company of a woman he was not conscious of Lizzie's presence. Everything felt correct, in its place. And, most astonishingly, he had no sense that he was betraying his lost family or guilt at sharing these little moments with another man's wife.

'I feel the same about my scar, Maggie. But despite what you say, maybe a day will come when we find it easier to exchange our stories.'

No more was said. It was enough for the moment. Below decks, in the gloom, one of the cabin boys began swabbing Rag's blood from the floor of the brig.

58 Decisions, Decisions

On the way to the fresh water store on the lower decks Jack Zurich and Walter came face to face with apprentices 'Nipper' Harris and Dungannon, who appeared through a hatch heading topside at a rate of knots and in a state of obvious excitement. The older boy was carrying a great coil of inch rope over his shoulder. The subtle odour of tarred rope hung in the air.

Just before being confronted by the apprentices Jack thought he had heard one of them shouting something about the chance of a lifetime.

'Easy, easy 'tween decks, you pair!' The boys almost careered headlong into the skipper and the emigration agent. 'You'll knock some old soul flying,' Jack smiled across at Lumsden.

'Yes sir, sorry sir.' They headed off towards the daylight, still clearly choking with excitement.

'Less of the old soul, Zurich,' said Walter stooping to follow Jack through the low doorway of the store and into one of the smallest but important spaces on the *Broomielaw*.

For people accustomed to an endless supply of fresh water streaming off the Border hills or roaring down the glens of the West Highlands and emptying into vast, dark, bottomless lochs, the very idea of rationing water supplies had been peculiar.

The main problem on board ship was that the precious drinking water had to last for an unknown period, up to six months in the worst scenario, and none could be spared for toilets or washing. Buckets of sea water were the order of the day.

In the Doldrums the downpours had provided a welcome and unexpected bonus for the passengers on the *Broomielaw* with every available container being called into service. The children particularly loved every second of these tropical rainstorms and raced around the deck with their buckets and pails looking for the most productive stream of rainwater cascading from canvas or crosspiece. This was followed by a mad frenzy of clothes washing.

However, it could only be a temporary respite.

Generally fresh water was in such short supply that much effort went into the management of water rations. What was left over from the day's allocation after the cook had taken a share for the galley was bottled for later use. Water loaded in Scottish ports, Jack Zurich knew from experience, tended to be better lasting, the casks were freshly coopered and the hoops efficiently tapped down; but even on the emigration ships operating out of Greenock and Leith, bartering of fresh water was common.

On the *Broomielaw,* as far as the Equator, the supply lasted well. On New Year's Day Jack had been able to order an additional allocation of drinking water which brought the loudest cheer from the emigrants over the entire holiday period.

But now they had a serious, potentially disastrous, problem. The entire reserve water supply, some 500 gallons in a separate tank, was found to be contaminated. Walter Lumsden cupped his hand under the outlet, sipped a few drops and immediately spat it on the deck.

'My God, that's awful, undrinkable. It tastes as if someone had poured a jar of paraffin into the tank.' He took the flask of potable water and rinsed out his mouth.

'Yes, and that's not the worst of it,' said Jack Zurich, bending to close the valve on the reserve tank and then straightening up. He pointed to a metal tun wrapped around by pipes which sat in the corner beneath the curve of a cross beam.

'With the help of Innes and his boys we got the condenser here up and running after we discovered the foul water; it would have kept us going for the rest of the voyage. It worked perfectly for half-an-hour, then bang, it seized. Innes has ruled out running repairs.'

It was apparent to the emigration agent, without Jack saying another word, that they were in the midst of the biggest crisis on the voyage to date. Together they made for the first mate's cabin to pore over the nautical charts of the South Atlantic and after throwing a few ideas around the captain and the agent came to a decision.

'We have to get fresh water on board and that condenser repaired before we get down to the Roaring Forties. If we rule out Rio or Montevideo then it's a straight choice between Cape Town and Tristan de Cunha, down here...' Jack pointed to a tiny speck on the chart almost on the same latitude as the Cape but in the midst of the empty South Atlantic Ocean. The island looked, at least to Lumsden, like the bleakest, most isolated place in God's creation. Thinking aloud Jack Zurich was making some swift calculations.

'With the Trade Winds unusually strong for this time of year, we're already several degrees off our planned course. Tristan da Cunha would take us only a touch further off our route. We can soon make up time once we're in the Forties with the wind behind us.'

'So it looks like Tristan da Cunha, skipper?' 'It would seem so, Walter. Docking in Cape Town, in any case, as well as taking us from the faster, more southerly passage, always brings a risk of allowing disease on board. But they're well used to servicing stray ships on that little island. A couple of days there and barring any unforeseen delays, we should be on our way.

With a rather half-hearted grin Walter replied: 'Yes, but the way this trip is unfolding we really must learn to expect the unexpected.'

59 Out of the Deep

On that same day as the decision was taken to head for Tristan da Cunha the great sea serpent scare unfolded causing the most amusing stir on the *Broomielaw* in weeks. A common jest among sailors on the emigrant ships was to tell tales to the wide-eyed voyagers of the leviathans of the deep, the titanic monstrosities which skulked around the death-black ocean canyons, rising silently, menacingly from the unfathomable depths towards the surface every so often to devour some poor ship and its unfortunate passengers and crew.

At least once every voyage the call would go up – 'The great sea serpent, off the port bow!'

Travellers would stumble and stagger on to the deck, rushing to the gunwales for a better view of the sensational event. This would be followed by a burst of laughter from the sailors and the less gullible. Often the great monster was merely a long, barnacle-encrusted tree trunk bobbing amongst the waves like a Mississippi alligator which had lost his way. Mothers would reassure the wee ones and the older children would laugh nervously at the sailor's yarns, all the time glancing over their shoulders at the sea, and wondering.

That afternoon Jack Zurich was deep in thought, still calculating how he might get away with a twenty-four hour turnaround at Tristan da Cunha when David Macgregor appeared at his side. Begging your pardon, Jack. But what to you make of that astern?' The stand-in skipper glanced aft, scouring the skyline.

'About a cable astern. Right in the eye of the sun.'

Jack homed in on a long, seemingly sinuous object swimming in the ship's track, cutting across the wake in a zig-zag pattern, yet seeming to keep pace with the ship. Occasionally its head, a ghastly spiked affair, would dip beneath the water then a writhing tail would stand six or eight feet proud of the water, its forward momentum throwing up a bow wave.

Because of the dazzling sunlight it was impossible to determine its colour or precise shape but it was clearly up to forty feet long and a marine monster unlike any known to science. In minutes word spread to the steerage and the rails of the *Broomielaw* were soon lined with families straining for a view of their pursuer.

'Do you think it's a sea serpent, Mr Zurich?'

'I wonder, Torrance, I do wonder.' The youngest Macaulay boy had sprinted for the deck with the rest of his classmates when news of this exciting event reached them, the teacher helpless to halt the floodtide of excited children who were soon lapping the quarterdeck in search of the best vantage point. As he spoke Jack glanced discretely over the side.

Soon the whole ship knew that the never-authenticated sea serpent had chosen to pay a courtesy call on the *Broomielaw*. Jack Zurich had been convinced that something was afoot ever since their encounter with the excited apprentices below decks but this was proving to be an entertaining diversion and with tougher times ahead he was happy to let the amusement run its course although he had noted that the *Broomielaw* had slowed markedly in her course. He looked across at the two apprentices who were hanging over the rail and seemed to be enjoying the spectacle more than most.

'Mainsail haul,' shouted Jack Zurich. 'Lee braces there!' The ship was turned closer to the wind and after a moment the serpent veered and appeared to dive.

'It's under,' a score of voices yelled in unison.

'She'll ram us for sure, cried the steerage pessimist.

'It must have been fifty feet long,' declared one of the emigrants.

'No, a hundred feet if it's an inch!' shouted another.

'Should I record the incident, Jack?' It was the second mate.

Log, tarred rope, apprentices. Yes, it all fell into place, concluded the skipper.

'No, I think not, David. Just let our travellers enjoy the excitement for a moment.' In his day Jack Zurich had been a prankster. After a few minutes he pulled the boys to one side. 'I think it's probably about time you freed that rope wherever

206

you've secured it. Too much of this monster business will over-agitate our emigrants and besides we have a schedule to keep to.'

The boys looked sheepish.

'And the cost of the rope will come out of your pockets.'

From being sheepish, the apprentices were now distinctly downcast. But as they moved away below decks Jack shouted after them: 'By the way, it was a very passable prank – one I'd have been proud of myself.' They brightened visibly and went off to set their sea monster free.

The skipper had guessed correctly that they must have passed close by a raft of tangled branches and trees and that the boys had got on deck in time to snare a huge, twisted trunk which had probably been carried down the Amazon or the Orinoco to the ocean. For the past 15 minutes the *Broomielaw* had been towing the monster at the end of the rope. In the eye of the sun it had looked every inch a creature of the deep. Yes, it was a neat prank, thought Jack.

60 Bread Day

Twenty-four hours later the captain's log noted that they had sent a boat across to barque *Oceanica* which was en route from Sydney to Aberdeen. It was the first opportunity that passengers had enjoyed to send mail home since the North Atlantic and this time, forewarned, the sealed leather mail satchel was well stuffed with letters.

Even though most were prepared, up to the lowering of the boat, some folk were scribbling messages to family and friends back in Scotland. The boat crew returned from the *Oceanica* with stories of a vast bush fire in Victoria and of fierce summer heat in the vicinity of Adelaide. Again the emigrants wondered – and worried - about what lay ahead for them.

Most important despatches in the outgoing mail satchel were from Jack Zurich and Walter Lumsden to the Clutha Company's agents in Glasgow informing them of the change of captaincy and the circumstances which prompted this dramatic action, the delays in the Doldrums, the catalogue of sinister incidents and the planned change of course to resupply with water and effect a repair on the condenser.

From the stern windows Walter watched the return of the day boat to the *Oceanica* and tried to determine, from the aromas permeating from the cabin area what Wallace had on the stove for the evening meal. A variety of vegetable smells suggested a pot of Wallace's famous broth was already simmering and the sweet vapours of baking bread reminded Walter that this was a special day in the galley.

All the food on board ship was cooked on a rota basis in a common galley, housed in the case of the *Broomielaw* in the sturdy, wooden deckhouse where the fireplace was completely enclosed in brickwork to reduce fire risk.

Normally Wallace, the temperamental Negro cook, was assisted by a few chosen emigrants. He was known on board by the nickname Spike, owing to the forefinger of his right hand being stiff in the middle joint and resembling a marlin spike. That and his tight curls of purest white hair were his distinguishing features. He had been at sea since he was a boy, and a cook for the past twenty.

It was his proud boast that he could make a meal from a bucket of water and a bone. The truth was he was no better than an average cook. His pea and ham days were infamous. The soup was either too thick or too thin and invariably the salt pork was either over-boiled or still red raw.

However, today was bread day, each compartment supplying its own quota of flour. Loaves, scones and oatmeal cakes were churned out by the cooking detail, the delicious aromas snatched away by the breeze must have betrayed their position for twenty miles around.

On this particular afternoon Maggie Gilchrist had been excused kitchen duties. She had important duties to attend to. Her labour pains had started. Instead, May and Flora joined Belle Macaulay in the heat of the galley where, with flour-flecked faces, they worked preparing doughs, clinging on tightly to the table with one hand and kneading deftly with the other whenever the ship began to pitch.

The girls took it in turns to steal down to the infirmary and visit their mother. Otherwise they worked quietly under the supervision of the cook who made it clear to anyone that would listen that he found this extra thrice-weekly chore aggravating. He was always anxious to rejoin his companions on the off-duty watch in the deckhouse card school. If Wallace had a fault, it was his lack of patience. The galley was his kingdom and he made sure everyone knew it. He would wave his rigid finger and his vocabulary of foul and abusive epithets was as stunning as it was extensive.

As often as not he vented his wrath on some poor victim of circumstance who carelessly dropped a loaf or allowed a tray of scones to darken overmuch. The Macaulay girls, however, proved more than a match for the surly cook. When he rounded petulantly on them over the speed at which the mixture was being produced, May let him have it with both barrels.

'You'd be better concentrating on your ovens, Wallace, rather than losing the place over silly wee things. We could do your job with our eyes shut'.

The chastened cook returned to his duties with a 'Hmmmph'.

Annoyed and stunned by this rebuke he may have been but it did seem to have a very positive effect. Soon a stream of piping hot bread was being distributed throughout the ship, excited children running with baskets along passageways and down companionways. In the calendar of shipboard activities, bread day was always circled in red.

61 A New Passenger

In the makeshift hospital a canvas screen had been erected around the end bed where Maggie would give birth to her fourth child.

She ran her hand over her distended stomach and waited; something at which she had never been particularly adept. But it wouldn't be long now, the baby was evidently anxious to be out and about. If only it knew what sort of strange, swaying, salt-charged world into which it was to be born, it might not press on so forcefully, thought Maggie.

An oil lamp flickered beside her and as someone tramped along the corridor, past the hospital with a laden basket, the sweet aroma of freshly-baked bread filled the air for a moment. It reminded Maggie of the baker's shop below Mrs Penman's in the High Street, just down from St Giles; it reminded her of lying, staring at the ceiling, crushed beneath a bulky, red-faced banker or a groaning fish merchant from the mart next door. God, the fish merchants. The smell from those men would linger for a week; she much preferred to recall the delicious, drifting scents of the bread.

James Gilchrist had eventually been persuaded that morning to visit his wife briefly, soon after her confinement began, but he soon disappeared again to the steerage, clearly with other matters on his mind. He seemed particularly preoccupied ever since with the terrible fate of Rag at the hands of Mrs Sinclair.

The woman in the next bunk, slowly recovering from the measles outbreak, was humming softly, comforting herself with a familiar refrain. It was *The Rowan Tree.* Maggie remembered one line from that melody in particular, a song which her mother had often sung to her and to her little brother in happier times in the drawing room at Melrose: *entwin'd thou art wi' mony ties, o' hame and infancy.* She felt a tear in the corner of her eye. Why was she weeping - for her disinterested husband James, for the childhood that was stolen from her, for Scotland left behind, for the uncertainties that lay ahead? She wasn't sure.

In the bunk nearest to the passageway Mrs Sinclair, who had shown no sign of remorse since her attack on Rag sat reading her Bible, the sampler with the Ten Commandments which she had been sewing lay on the rough sheet beside her. It was unfinished – halfway through the Sixth Commandment. She was whispering quietly to herself.

Apart from that violent, unheralded attack, she seemed to be the same concerned individual who got the Sunday school up and running and who had happily visited the sick and bereaved throughout the ship. Slowly she was being permitted to return to the fold, having been removed from the locked stateroom to the infirmary. It was as if she felt certain that she had done the right thing. Hadn't the Rev. Shade, confidentially in the aftermath of her assault on Rag, said as much to her.

Despite Elijah Shade's best ministrations Rag had died from shock and a catastrophic loss of blood the night after Mrs Sinclair's attack.

Jack had already told the woman that he would have to report the affair to the authorities in Adelaide but Mrs Sinclair had appeared very much at ease with herself; to such an extent it was eerie. It was as if she knew she would never be called to answer for the mutilation of the crewman.

'There is some sympathy on board for your action, Mrs Sinclair. But that does not disguise the fact that a man has lost his life. We will, of course, explain all the circumstances and Rag's assault on Jessie to the authorities but...'

She had simply responded: 'It will be many weeks before we reach Adelaide and there are still people on this ship in need of my help. You must do what you have to do, Mr Zurich. I know only that I was on the Lord's business.'

Mrs Sinclair smiled across the sick bay at Maggie who nodded, then grimaced and shifted her position. That was more comfortable, for the moment. This new arrival was sure to be a lively bairn. The child kicked so hard she felt stretched and sore. High time the wee soul was on his or her way into the world, no matter how strange these first surroundings.

In these moments her thoughts wandered to the long heart-searching hours beside the fire as they debated the idea of emigration. At that time she had surprised even herself by her steadily growing enthusiasm, even as she and the more reluctant James weighed up the pitfalls and possible problems which her pregnancy might involve at sea. And James's sudden, sombre conversion to the idea of emigration still baffled her.

So little had he contributed to their family life or their relationship as man and wife in the past months that Maggie no longer felt any need to try to excuse James's sullen behaviour to her fellow emigrants as she had been doing on an almost daily basis for the first week or two after they left the Clyde behind.

There were truths which had to be faced here. Maggie missed neither his physical contact nor his emotional support. For months he had offered neither. Yet, there were times, shared times past. These were less easy to erase. As she lay awaiting the next burst of labour pains she recalled how they met at the feeing market in Kelso. How James had persuaded the old factor, Brocklebank's predecessor to take on this young woman with her baby at the big house, at Fernieclough. For the first time since she had been cast out of the family home she had felt that she had a protector. But love, it had to be said, had never entered into the equation.

And yet this little person struggling to make his or her way into the world was their child.

Maggie shifted position again. The contractions began and each renewed surge of pain and purpose swept outwards from her womb to encompass her entire body.

Directly opposite Maggie, pale and silent, lay a lass from the single womens' quarters whose consumption had developed dramatically in the past week. Her name was Elizabeth McMichael and she coughed a weak, strangled cough – and stood at death's door. Auld Agnes, having passed a moment or two in conversation with Mrs Sinclair and smoothed the sheets on Miss McMichael's bed, appeared at Maggie's side and gave her a comforting pat on the arm.

'Keep breathing the way I telt ye, lass. You're an old hand at this by now. Shade is on his way down to see you, and for once he has put on a clean shirt.'

The surgeon cum minister skulked into the infirmary on cue and spoke briefly with the orderly who had been doing most of the work down in the confines of the sick bay since the *Broomielaw* left Greenock. Shade washed his hands in a steaming bowl of water which the orderly had just collected from the galley.

Then he was across at Maggie's side. He nodded to Agnes who was seated on the far side of the bed then turned to his patient.

'Well, I can foresee no complications, Mrs Gilchrist.' He took her pulse and began to probe cautiously with his fingers. Then his little brass ear trumpet was pressed to her stomach.

Maggie closed her eyes and was back at the Kelso feeing market. James had run in the men's distance race that afternoon, chasing through the hills and leaving the other young Borderers trailing in his wake. She had thought, even then, what fine children they might produce. She recalled the little vase James had collected for that victory. It was packed in one of the boxes, deep in the hold below them. Just then, opening her eyes, Maggie knew how she would name this baby.

But sweeping into her daydreams as he often did now was Walter Lumsden. It had been so long since she had felt at ease with a man in the way she did with Walter. No demands, no unsettling approaches, little more than a friendship. And yet. He was kind. Until that moment she had never allowed herself to even think such a thought but Maggie resolved to tell him about Brocklebank. She must. As soon as she had recovered from the birth.

'You're young and strong, Margaret, and the baby seems to have inherited your vigour. It's in the correct position for a normal birth. I'll leave you in the care of the midwife. And I won't be far away should you need me.' The gentler side of the Rev. Shade, his caring efficiency made his strange behaviour in other aspects of shipboard life all the more baffling.

Maggie's contractions were more violent now. The midwife arrived and within minutes the baby's head appeared.

'Keep pushin' lass! Now rest for a moment. Wait for the next contraction.' The midwife, a stout, genial woman from Argyllshire was the calmest person Maggie had encountered on the *Broomielaw* and the shepherd's wife had been quietly delighted that Shade had other business to attend to. He was clearly a good surgeon but he made Maggie's flesh creep.

'You're doing grand, lass; now push again.'

Beads of sweat gathered on Maggie's forehead, trickling down her cheeks. The pace of the contractions and their intensity, now feeling like little explosions deep within her, seemed suddenly to increase as the baby's shoulders appeared. Agnes mopped her niece's brow.

Maggie gripped the rough sheet and clenched her teeth. She had quite forgotten the unspeakable, tearing agony of contractions and the feeling of being turned inside out as her baby struggled to be free and was rhythmically evicted by the body.

'Push now, Mrs Gilchrist! Push now!' There was more urgency this time in the midwife's voice, as held a damp cloth to Maggie's brow.

*   *   *   *   *

A few feet above the women on the main deck Jack Zurich followed the pointing finger of the lookout aloft. It was a clear day with good visibility and they were making fully ten knots. Out there, still perhaps forty miles away across the heaving swell, hugging the sweep of the horizon like the back of some huge mythical sea beast, was the island of Tristan da Cunha.

It was said that in prime meteorological conditions often with strange refractions at work the volcanic island peak could be seen from 90 miles away, even around the curve of the earth. What the emigrants couldn't see as yet was the tiny Edinburgh settlement on the north side of the island. Hardly more than a collection of huts on a gentle sloping greensward, the dwellings were surrounded by vegetable plots, and all this lay in the shadow of the soaring cliffs guarding the volcanic heart of the isle. First garrisoned by British marines some four decades previously during the war with France the community clung precariously to existence beside the dark, volcanic beaches, most of the residents being ex-soldiers and their families.

Jack Zurich had never made landfall on Tristan but had heard stories of the hospitality of the islanders in this lonely outpost and their remarkable self-sufficiency. This also enabled them to happily turn their hand to any necessary repair work for passing vessels.

They had made good time on this brief deviation and if the water condenser could be restored to working order in a day or two the *Broomielaw*, her crew and passengers would soon be back on schedule and ready for the severe test that was the last and longest leg of the voyage – the dash along the Roaring Forties.

News that land had been sighted, as ever, brought the emigrants to the rails wondering what strange, new place they were about to encounter. With them they brought the glad tidings that the complement of the *Broomielaw* had increased by one. Deep in the ship a baby cried lustily. Little James 'Law' Gilchrist, receiving his middle name in tribute to the vessel where he saw the first light of day, had joined the adventure.

62 Tristan da Cunha

The skiff, peaked at the bow, with a broad beam and under full sail, bounced past close by, almost beneath the slanting bowsprit of the at-anchor *Broomielaw,* heading for the open sea. A tall, young man who had been working midships with the nets stood up stiffly and waved. It was William, third son of the laird of Doomy Hall.

'Hey there, you two! Alright for some folk taking their leisure!'

Hugh Macaulay and May Gilchrist were occupying their favourite perch towards the bow of the clipper, just above the stout port side anchor chain which dipped into the choppy, metal grey waters. They watched the lines of the elegant little craft as she turned into the wind and waved enthusiastically in response as William turned to resume his duties with the nets, lifting and folding in preparation for casting.

Several other skiffs of a similar design were already at sea and quickly disappearing towards the eastern horizon while others were preparing to ride out through the surf from the exposed landing stage below the village.

Every emigrant had found different ways of spending the past twenty-four hours in and around what the locals called the Edinburgh settlement. The womenfolk had gone ashore to try to stock up on personal provisions, to make their meagre larder a little more varied, while the men helped replenish the fresh water supply from the spring above the settlement, the barrels being transported to the shore in the back of a rickety cart by a moth-eaten pony. In the surf the day boat waited.

It took everyone a good while to regain their land legs but the opportunity to meet and chat with new faces, the Glasses, the Greens, the Laverellos and the Pattersons, to swap stories and learn about this very special place, was not to be missed. It would be an episode in the epic voyage to the other side of the world which would be passed down through generations of emigrant descendants – the Tristan da Cunha stopover.

The *Broomielaw* lay in a good depth of water, but no more than 100 yards offshore, riding patiently in the exposed anchorage, within hailing distance of the cluster of compact steadings, fringed by bushes and wild flowers, which made up the little township.

On board the crew were taking advantage of the enforced stopover to carry out repairs to the rigging and the bulwark which had been required since the tropical storm of December 21. Masts were oiled, sails were repaired and water pumped out. After the weeks at sea everyone that was mobile seized the opportunity to stretch their legs and explore this odd, other-worldly location. The infirm and the elderly listened eagerly to the descriptions of the islanders, the stark, volcanic landscape and of the wildlife, accounts which the shore parties brought back to the ship.

However, Walter Lumsden had spent the first few hours at anchor writing letters to the company back in Scotland. Hardly a week passed, the islanders told them, without a vessel calling by the tall island to effect some repair or other. It transpired that *The Spirit of Speed* had been there only hours before them. They were keeping well in touch with her and Walter, more than ever, felt convinced that Jack Zurich would still give that old sea dog Ritchie a run for his money. Sitting in the poorish light at his writing desk, Lumsden had much to report, particularly the growing suspicion that somewhere on the ship someone was deliberately attempting to undermine morale and working to slow the passage.

It was different, oddly soothing, to feel the clipper swinging gently at anchor and waves slapping almost playfully around the woodwork. For the moment the all-pervading groaning and creaking of the timbers of a ship at sea was silenced as the *Broomielaw* gathered herself for that last mad sprint to Australia. Just as importantly, this was a last opportunity to fling every hatch wide and let the South Atlantic breezes clear the fetid air from the steerage.

Lumsden also found that he could spend thoughtful time alone now without the constant torture of the Hunter River returning to him. Of course, it was still there in the corners of his mind. He didn't expect ever to escape it completely but now it was more manageable. He looked from his papers to the hatch and the panorama beyond and back to his documents again. Lizzie was still beside him, he was sure, but her presence no longer filled him with the same despair.

*   *   *   *   *

For his part Jack Zurich, with Innes Macaulay in tow, had made contact with Jacob Maddock, the island blacksmith. While life on Tristan da Cunha generally seemed to progress with more reference to the sun and the tides than to the ticking of a clock, the smith, a massively strong, Hispanic-looking individual with a neck like a fighting bull, saw every ship arrival as a brief opportunity to show the wider world that he was an engineering marvel. Each new sail signalled a chance for a burst of impressive activity.

Most of the residents of the island were members of the original British garrison who had opted to stay and carve some sort of life for themselves on this seemingly inhospitable dot in the South Atlantic. Jacob was one of them and proudly sported a long service medal on the leather shoulder strap of his smith's apron.

With a limited supply of spare parts he had set about re-fashioning the condenser in his stuffy, turf-roofed smiddy overlooking the anchorage. It was late afternoon and Jack, an interested spectator, leant against the door jamb, silhouetted against the sun, puffing on his pipe. It was a quiet, restoring moment after the responsibilities of captaincy had been so suddenly and dramatically thrust upon him.

While he worked the smith was silent, occasionally humming quietly to himself. From time to time he would fire a technical question at Innes. However, as he prepared for each new stage of the job he opened up, chatting in a strange, indeterminate English which confusingly betrayed traces of both the Black Country and possibly South Wales.

Jack discovered that *The Spirit of Speed* had spent twelve hours at Tristan only twenty-four hours previously, to take on water and to attempt repairs on a storm-damaged oven.

'Yes, the work, I have to say wasn't completed to my satisfaction but it should see them to Australia,' said the smith as he turned an iron in the hot coals. 'The skipper was so anxious to get under way. It was as if the very devil was on his tail.'

'Indeed,' responded Jack, 'that would be Ritchie for sure. And I'm afraid to say I would be that very devil!'

The skipper of the *Broomielaw* turned to look out on the scene - along the shore to where his ship lay anchor. It was his command, his ship. The idea filled him at one and the same time with pride and terror. Despite the storm damage the clipper still looked as elegant a vessel as any that had ever taken to the water. This was his first command – a sore test bearing in mind the unusual circumstances but also one he would never forget.

The smith was at his side, rubbing his oiled hands on a rag. 'Another couple of hours in the morning Mr Zurich and we should be able to test your condenser. With luck you'll be away on the afternoon tide.'

'Please, Jacob, call me Jack. And isn't that a marvellous sight.' He pointed out beyond the boulder strewn strand. The fishing fleet was returning to the rough jetty. Already some of the little boats had been hauled up on to the track. Jack counted eight skiffs still dancing across the foam-flecked waves towards the shore where some would also be raised on hoists, beyond the reach of the often angry ocean.

'One of your young men has spent almost every hour with our fishermen, Jack. He seems a natural with the nets and sails.'

'That'll be William Bigland, I'll wager, Jacob. He hails from an island not so very unlike this. He's an Orcadian who was fishing deep, dark and dangerous waters almost as soon as he could walk.'

The men talked for a few minutes about the weather conditions the *Broomielaw* could expect to meet as she headed south against into the colder waters of Southern Indian Ocean, towards the Antarctic, then Jack and Innes marched off down the brae to let Lumsden know the encouraging news that they would soon be under way. His eyes swept the circle of the vast horizon. It was possible from this slightly elevated vantage to make out the curve of the earth sloping away in all directions and to his astonishment, to the northeast, there was a sail. In this vast expanse of water a fellow traveller on the Atlantic swell could only be heading for Tristan da Cunha. Just at this moment.the island indeed did seem to attract passing strangers like a magnet.

'It's like Argyle Street on a holiday Friday, Innes' Jack observed as they made their way down the stony path.

The fishing skiffs which had been hadn't winched up on to frames were hauled up and lay side by side at the pierhead, secured for the night. In the gloaming oil lamps began to flicker into life in the narrow windows of the cottages around the settlement.

William Bigland shook hands with the new-found friends, Peter Repetto, a master fisherman, his son Nathaniel and members of the other crews. There was mutual respect between the da Cunhans and this man from the Scottish islands. It was a deference born of a shared knowledge of the awesome power of the ocean. Bigland had already proved himself brave and fit, yet willing enough to learn. He had hauled with the best of them.

More than that, the people here treated William as an equal. On Stormay he had always felt at a distance from his father's tenants. He had always been Master Will from the big house.

'If you find Australia too hot and dusty for your liking, William, then remember your friends, the fishermen of Tristan da Cunha.'

Peter, a swarthy individual with a weatherbeaten, lined face and strong, square shoulders slapped the young Scot on the back and they walked together up and on to the track. The truth was that Bigland was already giving serious thought to his fishermen friends and their island and of how they might fit into his own plans. As soon as he reboarded the *Broomielaw* he set off to find Queenie.

63 A Letter from Home

Walter Lumsden was bringing his voyage journal up to date in the cramped little cabin he had been allocated on the starboard side. He reflected on how this unexpected pause in the middle of the journey, this island interlude, had allowed emigrants and crew alike to take stock of how they were coping with the rigours of the adventure.

The passengers had learned the stories of earlier travellers at talks organised by the emigration company and in letters from family and friends who had left the homeland; but there was no substitute for the real thing. Most felt like seasoned seafarers by now, others suffered in silence longing for the journey to be over but fearing that the worst was still to come.

It was true that there had already been deaths, five children and six adults including the two crewmen who fell from the mast and the rapist Rag. Sad though these statistics seemed as Walter entered them in his company journal he knew that it was, if anything, less than the average for the Australia/New Zealand run.

Yes, and there was also much to be thankful for. So far they had avoided a serious outbreak of dysentery or whooping cough although measles was making its presence known. The general tidiness and desire of the Scots to keep their own compact corner of the ship spotless despite the impossibly cramped conditions, a kind of competitive edge, all this helped contain disease.

Despite his apparent fondness for drink and his strange ways with the womenfolk Shade, the minister/surgeon appeared to be a knowledgeable physician. His pastoral skills, well, that was another matter.

Lumsden corrected himself as he was about to fill in the figures; the total of adult deaths should have been seven. Elizabeth McMichael, the poor lass who had suffered terribly from consumption, and who had occupied the bed opposite Maggie in her confinement, had slipped away just as the *Broomielaw* put down anchor.

But with a complement of 220 passengers there would be deaths. Generally the shipping companies were agreed that a loss of ten per cent of passengers en route might be expected. No-one said it was an acceptable average but it was to be expected.

Sadly, by far the largest numbers of losses were usually among the children under five and the elderly who were just not strong enough for the trials of the voyage. According to press reports reaching the United Kingdom from Adelaide, Melbourne and Sydney which Walter had scanned carefully before departure, some ships arrived in the Antipodes without any child survivors, as many as sixty or seventy wee ones on a single ship having perished on the voyage.

Walter stirred himself from his reverie and returned to his journal just as the sound of wood on wood, the shipping oars from their rollocks and a series of shouted instructions indicated that a large oared boat, larger than their own craft, had pulled in alongside the *Broomielaw* just for'ard of the officer's accommodation.

On deck Innes Macaulay had been sitting listening quietly to the bustle of the returning boats and enjoying the last of the evening sunshine on his face. With him was his middle son Guthrie who had spread a pack of cards on a convenient barrel top and was absorbed in a game of patience.

Innes made use of these quiet moments to travel in his mind's eye back to the Lanarkshire haunts of his youth. Along the river, below the village, where the branches of the alder trees hung low over the bubbling waters and where he had guddled for trout. So many places to visit, so many interior landscapes, as real

220

to Innes as the South Atlantic breeze on his face and the salt tang in the air.

He had been as proud as he could remember when Jack Zurich asked him to discuss the options for the condenser repair on his behalf with the island blacksmith.

'You're the only man on this ship who has the slightest idea how this repair can be achieved, Innes', the skipper had said. 'Just you keep us right.'

Innes couldn't recall when he had last felt so functional, so pleased with himself.

And this came on top of his soul-stirring secret. For days he had convinced himself that it must be pure imagination, just little charges running around beneath his eyelids such as you can experience when you close your eyes tightly, suddenly. But this was much, much more. He was getting impressions of light and shade.

The doctors had insisted that with the degree of ocular nerve damage he had sustained, it was impossible that any vision would return but now, here on deck, when someone passed in front of him blocking out the bright sunlight momentarily, he was convinced that shadowy images were moving across his line of vision. As he heard footsteps approach Innes waited for the odd effect to come and go. There was no doubting that something unexpected was happening.

In addition, up at the gloomy smiddy on the hill, as Jacob worked at his bellows, Innes had been almost sure he had registered the sudden fiery eruption of flame from the furnace visually – and not just by the sudden blast of heat on his cheeks.

Already he has decided that he would bide his time before he confided this stunning information to Belle. He wanted to be sure damned sure. God forbid that it might only a temporary and very limited improvement. That would be almost too much to bear.

'Take your eyes off the cards for a minute, son, and tell me what's going on,' said Innes, reaching out to touch Guthrie's shoulder. 'By the sound of it the ship is going like the Lanimer Fair.'

Indeed the deck was a nest of activity, swarming with family groups and little knots of seamen. Not only had the day boat just arrived with more barrels of fresh water which were being swung aboard on hoists and a cargo of excited, chattering passengers, digesting the news that they would be under sail again the following day but another, larger day boat had also drawn alongside.

'Looks like an official visit from the ship which dropped anchor north by an hour past.'

'Did you get her name, Guthrie?'

'Aye, faither, a fine looking vessel, *Helenslee*, out of Leith. A bittie bigger than the *Broomielaw*, I would guess.'

Young Guthrie watched the man he took to be the skipper of the *Helenslee*, a man of middle age, a serious looking individual being respectfully welcomed aboard by the second mate and ushered toward Jack Zurich's quarters.

'Mr Shade is having a right good blether wi' the cox of *Helenslee's* boat, faither.'

'Aye, Guthrie, it seems there's not much that goes past the reverend gentleman.'

A few yards away along the deck Queenie Stout was completing her evening chores. This regime of punishment had now become a routine for the island lass who had turned stowaway.

'I think we've said all there is to say, William'.

With her sleeves rolled up beyond her elbows, her hands were sunk deep in the washing tub. She paused to flick a strand of hair out of her eyes and fixed William Bigland with her small, dark eyes.

'There really isn't an 'us' any longer, William, is there? Whatever this is you're planning you have no obligation to me.'

William shuffled uneasily beside Queenie as she started to wring out the clothes, the impressive muscles of her forearms, evidence of hard work throughout her young life in field and hearth.

'The truth is Queenie, I don't remember being happier in my life than I have been in the past two days, Look at my hands.' He showed her where the fiery salt water sores were rising around the finger joints. And he smiled proudly.

'Sitting listening to my father on his high horse ranting about the heavy responsibilities of the landed classes or during those tedious law lectures in Edinburgh I often wondered if I would ever find a way of life I felt comfortable with. Now I've discovered paradise….'

With a dramatic sweep of his arm William gestured towards the impressive panorama of Tristan da Cunha, the little settlement nestling on the grassy slope beneath the towering cliffs which in turn guarded the volcanic heart of this remote outpost. The sun dipped away to the west and the island was bathed for a few moments in a magical golden light.

'I aim to stay here, possibly for good.'

'But what about Australia, the shipping office? Your father will burst a blood vessel.'

'I think not. He's just glad to have me out of what's left of his hair. Out of sight, out of mind. He's probably already accepted the post of Lieutenant of the County. But never mind that old bugger – why don't you stay with me, Queenie?' She stood drying her hands on her apron. The deck was quieter now and a light evening rain had started to fall.

'I'm going to Australia, William. Having torn myself away from Stormay, I've no wish to swap one small island for another. I never realised that the world could be such a wonderful place.'

Will looked genuinely concerned. 'But wait, who'll look after you. You have no family or friends. I know it seems very late but I feel a responsibility for you. You'll be destitute.'

'Not so, William. Already I've met so many kind people – I have no fears. We were both willing partners to what happened on Stormay. You owe me nothing. I'll put my trust in God.'

For week or two Queenie had suspected she might be pregnant. The morning sickness of the past days had dispelled any doubts. She had decided there and then as she retched in the water closet that William would not be told. Certainly, it made more sense for her to stay on Tristan da Cunha with the youngest son of the laird of Stormay, especially now she knew that she was carrying his child, but she was caught up in a great adventure. Queenie longed to see Australia. And besides, there was Jack. She felt warm inside at the thought of him.

* * * * *

Jack Zurich had been reading the official document for several minutes, moving slowly, incredulously, from line to line trying to take on board the stunning information and allegations it

223

contained. The parchment creaked as he carefully turned a page. He needed to make time for himself, time to think. The despatch was crammed with legal jargon but effectively it was an arrest warrant from the Crown Office and signed by the Sheriff at Haddington.

He resisted the temptation to question the authenticity of the document, to stall for a moment or two. It was clearly the genuine article. Besides he was too preoccupied with its implications.

The skipper of the *Helenslee*, growing more impatient as the minutes passed, paced the cabin as Jack seemed to take an eternity to digest the details of the warrant.

Walter watched him over the half-moons of his steel reading spectacles. It was clear that in connection with this life or death matter the older man that did not feel comfortable dealing with the stand-in captain of the *Broomielaw*, a man almost half his age and with only a fraction of his seafaring experience – and apparently also a bit slow on the uptake. He coughed noisily.

'Come, come, Mr Zurich. It's a straightforward enough business this.'

Desperation now seized Jack as he frantically sought some sort of solution before the roof fell in. 'Yes indeed. But before we go any further, Mr McMaster, I have some unfinished business. It'll only take a moment.'

Jack called in the quartermaster and sent him with a scribbled note to the emigration agent asking Walter to head for steerage. His task was to keep the Gilchrists out of the way for the next hour.

'In simple terms, Zurich, if you're not willing to break your journey and take the prisoner to Cape Town for transportation back to Scotland, I'm authorised to do so.' He took the document which Jack had finally held out to him. 'We can resolve this matter now and I'll be off on the morning tide.'

Jack's mind was racing. Surely, this was impossible; it was certainly unbelievable. He needed more time to think. Should he allow instinct to direct him or should he follow the letter of the law – as his father, behind his counter in Portsmouth, would surely have counselled?

For one hovering moment he was about to recall the quartermaster who waited outside the door, asking him to bring the individual named in the document from the steerage berth. Instead, he bit his tongue, sat down again, refilled the brandy glasses at the same time taking a deep breath. A serious decision had been taken.

'God knows, it would be fine indeed to think Mr McMaster, that we could resolve this sad affair here and now. However, there will be no need for either of us to break the journey at the Cape. I fear that the person you seek is already called to a higher court. You see, Maggie Gilchrist died this morning.'

64 A Grave on the Hill

Through the gloaming Jack Zurich sucked anxiously on his clay pipe and watched the day boat smack into the waves on her return journey until finally she snuggled up tidily against the *Helenslee*.

The arrangement, the only way he could get McMaster off the *Broomielaw* without an on-the-spot inquiry, was by agreeing to take him to the hillside cemetery to see Maggie's grave before the *Broomielaw* resumed her voyage. He had also guaranteed to write a sworn testimony as to the circumstances of her death.

In the midst of this he was vastly relieved that he hadn't yet got round, mainly due to the urgency of the condenser repair, to adding Elizabeth McMichael's name to the daily log. By the time he showed it to McMaster the following morning over a cup of strong coffee it would clearly outline details of Maggie Gilchrist's death in childbirth and as far as the world beyond the ship was concerned Elizabeth McMichael, single serving lass, bound for Adelaide, lived on.

As he thought about this dramatic turn of events, the sheer enormity of the deceit began to fix itself in his mind. Poor, sickly Elizabeth, an orphan, with no relations in Australia and no fixed employment awaiting her was, by the strangest twist of fate, a Godsend. Hers had been a death of the utmost convenience.

When the skipper of *The Helenslee* suggested that he should go and pay his respects to the bereaved husband Jack took a deep breath – and lied again. 'The poor man is distraught. He's been given a quota of rum and is calm and asleep for the first time since his wife passed away.'

His mind was still racing. 'What are you doing, Jack Zurich?' he asked himself.

He swung away from the rail and pondered the next move. A catalogue of possible offences rolled before his eyes – conspiracy to pervert the course of justice, not only jail but the loss of his ticket and any chance of another command, disgrace and the condemnation of his parents and family. Perhaps even accessory to murder. He was risking all that and more.

On the other hand he was doing what his mother and father, locked into their predictable lives in their little south coast grocery empire had never done – he was acting instinctively, listening to that small, insistent voice inside his head, just as he had done when he decided to make the sea his life.

Listening to that mysterious mentor had kept him alive through a score of Atlantic storms, enabled him to deal with the unpredictable, tough-as-nails crewmen on the clippers and won him the respect of those same men whose lives depended on his decisions. He had learned over the years to trust these instincts. This plot, however, was something totally new.

More importantly Jack found that it was easy enough to sniff out the bad penny but recognising a braveheart or a thoroughly good soul was an altogether more demanding exercise. The little kindnesses which Maggie had shown to her fellow travellers in the past weeks, despite her own personal troubles with her surly, uncommunicative husband surely said more about the woman than any Crown Office document. He felt he could stake his life on that.

He hoped, prayed, his judgement had not let him down. And he must tell Walter and Maggie soonest – it was a matter of the utmost urgency. Going below deck he found Walter Lumsden poring over a map of the sea route with a group of his emigrants and suddenly realised that he might, at the end of the day, have to do precisely that, put his life on the line.

Passing the little huddle around the map at the head of the companionway he laid a hand on the agent's shoulder.

'Can you find Maggie and come to the day room. I think I owe you an explanation about that note. Just as soon as you can, Walter. We have a problem,' he whispered.

There was no time like the present to adjust the log to cope with these sensational and worrying developments. He reached the day room and began to put pen to paper. As he waited on Maggie and Walter Lumsden Jack Zurich wrote:

Died this day, Friday, January 15, 1858, in the ship's infirmary while in labour, (child stillborn) Gilchrist, Margaret, farm of Sweetshaws, Haddingtonshire, wife of James Gilchrist), buried in the community kirkyard, Tristan da Cunha, South Atlantic.

A burial at sea might have been better, he reflected, but circumstances made that impossible. Well, that was that. There was no way back. Jack could visualise his father standing before him, his face locked into that stern, disapproving scowl which he always reserved specially for his eldest boy.

'Too late, father', Jack murmured to himself. 'I've made my bed.'

Seeing the couple at the door he signalled them to enter while he blew gently across the page to dry the ink.

'What in God's name is wrong, Jack? You look as if you've seen a ghost.' Lumsden had never seen the young seaman looking quite so serious, even in the teeth of that fearsome tropical storm.

Jack glanced up at Maggie, as if looking for something in this woman that he hadn't noticed before. She had recovered rapidly from the birth of her son and looked in fine fettle. Now Jack understood how she might have come by the bruises on her necks and bumps on her face which he had noted on embarkation; the injuries had now all but vanished.

'Actually, Walter, you're nearer the mark than you might imagine; perhaps in a way I am seeing a ghost. Sit down, both of you, while I work out how to break this to you.'

65 Maggie's Confession

The get-together in the day room now had the air of a conspiracy which, chillingly, Jack realised was precisely what it was. The low ceilinged space, sparsely furnished with a few chairs, a stout table and a rather battered oil painting of fishing smacks on the Clyde was, however, replete that evening with an uneasy dusk.

Walter Lumsden lit the lamp above the table and immediately the flames brought the scene to flickering life.

Slowly, giving time for the other two to absorb events word by word, Jack described the arrival of the *Helenslee*, the serious allegations contained in the legal warrant, the accusations in detail against Maggie and his testing interview with McMaster. As he spoke Maggie's heart raced and she sank her head into her hands. After all these miles!

'In among that legal jargon, what you're really saying, Jack, is that they have Maggie down as a murderer and she's to be taken back to Scotland for trial?'

For long moments there was an uncomfortable silence. Clouds which had been threatening all day closed in over Tristan da Cunha. Big spots of rain pattered on the day room skylight.

'That's about it, Walter. If McMaster had had his way Maggie would already be in the brig of the *Helenslee*.'

Walter Lumsden looked at Maggie who was staring steadfastly at the faded fishing smacks on the wall.

'Well clearly, Jack, there's been some dreadful mistake, a case of mistaken identity. I know this woman well enough now to be certain that she's incapable of such violence. You must surely be of the same opinion. What did you say – the man Brocklebank, the factor, was battered to death. Tell him, Maggie. Tell him it isn't so.'

There followed moments of strangled silence before Maggie turned to face the stand-in skipper of the *Broomielaw* – a man who had become her friend and protector and his companion Walter Lumsden who was beginning to mean much, much more to her. She sobbed, choking on sighs which seemed to come from deep within.

If this was an act, thought Jack Zurich, it was an impressive performance.

'Tell him, Margaret. Tell Jack that they have the story wrong.' There was just a hint of panic in Lumsden's eyes. She reached forward to take his hand in hers. Without a word being spoken the emigration agent knew the response would not be what he wished for.

The distance between Maggie and the horrors of the Bluebell Woods had seemed vast. Unbridgeable. How could the consequences of that terrible day have followed her around halfway the globe? Yet, it was happening.

Jack Zurich spoke again. 'Yes, Margaret, take your time. You know you are among friends here. This will be upsetting, I can see that, but I truly think you owe us both some sort of explanation.'

Squeezing her kerchief and occasionally dabbing at her eyes, Maggie walked to the sloping windows and looked out into the gathering darkness. Beneath the stone battlements the lights twinkled from the cluster of fishermen's cottages, pinpoints of light on a uniformly dark scene. She had never felt so vulnerable, and so genuinely dependent on others. It was a new and disturbing sensation.

Maggie told them of the months of planning for emigration, of the long hours of discussion by the fireside at Sweetshaws, which more often than not concluded with an argument. She spoke of the inexplicable fear which initially overtook James at the thought of leaving his valley.

'After his father's death in Glasgow he suddenly became determined that we should make the voyage but when Brocklebank refused to free James from his contract, I saw all our hopes and dream crumbling around us. I couldn't let it happen. My sister-in-law needs me; my girls deserved the opportunity to make something of their lives, an opportunity which I never had.'

As if she sensed that her tone had become over strident Maggie drew breath.

'The only way I could persuade that beast Brocklebank to release James from his contract was to come to, well, to come to an arrangement.'

The men looked at each other; the realisation of what was suggested was clear enough.

'You must understand. It was for the girls, only for the girls. I was desperate.'

She held her head in her hands and wept. It was some minutes before she had recovered sufficiently to resume her tale. In the meantime, through the wooden wall, Silas Ratter was at his keyboard. The plinking strains of *What a Friend we have in Jesus* sounded out along the passageway.

'Ever since I moved to Sweetshaws I had known that the factor had a hunger for me in that way. I could see it in his eyes … what else could I do? Tell me, what else could I do?' she pleaded. As Maggie looked set to dissolve in tears again Lumsden put a comforting arm around her shoulder.

'We understand, Maggie. We do. But is it true? Did you leave that man dead on the ground?'

It was clear to the survivor in Maggie Gilchrist that she had already won both of these men over to her cause. What greater test could there be than this. She spilled the remainder of her story.

'We met in the Bluebell Woods on the afternoon before we caught the Glasgow train and I did what he wanted. It sickened me, but I did all he wanted.' Her stomach churned at the recollection of how she bent over the factor as he encouraged her, whispering obscenities, his hands inside her clothes, roughly probing, his hips thrusting to meet her lips.

'But he became violent, he just seemed to explode. He wanted me to pleasure him in other ways, unclean, disgusting ways, and I refused. Before I knew what was happening his hands were around my neck and he was choking the life … I freed myself and took a branch to him. I struck him again and again until he stopped twitching. I wanted to make sure he would never again treat a woman that way.'

Maggie paused. The ship was quiet now. The shore parties had returned. Families would be at their evening meal. Her breasts ached. Little James would soon be needing his feed.

'But how, Jack, did the constabulary know to look for me?'

'This is very awkward for me, Maggie. Difficult, you understand.'

'Difficult, difficult for you, for God's sake! I've opened my heart to you both. You must tell me.'

'Well Maggie, it seems that the night before this encounter you describe, at Lauder, at the inn, Brocklebank had been bragging about his meeting with you and what he was going to do to you. More than that there were the marks of a woman's boots at the spot where the gamekeeper found him.'

Maggie recalled how, like a crazed woman, she had gathered a pile of dead branches and rough grasses to heap on the bloodstained body.

Walter Lumsden stood up, fists clenched, jaw tight. 'This evidence is circumstantial at best. They can prove nothing. In any case, she was defending herself. I tell you now, Jack. I will return to Scotland with Maggie. The court must hear the whole story. We must surely let James know what is happening'

Jack looked across at the others. Lumsden was shaking with emotion while Maggie now looked composed. But her distress seemed genuine enough and Jack realised how this confession must have drained every last ounce of energy from her.

'Do you think for a minute, Walter, with that sort of evidence stacked against her that the court is likely to take a lenient view? Never! In any case, events have overtaken us. I don't think that either you – or Maggie – will be going back to Scotland.'

He then explained his impulsive decision to bend the rules and manipulate the truth, to use Elizabeth McMichael's timely death to write Maggie out of the picture, of how this deception would place her out of harm's way. He spoke of fears and friendships – then waited for a reaction. Maggie sank into a chair and Walter Lumsden looked out at the ocean.

Eventually, shaking his head in disbelief, Lumsden managed to blurt out: 'Jack, you've truly taken my breath away. It's a bold plan, and a risky business. But between us we could carry it off, couldn't we? What do you think, Maggie?'

'We should not, under any circumstances confide in my husband. He must never know about this. It would finish him. And you did all this, Jack Zurich, without having had the time or the opportunity to hear from my own lips if I was guilty'.

'There just wasn't time consult, Maggie. It was a desperate situation and it called for desperate measures. And after all you've an honest face.'

Then all three laughed, breaking the tension which had swept around the day room like a flood tide. She sat forward in her chair and looked intently at the stand-in skipper of the *Broomielaw*.

'Our little stowaway, Queenie Stout, says you are a very special man, Jack Zurich. I think I now know what she means.'

66 Deeper and Deeper

McMaster wouldn't have noticed but Jack Zurich had his fingers tightly crossed as they trekked along the rough, rubble track to the graveyard, lying above the shore on the edge of the little community. Bent forward and feeling every step the plump skipper of the *Helenslee* was too busy trying to catch his breath.

Behind the village the huge cliffs climbed to the sky dwarfing the cluster of homesteads and the two sailing ships at anchor. The island, thought Jack, was truly a magical lost world, a place where anything was possible.

He knew that Walter had recruited the ship's carpenter to help fashion an imposter of a cross and inscription for Elizabeth McMichael's grave – but he remained edgy. This sort of strategy formed no part of his master mariner's certificate

He would be relieved beyond measure to see the morning past and the *Broomielaw* under way again.

'You understand, Mr Zurich, why I have to see the woman's grave for myself,' wheezed McMaster, planking his ample rear end on a low dry-stone wall of dark rock. Two scruffy goats, content in their patch of scrub, in their uncomplicated little world, grazed beyond the wall, stopping every so often to gaze at the two men, jaws grinding rhythmically on the cud. They had an appearance of absolute contentment which just at this particular moment Jack envied.

'Otherwise, I would not have felt able to complete my despatch to Edinburgh. No reflection on you, you understand.'

The portly skipper of the *Helenslee* had made to stop at the trackside as if to inspect the view, a marvellous skyscape right enough, a sparkling ocean seeming to stretch forever. In fact, he was peching and panting at a furious rate. He produced a handkerchief from his jacket pocket and proceeded to mop his brow.

Jack scuffed the dry track with the toe of his boot. 'And no offence taken, Mr McMaster. You've been commissioned by the authorities to do a job and you must complete it to the best of your ability. I'm sure you are just as anxious to resume your voyage as we are.'

More sedately, they resumed their hike moving forward finally to the open level ground where the cemetery was laid out and through the creaking iron gates, peeling and patchy, rusted by the salt Atlantic air. The place wore a cloak of lazy dereliction. Walter had remarked that morning how odd it was that graveyards so often had spectacular views, as if it was some consolation to the occupants.

A strange, unsolicited remark, thought Jack. He could not have known that at that precise moment – a few yards away - in the graveyard, Walter Lumsden was thinking on three plain wooden crosses on a grassy knoll above the Hunter River.

As they picked their way between the scattered gravestones, some ornate stone affairs, presumably imported, others mere rough wooden crosses which Jacob said marked the graves of unknown mariners washed ashore on this lonely outpost, Jack suddenly felt more at ease. In the distance he could see Walter Lumsden standing head bowed beside the mound of freshly heaped earth which was topped by a spray of wild flowers, presumably from the strip of meadow at the base of the cliffs.

Lumsden introduced himself as the two men halted beside the grave. Jack removed his cap. They had chosen a sheltered corner for Elizabeth and at the moment the skipper pledged to himself that one day he must return to Tristan da Cunha and set things here to rights. He had already asked the smith to see that the grave was kept tidy. With a handshake the men had agreed on a bottle of Scotch and a fine new hammer to be sent at the first opportunity, as payment in kind.

'A sad business this altogether, Mr McMaster,' said Walter Lumsden. 'According to what Jack here has told me, we may never know exactly what transpired all those weeks ago. Somewhere in the Borders wasn't it?' The agent shuffled nervously.

McMaster bent his chubby frame with difficulty, dropping on one knee to examine the inscription burned in the plaque which in turn was nailed to the rough cross. It read:

Margaret Gilchrist, 1820-1858, beloved wife of the James Gilchrist and mother of May, Flora and Hilda – Let Thy Will Be Done.

'Aye, right enough Mr Lumsden, a sorry business, indeed. In a way the lass is maybe better off here what with the journey back, a trial, a public scandal, aye and more than likely the hangman's noose at the end of it all. Yes, strange to say, for the family at least, it all might be for the best.'

It was going to work! Hell, it was going to work! Jack, for the first time since he had launched himself blindly, spontaneously into this crazy plot, really believed it. All being well they would be under way within the hour. From the cemetery Jack could see the busy preparations for the departure, on the deck and among the rigging of the *Broomielaw*. He felt the sea breeze on his face and for the first time since Ratter's mad breakdown, he genuinely felt in control of the situation.

That morning McMaster had examined the ship's log and taken appropriate notes on Maggie's 'demise'. He had been persuaded that James Gilchrist remained in a dwam and that his girls were all poorly with measles and totally distraught at the loss of their mother. McMaster immediately agreed that he shouldn't risk taking the illness back to the *Helenslee* by insisting on interviewing them.

Jack had supplied a sworn statement witnessed by Walter Lumsden. The die was well and truly cast and both men had made it their priority to keep the preacher Shade well away from McMaster – just in case.

The creak of metal made Jack Zurich look up from his contemplation of the grave. Over Lumsden's shoulder, back toward the rusting iron gates which guarded the only break in the whitewashed walls surrounding the burial ground, Jack peered and felt the blood drain from his face. Weaving between the stones wearing her best Sunday bonnet and carrying a bunch of flowers came Jessie, the Sinclair girl, apparently fully recovered – physically at least - from her ordeal at the hands of Rag.

Jack recalled in a rush that she had befriended the poor McMichael girl almost as soon as they met at Greenock. They had been inseparable in the single women's quarters and here the lass was doing what was only natural – paying her last respects to her friend before they sailed.

However, if she got a glimpse of the cross with Maggie's name, the entire devious ploy would disintegrate in confusion and they would all be heading back to Scotland in chains.

Frantically Jack raised his eyebrows and indicated the direction of the gate. The emigration agent looked at him vaguely for a moment, as if Jack was temporarily sailing without a rudder, then glanced over his shoulder. Lumsden backed away from the graveside.

'Excuse me, gentlemen, that's one of the girls from the ship. She's obviously got herself lost. Forgive me a second while I set her on the track back to the shore. Wouldn't do to leave paying passengers behind, eh?' Lumsden trotted off across the boneyard. Reaching Jessie, he took her firmly by the arm and steered her out of the burial ground and back along the track towards the settlement.

'If you don't mind Mr McMaster we should be heading off too…if you've seen all you want, of course. I would like to sail with the tide.'

The return leg, slightly downhill proved much less taxing for McMaster. He had turned out to be quite conversationalist. 'It must be difficult for the emigration agent, Mr Lumsden, encouraging folk to leave everything familiar behind, then seeing them drop like flies on the voyage.'

'I imagine you have to believe firmly in what you are doing. I know that Mr Lumsden is convinced that he's offering these folk a chance to make a better future for themselves.'

His own words made Jack Zurich reflect, not for the first time, on the terrible burden of responsibility Walter Lumsden had to bear, especially now after this piece of subterfuge. Jack had responsibility also: getting folk from safely from Point A to Point B, but there it ended. He imagined that in some cases Lumsden's liability might last a lifetime. And there were certainly occasions when Walter appeared to be struggling with his own internal demons.

They reached the fringes of the settlement where a gaggle of children and a mangy dog were playing on the track. It was a fine, fresh day, the sort of day when sailors become restive if circumstances kept them on dry land, days when the salt in their blood draws them to the ocean.

Rejoined by Lumsden they walked to the shore.

Walter explained: 'Aye, it was Jessie. She's been a bit wandered and unpredictable since she was attacked. The graveyard is just the sort of place she would be likely to turn up.' After the first lie others seemed to materialise more readily.

It was clear from the way he spoke that McMaster took his task as the Sheriff's agent very seriously. Unable to deliver the prisoner as requested he was now going to make damn sure he had noted every possible angle for his report: 'You wonder, don't you, if the Gilchrist woman ever confided in her husband. Women, I've found are capable of great inner strength if the occasion demands. It's a strange, strange business.'

'Probably stranger than we'll ever know,' said Jack, tasting the salt on his lips and suddenly longing again for the motion of the sea and the cracking of the canvas.

67 Choices, Choices

The shoreline was overflowing with activity. Most of the community had abandoned work for the morning knowing that the two ships were set to sail. Both the *Helenslee* and the *Broomielaw* day boats lay hauled up on the dark shingle and folk were saying their farewells.

Jacob the smith was among them with the stand-in skipper of the *Broomielaw* and a couple of crewmen. They were congratulating each other on the successful repair and installation of the water condenser.

Sitting on the stern of the boat was Innes Macaulay who had walked the shore with Belle and was now recounting the unusual sounds and scents he had encountered on his walks to an intrigued group of islanders, who were standing in the surf.

It was another fine morning and the shadows which swept past Innes had more shape and form than they had done a day or two ago. When he opened his eyes each morning he wondered if he would continue to see just a little more clearly or if the black veil would descend again. It was an agonising time.

To date he had not been disappointed.

As the group around him dispersed he listened to a nearby commotion, able with ease to pick out the strident voices of his three sons. Along the shore the younger men – led by the Macaulay boys – had improvised a game of football against the local lads on the sloping beach. They were using what Innes was told was a pig's bladder for their sport.

However, the ball spent more time in the water than on dry land and threatened more than once to float off on the swell. The game ended abruptly when a huge, flop-eared hound which had been trying to join the action reached the ball in the surf before the players and sank his teeth into the bladder.

Back towards the rowing boats, strolling above the surf, came William Bigland and Queenie, who squealed with delight when she saw the hound take off along the water margin pursued by a pack of sportsmen deprived of their game. Guthrie Macaulay mistimed his flying leap at the beast and took a header into the foam to the delight of emigrants and islanders alike.

Up on the banks lay William's bags and boxes, the few possessions in the world that he could now call his own. Just for a moment, a fleeting moment, as they were being unloaded from the boat and carried up over the crunching dark shingle by a gang of willing helpers, William questioned his decision.

What if he didn't settle here on the island…what if the isolation proved too much…what if? Truthfully there were a thousand and one 'what-ifs'. And then he would think of a gloomy shipping office in Sydney with the lines of clerks hunched over their ledgers, the only noise, the scraping of quill pen on paper. The thought sent a shiver through him.

However, if he found himself ill at ease, he could hop on the first ship to call by. It was as simple as that, he thought.

But for the moment, for the foreseeable future, he could think of nothing he would rather do than go out every morning with the island fishing fleet. Lodgings had been promised with the Repetto family for as long as he cared to stay, in exchange for maintenance duties around the steading.

Yes, he would have like to try his hand on the goldfields, like his cousin Thomas Bigland who was in Victoria. He might yet, he reassured himself as he and Queenie rejoined the group from the *Broomielaw*. Meantime he was content.

'I wish you would stay, Queenie,' he said, looking at his companion with undisguised affection.

'You'll do fine here, William. You've taught me a lot in this past year, whether you know it or not – about life and about people. I now realise I have my own life to lead. What happened between us on Orkney has set us both on a wonderful new course.'

She watched Jack, Zurich and McMaster scramble down the shore. Jack, she thought, had the kindest face she had ever seen. When he smiled he sent a ray of sunlight right into her heart. But for the past day he had seemed so preoccupied, somehow anxious.

'I must go now, William. God will smile on you. I'm sure of that, and who knows, fate may bring us together again.'

Bigland took his gold fob watch and squeezed it into her hand. 'You must take this, Queenie, as a keepsake. It's the only thing of any real value I have to give you.' She smiled and placed the watch carefully in his jacket pocket.

'You hang on to it, William. I'm already carrying something much more precious which will always remind me of you.'

And with that she was gone, waving from the stern of the boat as William Bigland stood amongst his new friends puzzling over Queenie's parting remark about 'something' precious.' Then came the sudden realisation. And it was too late to shout after her.

68 Gilchrist Surfaces

It was the end of the afternoon. The bulk of Tristan da Cunha had disappeared over the northern horizon. Above James Gilchrist's head there was perhaps eighteen inches of space before his gaze came to rest on the low wooden ceiling, the base boards of the upper bulkhead, a space which for the past ten days had defined his world. The planks of wood were roughly hewn and hastily constructed – these bunks and compartments had to be dismantled at Adelaide to take on another lucrative return consignment of wool.

With a venom which he hardly believed himself capable of the shepherd slammed his fist into the hard board directly above him. Pain shot to his elbow and he felt his knuckles rasp on the wood. In his hand was a single, crushed, sheet of paper.

But the blow brought him careering back to reality. It was high time he focused on the awful task that lay ahead.

A few people in the compartment opposite and passing along the steerage stared across but seeing it was only surly, slightly mad, Gilchrist in his bunk as always they returned to their reading or their chores.

As he had done every afternoon since satisfactorily identifying his brother's killers amongst the crew, Gilchrist had been lying silently in his bunk staring at the landscape of knots and whorls, sweeping curves and deep, dark recesses, inscribed by nature on the bedboards. In this fantasy land he had been able to make out the curve of Ward Hill, the back of Craignethan, the entire stretch of Bracken Bank. Yes, and wasn't that Ward burn running across the scene from left to right?

And the longer he stared at this mythical landscape the more at ease he found himself in the setting. There were alarming moments when he thought he might never find his way back out of this tableau constructed by his own tortured imagination.

He knew people were talking about him behind hands. He had been eating, but in a mechanical, disinterested way. And it had been days since he said more than a few words, even to his family. He had hardly seen anything of his new son. The girls had taken to looking after Gip who would, nevertheless, faithfully curl up beside his bunk. She was there, today.

However, something had happened just moments before which had shaken him from his lingering reveries; he had overheard a couple of passing kiddies looking across and pointing. He heard himself described as 'daft Gilchrist'. That had stunned him. The shepherd resolved there and then that this dangerous daydreaming had to stop.

He had been set, or had set himself, a dreadful task on this voyage and he was determined that self-pity, and in particular this unhealthy preoccupation with the places from his past must end, must not deflect him from undertaking the final act avenging his dear brother Robert.

Across the steerage Mr Broadfoot, father of the little girl who had died, was reading from a battered old family Bible to his other child, a boy of about seven. They sat side by side on the lower bunk reading the story of how Jesus calmed the storm. The child, elbows on his knees and chin cupped in his hands listened, and every so often asked a question nodding enthusiastically when

239

provided with the answer. Gilchrist remembered his own father reading from the parables before he and his brothers went to sleep. The echo of the old man's strange lilting accent and his occasional lapses into his native Gaelic lived with Gilchrist. Life had been much simpler then.

As a child James's particular favourite was the story of the miracle of the loaves and fishes – hadn't Jesus always managed so often to make so much of unpromising situations.

It had taken Gilchrist long enough, far too long to rise above his melancholy. He had been unsure of their emigration plans in the first place and now the realities of his quest for vengeance were crowding in on him. He felt caught between two worlds. Every day took the family hundreds of miles further from the hill, his hill, and nearer to – God only knows what, thought the shepherd.

He took from his pouch the pebble from the Ward burn, a treasured keepsake, and placed it on the narrow shelf above his head where he kept his razor and cufflinks. Then he slid his late brother's pocket watch from the jacket which hung on a wooden peg at the head of his bunk. He glanced at the timepiece. Doig would be on deck for his evening pipe. This was it. The moment had come.

Gilchrist took several deep, rhythmic breaths, fillings his lungs then, stiffly, he rose from his bunk rubbing his knuckles. When the sinister task he had set himself was done he would find another hill to call his own in Otago. He would let them see that James Gilchrist was no daftie.

Just then Maggie reappeared from the afternoon infants' class where she had been showing young James to the little ones. She looked tired and massaged her stomach and laid the sleeping youngster on the bunk before dropping with a great sigh on to one of the half barrels covered by rough cushions which served as seats in the steerage.

'I'm away up on deck for some fresh air, Maggie, I'll tak' the dog'

This development caught Maggie completely by surprise. Unable to come to terms with the sudden change of temperament, she hesitated, but after a moment was able to say: 'Do you want some company, James? If you give me just a moment to brush my hair and put on my bonnet…'

'No, a few minutes on my own, Maggie, You sit yourself down. You should be resting. I'm feeling a bit more like myself…sorry if I've been such poor company lately. We must talk more on our plans…'

69 The Best Laid Plans…

The Sweetshaws shepherd's last contact with the sinister Aaron Malise had come a few hours before sailing from the Clyde when he collected a note at the Shipbank Inn – the scene of their fateful rendezvous after his father's funeral.

There was no question but that the man in the cloth mask was mentally unstable. However, for Gilchrist a brief meeting with another crewman, Effort Handler, set up by Malise, in a rat-infested Greenock tenement building, had been the clincher. As he sat in his squalid single room, the moisture soaking through the walls and angry shouts from the apartment next door, this timid, clearly frightened, man refused steadfastly to become involved in any revenge conspiracy. But he was rational and confirmed to James Gilchrist, in every emotional detail, the story of his brother's death.

Brief, and chillingly to the point, the last message from Malise which had been waiting at the Shipbank had been scrawled on a piece of rough paper and sealed with red wax in a re-used envelope. Most days since leaving the Tail of the Bank , sprawled in his bunk, the ocean crashing against the wooden walls, Gilchrist had read and re-read this despatch. By now, he knew it by heart:

'A few weeks ago, James, there were six to answer for your brother's slaying – now there are but four. Connelly and McKinstrie have already paid the ultimate penalty and will have answered to their Maker. By tomorrow night Cartwright will have joined them in eternity. Now you must ensure that the other three pay the penalty. Can I repeat their names which I have already given you to ensure there is no mistake – Evan Richards, an evil Welshman, a scoundrel called Dermot Rag and Davie Doig, a

deckhand. The Lord and the spirit of your brother Robert walk beside you on this sacred mission. God speed.'

Malise had dealt with three of the conspirators; now Richards was lost in the ocean after his fall from the mainmast and the *White Rat*, Dermot Rag, was dead thanks to the remarkable Mrs Sinclair and her blade. It was so clear that Providence had taken a hand on his behalf, thought Gilchrist.

That left Doig, a small, shifty-eyed, toothless individual who seemed to be everywhere on board the *Broomielaw*. However, Gilchrist had quickly discerned a pattern in his activities and set to planning. The remaining murderer was a creature of habit and this, Gilchrist realised, would simplify his end.

With Gip at his heel the shepherd headed for the deck, looking just once more over his shoulder at his stunned and disbelieving wife. The sharp blast of sea air, the smell of salt on the wind, so fresh compared to the dank dungeon of the steerage, momentarily took his breath away and ruffled his thinning hair. Dusk was already seeping over the *Broomielaw*. Two wee boys who had been playing in a corner with a small leather ball, stuffed with cork, halted to pat Gip, who happily swished her tail across the boards. Then, as they resumed their game, Gip followed their leaps and kicks, her every muscle taught, straining, ready at the command to join in the fun.

Gilchrist's gaze swept around the deck. There was no sign of the afternoon watch. Half way up the rear starboard companionway was Doig, silhouetted by a burnished sun which was dipping behind distant clouds. Conveniently, just below his smoking stance was a section of the bulwark which had been shattered in the storm and roped off where repairs were being undertaken. He sucked thoughtfully on his pipe, staring out over the deep. Apart from the youngsters there was no-one else around.

For weeks previously Gilchrist had determined that there would be never by any discussion with the killers, no time would be given for last minute explanations, for lies and excuses. The deed would be done, and done speedily.

At the foot of the companionway Gilchrist saw a pile of redwood batons where the carpenter and his apprentice had been working on the storm damage. The shepherd picked up a length of wood then took the companionway steps three at a time before launching himself at Doig.

For James Gilchrist the next moments had a dream-like quality.

'This is for my brother, you bastard Doig!'

Gilchrist swung the heavy baton through the air and caught Doig a fierce blow across the side of his face as the seaman turned to confront his attacker. His clay pipe shot from his mouth and with a look of agony and bewilderment on his face the sailor was catapulted across the rope and broken rail and dropped out of sight towards the waves.

However, before he knew what was happening Gilchrist stumbled through a confusion of ropes on the companionway, his momentum carrying him forward to the storm-damaged section of torn and splintered wood. Propelled by the weight of the baton, he tripped and staggered above the abyss. For a second he teetered on the open stairway having let the weapon drop into the ocean and then, almost in slow motion, he felt himself plunge over the edge. As he spun in the air he caught a glimpse astern of Doig, face down in the whirling creamy wake of the *Broomielaw*. Then he too hit the water.

Down and down Gilchrist sank from the light into the green darkness, conscious all the time of the rushing in his ears, the bubbles running up from the corners of his mouth, the great emptiness below him and a curious, cold feeling of detachment. Then coughing, spluttering, arms flailing, he broke surface only a few yards away from the baton.

The shepherd could swim after a fashion – hot summer afternoons in the lochan above Melrose as a child had provided him with the basics of a stroke – but he had not been in the water for twenty years. He broke surface at the bottom of a wave trough, the dark walls curving upwards on either side of him, the white-edged crest, impossibly high. Yet he rose with the swell and having swum a few strokes threw himself across the baton which floated close by and was able to gulp air and survey the scene.

There was no sign of Doig but in the gathering gloom the *Broomielaw* was already perhaps a couple of hundred yards distant, her tidy beam and stern windows becoming smaller each time Gilchrist rose from the troughs. He thought he could just make out two small faces peering over the gunwale, staring back in his direction.

Then suddenly, to his utter amazement, at Gilchrist's side, paddling strongly was Gip. He realised that his faithful collie must have followed him over the side.

Together, man and dog watched the ship slowly disappear below their line of vision. Now they were alone, caught halfway between worlds, below them thousands of feet of ocean and above a soaring, darkening blue sky with the first evening stars appearing. So far behind them lay the beloved hills of Scotland and somewhere ahead, the land of opportunity.

His heart had stopped thudding in his chest. He was strangely at ease. Crazy thoughts circled in his mind. He had so many things to do now that he had the vengeance he had so desired. He must speak with the shepherds in the single mens' quarters. There were at least half-a-dozen Maggie had said, mainly West Highlanders. Most would be going to the sheep stations in South Australia and Victoria but perhaps one or two might, like the Gilchrists, be bound for New Zealand. They would have much to talk about.

It promised to be a beautiful sunset and as he gently eased Gip up on to the baton Gilchrist thought how these waves and the deep, drowned valleys between were almost familiar, so like his precious Border hills. It was almost comforting. Darkness would come in an hour or so. The Sweetshaws shepherd stroked the dog and hummed a familiar Border ballad to himself. After all the heart-searching and anxiety of the past weeks he was now calm and focused – that was until he felt something substantial brush past his dangling legs.

70 Lost at Sea

The oil lamp, teased by a draught from the bottom of the door, flickered briefly casting strange, dancing shadows around the walls of Walter Lumsden's cramped cabin. Maggie Gilchrist was in his arms. For the moment he played the role of comforter.

'It's just inexplicable, Maggie. James must have suffered a complete breakdown – to attack the wee man Doig like that, the way the children described.'

It had been forty minutes before one of the boys plucked up enough courage to whisper to his mother what he'd seen unfold on the deck. It was a crucial delay.

Sadly the two men and the dog had gone overboard just at the change of watch and in the gloaming the crewmen had been preoccupied. It seemed to have been a fatal combination of circumstances. In addition Maggie, weary yet cheered and relieved by the seeming improvement in James's appearance and attitude, had fallen asleep on her bunk.

'Oh Walter, if only I'd gone on deck with him. I just can't believe what the children are saying. They must have misread what was happening. James was surely going to the crewman's rescue? Why would he attack him the way the wee ones say. He was not given to violence.'

Lumsden sat Maggie on his bunk, poured a brandy and placed it gently in her hand. 'I do believe the close company kept on board ship can send some of us a little crazy. Take another. It'll help. Then we must get Shade to have a look at you. You have young James to think on.'

The cabin door creaked open and a solemn Jack Zurich stepped wearily inside across the coaming at the base of the door, designed to keep thunderous green seas from pouring inboard during storms. He looked tired and dispirited, and clearly brought no glad tidings.

'It's starting to blow again. I fear there can be little hope for your husband, or my crewman, Mrs Gilchrist. We can only guess roughly where they might have gone over and, as you know, it took us fully an hour to tack around – and now with the darkness…'

'I know, Jack, I know. Thank you for trying.'

Maggie Gilchrist looked at the two men through tear-filled eyes. She suddenly felt as if she wanted, needed, to regain some sort of control over events. For the past three hours as the fruitless search had been under way and all the activity of the ship had been directed to finding the two men, she felt like a bystander. It was a most unnatural and unusual sensation and one which she felt compelled to put behind her.

However, she did experience some relief knowing that James had never learned of the sacrifice and the murderous rage she had shown on behalf of the family just before leaving Sweetshaws. Now James was gone forever, swallowed by the ocean, and would never know.

'I must go to my girls and James. Are Mrs Macaulay and Agnes still with them?'

Jack Zurich nodded and went to help her to her feet but Maggie waved him away. She was pondering new beginnings – and self reliance. She rose, steadying herself with one hand on the bunk.

'No, leave me, from now on I must be mother – and father - to these children. They will need my strength in the miles and months ahead.'

As the emigration agent watched her go he had to admit to himself a special concern for this tough, beautiful woman; no, it was an affection which grew by the hour. Clouded for the moment by tragedy, it was still not to be denied. He longed to reached out again and comfort her. Lumsden had never expected to be drawn ever again in this way to a woman.

He still felt Lizzie and the children close by, there beside him, as always. And yet, somehow, their presence was no longer quite so pressing, or demanding. He had feared that the more he warmed to another human being, the more his memories would torture him. This was not happening. Were they indeed clinging to him, Lizzie and the kiddies, as he had always imagined, or had he perhaps been refusing to let them go? He had never properly considered this possibility. And was he losing his heart to a woman who merely saw him as an authority figure, an official shoulder to cry on?

'No, I'll find my own way along to steerage.' Maggie was at the cabin door thanking Jack Zurich for his offer of help. 'I'd like a moment or two on my own.' With that Maggie Gilchrist – now the widow Gilchrist – was gone

71 The Vulnerable Persona

Sunset had always been Maggie Gilchrist's favourite time of day. At Sweetshaws, when the girls were small, she would often wander to the door of the steading at the end of a busy day and simply stand and stare, out along the Border valley to where the big house of Ferniecleugh lay beyond the stands of trees, smoke drifting from its high chimneys. What adventures she had planned in those quiet moments.

She would watch the sun splashing the hill slopes, the chequerboard of fields, winding tracks and woodland, everything beneath a soothing wash of orange and gold. And she would imagine herself far from the valley in romantic exotic locations.

In earlier years similar reflections had kept her sane when she found herself on the street, hardly more than a child herself. She would look beyond the dark vennels and stinking closes off the High Street and up to the castle. She would imagine herself as Mary Queen of Scots wandering the battlements. Such daydreams would sustain her in the blacker moments at Mrs Stockan's when she felt dirty and used and without hope, or even more recently when James descended into his sombre silences, leaving her alone as he retreated into the dark corners of his mind.

Having settled baby James and leaving Hilda to sing him to sleep Maggie climbed on deck and took up her favourite niche, forward on the port side, filling her lungs with the sharp air of the southern oceans. At these moments she felt oddly detached from everything that was happening around her. Walter had warned the emigrants that as the voyage progressed they would experience the odd sensation of existing in a kind of limbo between their old and new homes, but being part of neither, cut off from everything familiar, undergoing a strange almost mystical transition.

Like a caterpillar shedding its skin or a lobster its shell, they were being born again, renewed. In the words of *The Book of Revelation* Maggie's first heaven and earth were passing away and with it had gone her husband, James. Now she and her family awaited something still hidden yet surely ordained. What would that future hold? Nevertheless, she felt that despite the terrible additional strains and stresses of the past weeks she was coping, just, and now longed for a sight of the Otago coast and to be with her sister-in-law Elspeth beside the Clutha.

And yet, by rights, she should have been in custody and on her way back to Scotland. How often over the years she had exploited her charms to get what she wanted? Too many times to count. It was never deceit, just practicality. And men, all men, or so it seemed, somehow felt she needed protection. Maggie was happy enough to encourage that particular myth.

Look at James, poor dead James, the only one to get close enough to her to learn how calculating and emotionally sterile, Maggie actually could be. Yet, she asked herself, was a cold heart such a handicap? She could give purpose to another life and Walter Lumsden would be blissfully unaware of the role he was playing, as a vehicle for her ambitions as a woman and a mother. After all, the world still looked for a man to head up a family; it was particularly necessary in the pioneer lands such as New Zealand.

Since leaving Tristan da Cunha the *Broomielaw* had been moving sweetly with a side wind and cold, clear weather. She had quickly left the *Helenslee* in her wake. Soon the inky blackness would descend on the vessel as she followed her course across the deep and a nightly wonder would unfold, way up there beyond the mastheads. Maggie snuggled up to one of the smooth companionway posts and waited.

Stars would begin to appear, one by one, on a backdrop of sky which shaded from indigo and orange in the west to darkest blue and then black, above them and then dead ahead, where their destination lay shrouded by the night. On clearer nights the stars could be so bright that they cast a silvery hue over the water, almost as luminous as moonlight. Tonight the occasional cloud scuttled across the face of the moon. The ocean hissed beneath the keel. Yes, this was the adventure Maggie had longed for, striven for, all those brutal years.

Behind her two or three families with young children emerged on deck to gaze at the pinpoints of light in the dark canopy above them. Led by their mother a group of the wee ones sang *Star of Peace*. It seemed to Maggie that the third verse of Jane Simpson's hymn had a particular poignancy for every soul on the *Broomielaw*.

Star of faith, when winds are mocking
All his toil, he flies to thee
Save him on the billows rocking,
Far, far at sea.

'Stargazing, Maggie?' Walter arrived at her side having completed his regular evening tour of the steerage listening to complaints, arbitrating on one hundred and one niggling problem which arose with so many folk crammed in such close proximity...a disputed peg for hanging clothes, the rota for baking or washday. It was always the work of an hour or more. So many judgements to make the emigration agent occasionally felt like a storm-tossed Solomon.

'No, just a few quiet moments. I was just thinking how fortunate I've been to have fallen in with people who trust me, believe in me. I don't think it has happened before.' She was slipping effortlessly into her vulnerable persona.

'Do you believe that our destiny is planned out, up there, among the stars, Maggie?'

She looked at Lumsden then back towards the heavens.

'I believe Walter that we must make our way towards our destiny as best we can. The beauty of these stars simply reminds me that wonderful, remarkable things can be done, if we only believe with all our heart in what we are doing.' She paused, gathering her shawl around her. 'I've spoken to the girls and explained everything...about Brocklebank, about what happened.'

'This has been a hard time for them, Maggie, the deception and now the loss of James will surely hit them hard....'

Maggie drew herself up and reached to squeeze his hands. 'They are my girls. They know everything that was done, was done for them and given time I know they'll understand.'

'Maybe so, Margaret, but I fear you will have to be patient with them. Their father drowned and you are accused of murder. That's a terrible lot for young folk to deal with.'

They stood together for long moments in silence, listening to the *Broomielaw* cutting her path across the ocean and observing the stars come ever more sharply into focus as night descended. Walter shivered, as if suddenly remembering how few moments of such tranquillity had figured in his life of late.

As for Maggie her thoughts had turned to her husband once again, the mystery over his death and to Elizabeth McMichael, cold in the ground, in a grave with Maggie's name on it. It didn't make Maggie immortal but just for that instant, it felt that way.

She could, she felt, deal with anything that life flung in her direction.

'There are so many things I want to say, Margaret. But only one seems important now. I've longed to tell you, almost since that first night I caught sight of you in the hall at Haddington but...'

Maggie lifted her finger and placed it against his lips. 'Shhh! I know, Walter. I know. But let's take a little while. These have been difficult days. Just a little while.'

72 Fit for Duty?

Below decks, passengers were going about their evening business congratulating each other on how speedily they had regained their sea legs. But while they were playing draughts, reading, blethering by the precious light of the oil lamps and carefully guarded candles, a sinister interview was taking place in the day room.

It had opened in a genial enough manner but was destined to conclude in bitter recrimination.

Jack Zurich's mind was in two places because as he listened to a scrubbed-up Silas Ratter asking to resume his role as skipper, Jack could hear the wind building, the sails cracking and the motion of the ship had changed perceptibly. He was anxious to be up on deck.

'With time to contemplate my own actions I now realise that you took command quite legitimately, Zurich. I was out of my head but I'm fully recovered – Shade insists I am – and I should resume my captaincy.' He shifted in his seat, obviously ill at ease.

'I think not Mr Ratter. I'm happy – we're all happy – that you feel you are on the mend but your behaviour was so erratic, I must insist in retaining control of the vessel. Back there, in that storm, you almost sent us all to the bottom.'

'Within a week, Zurich, we'll be among the greybeards – do you truly feel ready to command in such circumstances, boy?' The conciliatory tone had evaporated.

Jack experienced a surge of both anger and fear. How dare this drunken oaf question his skills as a seaman. And yet – in an aggravating way – Ratter had the rights of it; he had never commanded before and the conditions they were soon to meet would be the most testing of the entire voyage.

'And so, Zurich, your intention is to act against the good doctor's advice?'

'If needs must. I will bow to him on matters medical but when it comes to the welfare of this ship and her passengers, I must be the sole arbiter. My first concern is for their safety.'

'You're a cocksure young bastard and no mistake.'

Ratter scowled menacingly across, his eyes narrowing, his voice lowering. 'Remember then whatever happens from here on in, you carry the responsibility.'

'I will return command to you Mr Ratter when the *Broomielaw* is safely docked at Port Adelaide and not a moment sooner. For now I will, of course, formally record your request to resume command and my response.'

The men glared at each other.

'More than that Ratter, if I have any trouble from you or suspect you are undermining my authority you'll spend the remainder of the voyage under lock and key.'

Ratter's face was blotchy and swollen, his eyes bloodshot and fierce and his ruddy nose threatening to explode. He slammed the cabin door behind him and strode off down the passageway to find solace in the company of the estimable Rev. Elijah Shade.

73 That's Entertainment

Tuesday, January 22, 1858 in the Southern Indian Ocean was a day of sleet showers slanting in across the deck from a low, oppressive canopy of cloud.

The *Broomielaw* was well beyond the line of thirty degrees south latitude and heading east south east, almost back on her original course after the Tristan da Cunha interlude; the voyagers were beginning to note a sharper edge to the breeze, a reminder of the great Antarctic ice cap lying beyond the heaving waves and the southern horizon.

Mid-morning, just after school, a group of kiddies tumbled down the stairway into the steerage, the oldest boy spluttering out the news which had their elders grabbing for their bonnets and scarves.

'Mammy, there's a flock o' doos fleeing roun' the ship.'

The arrival of the cape pigeons - a sign of land, distant, but land for all that, the southern tip of the great African continent - brought the emigrants, young and old, on to the deck; the constant sameness of view, the undulating monotony of leaden-coloured seas tinged with curling foam under an expanse of lowering sky could wear down even the cheeriest of souls. They were, in fact, halfway between the southern point of Africa and the great continent of ice.

Two of the crewmen decided to have a pot at the birds - larger and easier targets than the Scottish wood pigeon - with a slingshot. But intercepted, they were quickly engaged in serious debate by May Gilchrist over the morality of killing fellow travellers on the ocean deep. The girl stood, hands on hips, her curly auburn hair tossed by the breeze. Tall and confident like her mother she proceeded to lecture the stunned crewmen on the sanctity of life. In the background Hugh Macaulay watched his sweetheart in action. He was impressed and slightly awed.

And May's decoy action was successful because by the time the sailors, cursing under their breath and shaking their heads, reached the rail, the pigeons had swept away towards the north-east. Deprived of their sport the crewmen returned below decks muttering colourfully about wee lassies who didn't know their place or understand the ways of the ocean.

The ship was heeling more dramatically now in increasingly powerful winds and building seas which occasionally poured down the hatches and flowed under the bunks. Tumbling out of bed cases were being reported on an almost daily basis. The latest was a little boy of about five, Peter Maclean, who was berthed with his family along the way from the Macaulay/Gilchrist 'partment.

After a dull thud halfway through particularly rough evening he was seen, by the lamplight, standing on the boards, looking dazed and scratching his head, having only seconds before been fast asleep in his bunk. Fortunately his fall had been from a lower bunk. Asked how he came to be out of bed he replied earnestly: 'Ah dinna ken, but I've cracked me crown, mither!'

Seeing he was confused but unhurt everyone relaxed and laughed as the wee fellow was given a treat, a comforting glass of milk, and tucked up in his blankets again. The Jersey cow once again had proved her worth in providing a reminder, a little flavour of things familiar, now far, far behind.

Adults were occasionally hurtling out of their bunks also in the stormy conditions and Hugh Macaulay had come to the rescue of his section of the steerage by designing a rope screen affair for the upper bunks. It was one hundred per cent successful in preventing further accident. The young man was for a few hours, a hero of the steerage.

Generally people had amazed themselves by adjusting successfully to the strange, cramped and very public living conditions below deck. Getting dressed in bed beneath the blankets or behind an improvised screen was just one of the skills most had mastered by this stage in the journey. Country folk seemed to accept with a sort of quiet fatalism and stoicism that their lives – for a little while at least were not their own. When trouble on board ship came to one, it generally came to all.

*   *   *   *   *

That Tuesday in January was also a significant day in the social calendar of the *Broomielaw* – it was concert day.

With the weather deteriorating almost by the hour it was decided that the event should be held in the steerage and a rough stage of boxes and boards with Belle Macaulay's second-best curtains, retrieved by special permission from the hold and serving as a screen stretched along one of the crossbeams, was erected in the single men's' quarters for'ard. The choice of venue was quite deliberate – it was at the opposite end of the deck from the little infirmary where victims of the measles outbreak were still recovering.

The show had already been postponed twice because of the storm and the unscheduled landfall at Tristan da Cunha but the young people had been rehearsing at every opportunity and the ways and means committee were able to put on a show worthy of the Glasgow music halls.

There was a ventriloquist, a young Perthshire man who could drink a glass of water while his dummy, a gruff old Highlander, sang *Annie Laurie;* the Coocaddens Gutter Band volunteered to batter out a few rowdy numbers; another young man juggled oranges while standing on his head and Queenie, as promised, had

253

perfected a few card tricks; the Celebus Midgets did a fine tumbling act, there were poetry readings, the wee ones offered a few Scots songs arranged by Mrs Sinclair and finally Jock, the Falkirk fiddler, was to offer a couple of toe-tapping jigs to round off the evening.

A few hours before the performance, the younger Gilchrist girls had ambushed Jack Zurich on a companionway and were trying to persuade him to act as Master of Ceremonies at the evening's entertainment. Despite their pleading, he was unmoved.

'But oh, Mr Zurich, it would be just perfect if you could introduce the acts. You have such a polite way with words.'

Flora Gilchrist was at her coy persuasive best. She smiled sweetly and, with a skill of which her mother would have been proud, she played her trump card. 'And Miss Stout did say if we asked you nicely, you were sure to agree. Young Hilda giggled.

'I see. Queenie said that, did she? It's not one of the duties which I'd expected as stand-in skipper, ladies. But if you insist, and clearly you do, I will do my best. Half-past six I think you said.' The girls danced on the spot then hurried off to spread the glad tidings.

From the top of the companionway Queenie had watched the encounter with a wry smile. She had guessed what was afoot when the girls cornered him. She shouted after Jack: 'You'll make a fine compere, skipper, and I'll be there to cheer you on. You really are a big softie at heart, Jack Zurich!'

Queenie continued to blossom as the journey progressed. It didn't take a sleuth to detect the change. And she also appeared quite at ease about her friend Bigland's decision to come no further than Tristan da Cunha. Jack was also fairly sure there had been than just a friendship between them but he hadn't found a suitable moment to raise the subject.

'Mr Zurich to you, my girl. If you don't mind!' he said with a grin.

'MY girl - I think you are being a little presumptuous there, sir,' she responded.

Good God, thought Jack. This young lady is flirting.

For the evening of the concert both Jack and Walter Lumsden put aside their anxieties about Ratter and his mental condition and questions about the strange medical officer cum clergyman.

However, they were uneasy. There was something disturbing – if unspecific, about the two men which they were unable to pin down. But for the moment the acting skipper was determined to let that spectre lie.

Jack knew that concerts, dances, debates, any change in shipboard routine, in fact, helped break the monotony of the long voyage for the travellers and were important markers on the passage just as were the births – and sadly, the inevitable deaths.

Three hours later he peeked around Belle's curtain at the crowd which was gathering, teenagers jostling, adults chatting to their neighbours, kiddies running around, everyone excitedly anticipating the evening's entertainment.

74 The Drama of It All

The skipper of the *Broomielaw* had borrowed the sailmaker Jontot's large red, white and blue cotton tammy, complete with pompom - and he looked memorable. Peering out from behind the curtain, he was astonished minutes later to see the lines of eager and enthusiastic faces illuminated by the row of oil lamps at the front of the makeshift platform. To loud cheers he took centre stage. One of the young men produced an impressive drum roll on the top of a water barrel.

'Ladies, gentlemen, children and any others who've sneaked in – it gives me intense pleasure to introduce the talented *Broomielaw Minstrels* who will provide tonight's entertainment.' Jack was warming to his MC's role.

'No expense has been spared to bring you leading artists from all parts of the vessel. The performers say that while applause is welcome they would rather that you threw coins or this week's flour ration!'

There were cheers and laughter.

'I have here in my hand a joke given to me by Mr Macaulay.'

At the back of the throng Innes raised an arm in recognition.

'Obviously I can't take credit for it but Innes assures me that it will go down a treat. What do you call a Glasgow man who takes a small shoe size. Why – wee Shooey, of course! Being an Englisher I don't pretend to understand that one.'

And so to hoots of derision and shouts of 'Get Aff!' the show began. Almost everyone had found a vantage point, the wee ones sitting in ranks in front of the improvised stage, adults perched on bunks and barrels and one or two off watch crewmen standing in the shadows.

Jack had given over care of the ship to Macgregor the second mate who was at the helm and for a couple of hours everyone put the grey ocean beyond the wooden walls as far from their minds as possible, despite the constant pitching of the ship. Every act, good, bad or indifferent was wildly applauded with much stamping of feet and cries of 'encore!'

Queenie's card tricks had the audience spellbound. She had auld Tam to thank for this special skill, learned on cold Saturday nights beside the peat fire at Cott. Tam would surely have been thrilled to see his card skills reach such a vast, enthusiastic audience and to see volunteers scratching their heads in disbelief as Queenie pulled the missing Ace from a pocket here or from behind an ear there.

Immediately after the juggler, the show took a dramatic unplanned turn. Jack was about to introduce the Sunday school choir when from the just out of the compere's line of vision the manic figure of Ratter appeared.

'To round off the evening entertainment we have the boys and girls from….'

Ratter stepped nimbly behind Jack and held him fast round the throat with his forearm. As Jack Zurich struggled for breath he could feel the sharp, cold point of a knife or a hand spike being pressed against the soft flesh of his neck.

Initially there were gasps from the audience, a few men rose from their seats then, strangely, they settled again, most clearly feeling, hoping, that this was all part of the show.

Out of the corner of his eye, with immediate relief, Jack saw the two older Macaulay boys edging towards the corner of the stage.

'Sorry to break up the show, folks. But this lad here has taken command of my vessel without as much as a 'by your leave' and it's high time correct authority was re-established. The laws of the sea have a very specific way of identifying Mr Zurich's action – mutiny – that's what is – mutiny!'

Jack felt the blade nick the skin below his chin and he hissed: 'Put the weapon down Ratter. You've lost the place, man.'

At that moment little Peter Maclean who had taken the fall from his bunk left his companions and walked the two or three steps from where he'd been sitting to the front of the stage. He stood directly below Ratter and stared up at the two men, frozen for the past minutes in their dramatic and potentially deadly tableau.

The little fellow's gaze came to rest on Ratter. Their eyes met.

'Are you supposed to be a pirate, mister?'

'Clear off back to your seat, son.'

Without thinking he took the knife away momentarily from Jack's throat to wave the boy back towards the audience and in that fraction of a second, the Macaulay boys were on him, throwing him to the deck, tearing the spike from his grasp and sitting on him for good measure.

Jack ran his finger along his neck – there was the merest trace of blood.

'Well done, lads. Mr Ratter will be spending the remainder of this voyage in the brig.'

The audience who had been on the edges of their seats during this unexpected drama applauded as Ratter was half-walked, half-dragged away from the concert. 'As I was saying before we were so rudely interrupted. We now have the boys and girls of the Sunday school to sing some favourite hymns.'

As the children clambered on to the stage and stood in their pre-arranged rows and Mrs Sinclair seated herself at the harmonium, little Peter Maclean was heard to whisper to his contemporaries: 'Yon mannie was never a pirate. They aye have a parrot and an eyepatch.'

75 Scrubbing Day

Every second Wednesday, providing the weather held fair, the main deck of the *Broomielaw* would look more like the organised chaos of a street market than anything else. Amid much scurrying to and fro and lively exchanges, mattresses and bedding were hung from every part of the lower rigging and on any available peg or pin; it was an event the migrants had come to know as 'Scrubbing Day'.

While mattresses were being dragged up the steep and narrow companionways to be shaken then beaten with switches, the berths below were cleared, brushed and tidied. It was a scene of hectic activity, everyone running here and there and the animals in their deck pens working themselves into a real lather.

But yet again, these days were important watersheds in the long voyage.

This particular Wednesday, in the midst of all this activity, Torrance and Hilda were busy examining a formidable many-legged beastie which had been shaken from Flora's mattress and which scurried off across the deck boards in search of some dark corner. Poor, sadly missed, little *Beetles*, who had died tragically from the choking fit in the early days of the voyage, would have happily adopted this creature whereas most youngsters would rather have run a mile.

The children watched it scuttle off across the boards then ran to break the exciting news to Flora that there had been a monstrosity lurking in her pillow. First person they encountered was Innes Macaulay. They told him of their find.

'Do you think that beastie came all the way from Greenock, Mr Macaulay, asked Flora.

Torrance wasn't slow off the mark. 'I don't see why not,' said the boy, 'it's a wonder it didn't crawl into Flora's ear and have a wee look around!'

'Away you go you pair and don't be terrifying Flora with your tales.'

Innes Macaulay, who played no active part in Scrubbing Day was wandering the deck, feeling his way, hand over hand along the rail as usual, picking up snippets of conversation where he could, between the sharp thwack of the switches on the blankets and the excited laughter of the children. He was sifting the bustle for any gems and would halt for a minute or two if the exchanges became particularly meaty

or gossipy.

For some reason his blindness on these occasion also allowed Innes to don the cloak of invisibility among the crowds of emigrants and he could stand on the fringe of some very colourful conversations, head bowed, apparently deep in thought as the protagonists went at it hammer and tongs. It was as they imagined his blindness had automatically rendered him deaf also.

Innes was so aware of sounds now – of the constant thud of the sea on the hull, of feet on the decks, occasional male cursing. Groans, squeaks and knocks from the rigging. Already on his stroll this particular afternoon he had collected more details of the alleged indiscretions by the matron which had been the talk of the steerage for days. It was said that this brazen woman who was supposed to be a pillar of morality and an example to others had instead been organising drinking sessions in her cabin and inviting crewmen and some of the single girls along to join the fun.

She was directly answerable to Shade, the surgeon/clergyman and why he had not acted to halt this nonsense was baffling.

Macaulay knew that whooping cough had made an appearance in the steerage and one or two of the younger children had it severely. He had also learned by keeping his ears open that the measles outbreak was almost over. There was another baby due, slight complications there apparently and the consumptive boy who was to have been dumped at Madeira had had another setback.

The day's highlight for Innes, as he stood bracing his legs against the motion of the ship, was to listen to a heated discussion between one of the male passengers, a young man with a well-educated tone, who stupidly had expressed disappointment that they had not yet encountered a proper storm. He was getting a telling off from a group of mothers. Although Innes arrived towards the close of the exchange, one woman, with a restrained, almost genteel, manner, was lecturing the young man.

'For the mere curiosity of seeing the wild ocean fling this vessel about you would have out little ones in discomfort and alarm, Mr Cuthill. Eternal shame on you!'

The young man, notebook in hand as ever, protested his innocence in the face of this onslaught. 'All I meant was that it would be unfortunate for us all to have made this one-in-a-lifetime journey and never have seen the true majesty of the ocean. Have none of you any romance in your souls?'

Unrepentant the first woman made to go but from the sidelines a rough female Glasgow voice was having none of it.

'Romance is it? Look son, the best thing you could do is away an' bile yer heid!' There was noisy applause at this comprehensive and traditional put-down.

From what Walter Lumsden had indicated in his emigration lectures up and down the country, the chances of escaping a severe storm, or even a hurricane, during the passage through the Roaring Forties which they were now preparing to face, were on the thin side of nil.

Despite being put in his place this time by the regiment of women, Cuthill the notetaker and stormseeker looked likely to get his wish sooner rather than later.The wind was freshening from the Sou'west and the cleaning was progressing at a good pace. Innes noticed that the sun had come out as his hazy view of the world was suddenly illuminated and he felt the warmth on his cheeks. The rays seem to penetrate to his very soul. He felt invigorated.

Clearly, he knew, he would have to say to Belle that he was noticing an improvement in his eyesight. Formless shadows of a week ago were now achieving vague definition. Now his sight was sufficiently improved to allow him to avoid large objects in his path. It was a wonder Belle and the boys hadn't noticed how much more mobile and alert he had become.

Actually, if he was honest with himself, he wasn't quite sure what was holding him back from saying; and he worried that perhaps he had been carrying his handicap as a sort of badge of courage. Yes, he must tell Belle. Meantime he would have to check just how much his vision had improved in the past two or three days, He moved forward towards the bow of the *Broomielaw.*

76 Brothers-in-Arms

Through the iron grill of the brig the Rev. Elijah Shade, Bible beneath his arm, announced his arrival to the prisoner Ratter who was stretched out of the rough bunk.

'I'm told Mr Ratter that you are in need of either urgent medical or spiritual comfort.'

The crewman twisted the heavy key in the loch and pushed the door open. Shade entered and seated himself on the bench to one side of the bare, windowless box.

'Leave us now, Cobb.' He dismissed the sailor with a disdainful wave of his hand. The brig door was slammed shut behind the crewman.

Shade was smirking. He whispered: 'Now, Mr Ratter, we could start with a prayer. Something along the lines of the Lord assisting those prepared to help themselves but leaving the limp brains to fend for themselves in the brig. That was, by the way, some performance you put on at the concert last night.'

'Bugger off, Peter. By the way, where in God's name did you come up with Elijah Shade. Mind you, it suits a sinister, shadowy devil like you. It beats me how those folk in Argyll fell for that itinerant preacher line. Now, what do you want? I've no time for this. I've a lot of thinking to do.'

Shade produced a small flask from inside his jacket and carefully unscrewed the cap. He offered the drink. 'Here, calm yourself, dear elder brother of mine. Everything will fall into place. Take a sip of this malt and everything will seem less fraught.'

Silas Ratter grabbed the flask and threw a good measure over his throat, wiping his mouth with his sleeve. He looked across at the other man, clearly shaping his thoughts.

'Listen, Elijah Shade, high priest, father confessor and medicine man, if it wasn't for the fact that you've stashed those Lochgilphead jewels somewhere on my bloody ship, I'd shop you, brother or no brother. There are strange things happening on this voyage and from what I can see you are just too close to events.'

The captain hauled himself into a more comfortable position, belched noisily, and gulped another shot of whisky.

The phoney preacher raised his hands in supplication.

'Innocent of all charges, I assure you. And I would caution you strongly, my sibling against that course of action; that would be very much against your interests.

'As they say, if I sink, Silas, I'll be taking you with me. You knew my background when you found me a posting on the *Broomielaw*.'

Adopting a new tack the captain sat up straight: 'Well, where were you when I tried to take my command back at the concert?'

'Listen, I warned you often enough that Zurich, having put Matt Bostock on his backside, had the support of the crew and the goodwill of the passengers. But did you pay any attention? Oh no! It was a lost cause before you started. As soon as you get near the bottle there's a disaster waiting to happen. It clouds your vision.'

Peter Ratter, aka Elijah Shade, peered over the top of his reading glasses at his elder brother: 'What exactly were you planning to do, man the *Broomielaw* single-handed? You're better off in here.'

'Christ almighty, you really should have been a preacher, Peter, like our father. You're such a self-righteous, sanctimonius bastard sometimes. Anyway have you considered the fact that if anything happened to you, the jewels might be lost forever.'

The 'minister' stood up. 'Take it from me the jewels are safe enough where they are for now – like yourself; they won't be going anywhere until we reach Adelaide.'

'You expect me to swallow all your explanations. For the moment you hold all the cards, Peter, but there's still a lot of ocean between here and South Australia.'

Silas Ratter looked his younger brother up and down. In appearance they were certainly similar, the same puffy face and baggy, close-set eyes, the same small mannerisms, picking at their nails, opening their eyes wide when asking questions. Yet, so far at least, no-one on the voyage seemed to have made any connection Having got away with their deception thus far both men were privately convinced they would see it through to Australia.

'Just remember, we still have a palm or two to grease. We're not home and dry yet. Neither of us would have been allowed on board this vessel if our backgrounds and our connection had been known, if our service records had not been conveniently filed.'

The minister/surgeon turned for the door, tugging at his dog collar. He hadn't checked the jewels in the past week or so. He must do that as a matter of urgency.

*   *   *   *   *

Up above Innes had almost finished his daily ritual of gazing intently, from his seat on the hatch cover, fifteen or twenty feet across the rolling deck to the rope fretwork of the lower rigging which stretched upwards, way above his head to the foremast. It was happening. There was no doubting it. Every day the outlines had become sharper, more clearly defined. He was regaining his eyesight.

The clamour of 'Scrubbing Day' was over and just in time. A chill and clinging sea mist swept over the Broomielaw and the mattresses and blankets were speedily dragged down to steerage.

Just as he prepared to return below deck to complete one of his allocated daily chores, putting out the plates and spoons for dinner, Innes was suddenly on the alert. What was that acrid aroma he was catching? There was the vaguest hint, the merest whiff of burning timber.

He stopped, pinched his nose tightly, and then breathed deeply again. There was no mistake. Close by he could hear a soft voice humming gently. Innes knew that Maggie Gilchrist was taking baby James in her arms for a stroll on deck before tea.

He shouted urgently: 'Is that you, Maggie? You must run and alert Mr Zurich. I smell burning wood.'

Maggie was quickly at his side.

'I smell nothing, Innes. And there's nothing to be seen through this mist. Do you think the fire is here, here below us on the *Broomielaw?* In the hold, perhaps?'

'No, no, it's being carried from a distance on the breeze, I'm sure. Quick you must fetch the skipper.'

As Maggie ran aft, baby in her arms the voice of the for'ard lookout rang shrilly through the moist evening air: 'Flames! Flames off the starboard bow!'

77 So Far From Home

'Away aloft!' The call from Jack Zurich sent crewmen scrambling into the rigging as frantic efforts were made to adjust the set-up of the sails allowing the *Broomielaw* to tack around towards the flames, manoeuvring all the time to keep the lurid orange and russet glow in sight.

Soon the rails were crowded with passengers peering into the gloom. As they neared the stricken vessel folk on the *Broomielaw* were aware of plumes of dark smoke amid the sea mist and gradually the outline of the burning vessel ghosted into view. It was like a scene from some appalling nightmare.

Across the swell it was clear that the other ship had been burning from stem to stern and was listing heavily to port and was well down at the bow.

The more experienced among the *Broomielaw's* crew saw by the way that the fire had spread that it had probably started somewhere midships. She could not remain afloat much longer. There were gasps of dismay as this realisation spread like an infection along the rail.

The sight of the catastrophe struck real terror into the hearts of the most hardened seamen. Fire is the constant shadowy terror that stalks every sailing ship. The hellish sight also left most of the passengers ashen-faced, gripping the gunwales with white knuckles. Women were shushing their children and crushing kerchiefs to their mouths; any of the men who had been wearing bunnets or caps felt a strange desperate need to bare their heads.

They edged slowly, carefully, into the raft of devastation which surrounded the stricken craft. 'Keep an eye aloft there for people in the water,' Jack Zurich shouted up through the mist and trailing smoke to his lookout.

From somewhere above came the response: 'Aye, aye skipper!'

It was early evening and it was obvious that ship had been burning for hours; it was all but consumed. The fire was moving towards the bow where crowded a group of passengers, mainly women and children it seemed, silhouetted in the face of the flames, a ghastly, beleaguered huddle, clearly to terrified to jump into the deep, some too young to understand just how critical their situation had become.

Clearly the ship was in her death throes. As they closed in, the blackened and blistered superstructure, stern and midships, offered a dreadful sight, broken spars and tangled rigging trailing in the water and what remained of the after deck glowing hot still in several places.

Spasmodic yellow tongues of flame and showers of sparks leapt skywards as beams collapsed with a creaking and splintering into the lower decks. Embers drifted upwards on the breeze. The pungent odour of scorched timber now filled the nostrils of the witnesses. There was also a sweeter, more sinister aroma on the breeze. It went un-mentioned.

Destruction was total behind the wall of fire which was creeping mercilessly on to the foredeck.

The three-foot diameter mainmast had collapsed and the jib hung in the water. 'Good God almighty, sir – there are people out there on that bowsprit trying to escape the flames.' The helmsman's voice quivered with emotion. Even a man who had witnessed so much in an adventurous life was stunned by what he saw.

'Watch your wheel Mr Macgregor. Watch your wheel,' Jack gently reminded the second mate , laying a reassuring hand on his shoulder. And in a quieter tone: 'Tuck us in there as tightly as you dare, David.'

But Macgregor was correct. There were people out there clinging on to the bowsprit like so many ants crawling along a reed. Every so often the great timber would dip beneath the swell and when it broke surface again there would be one or two fewer souls on the woodwork. Even as the *Broomielaw* made her approach people could be seen slipping into the water never to surface again.

Thank God the weather and the visibility close in was reasonable, thought Jack. If they hurried some of those folk might be saved.

As he stood with the helmsman, a slow, aching realisation was growing in Jack Zurich's soul. As he gave desperate orders he tried as best as he could to push it from his mind but it came screaming back at him, more forceful and insistent each time. It grew from possibility to certainty. This could only be one ship; it had to be *The Spirit of Speed,* the elegant clipper which had followed them out of the Clyde and edged them into Tristan da Cunha - the vessel with the other members of the Circus Caledonia on board.

'Only one dinghy standing off her that I can see, skipper,' came the stark cry from the lookout.

Jack Zurich's head was spinning. He recalled the blacksmith's remarks about the defective oven. Ritchie perhaps should never have left Tristan da Cunha until that repair was completed satisfactorily. But it was his style to press on. There had been upwards of 250 people on that vessel. One boat with survivors; surely there must be more, somewhere out there in the sea haar.

Now Jack could clearly see the distinctive figure of Mercury, the blistered and smoke-stained figurehead of the *Spirit of Speed*; any lingering doubts as to the identity of the ill-fated vessel evaporated.

78 Saving the Few

'Lower number three and four boats and stand by to pick up survivors. Mr Jones, open the captain's state room as additional accommodation and put extra beds into the infirmary and cabin passengers' saloon. Mr Paterson, clear the passengers away from the port side.' Jack looked down at the families lining the rails and shouted: 'If any of you ladies have nursing experience please report to the Rev. Shade.'

All Jack's intuition, training and common sense told him what was required. His orders to the junior officers were firm, authoritative and confident. Yet still his eyes ranged around the hellish scene. Somewhere out there in the thin, flesh-chilling mist there must surely be another dinghy, a raft, something to which survivors could cling. At most, in and around the dinghy, there would be 40 people; perhaps another 16 or 17 still on the foredeck and the sagging bowsprit.

Shade arrived at the skipper's side.

'Well, Mr Shade, I think your services are going to be in great demand this day.'

'What are you saying, Zurich, as a minister or as a surgeon?'

'From what we can see out there, I should think it will be both.'

At that moment the stricken vessel sank deeper in the water and with a sickening groan a section of the burning bulwark on the port side gave way, tumbling into the ocean, throwing up water and steam as it struck the surface. The emigrants gasped. The *Spirit of Speed* was breaking up.

'Yes, I would say most definitely both,' Jack whispered under his breath.

Conchita had appeared on deck and clambered on to the rail to survey the scene. She glanced across at Walter Lumsden as he passed among the stunned passengers. She looked ready to cry.

'It's the *Spirit of Speed*, Mr Lumsden, isn't it?'

'I fear so, Conchita, I fear so.'

*   *   *   *   *

The boats had already been lowered and the crews were rowing steadily across the debris-strewn gap between the ships. Hamish had been one of the first passengers forward to offer his services and now crouched in the lead boat. At the same time the dinghy from the *Spirit of Speed* was making some headway in the direction of the *Broomielaw*. Jack Zurich, straining to see through the smoke and swirling mist, was astonished to see the dishevelled, despairing figure of Alec Ritchie, the skipper, standing at the stern of the dinghy, staring back at the disintegrating vessel.

Dressed in his uniform of trousers and a salt-stained navy-coloured heavy wool jacket, decorated with tarnished gold buttons he stood erect, grasping the tiller. He seemed to be slowly shaking his head, as if in disbelief.

The *Broomielaw* boats, lifting and dropping with the swell, oars slicing clear of the sea and then digging deep again into the dark waters came upon the first survivors floundering in the lee of the burning vessel, hanging on to barrels and spars. The crewmen began dragging them like half-drowned rats over the gunwales, dropping into the water themselves on one occasion to help three kiddies who had been clinging to a hatch cover to safety.

In fact, there were significantly more people in the water than it had seemed at that first, terrible glance.

However, to the dismay of everyone watching, as the tongues of flame reached out the survivors now jammed together on the perilously slopping bow, a mother with a child in her arms stepped forward, stumbled to the shattered gunwale and stepped into space. She knifed feet first down into the dark water – and did not resurface.

A mournful keening rose from the *Broomielaw* emigrants as they witnessed this horror; then there was much pointing at the burly figure of Hamish who was now standing in the bow of the lead rescue boat, stripping off his shirt. He dived into the dark green water and appearing and disappearing between the troughs, struck out strongly across the twenty or so yards to the dying vessel. He clambered up a trailing section of the forward jib to reach the terrified passengers on the foredeck which, with minutes, was certain to be engulfed by the flames. It was clear he was trying to calm the distraught survivors.

In a desperate manoeuvre the sailor at the helm of the lead boat edged in under the bulk of the sloping forward section of the *Spirit of Speed*, in among a tangle of stays, shrouds and shattered timber, almost within touching distance of the timber walls. Flame and shadow danced on the water as, one by one, Hamish assisted the emigrants ten feet down the angled forward deck and into the arms of their rescuers.

Meantime the second boat was picking up the scatter of people who were still floundering around the now half-submerged bowsprit and its accompanying debris.

It took perhaps fifteen minutes to complete this exercise and by the time the last victim had been escorted to safety the flames were only feet away and the gunwale of the rescue boat felt hot to the touch. Hamish returned for one last time, clambering up the wooden slope to check that everyone was clear. To his horror he saw rats crowding a corner of the tilting deck, squealing before leaping like lemming into the Indian Ocean.

'Get down here, man, afore she goes!' Was it a trick of the eerie, shifting light or was the stricken ship beginning to roll? The alarm in the helmsman's voice was unmistakeable. What was left of the *Spirit of Speed* was now making odd, heart-stopping rumbling and creaking noises and Hamish had reached the highest point on the bow.

'Stand off, Donaldson, and I'll dive for it!' The shrill voice bounced across the water and almost as soon as the oarsmen had pulled boat into open water, Hamish arced into the water, remarkably gracefully for such a big man, surfaced, and made for the hands which already reached out to haul him aboard.

On the deck of the *Broomielaw* Jack Zurich hissed: 'Oh, sweet Christ, No!'

With the gentlest of motions, in the space of a few seconds, the Spirit of Speed rolled over on top of the Highlander and in seconds she slipped, escaping air bubbling and still hot timbers hissing, beneath the waves.

For just a moment the gusting wind was the only sound to be heard across this forlorn scene. Then in the second boat, from among the shivering collection of survivors, a strange, bedraggled, lanky figure rose from the middle benches and before the crewmen could reach out to restrain him, and without a word or gesture, he slipped, almost slithered, over the side, the fathomless waters immediately closing over his head.

There were more groans from the onlookers aboard the *Broomielaw* convinced that this was another poor, tormented, demented soul taking their own life. But they had failed to notice that in entering the cold, dark water, the gangly man was in control, purposeful, in what did seem from a distance like a last, despairing act.

Having witnessed Hamish vanish Conchita was now being comforted by the folk around her, But through the rail she saw the thin man follow Hamish into the water and seemed immediately re-energised.

'It was the Eel, Mr Lumsden. I mean Mr Eales. I'm sure it was.' She had visibly brightened.

Walter thought it a strange reaction to having just seen two of her best friends disappear into the deep.

*   *   *   *   *

A minute passed, then two, as the boats began to pick their way through the debris field of barrels, spars and rigging searching, searching in the vain hope that Hamish might have forced out from under the sinking ship.

Then, a few yards astern of the lead boat, a thin head and beady eyes broke surface, dragging a mop of orange hair out of the water with him. Hamish had been returned to the land of living by the supposed suicide who, in a couple of powerful side strokes, had dragged the Highlander next to the boat. Both were hauled to safety.

On the brief return leg to the *Broomielaw,* The Eel began to press Hamish's chest and to the amazement of the oarsmen leant across the big man who lay on the bottom boards and appeared to kiss him several times forcefully on the mouth. They saw Hamish's chest rise and fall as the air was forced into his lungs.

Then, just as they drew alongside the *Broomielaw,* Hamish retched violently again and again, threw his head to one side and

269

spewed up what looked like half the Indian Ocean. The gangly man slumped back against the bench and with a smile of relief watched the big man coughing and grabbing great gulps of air, but slowly recovering.

One by one the survivors were helped, some half-carried up the rough rope ladders to the deck. Blankets had been laid on the boards to allow Shade to check quickly on those in a collapsed state – and there were many. Each face bore the imprint of that day's terrible events, their eyes, glassy mirrors of a disaster which would live with them waking and sleeping for the rest of their days.

The scene, with the stark realisation that most of the complement of the *Spirit of Speed* had been lost, was a heart-rending one. Walking 'wounded' stood in despairing groups, nursing cuts, bruises and minor burns; clinging to each other. A few numbed individuals stared out across the gap to where flotsam still swirled on the water, to the spot where the *Spirit of Speed* had broken up.

Eales was reunited with his comrades from the Circus Caledonia and they consoled each other over the loss of their companions. Conchita and Hamish went to sit together on the nearby companionway. All the little lady was heard to say was: 'That was such a brave act but I've said this before, Hamish, you have nothing left to prove. You must stop torturing yourself.'

Shade moved along the line of casualties, nodding reassuringly and speaking quietly to each person in turn, then summoning crewmen to help carry the injured to the infirmary.

* * * * *

Finally, when the deck was almost clear and the two lifeboats were being hauled up out of the water Shade was confronted by a young woman, about twenty years old, face blackened by smoke, sitting with her back to the mainmast housing. Her eyes were closed and she was breathing deeply and deliberately, as if she had just run a long race.

'Are you injured in any way, young woman,' said Shade, bending to look at her.

'Why, Mr Shade, this is a surprise!'

Her bright blue eyes, now wide open, fixed him to the spot. The physician gulped. Anne Dagger, the impertinent, provocative lass from Tarbert who had served him tea and scones at the Meek mansion on the hill just before his departure, smiled a conspiratorial smile. This was the serving girl's great adventure. She had been Australia-bound.

'So this is where you ended up, Rev. Shade.' He crouched nearer and laid his hand on her forehead. This is most inconvenient, thought Shade. In fact, he realised, it was more than inconvenient; it was bloody disastrous.

'Am I injured, you ask. Just a few scratches, really. I'm a lot better off than those poor folk. She pointed out to the open sea. 'But you're a surgeon, also, I see. My, my, is there no end to your talents?'

'Yes, well, I'll explain this to you later…'

Shade glanced nervously over his shoulder. In a rush, came memories of the smiling parade of trusting old widows, handing over their family heirlooms. 'There were a lot of folk around the loch wondering where exactly you had disappeared to, Mr Shade.'

He didn't respond. Most of them had more money than they knew what to do with, Shade reassured himself. He made a very plausible missionary in all the moribund parishes he had visited, even if he said it himself. The old dotery ministers were usually happy to let him do the foot-slogging round the parish.

But he was not about to let his Australian nest-egg, his entire future slip away. This needed swift, and decisive action.

'Listen, Miss Dagger. Keep all this to yourself, would you? For the moment, anyway. Not for my benefit, you understand. Rest assured I had my reasons for leaving. I wouldn't mind who you told but it could be embarrassing for others on this ship.'

'Really? Whatever you say, Mr Shade. Happy to. But I fear this going to cost you something shiny, or my name's not Anne Dagger.' She looked to be in control.

'I'll meet you on deck just before curfew, Anne.'

Theatrically Shade rose, patting the girl on the head. In as loud a voice as he could reasonably allow himself given the tragic circumstances he said: 'Just you calm your self, lass. And get those daft ideas out of your head. You'll think differently after a few hours sleep.'

Anne looked up, confused, wondering what that performance had been all about and a few folk close by cocked an ear. The man was clearly two ha' pennies short of the shilling. But as he moved off across the deck to assist other survivors Shade was thinking: 'Mission accomplished.'

The sea mist vanished almost as quickly as it had arrived, as if its task of screening this tragedy was complete. With the clearance it was heart-achingly apparent that no other lifeboats lay out there on the deep. Behind the *Broomielaw* the most dramatic coloursplash sunset of orange and burnished gold illuminated the horizon, as if mimicking the inferno which had taken the *Spirit of Speed* and 200 poor souls to the bottom.

79 Reliving the Nightmare

Walter and Jack Zurich stooped low under the deck beams as they left the now overcrowded infirmary and made their way through the ship to the state room where mattresses had been laid out and where the bulk of those rescued were recovering and were being fed and watered.

More than ever the two men felt, having witnessed the loss of their travelling companion, that their ship, their precious *Broomielaw,* was now a sanctuary as much as a sailship. For the moment, however, it was also, understandably, a vessel in shock.

Jack had seen ships go down before, had plucked poor drowning souls from the water but he had never experienced anything quite so painful, and yes, personal.

Through the open skylight of the state room drifted the hum of the breeze through the taughtened weather rigging high above.

It had seemed improper somehow, almost an insult to those lost, to have sailed away so quickly from the wreckage-strewn patch of ocean where the *Spirit of Speed* had been lost. Yet he knew they had a greater responsibility to the living.

Now there were a whole series of logistical problems to be faced – dozens of extra passengers meant drinking water would have to be even more severely rationed, the same applied to the food supplies. Space was at a premium and the risk of the rapid spread of disease all the more acute in these unusually cramped conditions

Jack felt the bereavement of the ship and its passengers almost as if it had been his own vessel. Perhaps it was because both sailing ships left the Clyde together, perhaps because he had sailed with Ritchie and knew him to be one of the most experienced skippers at sea. For his part Walter had begun to believe in the past month that he was coming to terms with his dread of the ocean, if not quite yet with the black memories of the Hunter River. However, this new catastrophe had shaken him to the core.

Entering the state room they were both wrapped up in these thoughts. There were two serious burning cases in the infirmary but here in the upper deck most were suffering only minor burns, superficial cuts and bruises. A few, not surprisingly, were slowly recovering from exposure and shock. Some were sleeping, a few wept into their straw-filled pillows or comforted each other.

Jack spoke to an orderly and arranged for a register of survivors, and where possible a list of those lost, to be compiled. Ritchie's log had disappeared in the scramble to escape the burning ship.

Belle, Queenie and their helpers moved from bed to bed offering hot drinks and comfort as they went. After seeing baby James settled and with May and Hugh baby-sitting, Maggie Gilchrist had joined the women helpers.

In one corner Shade was seated on the end of a mattress talking to two young men, the older of the two had his head swathed in bandages. A crosspiece had tumbled on him as he had desperately tried to stay above surface. It was a minor miracle that he had survived but both men wore a haunted, questioning expression as if they were constantly reliving the events of the day and that even now they did not fully understand the enormity of what had taken place.

In fact, there had been 28 people in the lifeboat and another 18 had been plucked from the foredeck by Hamish or dragged out of the water close to the tumbled bowsprit. Forty-six rescued from a crew and passenger complement of nearly three hundred.

And yet if the *Broomielaw* hadn't made her enforced stopover at the Tristan da Cunha settlement, the *Spirit of Speed* would have been alone in her final hours, alone on an empty, unforgiving ocean, just another disappearance to cause the ringing of the Lutine Bell back at the Royal Exchange in London, another sad statistic of the great emigration adventure appearing on Lloyd's List:

> *Declared Lost, somewhere between the Cape and Port Adelaide, on or about January 23, 1858, the Spirit of Speed, out of Greenock, no known survivors.*

It was a small consolation but at least in this case there were witnesses to her final agonies; families would not have the gnawing pain, the lifetimes without closure.

The shipping companies, with almost fifty years experience now on the Australia and New Zealand runs, were unanimous in their opinion that most migrant ships which vanished without trace on the long haul were destroyed by burning rather than by any other marine hazard such as storms.

Walter stopped for a moment beside Charlie Eales, or as he was better known in the funfair business *The Eel,* a man who was able to hold his breath underwater for over five minutes and whose unusually long and supple body had earned him the obvious stage name.

'I'm the emigration agent, Walter Lumsden. We met at my office in Queen Street. That was an incredibly brave thing you did out there today, Mr Eales. The Eel hauled himself up on to an elbow.

'Charlie will do, boss. It was nothing to speak of. Hamish is a big, strong lad and the chances were that with the ship going down the way she did, he would have been pushed aside rather than dragged straight down. It was worth a look-see.'

'Nevertheless, it took a lot of courage.'

'Truth is Mr Lumsden, I'm more in my element down there than I am on dry land, or here between the timbers.' He patted the wooden boards beside his mattress. 'My mother used to jest that all I was missing were the gills and she could have sold me to the fishmonger.'

'But diving into the ocean like that…for most people that would be the ultimate nightmare. When you think of the miles of dark water below you….'

'Actually, the toughest part of what I did this evening was working in salt water rather than fresh – too buoyant you see. It's bad enough moving about in the cold and near total darkness, threading your way through ropes and timbers, but struggling down to any depth took time. The big man could only have been ten or twelve feet beneath the surface.'

'Well, you have our thanks, and that of your comrades from the Circus, I'm sure…and my sympathies, of course, for the loss of the other members of your troupe.'

Eales had been telling them that the swarthy sword swallower, the juggler, and Alice, their bearded lady, had all perished in the first hour of the fire crushed beneath the toppling mizzen mast.

They looked around in the sombre flickering lights at the other survivors. Maggie was bathing the forehead of an elderly woman who was still drifting in and out of consciousness while Belle and Queenie passed out extra blankets.

Jack now faced the task which he had been putting off, skating around for fully an hour. He must soon confront Ritchie, who had been lodged in the privacy of the skipper's cabin, vacated by the prisoner Ratter. 'Will you come with me, Walter. I've a feeling I'll need some moral support?'

The stand-in skipper knew he must question Ritchie just as soon as possible to try to get some formal account of how the *The Spirit of Speed* was lost. As much detail as possible had to be noted and an accident report completed and witnessed for despatch to the Board inspectors just as soon as they made port. And the questioning had to be done while events were fresh in everyone's mind.

* * * * *

Having already spoken briefly to the survivors – crew and passengers – Jack Zurich had a broad picture of the course of events. And it made for difficult listening.

Most telling evidence of all had come from the mate, Sam Welsh, a gruff, gnarled Yorkshireman who they found among seafaring friends in the cookhouse, nursing a glass of brandy.

He explained how the dreaded cry of 'Fire Below!' had rung through the ship just after breakfast had been taken. The fire had been discovered in a forward cabin, starboard side. A dropped

275

light, a toppled lamp or simply natural combustion - they would never know.

When discovered the fire had already worked its way down through the boards and into hold. It was already so intense that it had proved impossible to get near enough to force open the door and get to the seat of the blaze. With a sense of relief on behalf of the Tristan da Cunha smith, Jack learned that the fire had not begun in the faulty oven in the galley.

After initial disbelief and reluctance to stir themselves the passengers had crowded on to the deck, having gathered their few possessions from steerage and were milling about in a growing panic. The blaze had taken a fierce hold amd the deck beams were soon collapsing.Welsh recalled with a shudder how their shouts and screams mingled with the distressed cries of the cattle and sheep penned on deck.

The fire had progressed rapidly toward midships, wrapping spars and masts in wild flame until they collapsed, eating away at the structure of the boat and crushing the emigrants crowded below. As the mate talked through these harrowing scenes he began quietly to weep, his head dipped, all the time trying to stifle his sobs, as if, despite the immensity of the tragedy, it was still not the manly thing to do. It was the guilt of the survivor.

'You understand, Mr Zurich. The noise on the deck was unbelievable. It was panic, pure and simple. No orders could be passed and we managed to launch only one of the lifeboats as the ship fell to pieces around us. The rest of the lifeboats were destroyed.'

'That would be the boat which was standing off when we arrived, Welsh?'

'The same, sir.'

'Then how was it that with scores of his passengers still in peril your skipper ended up at the tiller of the only safe haven?'

'That I fear, only one person can truly answer. Suddenly he was just there. That's all I can say.'

Welsh went on to describe how firefighting efforts failed amid the chaos as the burning rigging and sails began to tumble around them and chillingly of how a kind of fever for jumping overboard to escape the inferno seemed to grip the emigrants. He bit his lip as he spoke. Every memory seemed to be driving a blade into him. Tormented by the heat, as the *Broomielaw* passengers had seen for themselves, women leapt overboard with their offspring in their arms – and sank to rise no more. Whole families, said Welsh, had linked hands, prayed briefly, then leapt from one terrifying element into another. Others, as they saw, had clung in clusters to the bowsprit and tangled rigging and wood until they too slipped below the surface.

The mate raised his head. He was more composed now. But his companions, sensing the delicacy of the moment had backed towards the cookhouse door.

'What more could we have done for those folk, Mr Zurich? They trusted us. What more could we have done?' The note of utter despair in the mate's voice left the skipper and emigration agent lost for words, helpless to offer any sort of meaningful consolation. If only they had got there an hour earlier. Welsh's plea hung in the air like a sorrowful farewell.

80 A Dismal Day

Any hope that they might get a coherent explanation about the course of the day's events by interviewing Ritchie evaporated almost as soon as they stepped through the cabin door. Stripped to the waist the skipper of the *Spirit of Speed* was standing with his back to them, tap-tapping at a barometer which hung on the boards above Jack's bunk. He registered their arrival without turning.

'Set fair, young Mr Zurich, do you see? Set fair. We should be in Port Adelaide in two weeks.'

He turned towards them and both Zurich and Walter Lumsden took a step back. Amid all the confusion as the survivors were landed the opportunity had not arisen to confront Ritchie. Now in the light of the half closed shutter he stood before them, a man of about fifty but looking fully ten years older. The sun had teased wrinkles around his eyes and the wind carved lines across his brow. His silver beard was knotted.

Ritchie must have been weather-beaten but that night his skin wore a sickly yellow pallor and seemed slack, somehow too big for him. His eyes were pain-filled, dark circles. He looked as if something monstrous had sucked the marrow from his soul.

He spoke again, this time more gently: 'They're saying I was pressing too hard, Zurich aren't they? That I didn't take due regard to sea conditions. But they're wrong. You know me better than that, Jack.'

They both looked at this broken, disturbed man with anger but mainly with an agonising pity.

'And I left no-one to perish. No, not a soul.' Again he turned to the wall and resumed his rapping assault on the barometer.

'Set fair, don't you see, Zurich? We should be putting on more sail. The rest of the passengers will have been picked up by now. It was only a matter of time…how can they say I was too hasty…set fair…best damned ship on the Clyde…second to none.'

Together they guided Ritchie gently to the bunk and pulled the blankets up. The man was on the edge of a total breakdown. Prior to Tristan da Cunha, the last time Zurich had seen Ritchie was eighteen months previously across two decks in Cape Town. He had been alert and alive, leaping on to the rigging with the fittest of his crew.

Now he lay shivering from shock in his bunk, clearly torn and cruelly twisted inside, drawn and devastated on the exterior. The sea was a cruel master, it surely was, Walter Lumsden reflected. One blessing was that Ritchie was calmer now. As they snuffed the oil lamp on the wall and drew the cabin door to, a weak, ailing voice whispered in the darkness. 'Set fair, lads. Set fair.'

'I think we need some shut-eye, Walter. The end product of this most dismal of days is that we have forty-six more souls to care for and many miles of difficult ocean still to cross.' Parting company, both men stopped for a moment and glanced up at the corridor ceiling. The sad, trailing notes of a pibroch sounded out through the ship as the Falkirk piper, directly above them on the poop deck, began the first bars of *The Flo'ers o' the Forest*.

81 Scenes from the Deck

It was twenty-four hours since the *Spirit of Speed* had been devoured by the ocean. The weather was markedly cooler and every now and then as she moved steadily south-east, the

Broomielaw was being struck by short-lived torrents which often made it seem that the vessel was more under the water than above it. This was more like the dreich Scottish winter weather they had left behind and unquestionably these were the most severe conditions since the North Atlantic storm.

The emigrants, trying to push the sinking to the back of their minds, were somewhat buoyed by having read in their journals and leaflets that this change of weather signalled the start of the sprint to Australia.

They would check the board beside the forecastle where the ship's position and distance covered the previous day was posted each midday. This always drew an interested crowd. The latest bulletin indicated that they were 45½ degrees south and almost 30 degrees east, still heading south east towards the Antarctic ice pack. It was also noted that in the past 24 hours the *Broomielaw* had covered a useful 220 miles. Youngsters ran off to spread the news.

In these squalls the crew were kept busy shifting sails. Amid bitter sleet showers which seemed to drive the sea into a fury, the banshee howl of the wind was everywhere as the men clambered across the rigging.

But all the time the *Broomielaw* cut a clear, determined path through the cream-crested breakers.

The most daring of the passengers – Maggie and Hilda among them – would wrap themselves in plaids and blankets and venture above, between the squalls, to watch the sea in that wild, wonderful state while below, others were returning to the misery of seasickness.

'Margaret, I must speak with you.'

Walter had intercepted Maggie Gilchrist and Hilda as they gingerly scaled the companionway from steerage to their favourite spot in the shelter of the foredeck. The ship sank into a trough.

Clinging to the rail with one hand and gripping her wicker basket with its precious gurgling cargo in the other, Maggie looked down at Hilda. The girl's brown hair was ruffled by the darting wind. Maggie gestured to her youngest daughter to pull the ribbon of her bonnet tighter under her chin.

'Now, Mr Lumsden, I think we womenfolk have important matters to attend to just at the moment, don't we Hilda?' She turned to Lumsden and smiled. 'Our afternoon art class. Had you forgotten, Walter?'

'But this is important, Margaret. We made an arrangement weeks back and I…well, I haven't kept my side of the bargain.'

Maggie and Hilda moved off again up the companionway.

'It cannot be so important that it won't wait an hour or two. After tea, Walter, after tea.' Maggie's firm instruction brooked no response and they parted. She sensed that events were careering towards a decision for which she felt ill-prepared.

But it would wait till after tea. With baby James wrapped up snugly in the basket, only his nose and eyes peeking out at this strange, watery world, and with big sister Hilda as custodian, the Gilchrist women got themselves tucked into their sheltered corner and Maggie resumed her charcoal sketches. Certainly the subject matter was inspiring. The waves would leap up, building on themselves as if to overwhelm the rolling vessel then break into great sheets of white foam; others would crest up, tossing and tumbling on either side of the ship which would suddenly dip between them before rising again, defiantly, magnificently, over the stormy scene.

With sweeping strokes of the charcoal Maggie tried to capture this furious ocean, the dramatic rush of the waves against the stiff, unyielding lines of the clipper as she dived into the maelstrom.

If only she could remember all the little techniques he had taught her, her uncle, the art teacher. As ever, at the thought of him her heart raced and threatened to burst from her chest. She relived the intimate touchings, the fear, the pain and finally the scent of a male body moving on top of her.

Although she had struggled endlessly to chase any positive thoughts she still felt a strange residual warmth at the thought of the man who treated her like a woman rather than a little girl, who praised her artwork, who spoke of sunsets and poetry and love and promised to care for her. How could she have told the family that the father of her child, her darling May, was dear uncle Forbes?

He might have been dead for ten years for all she knew yet the memory of him still had the power to inflame her heart.

Maggie scanned the deck for a suitable subject to bring a human aspect to her sketch. And there in the distance, weaving unsteadily across the deck came the ideal candidate. Discretely, Maggie drew as the surgeon/preacher Shade passed them on his twice-daily round-the-deck constitutional.

For most of the journey while on deck he had worn a dilapidated straw hat tied under his chin with string while up on deck, but now with chill winds and high seas he was going about in a fur cap tied down over his ears. A splendid, eccentric sight he made for any would-be artist.

Maggie showed the quick sketch of the big, stumbling, puff-faced preacher to Hilda and they both laughed. As he passed, head bowed against the wind, dancing a little jig to keep his footing against the lurching of the vessel and hugging the collar of his coat, Shade raised a single digit.

'Greetings ladies. Rougher than yesterday, I'll warrant. You remember, Mrs Gilchrist, I'm happy to offer advice and quiet prayer at any time. I'll be seeing you, I hope.

'Not if I see you first,' muttered Maggie under her breath and again mother and daughter giggled like schoolfriends and tickled James who joined in the fun, happily blowing bubbles and watching them being snatched away by the breeze.

Already Maggie had received disapproving looks from parents who saw her determination to venture on to the deck with the young ones, ignoring the stormy seas. But she so wanted this experience for her children. Who could guess what lay ahead? Every experience was, she felt now, important; even the wild ocean, perhaps especially the ocean, since it had come to form such a major part of all of their lives.

She had to hurry with her drawing; if the weather worsened just a little, they were sure to be ordered below decks but for now, the moment was exhilarating, almost sensual and punctuated with ooohs and aaahs from Hilda each time a wave threw itself at the *Broomielaw*. The girl also had a rough pad on her lap and tried to match the flowing lines of her mother's hand.

Maggie was determined that Hilda would no longer be left out as her sisters went their own way on board ship. May was closer than ever to Hugh Macaulay and Flora was the steerage spokeswoman on every topic from the constant running debate about whether hatch covers should be left open at night to the proper consistency of Wallace's pea soup.

*   *   *   *   *

Down below the survivors of the *Spirit of Speed*, although still recovering from their ordeal, were slowly adjusting to the routine of their new home and had been allocated kitchen, cleaning or teaching duties according to their particular skills. Shade had held a rather faltering on-deck service for those lost but it seemed to be a ritual much welcomed by those rescued.

However, amongst the survivors Hamish Mhor McGrimmen had found a soulmate. The Carnegies were from Fife and the patriarch of this family was Willie, a watchmaker.

The two men had been scarcely introduced before Willie Carnegie – anxious for some work, any work, to keep his mind off the recent tragedy, had unearthed his precious instruments in their velvet wrap, lovingly carried from the sinking clipper, and off they went in the direction of the aft locker, chattering like a pair of canaries, their target, Napoleon Bonaparte's long box.

Hamish clearly felt he had found the very man to breathe life back into the little emperor.

82 Anne Overboard?

Anne Dagger had vanished – without trace. A search of the ship – including a

painstaking hunt through the baggage holds – had uncovered nothing. The survivor of the burning of the *Spirit of Speed* was nowhere to be found. Then, one of the cabin boys spotted her tartan shawl snagged low down near the bow anchor exit on the port side.

'She was upset, Zurich, but not in my considered opinion, suicidal - at least not when I saw her.'

Shade was at the door of the supplies cupboard in his cabin taking an inventory of bandages, splints, antiseptics and ointments, all heavily depleted by the rescue of the emigrants from the *Spirit of Speed.*

'That's really as much as I can tell you. When you think what she witnessed, mind you, it's scarcely surprising.'

'People saw you consoling her shortly after the survivors were landed.'

'True enough, but I say again, she seemed merely upset.'

Smugly, Shade congratulated himself on the carefully schemed piece of theatre which seemed to have worked a treat. The skipper of the *Broomielaw* looked the ship's surgeon up and down. His eyes betrayed a deep suspicion and something else which might have been a simmering anger.

'And you didn't think, Mr Shade, that perhaps you should have advised me or at least arranged for some of the other passengers to keep an eye on her for a day or two?'

'It must have been obvious, even to you, Zurich, that I was run off my feet dealing with physical injuries that afternoon. In any case there were more than Anne Dagger finding their way through the misery. How were we to know she would be the one to find comfort in the deep?'

'You feel that is what has happened, Shade?'

'It certainly looks that way.'

'Just a guide me for a moment, Mr Shade. A young girl, apparently level-headed and calm, according to all reports, rescued earlier from what must have looked like certain death, walks across the deck and throws herself into the ocean. You see nothing extraordinary about that?'

Replacing the remainder of the medicaments and shutting the cabinet door Shade turned to face Jack Zurich. He pulled nervously at his ear lobe.

'The human mind is an extraordinary piece of work. It's capable of great mood swings and incredibly contradictory behaviour. No, I'm not at all surprised by the actions of this lass. I wish I could have done more; I probably should have done more, but the truth is that I had another thirty or forty people with more obvious injuries to treat.'

Shade stepped forward and opened the cabin door to indicate that, at least far as he was concerned, the interview was at an end. Reaching towards the door handle his jacket cuff rode up to expose a series of long scratches down the inside of his right wrist. In almost the same motion, before Jack caught a glance, Shade pulled down the sleeve.

God, how she had hung on, he remembered, even when he had struck her three or four times with the belaying pin. He could still see the absolute terror, a fear beyond mentioning in her eyes as she clung to him and the dark water slid by beneath her. And then she was gone, forever.

'I fear Mr Zurich, we will never know precisely what prompted Anne Dagger to take such drastic action. Now, if you'll give me leave to finish my stocktaking.'

83 The Hunter River

By early evening the rushing seas had subsided, a kind of calm had wrapped itself around the boat and Maggie and Walter met up as arranged. Their conversation had, for Walter at least, a frustrating opening in his cabin as Maggie insisted on continuing with a portrait of the emigration agent which she had started weeks previously while they were becalmed.

'We can talk while I draw,' she said. Walter, who clearly had hoped for her undivided attention, sat rocking baby James on his knee.

'Now sit still, Walter. The light is desperately poor in here. At this rate I'll have you looking like something the cat dragged up from the baggage hold.'

'Honestly, Margaret. How can I talk with you when I'm expected to sit here like a dummy.' The agent squirmed uneasily on the edge of the bunk.

Maggie knew Walter had serious matters on his mind. She could tell by the way, for the past week, his eyes had started to light up whenever they met 'tween decks or at the morning service. She had seen that reaction before in the eyes of other men she had known. It almost always led to serious conversations. And these conversations were invariably prefaced by some sort of confession.

More emphasis on the eyebrows, she decided, as the charcoal skipped across the paper. She was flattering him just a little but she had found that often worked wonders with men. Walter, admittedly, had been the soul of kindness since James disappeared. And the girls liked him. She had to steel herself for the certainty that she would need a man around when they reached New Zealand. Would he do? She remembered asking herself that same question when she first met James at Kelso all those years ago,

284

when she was homeless, with a child in arms and three months pregnant with Flora.

Maggie was having difficulty with Walter's squarish, jutting chin, his impressive sideburns and straggly yellow locks. She tut-tutted to herself as she smudged the sharp outlines with her thumb.

'Walter, you've moved again! Sit at peace!'

Accepting the inevitable with a sigh she put her sketch pad and charcoal to one side as Walter rose to his feet with James in his arms and did a little dance to stretch his legs. She glanced again at her drawing. It was coming on.

What was it that Forbes had told her as he stood behind her, stroking the back of her neck: 'You have talent, girl, real talent.' But that was so long ago, in another lifetime it seemed. And he had also reassured her, hadn't he, that no-one would find about what her uncle described as their 'secret friendship.'

Only May, that lovely child grown to womanhood and with a man of her own now, remained as a daily reminder of that sad, desperate time when promises were made, innocence was betrayed and the heartlessness of a family was cruelly exposed.

Thereafter Maggie had quickly learned about men and their selfish ways.

She agreed with Walter that they perhaps might be able to think more clearly in the open air, amongst the salt spray and so they found themselves, moments later, well wrapped up on an almost deserted deck. It was a calmer evening than of late. They ducked out of the light breeze into the shelter of the deckhouse. It was clear that Walter was troubled. He frowned as if struggling to shape his delivery. And patiently Maggie gave him time. On this occasion, there was nowhere to run.

For a moment or two they were merely chatting – about baby James's healthy appetite, about Jack's growing confidence in charge of the vessel. Walter knew Maggie to be fully occupied in consoling her daughters who remained in shock and confusion over their father's vanishing into the ocean.

Most disturbing of all for the family was Hilda's insistence that her father might still be alive, that he may have swum to an island or been picked up by a boat. No matter how often her older sisters told her tearfully that it was impossible and to let the subject drop, she found an opportunity most days to express her forlorn, disconcerting hope.

The empty bunk in the steerage, Gip's wooden bowl (now consigned to the galley stove), James's shepherd's crook with the horn handle which hung from the bunk end – all were constant reminders of the untimely and staggering loss sustained by the Gilchrists.

But both Walter and Maggie knew they were skipping around the issue set against which all other paled into insignificance. There followed a lengthy silence during which the tossing seas on either side of the *Broomielaw* called the tune. Then Walter spoke.

'You've been avoiding me, Maggie. Ever since we left Tristan da Cunha you've been avoiding me. Why?'

'I've really no idea what you're talking about, Walter. We've both been very preoccupied, well, I certainly have, what with the loss of James, the arrival of the baby and keeping auld Agnes from fretting. Do you know she still believes that the sailmaker was the sneak thief. She won't rest easy until he's hung drawn and quartered.

'And worse, much worse than that, she's down to her second last bottle of *Dr Heinrich's Master Mixture*, that dreadful green concoction which she swears by.'

The agent huffed with frustration. The conversation was not moving in the direction he had hoped.

Maggie looked down at the baby who was snuggled in at her breast, gurgling and goo-ing. Here, in truth, was the little chap who was taking up all of her time. Religion had played only a small part in Maggie's life after being sent from the family home in disgrace. Even in her childhood all she remembered was the Shorter Catechism as a duty, Sunday services with old Mr Douglas either snoring at the end of the pew or trying to hook up the hem of her dress with his walking stick.

But when she looked into her baby's hazel eyes she could believe. Yes, there could be a pattern and a meaning to things. Even after the horrors she had witnessed. She thought of the great, perilous journey across the ocean which they were undertaking and of the parallels with this fragile little soul, ready to start another marvellous voyage – through life. His passage across the years might be rough or smooth, short or long, full of joy or sadness. Who could say? However, if she had her way James Law Gilchrist would be the happiest, most secure child the world had seen.

'If it was something I said, Margaret, please tell me.'

Lumsden stood directly in front of her, rocking with the motion of the ship. He looked pleadingly at her. She was attracted to the emigration agent, certainly. He had a strong face and a pleasant manner. Gentleness and consideration were not attributes she had often encountered among the men who had known her. But more than anything she needed someone to be assertive, courageous and to fill her life with certainties.

'Look Walter, I saw your face when I told you about my 'arrangement' with Brocklebank, the factor, what we did there in the woods and how I beat him to death. You were shocked, stunned. And with good reason.'

'Yes, yes, Maggie. For a moment I was, perhaps. But we said weeks ago that we would eventually share our secrets with each other. I now know the dreadful burden you've been carrying. It's high time you discovered that I also carry guilt, a guilt in many ways more terrible than your own.

'The Bible says it more clearly than I ever could – Let he who is without sin cast the first stone.'

What in hell's name was coming now, Maggie wondered.

'I am not, I never was, in a position to judge you, Margaret.'

Dear God, she thought to herself, this is surely a touch over-dramatic. What is he going confess – that he failed to keep the company log book up to date, or ordered too few bags of oatmeal for the voyage.

'I've told you about our little girl…'

'Yes, you said she died at sea, measles, am I right?'

'Whooping cough, Maggie, but sadly that's only the start of the story. With Lizzie and the two boys we…'

'You have two sons? You never mentioned any of this before, Walter.' She was genuinely stunned by this revelation and for a moment wondered why this should have been such a secret. For some reason she had never imagined Walter as the father of a clutch of kiddies. 'We really are full of surprises tonight.'

'Yes, I HAD two sons, but this is the part of me, of my story, I desperately want to share with you, Maggie. Above all else, you must know about this.'

He waited for some signal of assent. None came, so he pressed on.

'Like you and James we planned for months, no years, for our great journey. We settled with three other families from Stirlingshire on a land grant along the Hunter River in a wild part of New South Wales, back in '53'.

And so Walter Lumsden, emigration agent, began to relate his story, the way he had painfully rehearsed it so many times in front of the little shaving mirror in his cabin.

84 Walter's Agony

Despite the chill a few brave souls had drifted up on to deck to catch the last rays of daylight before the *Broomielaw* plunged into the darkness of the Indian Ocean night. Close by the watch was changing.

Walter slowly, clearly picking his words with the greatest care, told Maggie how in those first few months after the bullock cart trek into the outback, life had been hard, punishingly hard. The family had experienced flooding, drought, dust and dingos but with the help and support of the other settlers, stretches of level ground were cleared for cultivation, sufficient land along the river for a first sowing of crops by the end of that winter.

'Half-a-dozen farms had been constructed, roughly-built, but homes at last, two or three miles apart along the river course. I called our homestead *Balfron*, after my own father's village.

'We were so sad, of course, at losing our wee girl on the voyage south, but for the boys' sake we knew we had to find our feet. It was their future at stake. We sowed our crops, bought some goats and followed all the advice we'd given before leaving Scotland about the tricks of settling Down Under. Mind you, it's no easy matter for a schoolmaster to learn how to saw logs.'

Walter attempted a smile but it was forced and clearly out of place.

'So you were a teacher, Walter? What secrets are being unveiled tonight. I'd never have guessed.'

He looked downcast. 'But now you're teasing, Margaret.'

'No, no, go on with your story. You were saying, it was all sweetness and community spirit along the Hunter River.'

Even in the shadows of the encircling night Maggie could see Walter screw up his face as if someone had twisted a knife in his gut. More hurriedly now, he progressed as if desperate to complete his disclosure.

'There had been no problems with the local Aborigines. We were told they were friendly enough, interested in the settlers, and nothing had happened to make us think otherwise. That was until two army officers out hunting shot dead a native Australian who had made off with the wild duck which they had downed.

'Revenge, his friends were seeking revenge when they came to Balfron...'

Walter was now rushing towards the climax of his story. His voice was breaking and shaking.

He explained how he had come home one evening at dusk from the field to find a group of Aborigine men – all the worse for drink – loitering around the yard. When he tried to question them they turned on him and struck him to the ground with a spiked club. Maggie looked at the long wound on his face and understood.

Burned into his brain was the image of the decayed teeth of his attacker standing over him - the wild, red-rimmed eyes set in a leathery, sun-scorched face and the rabbit or dingo bone which decorated his nose. Until recently this memory had lived with him almost every waking moment.

Most of all in the retelling Walter recalled the sharp stench or raw alcohol on the man's breath as he peered into his face. Relating this part of the story Walter reached up to finger his wound as if it had been mysteriously revitalised simply by the power of recollection. It was apparent to Maggie that this was the first time he had related these terrible moments – to anyone. It was obviously a sore struggle.

Running to the house and barring the door, blood pumping from the wound on his face, Walter had found Lizzie and the boys huddled under the rough kitchen table. The inflamed Aborigines were soon stalking around the building, testing windows and banging the thin, clapboard walls with their clubs. It was Lizzie, he explained, who had demanded that Walter sneak out of the house once darkness fell to seek help from their neighbours, believing the renegades would surely never attack a woman on her own with her children.

'If I'd been stronger, I would have insisted on staying, Maggie. The simple fact is that I should have remained with them – but we argued. If I'd just ignored Lizzie and worked by my instincts – they might all be alive today.' The emigration agent was trembling visibly.

Almost without thinking Maggie stepped forward towards him and took him in her arms. Painfully slowly he now told her of returning with his neighbour Jim MacColl and his two grown-up sons perhaps an hour later to find Lizzie and his boys clubbed to death and thrown in the pig pen.

'You're the only person in this ship who knows the story. No-one must know, Maggie. They all trust me completely. They have relied on my honesty and believe I'm leading them to a bright new future and, of course, I am. But if they were to find out...'

85 Land Again – and Whales!

February 4, 1858, was notable for the emigrants on board the *Broomielaw* because of two memorable events which broke the long haul across the Southern Indian Ocean and appeared in every journal entry and letter home.

First of all in the morning a dozen or more blue whales were seen, tracking the *Broomielaw,* sometimes breaking surface to port then crossing beneath the ship and broaching magnificently to starboard.

These huge, inquisitive visitors – the largest creatures in the sea - appeared to be treating the clipper as one of their own kind and they swept along majestically, the ship and her shiny black-coated attendants, the sun glistening for a brief moment on their dark uniforms as they scraped the surface then slid under. Even the experienced seamen on board seemed impressed by the spectacular sight.

A great guessing game developed amongst the passengers who had crowded the deck to see this spectacle. They tried to estimate the size of these wonderful, sleek citizens of the deep and the concensus seemed to be that the largest must be almost sixty or seventy feet long from broad nose to sweeping tail, A sweepstake was organised to guess exactly how long they would stay in the company of the ship.

On the companionway to the foredeck Maggie was busy with her charcoal and paper trying to capture this magical moment. She wanted to banish Walter's confession from her thoughts and tried to convince herself that none of it was her burden. Yet she still felt shocked, confused, and involved.

Below her at the foot of the steps Innes and Belle Macaulay stood together. Tears were streaming down her face – tears of joy.

Tell me again, tell me what you see, Innes. Is it just a blur or do you see the whales and the wild water clearly?'

He turned to his wife and reached for her hand.

'I see a face, a beautiful face which I never thought to see again. Do you know, Belle, I never forgot a detail, the glow of your cheeks, your eyes.' They held each other close. 'Innes, you're squeezing the breath out of me,' said Belle, with a smile and a suggestion that he daren't stop.

'If I was offered one moment in this life to keep for my own, never to be clouded or tainted by time, Belle, this would be it. I've been so desperate to tell you, but I wanted to be sure.'

Innes Macaulay looked again at the sea and their dark companions on the ocean highway. 'My vision at a distance still has a way to go. It's as if I'm gazing through a rain-streaked window but it improves with every passing day, Belle.'

'I thought there was something, Innes. But I hardly dared ask. The boys will be so happy.'

The pod of whales tracked the ship for most of the morning, broaching and diving in splendid synchronicity, water spilling from their broad backs as they broke surface. From time to time, to a great cheer from the children, one of the creatures would shoot a jet of water high into the chill air. Dolphins, porpoises and flying fish were impressive in their own way but this was a sight none of the emigrants would forget, a saltsplash memory to be conjured up amid the arid bush or the dense kauri forest in years to come.

Jack Zurich spent most of this interlude moving about the deck chatting to passengers, particularly the survivors from *The*

291

Spirit of Speed. Everyone was full of questions as they suddenly felt the tug of their new home, each outlandish event seeming to confirm that they were nearing their destination. Questions, questions, questions. How long would they be in Adelaide before moving up country? How hot would it be?

Those going to New Zealand were pleased to learn that stopover in South Australia would be restricted to couple of days and then they would be on their way again.

The children, practical as ever, living in the moment, were relieved to be told by Jack: 'No, these whales are marvellous navigators; they won't collide with the ship.' But he knew it had happened, and more than once.

Yes, he told another family, the seas should be calmer for the next week or so now that the *Broomielaw* was close enough to the ice cap to feel its soothing influence. He told them to look out for paler clouds above the horizon which often indicated the presence of ice. He recruited whole families for this part-time ice watch.

No, he had to explain to another group, it was unlikely that the weather would get any warmer for the period when they were at the southern extremity of the voyage.

And yes, over the next hundred or so sea miles there was every likelihood that they would see an iceberg. This last piece of information was greeted with whoops of delight from the children who had been allowed away from morning classes to view the whales. They redoubled their cries of wonder as the closest of the creatures once again shot a powerful jet of water skywards with a splendid whoosh.

Belle Macaulay squeezed her husband's hand and returned to the care of the wee ones. She noticed that despite being wrapped in mufflers and caps the tots were shivering. 'Right, you little ones,' she ordered, 'down below into the warm.'

It was all relative, of course. Without any heating below deck it was scarcely any warmer but at least you were out of the wind which now had a markedly sharper edge. After Innes's news, however, that cramped and uncomfortable steerage, their temporary home, was for Belle Macaulay all she could have wish for at that moment.

*   *   *   *   *

For hours, just to keep folk on their toes, Jack Zurich, after checking his charts has asked the strollers on the deck to watch out for the Prince Edward Islands – two isolated lumps of rock, lost in the vastness of the Southern Indian Ocean. He fully expected to pass close by these lonely outposts in the early evening, according to his calculations and although he did not require notification of a sighting, the island spotting game seemed to have caught the imagination of the more energetic of the deck walkers. It was vital, Jack knew, to keep minds occupied. A bottle of rum was even offered as an incentive.

It was also too easy to dwell on the enormity of the tragedy they had so recently witnessed, not least because the survivors were a constant reminder, right there, eating, sleeping, breathing, amongst them.

Through the late afternoon and into the fading light of dusk passengers could be seen eagerly peering out from the fo'castle in the hope of seeing land once more. Most were disappointed. They drifted away saying they were almost sure they had seen something on the horizon. It might have been hills but Jack Zurich realised it might just as easily have been banks of cirro stratus cloud hugging the horizon.

Only a few of the older men, taking advantage of the official sanction to break the curfew, stayed about the deck well-wrapped against the chill, happily smoking their pipes and swapping yarns of home. Eventually they were able to report a distant sight of land and it was an early priority the following morning for Jack Zurich to evaluate six claims as the first sighting of the Prince Edwards.

Marion Island and Prince Edward Island, only 15 miles apart, protruding like sore thumbs above the ocean, were actually the summits of a vast underwater mountain range. They appeared to port and the ship passed close enough to allow the huddle of emigrants to see snow lying on Jan Smuts Peak on the larger Marion Island.

A barren and inhospitable place it looked. Much more exciting were twinkling lights of what could only have been a couple of whaling vessels tucked in under the impressive coastline. This caused a buzz of excitement. Were these British,

Scandinavian or even American? There was no way of knowing and no halt had been scheduled.

Jack, who had joined the smoking club on deck having received word from the watch of land sighted, was able to explain that the whalers often took on water at this location. There was also an opportunity for the whaling ships to replenish their pork barrels – pigs which roamed the island were descendants of animals left there by Captain James Cook during one of his expeditions at the end of the previous century.

As the islands were slowly left behind and the last of the passengers headed for their bunks an anxious cry summoned Jack to the animal pens in the shadow of the afterdeck.

Already on site were Walter and Willie Semple, the piper who had also happily taken on the lead role in feeding and mucking out Maisie, the Jersey cow, which had been doing such a sterling job supplying the wee ones with milk and as a result, keeping illness at bay. Apart from her role as the source of fresh milk, since the loss of the pigs and two lambs in the tropical storm, she had become the children's pet, spoiled and pampered. Any spare scraps from the tattie pot would always find their way to Maisie's enclosure.

Some of the older girls had learned to milk her and to the amazement of their parents two or three of the city children had taken a delight in helping in the mucking of the deckside pen, morning and night, up to their ankles in cow sharn and never happier.

But this night a sorrowful scene awaited Jack Zurich as he stood on the bottom rung of the enclosure and looked down at the prostrate animal and the two men bent over her, gently prodding her swollen belly. The grinding of teeth and the heaving stomach told even a townie like Jack Zurich who had made his life on the sea that the animal was suffering. 'For God's sake, Semple, what's going on here? Have those youngsters killed the old girl with kindness?'

'If only it was that straightforward, Mr Zurich,' responded the piper. 'It looks to me as if she's been poisoned.'

From a passage doorway at the other side of the foredeck a squat figure wrapped in a cloak watched the huddle around the dying beast – and tugged at an ear lobe with satisfaction.

86 The Evidence Mounts

A council of war had been summoned by Walter Lumsden. But anxious to keep a lid on his suspicions for the moment only the skipper and Hamish, as elected passenger representative from steerage, joined the emigration agent.

Walter opened the business. 'I have to say, Jack, that I was perhaps too cautious when we spoke about the faulty condenser at Tristan da Cunha and your concerns about the attack on the poor lass, Jessie.'

'How so?' said the skipper settling into the rough wooden chair by the writing desk. Hamish, hands clasped behind his back slowly paced the cabin.

'Well, if you now look at the loss of the woman Dagger and this dreadful business with the milk cow, on top of everything else that's happened, it adds up to more than a normal run of bad luck, surely? It's worrying.'

'I have to agree – Semple knows his animals and it was poison for sure,' said Jack tearing a strip of chewing tobacco from his pouch and popping it into his mouth. He offered it to his companions but both shook their heads.

'And as for the poor lass that went over the side, I have plenty of suspicion there, but not a shred of evidence.'

Hamish had ceased his pacing and perched himself on the wooden stool beside the bunk. However, it seemed he would either tumble off, or the stool might collapse under his impressive bulk. After some ominous creaking he stood up and examined the legs of the stool for signs of stress. So doing, he spoke.

'I'm thinking, gentlemen, that perhaps it's time we got out into the open what has been on all our minds these weeks past.'

He gave up on the stool and leaned against the door jamb. 'It's Shade, isn't it. He's a weird one.'

'Apart from creeping aboot the place and his, well, his enthusiasm for the womenfolk, Rag did accuse him o' some sort of involvement in the rape; he has the run of the ship and would have had no problem getting down to that condenser. It would be simplicity itself for him to concoct some diabolical mixture and feed it to that poor beast and it's odd that he appears to have been the only person to have spoken at any length of the Dagger woman before her disappearance.'

Walter Lumsden and Jack weighed up the Highlander's accurate summary, quietly pleased that, unprompted, he had homed in on what they had both been thinking. But there were problems, questions, they both realised. How could Shade have negotiated the vetting process if he was an imposter, a vagabond, or worse? Of course, he may have had an influential backer somewhere in the company to ease him through the system. Yes, and it did appear that he and Ratter were thick as thieves.

For a minute or two a thoughtful silence filled the cabin. Jack chewed rhythmically and Walter stared at the cabin floorboards in front of his bunk. For his part Walter was still analysing the strange emotions which had surfaced while he was confiding his terrors, those shadows of a dark time, to Maggie. It had helped to put everything into perspective.

Turning to the writing desk Jack Zurich flicked through the ship's log which he had brought with him looking for entries which mentioned Shade and his activities. Eventually he raised his head.

'For the life of me I can't understand what the surgeon would have to gain by slowing or even attempting to sabotage this voyage. He puts himself at as much risk as the rest of the passengers and crew.'

'When you can find no other explanation,' Walter chipped in,' then I'd follow my father's advice. He believed you'd find money at the root of most troubles. And he knew a bit about that.'

'Possibly. The simplest way might be just to search his room and his writing cabinet and get to the bottom of this before something else happens.'

'Maybe so, Jack. Certainly confronting him with our suspicions will achieve nothing. And if we're wrong and can't lay hands on any convincing evidence then this will be the last ship you'll skipper, I fear. What's more, any hope I had of landing a severance payment in Dunedin which would allow me to buy that land on the Clutha will be gone forever. Are you – are we – prepared to take that risk?'

Zurich was silent for what seemed like minutes: 'The same risk applies to simply slinging him in the brig, right away, no questions asked. Apart from the fact that he seems to be a pretty efficient surgeon we have no concrete evidence.'

'He may be a good surgeon but he's maybe the worst preacher I've ever heard,' was Walter's contribution.

'Aye,' said Hamish, 'he's no' what you might say – inspiring...'

The other two nodded in agreement. Through the hatch came the shouted order from the second mate for the crewmen in the rigging to trim the sails. Jack looked restless, as if anxious to be out on deck where he felt at ease and in control.

Hamish chipped in: 'There might be a less direct way of finding what we want to know; what this character is up to. If we can get a female volunteer....

Five minutes later the meeting broke up with a battle plan of sorts in place. Hamish headed off down the passageway bidding the agent and the captain goodnight. He bent low to avoid the cross beams. Sailing ships had not been constructed to accommodate men who had become mountains.

As Jack, anxious to see the set-up of the sails and gauge the changing weather, headed off Walter Lumsden called him back: 'Just before you go, Jack, a word. I wondered what you thought about Ritchie. When I called by to see him this morning he was just a picture of misery, staring at the wall and mumbling something about his crew returning for him.'

'Yes, I know. He's clearly disturbed. The shock has knocked him off course for sure...and we can only hope it's temporary. I even thought he might have a crack with Ratter, they used to sail together, but the two of them just sat there, staring at each other.

Jack Zurich felt great sympathy for Ritchie. He still struggled to imagine what it must be like to have lost not only your ship but most of your passengers and crew. For Jack this test of having taken on responsibility for a ship in mid-ocean was proving a dramatic enough introduction to captaincy. At this point he was in no doubt what needed to be done.

'I think you're correct, Jack. The security of the *Broomielaw* is under threat. We must find out what role, if any, Shade is playing in all this. That must be our top priority. And if you work your charms on Queenie, skipper, we should be able to do that in double quick time'.

* * * * *

There was a threat of open warfare in steerage a couple of nights later as the weather deteriorated further and the lookouts were posted on iceberg watch. To add to the creepy, other-worldly feel of this God-forsaken region, fogbanks, spawn of the ice walls, as Jack had predicted, could be seen gathering on the horizon.

The vessel had been pitching badly and most of the emigrants were taking to their bunks in the evenings long before the 10 p.m. curfew. Mothers sang lullabies, a few hardy souls played pontoon or brag, while one bright spark ground out some Scots airs on a mouth organ. Generally the atmosphere became more muted.

For the first time the hatches were being completely closed over, partly on account of the cold and partly to keep out the water. Every so often it was all hands to the mopping up when a wave crashed on to the deck and came cascading into the steerage. Night-time closure of the hatches had become accepted procedure.

But this way of working didn't please everyone. It was this difficult situation which almost brought civil war to the family department.

The dispute focused on the supposed need to close the hatch completely during the roughest of weather. Those whose children were still recovering from the measles were, naturally, afraid of the cold and were insisting on the closure.

Jack had brought Shade down to speak to the warring parties. He stood in his long overcoat and woollen cap at one end of the table and looked the assembled emigrants up and down. The surgeon launched confidently into his spiel : 'We all fully understand your anxiety about the cold. But you have to realise that foul air is quite as harmful as cold in hindering speedy recovery from all sorts of complaints.'

'Aye', shouted a husky voice from the back of the throng, 'if the hatches are nailed fast and old man Turner keeps breaking wind the way he does we'll all be suffocated.' The speaker theatrically pinched his nose between thumb and forefinger. There was muted laughter and a few further rude exchanges and sound effects before Jack gestured with his hands for the group to settle.

'Well,' continued Shade, 'this may be a joke to a few of you but that gent at the back has a very good point. There are a number of folk down here with troublesome bowel complaints. Fresh air is essential or we run the risk of more infection.'

Jack stepped in to explain that according to recent legislation there should always be ventilation and at the end of the day, like it or not, the hatchways would not be closed entirely, although he was prepared to let Hamish monitor the situation.

Another parent, surrounded by a brood of six or seven youngsters suggested: 'It's all very well for the folk back there, away from the cold blast of air, but here we're directly below the hatch in open berths and there are times when we might as well be sleeping on deck.' The man with one of his children, a freckle-faced wee boy with a winning smile, on his knee took the plaudits of his neighbours whose accommodation was closest to the hatches.

'Listen, we have a limited supply of extra blankets – for the kiddies, you understand. If you still believe it's too cold see the second mate and we'll distribute them; but the hatches stay open, I'm afraid.'

Jack waited for a reaction. This final gesture seemed to appease the opponents of 'fresh air' somewhat and the meeting began to disperse.

'Thanks for helping out there, Shade,' said Jack as they moved to the upper deck. 'A bit of expert guidance is usually enough to sort out that kind of problem.'

'As it happens, Zurich, I was merely trying to save myself some extra work. Don't put it down to my benevolent nature. I haven't got one.'

They parted. What a strange, thoroughly disagreeable character Shade was, thought Jack. With every minute that passed it looked more and more as if he may also have a scheming nature and another, sinister agenda.

Part Three – Arriving

87 The Mists Clear

Questions of open or shut hatches were of no consequence, mere distractions, for the Macaulays. Suddenly it was as if the whole family, right down to young Torrance, had taken to the home brew. They were intoxicated by the news of Innes's slow recovery from what they had all accepted long since as permanent blindness.

They were, without question, just at that moment, the noisiest, cheeriest, most animated family group on the *Broomielaw*. And there was no doubt that the steady improvement in Innes's vision was taking place – it was not wishful thinking.

Despite the increasingly bitter weather, each morning now on deck the boys set up a test during which Macaulay was required to read foot-high numbers and letters painted black on white boards and held at a distance.

The man of the moment stood at varying distances, the collar of his rough woollen jacket pulled up against the bursts of sleet which swept in over the deck and set wisps of Innes's greying hair dancing wildly.

He would stare fixedly ahead waiting for the next number to be unveiled, like a whaler poised to spear his quarry. Macaulay was a picture of concentration with furrowed brow and tight lips.

Over the next few days this strange tournament had ceased to be merely a family affair and became instead a bit of a feature of the on-board social calendar. Little groups turned up to cheer each of Innes's new visual achievements and sigh over any wee setback.

'That'll be a capital B, Guthrie,' said Innes, confidently covering first one eye then the other.

'Close faither - it was a capital E.'

Agnes Gilchrist tapped Innes on the shoulder and pressed a black, knitted bunnet into his hand.

'We're a' pleased for you Macaulay. This is my 10th tammy since leaving Greenock, so it's a wee bit special. I wanted you to have it. God loves you.'

'Thanks, Agnes – I'll treat it with care. It's a kind thought.' So saying he pulled it over his head and covered his ears. 'Perfect Agnes, just perfect.'

The reek of her patent medicine was almost overpowering. With a satisfied smile, the old crone shuffled off to commence hat number 11 and to resume plotting the downfall of the French Republic, starting with her mortal enemy, the sailmaker Jontot. She knew there was only a week or two left to wreak vengeance.

The boards were changed and Macaulay's challenge resumed.

When news of this wee miracle had spread through the ship he could hardly walks to the 'heads' without being intercepted by well-wishers who wanted to shake him by the hand and ask for an update on his condition. It was as if the entire ship's company wanted to lay claim to share of this miracle. It was a symbol of hope for everyone. Through it all Macaulay smiled politely and thanked them for their interest.

Shade had examined the Lanarkshire miner, peered into Macaulay's eyes and ran a few visual tests of his own, before declaring himself baffled.

However, as Innes's vision returned he realised that at the same time he was losing that strange ability to register events at a distance. Even his dream of the rock finger, whatever its significance, had ceased. The feeling that Bob, his staff and comfort in the hardest of times, was still around was fading also.

He was too busy to wonder what it all meant. To have his sight back was surely to be complete again. Innes felt strangely bereft without that strange unnerving ability, that sixth sense, which arrived as a companion with his blindness and which had allowed him to wander unbidden into other people's lives, to sense the unseen.

Perhaps he would never know what half the images he had seen meant. The beckoning finger would remain no more than a strange mirage.

Now for hours in their 'partment, as the seas smashed into the *Broomielaw* and the following gale howled around them, Macaulay and his boys talked with renewed vigour of their plans for the smithy at the market town of Comrie, on the South Australia/Victoria boundary and pored over their precious emigrant's map.

They drew sketches of the layout of the smithy, of their new home, discussed the appropriate size of the furnace and speculated about opportunities to go into machinery manufacture – Hugh's pet project. But Hugh himself was strangely quiet on it. He agreed politely with the various proposals during the planning but Innes knew, they all knew, that his thoughts were with the oldest Gilchrist girl and that the Port Adelaide parting which drew ever closer would be a testing time for the young couple.

It was cold, very cold, now. The rigging stood stiff and firm and the sleet froze on the hatches and gunwales. This was the penalty for their sweep south to catch the fierce following wind which was now throwing them towards Australia.

Conditions on the *Broomielaw* were approaching their most difficult. But as ever there were sweet moments of great joy to chase away the miserable cold which seemed to eat into the emigrants' bones and sap their energy.

Another birth was reported from the infirmary on Monday, February 8, and this time the word in the steerage was that the mother, a McNeil woman from Barra, was no less than 55 years of age and incredibly this was her tenth son, having just one daughter. Four of the oldest boys were already at the gold mining and sheep farming in South Australia.

This formidable lady had been given the nickname by the emigrants of 'Strong Sarah' – the fact that she was delivered of her eleventh child with the minimum of fuss had been a source of great wonder and admiration amongst the families.

A steady stream of well-wishers came to the infirmary to visit Sarah and the newest McNeil who had been named Colin. His father was a bony, worn-out individual, so frail that the avalanche of handshakes and backslaps which he had to endure threatened to do him a serious mischief.

However, the severe conditions were beginning to take their toll on social activities. The ways and means committee having achieved only partial success with their demands for smoking restrictions had to cancel their weekly meeting on account of the bitter weather and the fact that so many were in bed, and even those who struggled from their bunks were constantly complaining of the cold, rheumatism and toothache.

This cancellation followed another fearful night of rolling and pitching with water cans flying about and boxes bouncing from their fittings.

*   *   *   *   *

It was a source of constant wonder how in these extreme conditions when most adults found that a sleepless night, with the *Broomielaw* pitching through the whitebeards, was inevitable, the children appeared little disturbed and awoke refreshed each morning, ready for the day – all their routines of eating, sleeping and working now firmly established.

The crew of the vessel had their own description for this part of the voyage. They were into what they called the Burcoo Days. It was a tradition in the Roaring Forties, when the weather took a difficult turn, that seamen were given an extra ration to fortify them for outside work – oatmeal porridge and molasses – the Burcoo. It filled an empty belly in good style and refusal to provide this vital fodder for the fo'castle had resulted, over the years, in a number of so-called Burcoo mutinies, with hard-worked crews demanding that they got their porridge before resuming work high among the icy foot ropes and frozen canvas. At the best of times work aloft required nerve, physical strength and stamina.

Jack pushed open the door to his cabin – now occupied by the stricken skipper the *Spirit of Speed* to find Ritchie struggling to put on his gold-braided jacket.

'What are you up to now, Mr Ritchie, Sir? This is no weather for going parading out and about'

He placed the tin dish on the table beside Ritchie's bunk. 'Here, I've brought you a plate of burcoo. You've scarcely taken a bite of food these past few days. Try this – it'll put some warmth into your belly.'

Ignoring Zurich completely the skipper of the *The Spirit of Speed* finally dragged his jacket over his shoulders and reached for his skipped cap.

'I must get on deck. No time for food. They'll be coming soon. I must be ready to meet them.' It was clear there would be no arguing with the disturbed man and bar tying him up, Jack decided, it would be simpler for the moment to go along with his little fantasies. Chillingly, Jack knew precisely what form this obsessive behaviour was taking. Among seamen there was an odd notion that the souls of drowned mariners were adopted by sharks and if their captain had not drowned with his ship and his men, the dead would return to claim him.

'Don't you think it would be best if you went back to your bunk, Mr Ritchie. The weather topside is foul.'

'Time and tide wait for no man, Zurich, you should know that.'

The older man threw such a menacing stare in Jack's direction that the skipper decided it might be simplest just to take a turn around the deck with him, to calm him a little. It was bad enough having Ratter next door, pacing his cabin, playing the harmonium at all hours of the day and night without adding to their problems by tipping Ritchie right over the edge of insanity..

There had been moments in the past week when Jack Zurich felt that his vessel might have been more appropriately named *Bedlam* rather than *Broomielaw*. But you're learning all the time, Jack, he told himself, as he escorted Ritchie topside. Stick with it, boy, stick with it.

88 Downing the Albatross

There was something especially sinister about those great, rolling waves of the Southern Ocean, thought Jack. He followed Ritchie who marched, leaden-browed as if to meet his destiny, back and forward, back and forward, across the see-sawing afterdeck.

In his present frame of mind, the *Broomielaw's* skipper realised, it was more than possible that Ritchie would take a dive over the side. He needed watching.

Jack looked again at the iron grey, snow-laden skies and the sea. In these hellish conditions even the most sane individual could imagine the elements working together, conspiring to push poor lost souls, adrift on an endless ocean, towards the brink. Around here, just a century previously, these were the waters where sailors fully expected to fall off the edge of the earth.

Even when the waves were not being driven into a fury by the westerlies, they dwarfed the ship. Jack could feel the power, the surge of the greybeards rising through the soles of his boots as they dragged the *Broomielaw* this way and that. It was terrifying yet it was one of the reasons he loved the sea. The raw power of the ocean. And those waves… down here in their ferocity they were like no others he had ever seen.

The truth, perhaps, was that fragile ships and their crews should have left these far-flung southern waters to the salt-laden gales, the wave-skimming birds and the creatures of the deep ocean. Could it really be part of God's plan that ship after frail ship, packed with emigrants, should traverse the face of the deep along this bleak passage? If so, it was the most severe of tests for man and ship. Already many had failed to emerge at the other end.

Ritchie was talking to himself, mumbling incessantly as he moved from rail to rail. Sharks were nowhere to be seen. But now the skipper of the *The Spirit of Speed* stood silently, like a man whose soul had been snatched away, wringing his hands with frustration as he watched a crazy scene unfold below him on the main deck.

Three crewmen from the off-duty watch had managed to land a rare black albatross with a baited hook and having removed the vicious metal prong were set to decapitate the bird which flapped and squawked pitifully on the deck; one of the sailors stood with his foot on the great bird's neck; its huge wild eyes were filled with terror.

Not every sailor believed that killing an albatross brought bad luck. Catching one provided some excitement; the feathers made a decorative jacket and the webbed feet were occasionally fashioned into tobacco pouches. But Ritchie was one of the old school and this was to him, criminal folly. He brought his fist down with a crash on the teak rail.

He screamed in a desperate, panicky voice: 'Hey! Below there! Free that bird. Are you bloody mad, the whole gang of you? Do you want to send this ship to the bottom? Release the bird I tell you. Now!'

The sailors looked at the uniformed but unkempt and haggard officer who leaned glaring wildly towards them over the rail. There was definitely a mad glint in his eye but he remained, marginally, an authority figure. The knife remained poised above the bird. Then they saw Jack standing a few yards behind and his crewmen looked to him for guidance; the albatross all the while redoubling its struggles and shrieks.

Even as he gestured with a flick of the wrist for them to release the bird Jack knew the damage had been done. A group of intrigued passengers had been watching this odd exchange from the top of the companionway and were now glancing anxiously at each other.

Magnificent on the wing, a splendid pilot of the seaways, the huge albatross is the most ungainly booby of a bird out of its element and Jack's worst fears were realised when the terrified creature was set free by its captors. There just wasn't sufficient space for the bird to build up momentum, take flight and clear the myriad of obstacles to be found on the cluttered ship's deck. With a sickening bang and crack the albatross, its body as big as a goose and with a wingspan of perhaps ten feet, hit the for'ard mast a few feet above deck level and crashed to the boards.

If the passengers had seen this black omen bird slain for sport with such dire warnings ringing out from Ritchie, it would have for certain caused unrest in the steerage where the icy weather and the recent death of another infant were already having a demoralising effect. To invite bad luck was the way of fools.

But the bird would never fly again. In the collision with the mast its right wing had been shattered and as it flapped around the deck, it trailed a useless, broken wing behind it. Jack Zurich signalled again and the sailors fell on the injured bird. This time there was no hesitation as the albatross was freed from its pain. Ritchie held his head in his hands.

This is a bad business, Jack thought, but it was unquestionably the lesser of two evils since the seamen were obviously putting the bird out of its misery rather than slaying it on a whim.

Superstitions – Jack didn't really know what to make of them but you wouldn't catch him whistling at sea or mentioning the number that falls between twelve and fourteen. There was also an old tale about the risks of carrying a minister of the church on board. He already suspected, from recent experience with Shade, that this might prove to be the most solid superstition of all. They would find out soon enough now that Queenie had agreed to beard the shady beast in his den.

Looking concerned Walter appeared beside the folk on the bridge.

'I heard there was a commotion on deck.' He looked down on the trio at work below. 'My God, it's a slaughterhouse and no mistake. Albatrosses, isn't there some superstition about them being birds of....'

'Leave it, Walter. Leave it. We're in deep enough. Perhaps you can help me get Ritchie back to his bunk.'

'No sooner said than done, skipper. And I've had a final word with Queenie. She seems to see the whole business as a bit of an adventure.'

Ritchie was now chanting quietly to himself and had resumed his pacing of the deck while at the same time scanning the white tops astern, presumably for any sign of the anticipated shark pack.

'If we leave him here he'll either go over the side or freeze to death.'

As they moved to escort Ritchie below decks they realised that he was not moaning but almost silently mouthing one of the well-known of the old sea chanties in a monotone, tuneless voice: *'Five and fifty fathoms, my bones will never lie, haul away for the Cape.'*

Leaving the deck, without warning, Ritchie took Walter's wrist in a firm grip, digging his fingers painfully into the flesh and drawing the emigration agent again to a halt. Staring into his face he pleaded: 'Tell me, Mr Lumsden, tell me I won't die in the sea. They're out there waiting for me. Don't let them take me. In the name of pity, don't let them have me.' Ritchie's terror was genuine. He shook like a loose sail in the wind and started to sob.

'Don't you worry, skipper. You've a lot of sea years ahead of you yet.' Walter felt it had been the correct and obvious remark, but another, stealthy voice in his head told him that it was not so.

89 Don't Spare the Rod!

Queenie knocked firmly on Shade's cabin door. She felt reassured. Mr Lumsden and Jack were only a few paces away along the corridor and if anything went drastically awry while she was closeted with Shade, she had only to cry out and they would be there in an instant, they had assured her. This was surely an adventure. People were putting their faith in her, confiding in her, trusting her. It was a completely new experience for the kitchen maid, and one she found herself enjoying.

At Walter's suggestion but as much for her own peace of mind, Queenie had tried to persuade some of the handful of women who had been given the preacher's special benediction to reveal at least some of the detail of what had unfolded in the dim confines of the his quarters. But it was to no avail. Whatever his motive Shade had selected his 'candidates' with the utmost care. He picked the most reticent, modest and Godly of the womenfolk on board to receive his secret favour.

They would say nothing, but Queenie did sense a feeling of something – more like revulsion rather than fear – amongst the women she spoke to.

Belle told her all she could of her own encounter and the haircutting session but apart from sensing a dreadful frustration in Shade when whatever he had planned was cut short, she was unable to cast any light on the mystery.

One quiet, attractive matron of about forty who had been with the minister, in private, for Bible studies, as his official line suggested, went as far as to say: 'I think he's a good enough man at heart, lass. But he has perhaps got things just a bittie confused.' This had eased Queenie's mind. There had been no suggestion of violence implicit in any of the responses from the women. But there was more than a hint of something loathsome, disgusting, something she could not even start to fathom.

Armed with this information she had approached the minister about taking part in a session of private worship. Having brushed her auburn hair and tidied herself after her galley chores Queenie had been at her most demure, coy even, while making the request. And the clergyman had taken the bait, enthusiastically.

Now the moment of reckoning had arrived. 'Coming my dear, coming!'

Shade's voice reached Queenie waiting on the threshhold as she reminded herself for the umpteenth time of the purpose of her mission, to discover something, anything, which might confirm – or disprove – Shade's true identity and his agenda.

She was to await Walter's summons asking for Shade's presence in the infirmary. Shade would leave her in the cabin which was always kept locked and joined by Jack, they would seize their opportunity to turn the place over, quietly and efficiently. An adventure, she thought, truly an adventure.

The door swung open and Shade waved Queenie into the cramped accommodation.

'Come in – so pleased you wanted to share a few moments with me – and with the Lord, of course.'

He pulled out the seat and helped her sit before parking himself on the bunk opposite, his thick, leather-bound bible open on his knees. He rose to close the hatch just as a shower of hail rattled along the port side of the *Broomielaw*. Then Shade lit the oil lamp, secured to a wall fitting.

'A few moments of quiet contemplation, just to get us in the right frame of mind, I think.' He bowed his head.

Queenie looked at this peculiar man as he opened the Good Book.

Gasping for breath now, even at the slight exertion of moving around the cabin Queenie imagined, his face the texture of well-boiled ham, Shade began to run through some fairly racy verses from the Book of Leviticus….those referring to the spilling of seed and the soiling of neighbours' beds which Queenie remembered the boys giggling over at Sunday school in Stormay.

In so many ways Shade reminded her of the old laird, the 'parish bull' as he was known to the islanders. She tried to picture Shade with a ring in his nose and had to bow her head again momentarily to allow a smile to dissolve from her lips.

'That's the way my girl – take it to the Lord in prayer,' he said, noticing that his young guest had lowered her head.

Surreptitiously Queenie glanced around the gloomy cabin. Shade's writing desk tucked in a corner beside the hatch would be the first target for the search when the moment came. In the opposite corner of the living space was a sturdy tea chest which looked promising and there beside the bunk stood his familiar thin, walking cane, his constant companion almost, it seemed, like an extra limb.

Shade's puffed-up features, she thought, and his penetrating stare which appeared to fix to the spot anyone who it came to rest upon, that's what put her in mind of auld Bigland. That life, those people, even William on Tristan da Cunha now seemed so very far off, both physically and emotionally.

'Am I wrong in thinking we've met somewhere before, lass?'

'Oh, I think you must be mistaken, minister,' replied Queenie remembering the bar-room brawler in the *Bengal Merchant* taking the minister's splendidly delivered uppercut.

As she sat watching Shade trace the text across the page with his forefinger she marvelled at how much she had learned about men and their fickle ways in just a few shorts weeks.

Until she tumbled happily into the hay with William Bigland, men had not figured in her life, not at all. The premature death of her father, who collapsed on a scorching day during harvesting at the home farm and the loss of her brothers in the North Wick when their yawl sank within sight of their front door, meant that she had lived a convent-like existence with her mother down at the steading of Hookin'.

Now she knew that men could be selfish and demanding like William, or kind-hearted and thoughtful like Jack Zurich, paternal and helpful like Mr Lumsden, mean-spirited like poor Mr Gilchrist who had been lost overboard or just downright strange like the reverend gentleman opposite.

She was certain from her continuing bouts of morning nausea and an oddly contrasting feeling of well-being that she was pregnant. And the father would be at the fishing somewhere on the deep Atlantic waters off the rock outpost of Tristan da Cunha.

Shade looked up from the text: 'I am a sinner, my dear. And I feel my soul more restful for having brought this out into the open. And you, my innocent, have been sent to put things to rights.'

Queenie wondered what was coming next. Perhaps it was already time to blow the whistle and summon her helpers? 'Surely Mr Shade we are all poor sinners. But not you, being a reverend gentleman and all...'

'Why, yes, my girl. People seem to think that just because we wear the collar and wave the book that we are above sin. No, we are in the front line, as it were. Satan is at our shoulder night and day to tempt us from the straight path. It may be more often in thought than in deed but it is sin for all that.'

Queenie stumbled for a suitable response, beginning now to feel more than a little uncomfortable.

Although the cabin was unheated, bleakly cold, in fact, she saw tiny rivulets of sweat running down Shade's brow,

313

reflecting the shimmering yellow candlelight and disappearing into the forest of his bushy eyebrows.

'I'm just thankful to God that there are sufficient well-meaning ladies on board the *Broomielaw* to apply suitable and regular correction to me.' He was most definitely becoming overheated – it was plain to see. His own words seemed to excite him, He shook like some vast red jelly and his eyes threatened to pop from his head. A comic scene, for sure, if Queenie hadn't found it so disturbing.

'Now if we can proceed to the benediction, or the blessing, as we should more aptly title it. If you would face towards the door. For the sake of modesty, you understand.'

Yes, she was beginning to understand what she had got herself into. Queenie wanted that knock on the door, Shade's summons to the infirmary – and she wanted it quickly. Facing the cabin door Shade's voice reached her again: 'It's a sacred task I am asking of you, a sacred and most secret task. You may turn around now my dear.'

Turning, slowly, nervously towards the centre of the cabin Queenie almost slipped from her seat in disbelief. The sight which greeted her was an enormous pair of flabby, pink buttocks, folds of fat, layer upon layer. Shade had stretched himself, face down, across the table, his breeches at his ankles, arse up to the elements. She wanted to look away but she was transfixed by this mountain of male hinder flesh. An enormous dark brown mole with a single curly hair spiralling from the preacher's right buttock cheek drew her gaze like a magnet.

Queenie also registered the angry wealds across the minister's rear end superimposed on yellow-black bruising which seemed to be of a more distant antiquity. Punishment had been clearly applied – severely and regularly – since the start of the voyage.

'The stick, pick up the walking stick, miss, and lay on with all the force you can muster. Thresh me and dinna spare the rod, thresh me tightly with the flail of the Lord's wrath. Remember, it is his work you are about this day.'

There was a sharp double rap at the door. The last five minutes had seemed like five hours to Queenie.

'Lumsden here, Shade. You're needed at the infirmary, right away if you please. It's the consumptive lad.'

'Hell and buggeration!' – cursing, the preacher rolled from his improvised altar, staggered and hauled up his breeches. 'Forgive the language, Miss Stout. This is most inopportune.' Spitting and cursing he buttoned himself up and Queenie made to go.

'No, no, no! Stay! We have unfinished business. I'll return in a trice. You make yourself comfortable meantime.' So anxious was Shade to have his castigation completed that he had let down his guard and for the first time on the voyage he was about not only to leave his door unlocked, but also to leave someone in his cabin.

Warming to her performance Queenie smiled demurely and fingered the walking stick as if she was practising her scales on the flute.

Shade raised his eyebrows, made a noise like steam escaping from a kettle and left in a lather, banging the door behind him. Moments later Queenie flung the door wide to Jack Zurich.

'Jack, Jack…you'll never guess what he wants me to do…'

'No time for that now, Queenie. Lumsden will do well to keep him occupied down there in the infirmary for more than five minutes. You know the sort of thing we're looking for. Let's be quick.'

90 Shade Unmasked

The Council of War was ready to reconvene the following day as crew and passengers of the *Broomielaw* celebrated the fastest 24-hour run since leaving the Clyde – an impressive 282 miles, the westerlies pushing them along at a fearsome rate of knots.

The weather in the Roaring Forties remained cold, bitterly cold, but the emigrants huddled around the bulletin board, stamping their feet to keep warm, coat collars pulled up against the snow flurries, pointing at the new figures just posted and cheerfully debating just how many days might remain of their great journey.

The clipper was swallowing the miles; so rapidly that the great sweeping arc she was describing across the southern ocean would soon take them clear of the iceberg belt. Disappointment among the youngsters at the possibility they might not see one of the great green and white fortresses of ice was scarcely softened by the fact that the new home for so many of them was fast approaching.

Somehow the morning lessons and particularly Belle Macaulay's geography class – featuring stories of the timber-dry bush, vast forests and the snowy mountain peaks of their new homelands – now had the older children sitting up and paying attention; Belle had never seen them so enthusiastic and filled with questions.

Pleased as they were with the progress being made, Walter and Jack Zurich, having adjourned to the state room to join Hamish, now had a dilemma of major proportions on their hands. Shade was exposed as a fraud and probably much worse.

But first there was a discussion of the preacher's deviant behaviour as described by Queenie. His desire to have punishment inflicted on him – albeit with the tawse, the twin-tongued leather strap favoured by Scottish dominies usually applied across the open palms rather than the bare posterior– suggested, thought Walter, an English public school education.

'It's usually the cane at Eton or Harrow and the like but it has put so many so-called gentlemen of a mind to accept such punishment – as a reward of sorts. Don't understand it myself but it's an odd old world we inhabit,' observed Walter.

The way Queenie had described the scars suggested he had been welcoming such 'punishment' for most of his life.

However, the main issue was now beyond question. He had been unmasked as an *agent provocateur,* the troublemaker between decks. As they settled themselves, Jack Zurich had spoken, perhaps only half jesting, of happily waiting until they could keel-haul Shade in front of the entire population of Adelaide.

For long minutes in Shade's cabin it had seemed that their search would prove fruitless until, tucked in the purple silk lining of his sea chest, Queenie discovered a ribbon-tied folder containing perhaps a dozen letters. Among them was a single page, only two and three sentences but the implications of which, for the *Broomielaw* and everyone on board, were immense.

Written in very circumspect terms, innocent enough in themselves, the despatch thanked Shade for his work 'aboard the *Pomeranian*' and expressed the hope that his brother would assist in securing his next placement, on board the clipper *Broomielaw*. The letter wished him good fortune in Australia, mentioned cash withdrawal arrangements and was signed with the enigmatic initials *W-MF*.

However, Walter had seen this signature before on correspondence – it was the moniker of William Macmillan-Fyfe, a crooked Edinburgh business lawyer who operated from a sleazy bureau in Gladstone's Court, off the Canongate. Among his many dubious clients was numbered the Southern Cross Shipping Company. At the end of the letter were specific instructions to destroy the correspondence. Shade had blundered.

There had been talk, Walter told the others, of Macmillan Fyfe's involvement in shady land deals in the Hutt Valley behind Wellington, of emigrants finding that their promised acres had not even been surveyed.

'If the trouble on the *Pomeranian* was indeed the work of Shade, then it explains much of what has been going on. We must also wonder about his brother's involvement - whoever he might be. And you mentioned gold sovereigns, Jack?'

'Yes, they were in his sea chest, a small fortune for a poor seafarer like myself. Little wonder he kept his door tightly locked. Some sort of pay off from Southern Cross, I'll wager.'

'It looks that way,' said Hamish. 'Aye, and possibly includes a wee advance for work still to be completed.' This was said with a frown which clung uncomfortably to his normally jovial face. The possibilities were alarming.

Shade's clandestine task had now become transparent. It had been to slow the ship and cause as much confusion and delay as possible, presumably stopping short of actually taking the *Broomielaw* to the bottom. The failure of the water condenser, the attack on the servant girl, the poisoned beast; it was probable that all of these incidents and more might be laid at the clergyman's door.

317

And all three men were aware that if he was suspected of involvement in these matters why not in the dramatic collapse of Ratter into an alcoholic binge, the mysterious disappearance of the girl Anne Dagger from the *Spirit of Speed* and the early mutinous rumblings in the fo'castle. He did seem to have taken his work very seriously. How ironic, all three realised that the *Spirit of Speed,* the ship which was clearly meant to benefit from these deadly delaying tactics should have met such a terrible end.

In the past hour or so the icy blast seemed to have eased back and it was clear to all that the *Broomielaw* was failing to maintain the spectacular headway of the past two days. Jack knew from experience that the great ice sheets – so close by – often calmed the gales. Perhaps this increasingly sinister individual Shade had some sort of control of the weather too, Walter mused, before chasing the strange thought from his cluttered mind. Over Hamish's shoulder, through the half-open hatch, Walter could see the ominous blurring of the horizon which suggested they were slipping into the fogbanks. Jack had noted this change also and was uneasy.

For his part Hamish had been sitting quietly, arms folded, chewing on his lip and gathering his thoughts: 'If you ask me, this needs a lot of thinking about, Mr Lumsden. We'll regret acting in haste.'

'Well, from what we learned last night and heard from Queenie, it's clear as daylight that Shade is no genuine man of the cloth, but admittedly he does seem to have the skills of a first rate surgeon . We've all seen that,' said Walter Lumsden.

'The obvious response is to get him into the brig before his feet touch the ground – but let's not forget about the kiddies.' Jack was referring to the long-lasting whooping cough outbreak which had begun off the Cape and showed no signs of easing off. There were seventeen children in the infirmary or under constant care. With three or four of these it was already touch and go and Shade had unquestionably been diligent in caring for the wee ones.

'If Shade believes we're on to him,' said Jack, 'or if we simply confront him, he might simply abandon the sick.'

The three pondered Shade's likely reaction. Walter was the more optimistic. 'Then again if we assume he's a trained

318

doctor he'll be bound by his oath to care for the poorly…but I do agree, it's a huge risk to take with so many of our number sick'.

'With the *Spirit of Speed* gone he would surely see his task as being over.'

'You would have thought so, Walter,' replied Jack. 'But would anyone capable of taking on such acts of madness in the first place know when to call it a day? I shouldn't think so.'

The discussion ranged to and fro until it was agreed that, whatever the cost, they must take Shade out of circulation. The womenfolk had picked up enough expertise to cope with the whooping cough and any other ailments which might arise.

'We can only pray to God that no serious illness takes a hold or serious accident overtakes the *Broomielaw* over the sea miles left to Adelaide,' said Walter.

The Rev Elijah Shade was destined for the brig. It was unanimous.

'I'll get Davie Macgregor and we'll have him under lock and key before dusk. The sooner he's shut away, the safer I'll feel,' said Jack.

Hamish held the door wide for the emigration agent and the skipper.

'If you have just a moment, gentlemen, perhaps I can show you something to raise your spirits, Mr Carnegie, the clockmaker – he's turned out to be a Godsend. If you'll please follow me to the Emperor's apartments!'

91 Warlocks and Frenchies

Auld Agnes Govan pressed her cheek close to the rough-hewn wooden door through which only a minute previously the sailmaker Jontot had disappeared. She clung tightly to her medicine bottle and strained to see through a narrow crack in the planking.

The aft locker hatch which had been jammed half open scarcely drew any grey light from the southern ocean into the space but she could just make out three figures in a huddle at the far end of the locker.

What were that damned Frenchman and his cohorts up to?

Since Carnegie came aboard from the wreck, he and that big Jacobite monster McGrimmen had been in league. For sure, the old woman had convinced herself that a plot was being schemed; they would take over the ship and sail for some French colony in the Pacific. Yes, that was it!

Peering through the fissure she recognised two of the men – one was Jontot, easily identified by his black Normandy beret and the other with the beard was Carnegie, the watchmaker who had been plucked from the sea, rescued, then recruited as a conspirator. It was a scandal.

And the third person, a little chap standing the shadows; Agnes just could not place him at all.

Then, slowly, unsteadily this third individual began to walk towards her. With every step closer the identity of this mysterious individual began impossibly, incredibly, to crystallise. Agnes's heart thumped against her rib cage so powerfully she felt sure that those inside must hear its insistent beat. Her eyes began to open wider and wider. She realised that her teeth were chattering.

The little man, one arm jammed inside his greatcoat, had made his rather rigid, upright way to within a few paces of the door when his features came sharply into focus as he walked through the section of decking illuminated by the pale glimmer from the half-open hatch. It wasn't the beady eyes, dark eyebrows, pert little nose or sallow complexion which Agnes registered, although they all told part of the story; it was the neat curl of hair on his forehead which her gaze locked on to. Just like the drawings in the Illustrated London News.

From the back of the locker room came a voice. It was Jontot: 'Ah, bravo mon emporeur. This has just been a few small steps for you but a great stride forward for France.' Laughter followed.

That was more than enough. In dismay and disbelief, Agnes turned on her heels and bustled off along the corridor as fast as her creaking old legs would carry her, hugging her precious little bottle to her chest, arguing noisily with herself as she went. McGrimmen & Co. met her stumbling along, banging from side to side against the woodwork, still conducting a conversation with herself under her breath, her eyes wide with fear and shock and clearly determined to put the maximum distance between herself and the locker. She had a wild, hunted look her as if her most terrifying nightmare had suddenly taken form, along there in the gloom at the end of the passageway,

'Let me past,' she hissed. 'This damned boat is cursed, possessed. I tell you – there are demons, warlocks and bluidy Frenchies at work here!'

'Go after her Walter,' Jack urged, 'while we find out what the hell has happened down here. Although I've got a shrewd idea....'

Hamish had already squeezed his huge frame through the low doorway and when Jack followed him into the locker he found himself standing by the big Highlander's shoulder. As his eyes adjusted to the half-light Jack Zurich was conscious of a strange mechanical movement to his left. Walking, or more accurately, stiffly plodding towards him, one careful, deliberate step at a time down a path cleared between the stacks of boxes and bags came a small, neat figure with a peaked hat, grey overcoat and medallion. Napoleon was on the move.

'Carnegie, you've got him walking. I never thought we'd see him walking again. You're a bloody genius, that's what you are.' Hamish, who had seen the most complex automaton in the world smashed beneath the scenery in the Adelphi fire was clearly ecstatic and went towards Napoleon, rubbing his hands like an excited child, gazing at the mechanical masterpiece from all the angles.

Walter could see that back there in the gloom Carnegie and the sailmaker Jontot were seated on stacked boxes, admiring their handiwork. With a gentle clunk, his left foot raised, ready to take another step, the little general stopped in his tracks as the clockwork finally wound down.

'Brilliant. Brilliant, Brilliant. Still lots to do, obviously. But it's just brilliant. I really doubted that he would ever get mobile again.'

McGrimmen was joyful. He went across to the pair, slapped their backs and roughly shook the hands of the two men who had helped restore not only the Emperor's movement but the Highlander's hopes of resurrecting the Circus Caledonia from the disaster of the Adelphi theatre and the catastrophic loss of the *The Spirit of Speed*. Jack was equally impressed and he too could visualise the crowds flocking in Melbourne, Sydney and Adelaide to get a glimpse of this eighth wonder of the world.

'What an impressive job you've made of the clothes, Jontot. He looks a damn sight smarter now than he did in real life, by all accounts. You're right, Hamish – a real success.

'Well, not quite, Mr Zurich.' McGrimmen patted the automaton on the shoulder and gazed into the Bonaparte's vacant blue eyes.'

'There's just one more tilt device which so intricate that it's baffled us so far. The designer made sure his masterpiece wouldn't be easily copied. The tilt controls a rise/fall mechanism in his chest and if we can just get it operating than Napoleon will breathe again. It's a stunning, eerie effect, really quite exceptional.'

Walter rejoined them in time to see Napoleon walking again, four turns of the handle inserted at the base of his spine was enough to see him click into motion.

The agent blew air through his lips in admiration. 'My God, that's impressive. No wonder Agnes is lying down. This is her worst nightmare walking around as large as life.'

92 At the Mercy of a Maniac

Away to the north, as Walter headed aft to answer an urgent summons from the skipper, thunder drum-rolled perhaps twenty miles off and sheet lightning curtained the horizon.

The deep base echo of the thunder came bouncing across the waves towards the *Broomielaw,* as if signalling the start of some new on-board action. Walter consoled himself with the fact that the storm appeared to be drifting away from them. Fine. Already there had been enough tragedy and drama on this ship to last a good few lifetimes.

As he moved through the *Broomielaw* the emigration agent had been surprised to see Elijah Shade near the entrance to the family department chatting animatedly to a group of passengers. Walter had fully expected him to be already locked away in the brig.

More than that, the impostor had sent the most unsettling and knowing of smiles in Walter's direction as he passed. And didn't he also wink at me, thought Walter. No, I must have been mistaken. The emigration agent, with the collar of his greatcoat turned up against a raw bluster of wind was to quickly discover on the reaching the helm that Jack's mood was as grey as the weather.

The skipper's dejection immediately made sense when Walter listened to the crushing explanation of why Shade, the man who they were now convinced had toyed with the lives everyone on board the *Broomielaw,* was still so obviously at liberty and likely to remain so.

'No, it's not surrender, Walter. It's simply at matter of practicality, a trade-off, if you like.'

Jack Zurich's planned detention of Shade had taken a most unexpected turn. Trying to explain what had happened made the young man almost speechless with frustration. The emigration agent's first reaction was simple disbelief.

'But how could he have discovered the reason for McMaster's visit to the *Broomielaw* at Tristan da Cunha?' asked Walter.

'God only knows! He was seen on board ship and at the settlement speaking with the coxswain of the *Helenslee's* day boat. He might have someone listening at keyholes, he might even have the second sight for all I know. How he found out matters little. The fact is that he has the whole business, our little scheme to protect Margaret, chapter and verse - he knows every angle and has us cornered.'

'And what exactly did you agree to, Jack?'

'Well, after I'd dismissed Davie Macgregor, who owes me too much to be indiscreet, and Shade had stopped laughing in my face, he told me what he knew about our arrangement but promised to keep quiet under certain conditions. He was gloating, the bastard.'

Walter banged his fist on the rail. 'Dictating terms, was he?'

'That's about the stretch of it. He would, he said, continue to work with the sick, perform God's calling and retain his freedom in exchange for remaining silent about the way in which we had deceived McMaster and the Scottish authorities, to cover for Maggie.'

'So we've put our trust in a maniac. It's senseless.'

'What choice have we? Tell me, Walter, what choice? He only had to mention this to either of the government officials travelling with us and we'd be sunk. There was, there is – no choice.'

Was Walter imagining it or had the storm turned in its course, away there to the north, and was now tracking back towards the *Broomielaw*? What he wasn't imagining was the way Jack Zurich had had taken this body blow. The stand-in skipper looked breathless, deflated, perhaps even defeated.

'But what about the damage he has already wreaked on your ship, Jack? Is that just to be forgotten? This is a nightmare.'

Zurich turned to go. 'He says the loss the *Spirit of Speed* ended his interest in delaying our voyage. It seems he is now as keen to be in Adelaide as we are.'

'I'll wager he is. Damn his corrupt and evil soul!'

'If you can think of another way to proceed, short of actually disposing of Shade, losing him overboard, then I'll be delighted to hear of it, Walter.'

'Don't tempt me, Jack. Just at this particular moment I'd… No, we'll simply have to take this an hour at a time. But if we get any indication that he's still about his disruption then we must lock him up and take the consequences. I haven't brought these emigrants 10,000 miles to leave them at the mercy of a madman.'

'Think what you're saying, Walter. Push him and it'll be all three of us – you, me and Maggie in the dock at the High Court in Edinburgh, with the hangman waiting for us down at Leith.'

'An hour, a day at a time – that's all we can reasonably negotiate at the moment. Some breathing space. Meantime, Jack, let's try if we can to keep this sorry business from Maggie.'

Taking his leave Jack smiled across the deck at Macgregor who lifted one hand from the helm in salute and nodded dutifully.

'There is that one further matter to deal with, Jack. It is high time we confronted Cuthill, the young man who seems to have so many questions. It would be too much too hope that he's not tied up in some way with Shade.'

Jack Zurich turned at the top of the companionway: 'Leave it with me. Let's get clear of this God-forsaken place first,

Walter, then I'll tell Tully that we'll dine with the cabin passengers.

93 Battlements of Ice

Walter watched baby and mother. James Law Gilchrist, a smiling, pink bundle of fun and games, who lay gurgling on Maggie's lap, energetically stretching his stubby little legs, pointing his toes towards the wooden beams and blowing bubbles which he watched with mystification until the popped.

Above him a wooden fish with one beady eye, carved by Innes Macaulay as a birthday present, danced at the end of its twine anchored to the base of the upper bunk. Feed over, Maggie bent across the bunk as she prepared the baby for his afternoon nap. Hilda would sing him to sleep as usual.

Around them in the steerage there now a buzz of activity as early preparations for the evening meal began. Plates were gathered together and those on cooking detail tramped off in the direction of the galley. Hungry children patrolled the passageways or dived around the compartments playing hide-and-seek. One way to keep warm, I suppose, Maggie realised.

Wallace, as good as his word and goaded on by the cheeky youngsters, had proved that there were indeed one hundred and one ways of preparing salt fish. Tonight it seemed, they were to sample number 102.

Maggie watched Walter as he sat jotting some figures in his note book. There was no doubting that Walter was a restless, haunted soul. Perhaps he would never change. But equally, she was convinced that he could be a solid provider. Above everything else now it was what her family needed now that her husband James was gone.

And she had to admit to herself that she had a fondness for the man; for all his anxieties, she felt comfortable with him. Perhaps because his need for reassurance, companionship and security far outweighed her own. They had shared so much in such a short time. Again he had started to express anxiety that his background on the Hunter River and the nightmare which overtook him there, might become public property.

'I may have told you this a thousand times in the past few weeks. Walter, but you worry too much.'

'Yes, yes, you say that Maggie, but these folk have put their trust in me.' Suddenly Maggie felt that Lumsden was carrying some new, additional burden. He needed reassurance.

'Yes, and they will continue to put their faith in you. They know this vessel is merely oak, canvas, nails and pitch. It is really you who brings us to a new life. They will make what they can of it with hard work, a little luck and God's help. Don't let any guilt you feel cloud your judgement, Walter.'

The agent tucked his note book in his jacket pocket and examined the end of the pencil stub.

'I hope you're right, Maggie. I really do. But whatever way you care to look at it I've been less than honest with them. And now....' Whatever he had planned to say he clearly thought better of it. He tickled the baby's chin and was rewarded with the broadest of smiles and the biggest bubble of the day. Walter seemed pleased. 'Look at that! He hasn't a care in the world. That's the way I want us all to be.'

'Anyway, haven't you told me a hundred times of your hopes of securing a parcel of land on the Clutha,' she said, wrapping James in his blanket and laying him gently across her shoulder. 'What does it matter if the whole world knows, Walter? We are close now to our destination. Soon you will be able to start again, without any secrets, with a whole new life ahead of you.'

'That was merely one option, maybe it was only a dream. So much has happened since then...I don't think I could ever make a go of the farm on my own.' Silence.

Maggie paced up and down the narrow confines of the compartment, rocking her baby on her shoulder and patting him rhythmically on the back until he burped, then nestled at his mother's neck. Eventually when she stopped Walter stood directly in front of her and lifted a strand of hair and gently touched her cheek with his forefinger.

'Do you think you could ever come to love me, Maggie? With all my faults? I would try to shed this guilt and be more positive, I promise.'

'Oh Walter, you're a fine honest man but this is my future, this wee chap and my girls. After all you've been through, and all you know about me, we'd be fools to compound our misfortune. And you must know that there is no magical cure for this guilt you feel. Time is the only healer.'

The emigration agent clenched his fists, steeling himself, so it seemed, for a moment of some importance.

'I want to marry you, if you'll have me, Margaret Gilchrist. I know that we are different in so many ways and that James's loss must still be so hard to bear, but we'll be parting forever before too long. I couldn't stand to see you go out of my life without asking, without finding out if there is any hope at all that you…'

'Wheesht!' Maggie raised her finger to her lips. She had expected this eventually and had asked herself over and over how she would respond. All her eloquent certainty of the previous moment was gone and now, to her own surprise, she felt a whole deluge of emotions, elation, doubt, a touch of shame, guilt, and yes, a shiver of anticipation. But wasn't it odd that the enticing powers of persuasion which the emigration agent had so clearly displayed during the recruiting campaign for the voyage were so clearly missing from his make-up in this intensely personal and emotional moment.

'Well, Walter, I'm flattered. You know that of late there was little between James and myself as man and wife so that presents no problem but I must speak with my girls – this is an important moment in their lives too. There is much to explain'

'But you're not saying 'no, Margaret, are you?' His face lit up. She had never seen such a glow about him before.

'Let's say for the moment, Walter, that it's a definite maybe.' She smiled mischievously and settled baby James on the bunk where he snuggled down amongst the blankets, breathing gently and drifting off to sleep.

Just then, the second mate, a middle-aged sailor with a mop of thick curly hair, appeared, weaving his way between the family groups, stepping over a toddler playing on the boards with a set of wooden building blocks. 'Excuse me, ma'am. I hope this isn't an awkward moment; Mr Lumsden, the skipper would like to see you on deck.

*   *   *   *   *

'Well, Walter, you get your iceberg after all. And this really is something out of the ordinary! With a sweep of his arm and a raised finger Jack Zurich pointed casually to starboard.

The *Broomielaw* was cruising abreast of an iceberg, more like a vast island of ice, which dominated the entire southern horizon. The rugged sixty or seventy foot-high face, with its subtle green and white hues reached up to a knife-edged plateau surface. It was a huge chunk of the Antarctic ice pack which had broken free and was drifting north to destruction, slowly melting and disintegrating. It probably had already travelled hundreds of miles, suggested the *Broomielaw's* skipper.

It might be ten, twenty miles long, thought Walter, as he scanned the berg; and it was anyone's guess how broad. It had to be the size of a small county.

All work on the ship had stopped as if by some unspoken command, tea was forgotten and the emigrants and crewmen appeared from hatchways and deckhouses to view this awesome offspring of the great ice continent. Little ones were lifted at the rail for a better view and oohs and aahs were heard all across the quarterdeck as the emigrants pointed out the ever-changing features on the ice face as the moved along its length, the helmsman keeping the ship a cautious but sensible two hundred yards off the spellbinding silver-frosted wall.

The ice cliff was scarred and criss-crossed by clefts, crevasses and caverns where waves tumbled white-capped then squeezed themselves into the echoing, translucent interiors. Occasionally a shallow frozen valley would run up to the very level of the plateau giving a brief and tantalising glimpse of the smooth table top.

Somewhere up there, surely, an ice queen had her palace.

Every so often a section of the berg would creak and groan before breaking free and sliding spectacularly into the maelstrom at the cliff foot, setting up a miniature tidal wave which raced for the flanks of the *Broomielaw*.

'I've stationed a watch on the fore cross-trees to alert us to pieces of ice drifting in our path. This is dangerous work, Walter.' Jack Zurich blew on his hands. 'It's a sight to remember but pray God that we're well clear of the ice by nightfall.'

Within an hour the fresh sou'westerly had taken them clear of the plateau berg but into an infinitely more dangerous ice field, scattered escorts of the great floating table of frozen water.

Averaging less than four knots they had already crept past half-a-dozen towering bergs, the largest of which Jack calculated soared over 300 feet from the ocean surface to the summit, a veritable mountain round which they plotted a course.

But the smaller ice floes which hardly broke surface remained the biggest threat and into the dusk cries of 'Helm Up', 'Hard Down' or 'Stand Easy' rang out from for'ard as anxious hands were laid on the wheel.

'Have you looked astern recently, Walter?'

'No, to tell the truth, I've been more concerned with what's ahead.'

'It's a shark pack, maybe a dozen and they've been with us this past hour. It would be best, I think, if Ritchie did not learn of our new companions.

94 Calling the Ice Master

'And you can wipe that smirk off your face, Ratter. This is no climbdown. The only reason you're up here is so that you can advise me on how to pass safely through this damn ice field.'

'Aye, aye skipper,' Ratter responded, standing mockingly to attention and saluting: 'It's grand to know that you still need me for something. And you're right. Fifteen times to the Davis Straits and you can read the ice like the open pages of a book.'

Wrapped in a blanket against the cold, the deposed captain was enjoying his moment. He scanned the leaden, unfriendly waters around the *Broomielaw* with a trained and confident eye. The wind carried that distinctive chill as if cooled by contact with so much ice. It chaffed on the cheeks and explored the salt cracked lips of the seamen ranged around the wheel. Broken floes and occasional bergs still stretched in the dusk to the limit of vision, which in the eerie half-light was only a matter of a few hundred yards.

It was perhaps imagination, more likely wishful thinking but in the past few minutes as they ploughed eastwards Jack Zurich had sensed that the bergs were becoming smaller, that there was more open water, the floes more dispersed.

Tully, the steward, placed a wooden tray with some biscuits and mugs of steaming tea in the charthouse and disappeared down the lee companionway. Jack hadn't left the wheel for the past few hours and with darkness fast closing in he felt justified in having summoned Ratter from his cabin.

'You seldom see so much ice drifting this far east by north,' muttered Ratter, raking his fingers through his rough beard. Looking across at the younger man with an expression which betrayed mild contempt, Ratter spoke: 'Aye, this voyage is proving a real test for you, Mr Zurich, and no mistake. Not so damned cocksure now, eh?'

Ratter had been of little trouble lately, isolated from the rest of the voyagers, an almost forgotten man sitting the day through humming tunelessly to himself, flicking through his Bible. Escorted on to the deck morning and afternoon for exercise, his only visitor apart from Tully who brought his meals, had been Shade. And even these visits had tailed off recently.

Jack peered for'ard through the dusk in the direction of the ice watcher who had been posted at the bow and had been joined by an anxious group of passengers including Innes Macaulay and his two older sons. Looking astern Jack Zurich saw that the sharks were still with them, tracking the ship. It was certainly not unusual in these waters to be followed by a pack of sharks who had acquired a taste for the debris tossed overboard, but with ice around, it was somehow doubly unsettling to see the fins cutting through the languid wash of the *Broomielaw*.

The helmsman was tight-lipped, his powerful arms, veins standing proud, held the wheel as if it might at any moment assume a personality of its own and spin wildly out of control. Everything in the way he worked the wheel suggested that he was acutely aware of the burden of responsibility these manoeuvres placed on him. He was clearly glad that Jack Zurich was only feet away. The helmsman was also pleased to see the second mate Macgregor who held ultimate responsibility for steering the ship, reappear after thirty minutes shut-eye in his cramped cot in the fo'castle.

'Fortunate that you had to ask for my help,' said Ratter, tapping a dry biscuit on the rail and examining it with the trained eye of a seafarer who had bitten into more than one burrowing insect in his time. Even in the relatively civilised conditions on the *Broomielaw* it was still difficult for the old salt to break a lifetime's habit of checking for maggots and weevils.

'It's high time, Zurich, we had a talk about the goings-on aboard this ship.'

'Business to hand first of all, Silas, if you please; what advice have you for us bearing in mind that, as you say, you are almost a citizen of the Davis Straits.'

'Whatever you say. Steady as she goes – that's the best I can do you for you at the moment. Don't be tempted to race her out of the ice, especially with dark falling. That's been the downfall of many an ambitious skipper.'

'Why so?'

'The danger here is not above the water but just below the surface. There are ice reefs stretching out around these bergs and they are treacherous as any coastal shoals. Keep her on an even keel and stay alert. Now there is something you must know about Shade.'

'Oh, your old bosom and boozing companion? I heard that there had been a falling out between the two of you. What secrets could you possibly have to interest us concerning our esteemed surgeon and confessor?'

'Bosom companion – well you have the rights of it there, for sure. He's my brother, damn his black soul. And he's a dangerous, violent and unpredictable man.'

Stunned, Jack took a step back, held on to the rail and was drinking in the implications of Ratter's revelation as the cry – 'Bergs Dead Ahead! Port and Starboard!' rang out through the half-light.

Jack turned to the helmsman who was straining anxiously, perched on tip-toes, attempting to see what nightmare lay ahead. 'Keep her steady man till we see what we've got – then be ready to work like the devil.'

'Stay here Ratter, I'm going for'ard.' With two bounds Jack was down the wooden stairs and off across the quarterdeck.

The sight ahead, slowly emerging out of the gloom of evening was impressive, awesome. To starboard towered a huge iceberg with a twin-peaked summit that seemed to point the way to heaven like the glistening spires of some medieval cathedral. It was no more than eighty yards from the *Broomielaw*.

God only knows how much more of that is actually under the water, thought Jack as he reached the rail and the emigrants parted to allow him into a prime viewing position.

Already they were close enough to hear the water slurp around the base of the ice mountain and to hear the great berg groan and creak as it worked against itself, internal fissures opening and closing with the motion of the waves. It hung ominously over the *Broomielaw*.

'Lookout – up there, tell me man, quickly, what's to port?'

From directly above them came the shout: 'More bergs, sir, three or four, smaller mark you, perhaps half a cable from us.'

Jack was suddenly aware of Ratter's urgent yell from behind him. 'Look out for the ice raft! This has probably all been one large berg. We'll be right on top of her.'

'Hard to port, for God's sake to port! Ice just below us!' As the call came from the lookout the men at the bow could hear – and feel through their boots – an ominous scratching and scraping as the keel came into skimming contact with the platform of ice which now stretched all around them, probably only a few, terrifyingly few, feet below the surface.

95 The Glass Prison

Together the helmsman and the second mate dragged the great wheel around and everyone on deck waited, frantically, for the *Broomielaw* to respond. There was an ominous sensation of dragging, of the vessel slowing in her course, and a deep groaning like a beast in pain carried up through the timbers as they reached for the bulwark to steady themselves.

They were over the ice and if they were drawn to a halt, it would surely be the finish of them.

Below decks the emigrant families could only sit on their bunks and hug each other. Parents comforted the wee ones as the strange grating noises seemed to issue from the wooden floor and

332

walls. A few whispered prayers were heard and the menfolk who had been on deck hurried back to be beside their loved ones.

The *Broomielaw* was still stuttering along, bumping across the bed of ice, and as they turned to port the first of the clutch of smaller bergs could be seen through the rigging. It was perhaps a hundred feet high, soaring up into the gloaming.

The first of these pinnacle bergs, like a glassy minaret, could not be avoided. The ship brushed alongside, wood crunching and grinding on the frozen outcrops. The slender crown of the berg tipped, then tumbled, bringing tons of ice thudding down on the deck, sending up a spray of ice crystals.

The *Broomielaw* seemed, at that moment, to be locked to the iceberg, held fast. Jack sprinted back to the afterdeck. The crew were guiding the emigrants down from the deck, away from the danger of more ice collapse. Miraculously no-one had been caught under the ice fall but there were a few minor injuries caused by flying shards of razor sharp ice.

What happened next had the quality of another time and another universe.

In his full dress uniform, Captain Alec S. Ritchie of the *Spirit of Speed* marched up from the hatchway, picked his way through the scatter of ice blocks on the deck and hauled himself up on to the gunwale, port midships, clinging to the shrouds and waiting his moment. Close at his heels Walter Lumsden burst on the deck and shouted over his shoulder at the group gathered by the wheel: 'Help needed over here! Ritchie's lost the place. He's left a note in…'

As he spoke the *Broomielaw* dipped a few degrees to port, towards the berg and Ritchie leapt forward, like a man half his age, down some eight to ten feet on to the narrow ice platform which fringed the berg. He crashed to his knees as the ship regained an even keel but picked himself up and casually brushed the ice from his uniform as if he had just stepped ashore at Greenock.

He saluted the group on deck then turned to repeat his salute in the direction of the emigration agent who watched dumbstruck from the rail. He shouted: 'The sharks shall not take me, Mr Lumsden. I knew they were there. You kept it from me. It was only a matter of time…'

So saying, the sad, demented skipper without a ship, a man who could never again look the survivors of the *Spirit of Speed* in the eye, began to scramble, unsteadily, slipping and sliding up the forty-five degree slope towards the vertical base of the pinnacle. For a man who had not left his cabin for two weeks he pushed ahead confidently.

On the deck of the *Broomielaw*, on Jack's orders, ice anchors were lobbed across the gap between ship and berg. And all the time the *Broomielaw* was still making little headway, but seeming to spin the berg, every so slowly on its axis as she went. Only one of the ice anchors gripped, the others clattered on to the ice shelf and slid into the water. The crewmen hauled in the ropes and tried again.

Jack Zurich struggled with a terrible dilemma. He wanted desperately to be free of the berg but he knew that the moment that happened Ritchie, sad, mad Ritchie, up there on the ice slope, kicking into the ridges and still progressing upwards, was as good as dead.

Then fate, as fate often seems to do, took the decision out of Jack's hands. The berg lurched perilously and a fissure, which had been perhaps only a few feet wide and which ran down to the water at Ritchie's right hand, suddenly opened yawningly revealing the dark green, glassy heart of the ice island. At the same moment Ritchie lost his footing and after scrabbling for a few terrible moments at the ice with his fingers, he began to slide, slowly, inescapably, towards the dark crevasse. Without a sound he slipped over the edge and dropped into the dark chasm.

On the *Broomielaw* anguished, helpless glances were exchanged. The ice anchors were gathered in and as if at a signal, the *Broomielaw* lurched forward, freeing herself from the ice below her keel.

The moment of parting from Ritchie's berg was one which none of the folk on deck would ever forget – from captain to cabin boy. It was the stuff of future nightmares. The berg rolled again and to their utter dismay the watchers saw the crack in the ice where Ritchie fell begin to heal itself. The movement of the ice closed the gap, drew the frozen walls together until Ritchie's tomb was closed, sealed completely.

96 Sharing the Burden

Below decks the realisation among the emigrants that the *Broomielaw* had wrestled free of the ice was greeted with a relief which bordered on mild hysteria. Two or three women wiped away tears, folk hugged each other, some shook hands. However, the initial euphoria soon edged into moments of prayer and private thanksgiving. Everyone had been made aware that it had been a mighty close call.

Storms, even hurricanes, they had anticipated, but that cruel, frozen ocean with its shifting reef and treacherous channels, had been a truly alien landscape for which nothing could have prepared them.

By the following morning, however, thoughts, particularly among those who had survived the sinking of the *Spirit of Speed* two weeks previously were with the master, Ritchie, the tormented skipper who had been swallowed by the iceberg. Few forgave him his dereliction of duty during the sinking but most understood why he had chosen to end his torment.

The awful truth was that Ritchie, in his determination to be the swiftest on the Australia run, to ensure that the Southern Cross company left their principal rival trailing, had probably driven the *Spirit of Speed* – and himself to destruction. An accumulation of small errors had conspired to bring catastrophe. The details would probably never be known. It was a truth that would not now be spoken. It was as if they all, in some strange way, took on the burden of Ritchie's guilt now that he was gone.

The crew of the *Broomielaw* did their best to lift the dark mortcloth of gloom which enveloped the ship. But even patches of blue among the ceiling of grey cloud and a freshening, following wind pushing them ever closer to their goal, failed to cheer the emigrants.

Queenie returned from her private corner of the quarterdeck where she had been retching. No fresh bout of sea nausea this, although that was how she explained it to her concerned neighbours in the women's quarters. No, it was the confirmation of morning sickness.

Having completed her cleaning duties in the galley and water closets, a routine which she now felt she could perform in her sleep, Queenie kicked of her working shoes and sat on her bunk, legs dangling over the edge, back against the wooden wall. She thought she sensed a tenderness in her breasts, then poked and prodded at her stomach and wondered. Was she showing yet? Queenie hoped not. It would make securing work in South Australia all the harder.

'My, my lass. I've seen more fat on a skinny mouse.'

Maggie Gilchrist planked herself down beside Queenie and began to sift through and fold a basketful of nightshirts which she had washed and aired for the kiddies in the infirmary.

'If my weight was the only problem, Maggie, I'd be less anxious. I believe I'm going to have William Bigland's child and where is he, a thousand miles behind happily hunting crayfish at Tristan da Cunha.'

'But you must have known before now, Queenie?'

'Aye, well, I always hoped it was an upset stomach.'

Discretely Maggie looked the Stormay lass up and down. She certainly had the glow about her. There followed a serious conversation in which the dates since Queenie's last flux were scrutinised, her symptoms considered and the options discussed. For a moment the two women sat in silence.

'They say you develop cravings…you know…when you're pregnant, Maggie.'

'That's true enough. I even saw myself sampling some of Agnes's quinine wine when I was carrying Hilda.'

'Well, I've developed a taste for Jack's chewing tobacco,' She smiled. Then they both smiled. 'Honestly, Maggie, you're laughing but who's going to want me when I've got a belly like a baby elephant.' She made a sweeping two handed gesture which indicated an imaginary stomach of gigantic proportions.

Maggie chuckled. 'You'll still be beautiful, Queenie, whether you've a belly or no'.' But they both knew that inevitably there would be difficult times ahead for Queenie.

Maggie remembered another young woman, abused, misunderstood, betrayed and cast out by a family more afraid of scandal than their daughter's happiness. Cast out into a world where only women were fit to take the blame.

There had been moments in that first month away from home, Maggie recalled, when she had thought it easier just to lie down in the snow – and give up. Instead she had developed her God-given talents to survive. Nothing much had changed. This deadly serious game still continued.

The difference now was that she was responsible for four children. And they, she was determined, would grow up in Otago, in New Zealand, where they might have space to cast aside all the old ideas, the senseless values of Victorian Scotland – where success was measured only by a blind obsession for hard work.

And Queenie could make that fresh start too. Once she became adjusted to the idea that she was carrying another living being within her. That helped women adjust to almost anything.

Just look at this prison, thought Maggie, patting the last of the neatly folded nightshirts. Here there were eighty women, jammed together like bobbins in a box. Sensitive, intelligent creatures in the main, living, eating and sleeping almost on top of each other but generally managing to do so with good grace and without the fist fights and disputes which were daily occurrences in the single mens' quarters.

Three or four of the circular brass-rimmed scuttles were flung wide, just enough to clear the fetid night-time air but allowing a semblance of warmth to be retained on the lower decks. Pale morning light splashed all around the bunks.

A gang of squealing children, chasing a scruffy, flop-eared collie which had escaped from its pen on deck, thundered past.

Even the distinctive, lingering, vaguely medicinal lanolin smell of the wool bales which had filled the *Broomielaw's* holds on the last homeward voyage blended with the other aromas of the steerage to create a 'perfume' which would live in the memories of the emigrants for the rest of their lives.

Maggie rubbed at a cluster of flea bites, now matured to water blisters, on her forearm and glanced along the passageway towards the cramped water where a small, neatly formed queue of women had formed to use this, the only private toilet facility for the steerage passengers. Yes, women could adjust to almost anything, given time.

She thought again of Walter and his proposition, or should she admit to herself that it was a proposal.

Queenie dabbed at her eyes with a kerchief. 'For a wee while there I really began to believe that everything would work out for the best, even without William. But now I'm not so sure.'

Maggie took her hand. 'Listen, girl. If you think we're going to leave you standing on the pier at Adelaide with nothing but five dollars in your pooch and your hat box for company then you should think again. If no satisfactory work turns up in the days that the *Broomielaw* lies in South Australia, then you'll come on with us to the Clutha. This time you can work your passage as one of the Gilchrists.'

She patted Queenie gently on her stomach.

'Selfish motives, you see. This wee lad or lass will be grand company for my baby James.'

Queenie leant forward and kissed Maggie on the cheek then together, like mischievous playmates, the two women, arms linked and carrying a basket each set off in the direction of the infirmary.

97 The Brothers Grim

'I don't understand your problem. Lock him up! For God's sake, lock him up. If you think I've been trouble to you, then you haven't seen anything yet. The man is unstable. I've no plans to join those poor bastards who went down with the *Spirit of Speed*.'

Ratter twisted uncomfortably on his bunk and gazed at the manacle on his wrist, rubbing the joint with his other hand. More calmly this time he said: 'It would make more sense, gentlemen, if my dear brother was under lock and key.'

Walter Lumsden was struggling. 'It's not as straightforward as that, Ratter. The man is our surgeon. And there's illness on this ship. We need him.'

It might have been better to get the whole, sordid Sweetshaws business out into the open. Walter had questioned himself about this over and over, ever since they left Tristan da Cunha. Never! They had lied. They had plotted; all to protect Maggie. And Shade, if truth was told, had them over a barrel.

Both Jack and Walter felt haunted and helpless in the presence on board ship of Elijah Shade now emerging as Peter Ratter - man who held their futures in his hand and continued to smugly roam the decks and companionways of the *Broomielaw*, a loose cannon in their midst.

This resumed conversation between the three men, interrupted when the ship ran on to the ice shelf, had done nothing to ease the anxiety felt by the emigration agent and the stand-in skipper. The family history that Ratter, slouched in the brig, related that morning and the details of the dark career of his brother, set the two men back on their heels. Any doubt that they were dealing with a dangerous, devious and unpredictable individual was quickly evaporating.

Jack reflected how odd it had seemed that Ratter and the preacher should hit it off so quicky and enthusiastically bearing in mind the old nautical superstitions about having a man of the cloth on board ship. Now it all made sense. Ratter for his part, while clearly confused over the reluctance of Jack and Walter to put his brother, the phoney preacher, out of business was now desperately trying to justify his deceit over his brother's posting to the *Broomielaw*.

'What I hadn't realised was that Peter has totally lost any sense of right or wrong. I have to say I knew him as a fraudster, confidence trickster, impersonator and thief. But when you consider the events of the past weeks, we could safely add potential homicidal maniac to that list.'

'You've seen it yourself, surely. He has been acting like a man possessed. I don't understand this reluctance to take him out of circulation.'

Walter caught Jack's anxious glance. But once again they skipped around this very reasonable query.

'Are you telling us then that he is neither a minister or nor a surgeon? asked Walter.

'Oh, he qualified as a doctor right enough; at the University of Edinburgh but he soon drifted away from orthodox medicine. He made several voyages as a ship's surgeon then five years ago he was forced flee to Australia when he was involved in a plot to defraud the Christian Charter Bank of Dundee out of thousands of pounds.'

Walter Lumsden shook his head. 'And what exactly, Ratter, has prompted this change of tack on your part; you've been protecting him since we left Greenock? Presumably you helped him secure a berth on the *Broomielaw* in the first place.'

'I did. But I had no idea of this other agenda he seems to have. He would never have set foot on my deck if I thought he was a wrecker. When all this comes into the open, I want that understood. He simply asked my help in securing a passage south and I was to be well paid for it.'

The deposed skipper of the *Broomielaw* seemed to have lost so much of his confidence and aggression. He struck a pathetic figure as he lay on one elbow and stared at the floor. Almost in a whisper he continued: 'He also knew my weakness for the drink and was hardly on board before he was plying me with brandy. It truly brings the devil out in me. And my dear brother, he hardly touches the stuff...'

Walter Lumsden moved from the low doorway to confront Ratter.

'Come on now, man. That's bloody ridiculous! I've seen him half-seas over many a time on this voyage, staggering back to his cabin after a session with yourself or the boys in the fo'castle.'

Ratter chuckled, the corners of his red lips cracking and creasing. 'If you say so, chief. I told you he was a sharp operator. It suited him to have you think he was a toper; made him less of a threat, you see. No, he's far too interested in the other little pleasures of the flesh to allow alcohol to cloud his brain. If you take my advice you'll lock him up and throw the key into the ocean, or better still throw the maniac himself to fishes.'

God, thought Jack, if only....even now the agent and the stand-in skipper felt they were getting at best half truths from Silas Ratter, but over the piece, the story had a chillingly authentic ring to it. It was maddening to be hog-tied by Shade's threat to expose them.

At the same time Walter recalled that half-mad, half-mocking smile after Peter Ratter, alias Elijah Shade, alias God knows who else, had played his trump card. It was a smile which said he had them dangling on a string.

Even now, despite their supposed deal, this devil's truce, Walter feared that some piece of mischief might have been set in train by the false preacher which would affect the smooth running of the ship and which would only make itself felt in the coming days. He looked across at Jack and shook his head ruefully. He felt great sympathy for the man who had become his friend. But Jack's first command was turning into the stuff of nightmares.

Walter continued to ask himself how he had failed to register the phoney minister's stuttering performance at the first service on deck at Greenock, neglected to question earlier these bizarre, one-to-one meditations with the women of the ship and how he had lacked perception to see that his apparent comradeship with the crew had been merely a device to foment unrest.

Ratter's revelation that Shade had even been prepared to feed drink to his own brother in a successful attempt to disrupt the smooth running and slow the course of the ship, had stunned the emigration agent. He felt only slightly reassured knowing that the big Highlander Hamish McGrimmen had been the surgeon's shadow for the past couple of days, just to ensure he kept his side of the dubious bargain. But it was all desperately unnerving at a time when they could almost smell Australia.

'Yes, be warned, Silas Ratter concluded, 'Get him locked away as soon as might be. He's a dangerous piece of work, brother of mine or no'. And for God's sake don't put him in here beside me!

98 Undercover No More

The steward appeared, beaming from ear to ear, carrying the pie aloft like a trophy of war. Gusts of steam issued from the perforations in the crusty surface and a meaty aroma which reminded the company of Sunday dinners and busy firesides filled the air.

There were oohs and aahs from the cabin passengers and ritual raising of knives and forks as the dish was placed with utmost care on the table in front of the master of the *Broomielaw* who lifted the knife and prepared to slice the masterpiece.

This once-a-week meal with the cabin passengers gathered in the passenger saloon/dining room had become part of shipboard routine for the emigration agent and the young skipper.

Within a few days of taking command Jack Zurich had instituted a radical move to ensure that as the new skipper he knew accurately how his regime was being received between decks; the aim being to prevent him becoming a lonely, out-of-touch individual like Ratter. He resolved to spend more time with the crew, to listen to their complaints over a chew of tobacco, by the shrouds or as they prepared to reef or furl the sheets.

These were opportunities to hear grievances and try to deal with them informally before a thunder-browed delegation arrived at his cabin door. He had also introduced an open-door policy on complaints despite being warned by more experienced crewmen that it was unorthodox and might even undermine his authority.

And with the emigration agent by his side he had been regularly taking his evening meal in the noisy yet friendly chaos of the steerage mess or less often, like this evening, in the slightly more refined surroundings with his little band of cabin passengers...when he would normally just listen and digest. As far as Walter and Jack could judge, these manoeuvres had been a success, if only because both passengers and crew now felt Jack so much more approachable than his predecessor.

This particular evening the two men sat among the elite group, the Dunnets from Caithness, middle-aged hoteliers who aimed to give Melbourne its first truly respectable lodging house, two middle-aged gents heading for Adelaide to take over senior banking positions, a very serious government official called Minard Price who was to carry out mineral surveys up country and the Sinclair family from Dunbar.

There was a prim young governess who was going to join the family of a colonial official in Adelaide and a large, florid, corpulent gent with a port-wine voice who was a printer by trade and was taking his own press to Australia with the intention of producing a modest journal.

Also seated quietly at one end of the table was the thin, pale young man with the wire-rimmed glasses, the notorious notetaker Cuthill who had been taking such a keen interest in shipboard activities, yet somehow always seemed to stand apart from the action.

What was this chap up to with his questions about everything and anything to do with the running of the ship? On a normal voyage this behaviour would have raised no suspicions, but this was no normal voyage.

The oil lamp, squeaking and swinging gently from the beam above them cast a moving pool of yellow light back and forwards across the table as the emigrants ate enthusiastically. The conversation was light and the food, delightfully, surprisingly was delicious.

'Spike' Wallace had made an extra special effort that particular evening with a sea pie of fish and vegetables layered between crusts of pastry. This was a three-decker version normally regarded as a treat reserved for birthdays of crossing the line. It was followed by a duff of epic tastiness and in quantities which would have sunk a man-o'-war And this was washed down with as much lime juice as the body could stand.

It was 'Spike's' secret, of course, but having sailed the oceans for close on twenty years, there would always be a magical morning when he would wake and sense some unspoken change. He didn't need banks of cumulus cloud in an otherwise clear sky, rafts of driftwood and floating plants, lagoon glare, a greenish tint in the sky caused by the reflection of sunlight from coral reefs or unfamiliar birds, to tell him land was near. There was simply something in the air. Wallace knew instinctively while other people developed giraffe necks straining for a first sight of land, that the journey was approaching its conclusion. It was pastry time. Plates were eventually cleared away by the steward, and after chatting for a few minutes the cabin passengers began to drift back to their accommodation to dream dreams of their new home or venture on deck before turning in.

Walter and Jack Zurich, now convinced they had an almost complete picture of how Shade had schemed to sabotage the voyage of the *Broomielaw* were keen to tidy up the remaining, nagging loose ends.

'Mr Cuthill, just before you go – a few words, if you don't mind.'

Walter Lumsden studied the young man who sat down again opposite pulling at his cuffs and occasionally clearing his throat as if it was arid and tight. Jack waited until the steward had completed his duties then pulled up a seat. Cuthill was carefully avoiding eye contact.

'Thanks Tully,' said Jack. 'Leave the bottle, if you will.' Tray in hand, the steward closed the door behind him and his creaking footsteps disappeared down the passageway.

'A drink, Mr Cuthill, or can we call you, Gilbert.'

'No, I won't have a drink. Sorry, yes. Gilbert. That would be fine.'

'Here, let me pour you a little, in any case. I've a feeling you might be in need of a wee stiffener before we're through here.' So saying Jack filled the glass and slid it across the table towards the passenger, whose eyes suddenly narrowed with alarm.

'I recall you were off to take up some sort of municipal post with the council in Adelaide. Is that the way of it?' The question posed Walter leant back in his seat and traced a lazy circle with his finger on the rough tabletop.

'Yes, in the land office.'

'Hmm, you understand there's been a deal of, well, disturbance during this trip and although we now think we've rooted out the culprit – yet we can't figure out where you fit into the picture.'

Cuthill glanced nervously from Walter to Jack Zurich and back again. The *Broomielaw* dived into a wave and the brandy bottle slid a few inches before rocking to rest.

'What do you mean? Why I should I fit into any picture?' Jack took out his clay pipe and began to suck on the stem. In half-an-hour he could enjoy a smoke on deck - just as soon as they got the measure of young Mr Cuthill.

Jack tapped his pipe on the edge of the table. 'Well, for one thing young man, you seem to have an insatiable appetite for information about the way the ship is run. And Hamish tells us you've been asking around, odd questions such as: 'Has the food been satisfactory? Have grievances been properly dealt with?'

If we didn't know better we might think you'd been deliberately stirring the pot. Why don't you save us all time Gilbert, or whatever your real name might be. I'm sure you can clear up this misunderstanding.'

Jack sat back in his chair and eyed the young man. Cuthill showed no sign of responding. 'If not, we can just as easily hand you over to the constabulary. They tell me the process of justice grinds exceeding slow in the new lands. A few years in a fly-infested cell during the hot season in Adelaide would be just the ticket.'

For one unsettling minute the only sounds in the saloon were the creaking of the timbers and the occasional exchange of voices from along the wooden corridors. Walter became convinced that the young man – he guessed he was no more twenty years of age – was about to burst into tears. But he composed himself and pulled himself upright in his seat.

'There will be no need for that. My name isn't Cuthill as I think you'd guessed. I am James Gordon Anderson, a reporter with the *Bulletin* of Buchanan Street, Glasgow.'

'Aye, we suspected you weren't a member of the guild of actors!'

Walter grinned across at Jack Zurich. Events had taken a fearful turn since the start of the voyage but early on the two men had agreed on a wager as to the true identity of the mysterious Mr Cuthill. While Jack was increasingly convinced that he was either a criminal sidekick of Shade's or perhaps an undercover inspector from the Colonisation Commissioners, Walter had suspected all along he might be a writer, or worse, a newspaperman.

And so the real story spilled out. Cuthill told them there had been so much adverse publicity in the Australian press and so many letters of complaint reaching the United Kingdom about conditions on emigrant ships that as a public duty the owners of the *Bulletin* felt compelled to investigate. The Clutha Society in particular was the target of a series of vicious epistles received by the newspaper which claimed the company were operating their ships under a brutal and uncaring regime. More than once letters had described the Clutha fleet as 'death ships.'

'Anyway, such was the volume of complaint; my editor decided that there would be no better way to establish conditions on board than to actually make the great journey. And so yours truly, James Gordon Anderson, joined the emigrants.'

Jack sighed. Whether this had been an orchestrated campaign to scupper the activities of the shipping line by their rivals or genuine complaints from passengers, there were questions to be answered. 'Our journey is almost over, Mr Anderson. Are you prepared to honour us with your conclusions about the *Broomielaw* and the way she is being operated?'

'You want the truth?'

'It would be a help.'

'Well, frankly, I've been astounded at the way you've dealt with the troubles through which we've sailed. You seem to have had so many headaches – not least having to take command when Mr Ratter, well, took ill. And I should say that I personally had my worries over the Rev. Shade; call it journalistic instinct, if you like. I mentioned my doubts about him to the captain early on but he told me quite forcibly to keep my suspicions to myself. It would only cause ill feeling.'

'Now, there's a surprise,' Jack muttered.

'As it happens, Mr Zurich, the passengers have nothing but praise for you and Mr Lumsden. I fear my first despatch when I file from Adelaide will have to suggest that a false trail was laid for us.'

Jack began, carefully, to fill his pipe while young Cuthill, like a veteran, disposed of the glass of brandy which had been set in front of him.

'Well, Walter, we appear to be swiftly running out of loose ends. I think it might be best if we found half-an-hour over the next few days to brief this young man properly on the South Australia run, so that he can write with a bit of authority. What say you?'

99 Just Mild Euphoria

Every hour now felt warmer; the seas somehow less threatening. The ominous grey cloud cover had broken and vast tracts of deepest blue opened up above the white sails crowding. Spray arrowed from the bow.

The thought that every blessed mile was taking the emigrants further from the kingdom of ice and emptiness lifted their spirits. It was easy, so easy, in those precious moments to forget how treacherous and unforgiving the ocean remained. The *Broomielaw* was scudding nor'east – frequently making more than 250 miles in a day to the delight of the deck-walkers who had cast off their heavy jackets and glum faces and gathered expectantly each noon around the bulletin board beside the main mast.

They were fast approaching their first planned Australian landfall, the tiny community of Albany, founded only thirty years previously in King George Sound on the Southwest corner of the great island continent.

After the terrible ordeal in the ice fields normal shipboard activity resumed. There was even a lively *Matter of Opinion* one evening on the merits of the Scottish climate as opposed to that of Australia. In their pioneering mood and following the experience in the frozen wastes it was no surprise that the heat of Australia won hands down.

This discussion concluded with another lively session from the Coocaddens Gutter Band whose regular musical interludes had always helped to lighten the mood of the emigrants. This particular evening Erchie Bowers, the smallest of the players, seemed set on beating his drum into submission. He smiled his gleeful smile at his admiring audience and his enthusiasm mirrored the optimistic mood which had taken hold of the ship.

There was, without question, a kind of magic in the air.

Long-term repairs to the storm damage had been completed and the *Broomielaw* was almost back to her sparkling best. There was a feeling of expectation throughout the ship, a sense that all discomfort, pain and grief was behind them. Australia – merely a word of nine letters – but their destination, now the focus of every waking thought, had scarcely been mentioned in the past weeks. These days it was on everyone's lips.

People would stand gripping the rail, eyes closed tight, the wind beating on their faces, taking in great draughts of the sharp air as if they could already smell the shores on the new land on the breeze. Away to the north where sea met sky, under the vault of brilliant blue, the focus of all their hopes lay just beyond the edge of imagining.

Each day saw a little huddle of emigrants on the main deck, gathered to greet the rising sun with a prayer and a hymn. Even those who still had the Tasman Sea to cross to reach their new homes in New Zealand, joined in these faith-restoring reveries.

For a little while it was grand fun for the children to sprint for'ard, look mischievously at each other, point dramatically to distant battlements of cloud hugging the horizon and shout with all the strength they could muster: 'Land Ho! Australiee!' Parents allowed this game to continue for a couple of days but when it became aggravating for the elders, a belt round the ear brought the prank to a conclusion.

However, there was no doubting that even the most sober and patient of the passengers were keeping one eye on that northern skyline.

The mild euphoria seemed to transfer itself in particular to the youngsters in the teens of years and their early twenties who staged impromptu mid-morning ceilidhs on the main deck when the weather permitted. The Gilchrist and Macaulay boys and girls would lead the way, flinging each other frantically around the boards, dodging the hatch covers, capstans and ropes as they went.

Jack Zurich again found himself being constantly questioned on their progress and every command to put on more sail was greeted with delighted smiles among the company. The emigrants, who now considered themselves storm-hardened mariners would listen to the shouted orders and try to identify the various canvases which were being worked on.

After what seems like months of intrigue, agitation, double-dealing and tragedy, an unfamiliar calm wrapped itself around the *Broomielaw,* like the aftermath of the restoration of a child's misplaced favourite blanket.

Maggie continued with more urgency to complete her sketches of passengers and crew, taking advantage of bursts of sunshine to persuade her subjects topside. She planned a little gallery of portraits for her new home in Otago. In her folio of charcoal drawings was an incomplete portrait of her husband, James. Strangely over the past week or two she had been unable to call up a precise image of his face.

100 Lights on the Horizon

St Valentine's Day, February 14, 1858, dawned fine and clear. However, even in the bracing but pleasant conditions of mid-morning Jack did not like the feel of the wind. He took his readings and stood anxiously by the helmsman watching the movement of the sea and the clouds rolling away to the east like an armada of unfurling sails.

By the middle of the day the sky had become overcast, a menacing metallic grey; so low it seemed that if you stood on your tip-toes you might thrust a fist into the cloud cover.

Then, as the wind whipped angrily at the waves, came the unnerving order which everyone had hoped they'd heard the last of – 'All hands shorten sail!' Crewmen moved up among the stretched canvas, swarming through the rigging like a battalion of Gibraltar apes.

Wild squalls with stinging showers arrived and in those mad moments, it was scarcely possible to see more than a ship's length ahead. Aloft, the seamen fought to keep a secure foothold on the guide ropes with the rain stinging faces and the cold deadening all sensation in their hands. Memories of the loss of their two shipmates were still fresh in their minds as they worked on the high ropes.

Again Jack Zurich, who four months previously had expected no more than his usual responsibilities as first mate, was called to make yet another judgement of Solomon – whether to heave to and ride out the storm or to run before it. As ever, he confided in Walter who over the past 24 hours, like the children, could scarcely took his eyes off the northern horizon.

'We are close, damned close, Walter. But this storm threatens to be a beauty. We'll give it a couple of hours yet before snugging down and riding it out.'

Jack Zurich's voice was calm, confident as usual; inside he was wracked with doubt. He looked out across the white-topped rollers and after much agonising his decision was to run under two lower topsails, at least for a little while. However, the wind increased steadily and by mid-afternoon they were being battered by a full gale which screamed in the ears of everyone deck and sang a terrifying dirge to the emigrants down below.

Heavy seas, whipped into a lather, began to tumble aboard. The *Broomielaw* was plunging by the head now, too often for Jack's liking, taking avalanches of green water over the bow.

At around 2 p.m., in rapidly diminishing light, while a young seaman was trying to weave his way aft through the obstacles along the main deck on order to relieve one of his shipmates at the helm, the *Broomielaw* shipped one particularly enormous sea when more of the vessel seemed below water than above it.

From his position on the poop Walter could see a dreadful scene unfold in front of his eyes – and he was powerless to help. Hamish, who was with the skipper, moved to clamber down the port companionway from the quarterdeck to give assistance, as the boy struggled desperately to hang on to a hatch cover. But as he stepped forward Hamish of a sudden felt Jack's restraining hand on his shoulder.

'You'll be over the side with him if you venture down there.' Hamish slumped down on the top step and clung to the handrail. The main deck was waste deep in water.

Then in seconds the surging, rolling wall of water lifted the boy high and carried him clear of the safety net where seamen were normally caught like herring during heavy seas. From the quarterdeck a rope was thrown but he surfaced, just once, for a second, already astern of the ship; then he was gone.

Even in the teeth of the storm each man found a moment for silent prayer for their lost shipmate. Jack Zurich, in a quiet agony of frustration and helplessness, turned to deal with another crisis. He scrambled to the aid of Macgregor who was struggling at the wheel to prevent the ship broaching.

The other individual who had been at the helm, known to passengers simply as Harry the Greek, was being helped below, sobbing and dismally shaking his head. His swarthy face had taken on a ghostly, ivory tinge, reminiscent of the breast of the albatross. In the face of the blast he had lost all reason and had been standing, staring ahead into the storm, calling on all the saints in the Greek calendar to come to their aid.

It transpired that the man had briefly glanced over his shoulder to a see a regiment of huge seas building immediately astern of the *Broomielaw*, foam-crested leviathans, threatening to overwhelm the vessel. On voyages past Jack had known men to be strapped to the wheel to stop them being swept overboard by the sea but just as crucially to prevent them turning to witness that awesome sight.

Walter's latest mission was successfully completed – he arrived in the chart house with a pot of coffee. Jack threw a mug of the strong, scalding liquid over his throat realising he had been on deck for almost six hours. He knew the strange compression of time which mariners often felt during storms was at work.

But this was blowing up to be more than just a storm – the force of the wind was building towards a severe gale. Walter and Jack exchanged anxious glances.

A further hour passed, then two. Violent blasts were now bouncing off what remained of the stretched and shredded canvas. Mountainous seas were pouring over the stern and racing in torrents, flooding the waist of the ship. The scuppers could scarcely cope with the discharge of water before the next roller crashed inboard.

The light was almost gone; a brief glimpse of the moon was seen among the cloudbanks and then it vanished never to reappear again that night, almost as if it feared to look upon the vessel struggling against forces so enormous as to be almost incomprehensible.

There were brief lulls in the ocean's assault on the *Broomielaw* when the more optimistic might have thought, just for one crazy moment, that the worst was over. It was during one of these periods of relative calm that a disbelieving shout went up from Hugh Macaulay who had volunteered to lend a hand with the deck pumps.

'To port, Mr Zurich, lights to port!' he screamed over the thunder of the waves.

Everyone within hearing turned to stare into the murky afternoon.

'Walter, pass me the chart. This is impossible.'

But the sighting was genuine enough – half-a-dozen pinpricks of light seemingly spaced in a random grouping against the dark backdrop, disappearing and appearing with the vertical motion of the vessel as the enormous seas rose and dispersed beside, and over, her. They must be very close to Albany, Jack now realised.

A trick of the light – it was unlikely; stars low down on a cloud-clear stretch of horizon – implausible. The most likely explanation was, indeed, that they were seeing a small coastal community, a scattering of houses hugging the shore around King George Sound. It could only be Australia.

101 Hell and High Water

Over the siren din Jack screamed at his companions across the shuddering deck: 'We must have driven ahead at a fearsome rate in the past two hours. Watch for rocks – we're close to shore.'

Before they had a chance to make a proper assessment and guess at their position and distance from landfall the *Broomielaw* was struck by a ferocious squall abeam. For a moment only the roofs of the deckhouses could be seen. Men clung to anything they could find that was secured to the decks. When next they looked the lights were gone.

At the same moment the remains of the topsails were torn away, the wind now circling the *Broomielaw* was uttering a blood-curdling, demonic roar. She went over with her lee rail in the water and as the masts reached for the surf the remaining shreds of sail were claimed by the waves.

Chillingly, the *Broomielaw* did not fully right herself.

'Damn it to hell. Those mining engines below. The crates must have shifted,' shouted Jack as he watched men, ropes, torn sail and everything moveable floating amongst the foam. It was becoming impossible to move around or even to hear commands amid the cascades of water.

Below deck, the emigrants knew the drill for such situations well enough by now and as the able-bodied men rushed to help with the bilge pumps and tried to tie down deck equipment which had broken free, the women gathered their children around them in the 'partments.

Agnes Govan was found collecting her knitting, her precious potions and James Gilchrist's piece of pink rock from the Ward Burn from the shelf above her bunk and stuffing them in her bag. The women with their families, young and old then crowded to the foot of the main companionways awaiting instructions, grasping their little bundles of personal possessions, fearing the worst.

'We've been through hell and high water on this ship, surely we will not abandon her now,' whispered Maggie to Belle as they wrapped arms around each other for comfort. Maggie had the girls organised with extra shawls and they all carried an additional blanket. The Macaulay and Gilchrist families stood steadfastly by each other in the crush. Above them, as the *Broomielaw* bumped and bucked, beyond the fragile wooden boards they could hear the seas pounding on the hatches, demanding entry and the shouts of the crew and their menfolk as they worked.

Looking round at the faces Maggie saw fear in every one, old and young; a fear of the unknown and a sense of utter helplessness in the presence of the preternatural fury of the storm. Wee ones clung to their mother's skirts and angry cries went up from the throng: 'Make space there! Don't push!'

On deck, everyone who could stand was pointing into the rigging. Globes of pale blue fire, about size of footballs, could be seen at each yardarm and at the sheave holes by the mast heads. Like spectral lanterns they danced at their allotted positions as if providing illumination for the macabre dance which was unfolding way below them. Walter knew this strange phenomenon had been dubbed St Elmo's Fire but he had also heard the flickering light described by second mate Macgregor as *corpse candles*. He wondered how many crews had seen the 'candles' decorate the masts before their vessel disappeared from beneath them.

102 Hard Aground

'Broken water off the starboard bow! For God's sake turn her away!' The despairing cry came too late. The lookout had only a momentary, terrifying sideways glimpse of saw-edged reef before she struck.

One moment they were banging through heavy seas, everyone working away at their allotted tasks on the tilting deck, still confident that they would see the storm out, and the next moment the *Broomielaw* lurched violently, sickeningly to port, shaking, grinding, wood ripping along the saw-edged rocks for a second or two before she eventually jolted to a halt. The mighty masts and spars quivered like reeds on impact.

Immediately even heavier seas began to pile on to the decks and crewmen were thrown to the boards. One sailor was catapulted backwards and crushed against the gunwale by a tumbling spar, trapped by his midriff. He screamed once, waved an arm weakly then was silent and still – the frothing waters washing around and over him. All was confusion as lightning now crackled around the stricken vessel.

From beneath his feet Jack could hear series of muffled screams and the sound of fists thumping against hatch covers. The clipper was stuck fast on this partially submerged reef and no-one had to tell the emigrants below what had happened as the water crept up and along the lower passageways.

A hatch cover was thrown aside as crewmen moved along the deck knocking wooden pegs free and lifting waterproof tarpaulins from the frames. Tully, the Manx steward, his eyes filled with fear appeared through the hatchway followed by a stream of scrambling, wide-eyed, terrified emigrants clinging to their children, their bags and satchels, spilling out into the this angriest of nights.

They crawled and stumbled up the thirty degree angle, directed by the crew, heading for the high starboard side of the sloping main deck, seemingly oblivious to the storm which raged around them. Further along the deck other hatches covers were now being thrown aside as more emigrants emerged to face their destiny, relieved to be free at least from the dark, claustrophobic depths of the rapidly foundering vessel.

Tully reached the quarterdeck: 'Forgive me, Mr Zurich, sir. But I just couldn't keep the passengers down there. She seems to be holed in two or three places and taking water fast.' Vivid flashes of lightning now threw the vessel into strange relief, bathing the deck in a steely glare.

Immediately Jack Zurich ordered a sail passed over the bow to at least try to stem the leaks but it was impossible to achieve any sort of efficient seal, the largest hole according to Macgregor who had bravely crawled through the ship, was six or seven feet wide and ominously, mostly below the water line.

Tully had an additional piece of news. 'And Mr Macgregor saw the Rev. Shade down below, making for the aft sail locker. Perhaps he was lost, disorientated. Should I go back down for him?'

Jack bit his tongue. 'No, leave it, Tully. I can't imagine Mr Shade has ever lost his way. You're of much more value up here. Get down there amongst the passengers, please, and make sure folk are as secure as possible. I think we'll be filling the boats before long.'

'Listen, Jack. I'll go down below and see if I can find Shade', said Walter.

The two men looked at each other. In that moment an unspoken message was conveyed. Jack nodded.

'But don't hang around down there, Walter. It's difficult to say how long we've got before she starts to tear herself apart.'

Although firmly grounded the ship pitched and rolled as each successive wave smashed into her. Minutes sped past. Walter soon reappeared from the flooded depths of the vessel. The deck was now a mass of stumbling, scrambling humanity. The entire complement of passengers had found their way into the open and people were hanging on where they could on ropes, rails and rigging.

Walter, working his way hand over hand, along the high rail moved among his emigrants, patting the children's heads, trying to reassure the parents that all would be well.

Chances of the *Broomielaw* leaving the reef intact were now close to nil. The sounding rod had shown no deep water on either side of the stricken clipper. At this terrible juncture, when it was clear that his first command was almost over, his first ship about to disintegrate beneath him, Jack Zurich remembered Ritchie, a man driven to madness, a man who had simply given up on himself and the people who looked to him for salvation, who trusted him. He resolved at that moment to avoid the emptiness he had seen in Ritchie's eyes as the older man stepped on to the ice. The memory seemed to galvanise Zurich.

'Free the lifeboats – women and children to the port side. Abandon ship!'

The dread order given, his log and official documents retrieved from his cabin, Jack looked like a man with a burden lifted from his shoulders and he set about the task of saving his passengers as if it was the role he had been destined to play all his life.

It was at this moment that he noticed Innes Macaulay standing near the port rail, clinging to the rigging, up to his waste in sloshing water, struggling to keep his balance and staring out over the dark surf…and pointing, out into the night. Moments before he had seen something out there which made his flesh shiver; a familiar image, suddenly and hauntingly given shape and form.

Two bolts of lightning, crossing each other close by in their transit across the night, lit up the wild hellish scene for the briefest moment. Innes Macaulay gasped again, slipped and staggered back as if someone had switched on a lamp in a deep, dark cavern. Walter, Jack and many others saw it too. There, no more than forty yards to port from where the *Broomielaw* had locked into the rock shelves, sharply outlined in the electric blue light, stood a huge sentinel of stone, a dark weather-scarred column, a monolith reaching up into the darkness. Possibly fifty or sixty feet of the rock tower was visible and it seemed crooked at the summit – like a finger beckoning.

Macaulay waded through the swirling waters and dragged himself a few steps up the companionway to the quarterdeck from where Jack, having called Queenie to his side, was overseeing the clearance of the ship.

'Did you see it, did you see it, Zurich! The rock finger – that's the way to safety. I know it. Take my word on it!

'It's your rock or the bottom of the sea, Innes. No choice at all. Let's get on with it.'

Below on the decks the pumps had been abandoned and the crew worked to release the port lifeboats into the swell, working amid a tangle of lines, blocks and assorted flotsam, while the passengers still crowded the high side of the sloping main deck, drenched every so often by breaking seas. The *Broomielaw* groaned and squealed as her timbers were pulled this way and that. Death was checking in on the night watch.

103 The Fickle Finger

Jack Zurich peered through the gloom at the throng of emigrants and homed in on his target huddled together with Hamish, Conchita and the surviving members of the Circus Caledonia at the foot of the aft mast. Leaning across the rail he yelled over the clamour: Mr Eales, up here, if you please.'

Once the situation had been explained the thin man looked briefly out into the night then threw off his jacket and slipped, without another word or a moment's hesitation, into the black water. Eales had secured a rope around his waist and struck out, rising and falling on the swell with a stylish, easy stroke, just as if he had gone for a summer afternoon's swim. He was heading for the base of the rock pinnacle but soon he was swallowed by the cruel darkness.

Word got round the deck of what was afoot and all eyes came to rest on the spot where the human eel had vanished into the night. Again lightning cast the briefest illumination across the scene but it was enough for the company to see Eales scrambling across the boulders at the foot of the rock, trailing the rope behind him. A cheer rose from the throats of the crowd.

Seconds later the rope, which had been lashed to a capstan at the shipboard end, dragged taught.

'It's secure,' came the order from the skipper, 'now get the women and children into that bloody boat.'

One by one the females and kiddies, some whimpering, other displaying remarkable stoicism, were carried, led, slid or stumbled down the sloping deck and were hauled, manhandled and lifted through the surf and into the yawl. Able-bodied men were still needed on the *Broomielaw* yet and there were frantic scenes of parting. It rained, mercilessly.

A group of young men, perhaps a dozen, ignoring the shouted orders to assist with the evacuation to the rock, half ran and half flew down the deck before pushing off a second boat. Almost immediately, only yards from the *Broomielaw* and without the precious lifeline the boat was overwhelmed and capsized, spilling the occupants into the water. When the seas relented a little only three or four men could be seen clinging to the upturned boat. After the next heavy sea, they too were gone.

Walter Lumsden, on the nod from the skipper, nominated three more crewmen to join the four already in the lifeboat either receiving passengers or clinging desperately to the rope, their last hope of salvation. The first emigrants, crammed in the bow of the lifeboat had watched, mouths open, eyes wide with dismay, as the young men drowned almost within touching distance.

Short minutes later there were perhaps forty people in the boat. Walter Lumsden looked round and quickly calculated that it would require six journeys, perhaps seven, to get everyone clear.

Surely the *Broomielaw* would never survive such a pounding for the time necessary to conduct an evacuation.

Then he remembered with pride that she was built in a Scottish shipyard, in Aberdeen. Of course, she'll stay afloat he tried to reassure himself.

Stepping back Jack Zurich waved the boat away: 'Now pull lads! Pull like you've never pulled before, like the devil's at your stern.'

Buffeted and battered by the storm the lifeboat edged slowly away from the half-sunken port side of the ship. Standing upright in the rocking boat, hand over hand, with a co-ordination that defied the drastic circumstances, muscles straining, salt water running down their faces and hair plastered over their brows, the sailors pulled the lifeboat slowly out into the night. They passed over the submerged bulwark and into the teeth of the storm, towards the doubtful sanctuary of the rock finger.

Jack's voice rang out again over the waves in their wake: 'And whatever happens, for God's sake don't lose hold of that rope.'

The short haul to the rock, the unloading of the first emigrants and the return leg was completed in remarkably few minutes. The second boatload with a fresh crew of haulers set off. There were a few less folk on board this time but it was stacked with provisions, fresh water and tools.

Turnaround this time took fully fifteen minutes. And so the evacuation continued slowly, painfully slowly. Mercifully, the downpour had stopped but there was so much water flying about that the change was scarcely noticeable.

When it came to Maggie and Belle's turn to lead their families to the lifeboat, Maggie hesitated. Behind her Walter was carrying baby James and the girls were carefully leading the way down the sloping deck.

Torrance Macaulay had his mother's hand and Guthrie and Hugh were among those nominated to hauling on this trip. But Maggie stopped in her tracks.

'No, I'll just wait with you, with James and the girls here on the *Broomielaw*, Walter. We'll go together on the last boat. Get the Sinclairs instead'. Maggie made to move up the deck gesturing to the Sinclair family to take their place. 'Look, Walter, Queenie is staying behind. She's waiting for Jack.'

It was true enough. Queenie was clearly determined to stick by the skipper to the last and while he supervised the exodus she had been helping the less able into the boat, her hair plastered around her face by the drenching sea water, her hood thrown back. As he looked at Queenie Walter no longer saw the lost little girl who had emerged from the for'ard hold as a stowaway but a woman determined to begin steering her own course through life.

Through the water which ran down his face and into his eyes Walter confronted Maggie, this stubborn, self-opinionated, beautiful woman. Yes, he'd hoped she would stay. He wanted this woman and her children to remain at his side. He could hardly bear to be alone again. But at the same time he was achingly aware that they should be off the ship now. The *Broomielaw* was beginning to twist ominously on her rock anchor and could split asunder without warning.

Just as he had done on the Hunter River he was in danger of being persuaded by someone he loved to act against his instincts and against his better judgement. He wanted them to stay, desperately. But he would not make the same mistake twice.

'You're going on this run, Margaret. There's no argument. The Sinclairs are happy enough, they say, to wait on the last boat. And as for Queenie, she knows her own mind well enough.'

He moved forward through the knee high water and lifted the baby into the safe arms of Guthrie Macaulay.

'You watch out for that wee man, Guthrie.'

'I will, Mr Lumsden, I will.'

Turning to Maggie he was imperious. 'Now get in that boat, woman, before I throw you in. We'll see you on the shore. We should be there in twenty minutes at most. Two more journeys after this should do it.'

For just a moment Maggie looked surprised and then leaned forward and kissed Lumsden gently on the cheek. This man would do, she told herself.

Old Agnes Govan was cursing as she struggled with her heavy carpet bag. One of the sailors helping to load the boat took the burden from her when she reached the front of the bedraggled queue and threw it back to the foot of the mainmast.

'You'll have a better chance of making it without that bag, auld yin.'

'Less o' the 'auld yin' ya big galoot. That bag has my man's medals in it – and my knitting. As she spoke her bag was being rescued and handed over to her in the bow of the lifeboat. The little sailmaker Jontot smiled at her.

'Perhaps, Madame, you would look after my sailmaker's needles. They are also very precious to me.' He handed her a grubby leather satchel and stepped back.

Agnes was speechless, and astonished to find herself smiling back.

The Macaulays and the Gilchrists then climbed aboard and settled in the waist of the boat. Everyone that could do so set to baling with buckets, tin mugs, some even with cupped hands. Then off they went, dragging themselves into the darkness and, they prayed, to safety.

Forty minutes later as the second last crossing with the few remaining emigrants was set to go, the situation had become critical. The ship, having taken such an incessant pounding, was clearly breaking up around them. No vessel, even this splendid, solid clipper could withstanding the battering she had taken over the past three hours.

The deck of the *Broomielaw* was now at almost forty-five degrees. People stepped and slid their way down to the side of the lifeboat and were hauled aboard. Silas Ratter under escort, the Sinclair family, Wallace the cook, Jontot, the apprentices, looking like a family of bedraggled rats – were among those that made that fateful descent.

At the last moment, from the port companionway, Shade appeared. Like a bedraggled rat he scurried down the deck and was dragged into boat. He sat in the stern of the lifeboat, head in his hands and those around heard him groan: 'Under water, the aft sail locker. Completely submerged. God, after all that effort…'

104 Beneath the Rock

The remainder of the *Broomielaw's* complement, Lumsden with Jack Zurich at his side, Jack's officers and the more experienced hands, eighteen people in total had gathered at the starboard companionway. Theirs would be the final journey. Jack supported Queenie who for a moment almost lost her footing on the sea-spray drenched and crazily-leaning stairway.

'I think you should get on this boat, Queenie.'

'I've taken all of my nineteen years to find you Jack Zurich and if you think I'm sailing off into the night without you, then you're plain daft. I've booked a place on the last boat, didn't I tell you?' He laughed and hugged her close.

'I could just pick you up and throw you in the boat...'

'Just you try.'

Scarcely had the last of the emigrants been installed when a huge crested wave crashed in along the main deck effortlessly tipping the lifeboat with its precious cargo end over end catapulting it forward into the wooden walls of the *Broomielaw*. The little boat was smashed to pieces. And for a moment the water was filled with screams and struggling bodies. Two more tumbling walls of water broke in quick succession over the side of the ship and when the sea settled for a moment, two or three terrified, pleading faces could still be seen above the surface. Then the maelstrom resumed its deadly work.

Jack and his group watched helplessly, miserably, as the last occupants of the ill-fated lifeboat were swept from view by the boiling sea, amid the tangle of wood, sail and lines which clogged the water in the lee of the ship. Almost at the same moment, the *Broomielaw* rolled again in her final agony, or so it seemed, coming to rest this time with her deck only a few degrees off the vertical, her masts now almost level with the water, pointing towards Innes's rock and the shore. Those on the companionway were pitched forward, some crashing appallingly, sickeningly, into the superstructure as they fell, others dropping into the temporarily calm pool in the lee of the overturning vessel.

The *Broomielaw* groaned anew, slumped deeper into the frothing mass and threatened to topple over completely on the little group floundering in the surf.

As she floated Queenie suffered a smack to the side of her head from a piece of broken timber. She scarcely noticed it. Suddenly she felt tired, so tired, weighed down by her heavy clothes. She slipped easily below the surface. Only a second before there had been noise all around, occasional screams, the frenzy of the water as it rose and fell, the grinding of wood on rock, the snapping of spars and the distant, despairing shouts of encouragement from the folk on the shingle below the rock pinnacle. It seemed as if the voices had being coming from a million miles away.

But, mused Queenie, it was silent and peaceful down here. Queenie was back on the sands of the South Wick with her brothers. She could feel the warm sand between her toes and hear the seals calling across the bay. This was easier.

After what seemed a lifetime her mouth filled with water as she tried to scream. Someone was dragging her, painfully, by the hair, back to the world.

Unceremoniously Jack draped Queenie, coughing and spluttering but clearly very much alive, across a small hatch cover, and pushing his cargo before him he kicked out in the direction of the rock, aware all the time of the unstable mass of his ship which hung over him.

A few yards away Walter Lumsden had taken possession of a cabin ladder and likewise pressed forward. He looked across at his henchman: 'Stay close, Jack, we're no' deed yet, not by a long way.'

'Aye Walter, follow the line of the mainmast. That's our route to safety…'

The next wave carried them away from the wreck and towards the shingle shore.

105 Journey's End?

Far to the east, where clouds stretched lazily along the edge of the earth, first daylight caressed the sky with a vivid indigo hue and the stars faded as they gave chase to the night. With sunken, tired eyes those among the emigrants who had not yet found merciful sleep gazed bleary-eyed at their first Australian dawn.

Light spilled along the shore as if already searching for survivors among the tussocky sandhills and driftwood logs. The pinnacle rock with its natural causeway to the shore which had been the salvation for so many from the *Broomielaw* during the long, dark night, cast a narrow, crooked shadowy finger along the sand. The sun was rising quickly now, desperate to be on with its work.

Among the huddled, exhausted groups of emigrants in their sand burrows and makeshift tents at the top of the shore, a few began to stir and slowly take in their surroundings. A child cried. The screams and wailing which had followed the wreck and had filled the awful night had been replaced by occasional sobbing across the makeshift encampment.

With careful, measured tread, hardly disturbing the sand amongst the sleeping emigrants, walked the master of the *Broomielaw*. Jack stopped for a moment beside two little tots who had wakened and were busy building sand castles beside their mother. She lay in her plaid, eyes wide, as if in a drug-induced stupor. In her arms an infant slept soundly.

Let the child sleep a while longer, Jack thought to himself as move on. Time enough to face all of this.

Nearby a young man was trying to start a driftwood fire, working with flint, twigs and beach grass. He looked up and smiled in a half-hearted way at Jack Zurich.

At the enormous tree stump, bleached as white as old bone by the sun, where the Gilchrist and Macaulay families had found shelter Jack crouched down beside the emigration agent who had also finished his count. Walter sat, legs pulled up, his chin resting on his knees. His fingers were sewn into his thinning, yellow hair and he rocked gently. Sensing Jack's arrival he glanced up.

This is too much to bear, Jack. First my family, and now I lose so many people who pinned their hopes on me.'

The skipper considered offering some words of reassurance but knew that at this moment anything said would inevitably seem like echoing, empty platitudes. Besides, he had plenty to think about himself. He had seized command in mid-ocean, a drastic action at any time and now his ship had gone down. His own future looked endlessly bleak.

A family across the way stirred in the sand. A little girl with rosy cheeks and a head of curly hair and wrapped in a plaid came tip-toeing towards them in her bare feet. She stood directly in front of Walter, her oval blue eyes bright in the morning sun. She was no more than ten. 'Thank you, Mr Lumsden, thank you for bringing us safely to Australia.'

Walter took the little girl's hands and squeezed them gently. He remembered her name. She was one of the Stoddarts from Argyll, Lochgilphead he seemed to remember. The emigration agent looked across at the other members of the family who were, in turn, smiling.

'Thank you, Phoebe. That means much more to me than you'll ever know.' The girl skipped of to rejoin her parents.

Jack shook him gently by the shoulder and spoke solemnly. 'Well, Walter, what do you make it? I've got 216.'

'Well, I have 214 but, of course, I hadn't counted ourselves.'

'One hundred and eight lost, according to my reckoning, including some of the poor souls we took from the *Spirit of Speed.*'

'Without you, Jack, it might have been all of us.'

'Maybe so, but again we owe a great debt to Eales, a debt I fear we can never repay.' Hours after the event Jack could still not fathom the raw valour of the thin man who had swum off into the gloom to give so many of them an umbilical cord to the future.

They turned their gaze to the water margin where a dozen young men and boys, organised just minutes earlier and supervised by Eales himself, were already wading into the surf, carefully lifting bodies from amongst the debris and carrying them, ever so gently, up the sand to the privacy of the dusty hillocks which fringed the beach.

Already the queer brothers Silas and Peter Ratter lay side by side among the rough grass. Jack noted that in his drowning Peter Ratter, alias Elijah Shade, had acquired some severe head injuries. Hardly surprising, and yet... Close by the body of Jontot the sailmaker lay among around two score or more victims of the wreck.

Walter had hand-picked and woken the young men early. It was work, excruciatingly painful work, best done before the rest of the survivors rubbed the exhaustion from their eyes. It also meant there would be a degree of privacy for those claiming their dead. No-one had survived, it seemed, from either of the upturned lifeboats, only eight from the group which had been thrown into the ocean from the companionway when the *Broomielaw* tumbled. There would be burials to look to soon.

The Macaulay boys passed carrying the bedraggled remains of an elderly man, still loose-limbed, like an unkempt rag doll. Walter nodded to the boys gravely as they moved up the beach.

Curled up like a puppy at the end of the tree trunk Queenie Stout was restless in her sleep, her face creasing occasionally in a painful expression as if she was reliving the terrible night just past. Next to her Agnes Govan was quietly and carefully polishing one of Jontot's sailmaking needles. News of the discovery of his body had been passed to her moments before.

Perched on the log above her was *Erebus*, the sailmaker's monkey who had found his way ashore on a section of decking. Agnes stretched her hand towards him and the monkey examined her fingers, one by one.

The rest of the Macaulay and Gilchrist families sheltering in the lee of the log were gradually waking to what was sure to be a testing morning.

The ocean now wore a tranquil deceitful face, long-necked birds cruised along the tideline, surf slapped gently along the sloping beach. All this provoked a quiet fury in Walter's heart. How could the sea be such a merciless killer one moment and then a harmless, beautiful mill pond the next? The lightest of breezes, a merest zephyr, ruffled the canvas shelters which had been erected where only a few hours previously a howling banshee of a wind had mocked their efforts to save themselves.

Out beyond the rock tower, port side under water, lay the *Broomielaw,* her main and fore masts snapped and what was left of her rigging rising with the gentle swell. She seemed to have split amidships and stern section had collapsed completely. Yet the ship remained firmly fixed to the reef which had claimed her.

All sorts of debris was bobbing around in the surf. A scuffle of sand and Hamish trotted past them, followed into the surf by three of the Circus Caledonia midgets. They had spotted a wooden crate in the shallows – a long, wooden crate about the size of a coffin – near the rock causeway. Other crates had been dragged part way up the beach. A few yards from Walter and Jack stood a packing case on which had been stencilled: 'Gilchrist, Motherwell Mains, Otago – Wanted on Voyage.'

The immediate priority Walter knew was to find a suitable supply of fresh water and shelter. The lights they had seen could have been no more than ten or twenty miles west at most. But it threatened to be a day of fierce heat. The few clouds that had been there at dawn were evaporating rapidly and already the sand beneath their feet was warming.

The two men talked for a time about putting reconnaissance parties out along the shore towards Albany but their planning stopped abruptly as Jack pointed to a solitary dark figure, dressed only in a tan loincloth and carrying a tall spear. He had taken up station on the sand hillock immediately above their improvised encampment.

'A fisherman, perhaps,' said Jack, 'we're probably sprawled across his tribal territory.'

However, seeing the spear, he reached instinctively for the musket which stood against the meagre stack of water barrels, crates of food and medical supplies. With a shake of his head immediately replaced the weapon. What was he thinking? What foolishness on his part.

The man stood – spear resting vertically beside him – peering from beneath thick, dark eyebrows at the huddled victims of the shipwreck. His enigmatic expression betrayed nothing of what he was thinking. Shielding his eyes against the sun and gazing out over the sparkling surf towards the shattered remains of the clipper.

'He looks friendly enough – and if anyone along this God-forsaken strip of sand knows where we can get food, water and shelter, it'll be him. Walter Lumsden got stiffly to his feet. 'I'm going up there.' At that precise moment as the sun dazzlingly illuminated the clouds on the eastern horizon like the sails on some fiery galleon, Hamish Mhor McGrimmen arrived. He was soaking from head to toe and was gasping for breath. But his eyes were sparkling.

He blurted out: 'Mr Zurich, Jack – it must have been the bump…on the rocks down there, as the crate ran ashore, that's what did it. It must have been that.'

'Take your time for God's sake, Hamish. What about the crate?'

'Look, no wonder old Nappy was so short of breath.'

He opened his hand to reveal a leather pouch. He poured some of the contents on to his palm. Diamond and sapphire rings, a beautiful necklace, ear-rings. 'Jewels, a fortune in jewels.'

'Someone had stuffed this pouch down his gullet; is it any wonder we couldn't get the throat mechanism to work. But he's breathing now, Jack! Napoleon's breathing!'

Walter Lumsden was already striding up the slope of the dune towards the aborigine framed on the slope above him. He could see that the man wore a thin animal bone which had been threaded through his nose.

However, the emigration agent moved forward with a new-found confidence and belief. Little Phoebe's words of thanks still rang in his ears.

From out of a group of mothers Maggie came stumbling across the sand after him. 'Wait on me, Walter. Wait on me'. She slipped her hand into his and together they went forward – together – to meet Australia.

Cast of Migrants and Mariners

Aaron Malise: *A former shipmate of James Gilchrist's brother; a scarred individual, physically and mentally - and a man with black vengeance in his heart.*

The Gilchrists: *Border shepherd family bound for South Australia – James, Maggie, their three girls – May, Flora and Hilda - and James's elderly aunt, Agnes Govan.*

Robert Gilchrist: *Brother of James he had sailed for Australia five years previously on the Arran Dubh but never reached his destination.*

The Macaulays: *Family from a Lanarkshire mining village emigrating following a pit disaster, Belle, Innes and their three boys, Hugh, Guthrie and Torrance.*

Tam Swift: *A neighbour of the Macaulays who worked the same shift as Innes Macaulay at the Fraser Castle pit on the day of the disaster.*

Walter Lumsden: *Emigration agent for the Clutha Company; the man charged with seeing the emigrants safely to Australia and New Zealand*

The Sinclairs: *A middle-aged couple from Dunbar with their servant girl Jessie; heading for Adelaide where the husband is to manage a bank.*

Napoleon Bonaparte: *Circus Caledonia's remarkable automaton, a mechanical representation of the French Emperor which had caused a sensation across Europe.*

Hamish Mhor McGrimmen: *A huge, muscle-bound Highlander; the Circus Caledonia's strongman; his stage name – The Lochaber Ox.*

Conchita Rodrigues: *Also a member of the Circus Caledonia; three-feet tall, her Spanish dances were famed throughout the United Kingdom.*

Charlie Eales: Perhaps the oddest character in the Circus Caledonia contingent who found berths of the Spirit of Speed; Half-fish-Half-man, the posters described him.

Elijah Shade: The mysterious and somewhat sinister preacher/medical officer on board the Broomielaw; an individual with more secrets than most.

John Connelly: A crewman from the voyage of the Arran Dubh in 1852 and a target for the vengeance of the scarred sailor Aaron Malise (see above).

William Bigland: third son of the Laird of Doomy in Orkney; following a sexual indiscretion he has been 'sent' to Australia to work as a clerk in his uncle's business.

Queenie Stout: An attractive and clear-minded serving lass from the Hall of Doomy in Orkney, who was discovered in a compromising position with William Bigland.

Dougal McKinstrie: Yet another crewman from the Arran Dubh on the voyage in 1852 who was involved in the death of Robert Gilchrist.

Ezra Mooney: A crewman from the Broomielaw whose part-time speciality was arranging to hide stowaways amongst the mountains of freight on the Australia run.

Louis Cartwright: The third member of the crew of the Arran Dubh targeted by Aaron Malise for retribution.

Jack Zurich: A formidable young seaman, first mate on the Broomielaw, who knew the Australia run better than many seafarers twice his age.

Silas Ratter: Skipper of the Broomielaw; a veteran of the emigration voyages to the Antipodes but nearing the end of his career; over-fond of strong drink.

Leon Jontot: A French sailmaker who had made Clydeside his home and found employment on the Broomielaw - a meek and mild individual with a mischievous pet.

'Beetles': *A little boy from a Lanarkshire family, the first fatality on the Broomielaw's voyage, who died of a choking fit in mid-Atlantic.*

Ann Broadfoot: *Died from measles within a few hours of the first fatality*

Matthew Broadfoot: *Father of the measles victim Ann, a former burgess of the town of Lanark.*

'Spike" Wallace: *Cook on the Broomielaw, a tall, affable negro from out of Baltimore, Maryland*

Erebus: *The sailmaker Jontot's pet monkey, noted for his mischievous behaviour and his big sad eyes.*

Eamon Tully: *The captain's steward who was also responsible for looking after the cabin passengers; a survivor, so it was said, of three shipwrecks.*

'Chippy' Carlsen: *The ship's carpenter, a tall Dane, who had the appearance of a Viking warrior and a tool kit to match.*

David Macgregor: *Second mate on the Broomielaw; a man who had travelled far and wide in an adventurous life and was known along the Clyde as a master helmsman.*

Tommy Dungannon and 'Nipper' Jarvis: *Two of the shipboard apprentices, young men still in their teens who undertook a huge variety of jobs during the voyage.*

Jimmy Ducks: *A cockney crewman and a match for the second mate Macgregor with his strength and skill at the helm.*

Evan Richards: *Crewman from Cardiff lost overboard during the first major Atlantic storm when he fell from the mainmast into the ocean and implicated in the death of Robert Gilchrist.*

George Macdonald: *A teenage seaman from Gourock who died in the same accident in the rigging as Richards.*

Matt 'Barbarian' Bostock: *A Belfast lad and former booth boxer and up among the sails, one of the fittest and most agile of the Broomielaw's crew.*

Elizabeth McMichael: *A sickly young servant girl travelling to Australia to begin a new life in domestic service.*

Donald McMaster: *Skipper of the Helenslee which caught up with the Broomielaw at the lonely outpost of Tristan da Cunha in the South Atlantic.*

Alec Ritchie: *The confident, experienced skipper of the Spirit of Speed who expected to leave the Broomielaw in his wake in the race for South Australia.*

Sam Welsh: *Mate of the Spirit of Speed*

Erchie Bowers: *A drummer and one of the leaders of the Coocaddens Gutter Band whose members kept the emigrants spirits up during the voyage*

Previous Publications by Jim Hewitson

Tam Blake & Co – The Story of the Scots in America (Canongate – 1993 and OTCEditions)

Scotching the Myths – An Alternative Route Map to Scottish History (Mainstream – 1995)

Jim Hewitson's Scottish Miscellany (Black & White Publishing – 2003)

Far Off in Sunlit Places – Stories of the Scots in Australia & New Zealand
(Canongate – 1998 and OTC Editions)

Does Anyone Like Midges? (Black and White Publishing – 2006)

Island at the Rainbow's End (Mainstream 2005 – previously 'Clinging to the Edge' – Journals from an Orkney Island', (Mainstream 1996)

Astonishing Scotland – A Cheeky Thesaurus of Scottishness (Black and White Publishing – 2003)

The Scots at Sea (BBC and St Andrew Press – 2005)

Dead Weird – Scottish Attitudes to Death (Black and White Publishing – 2004)

Skull & Saltire – Stories of Scottish Piracy (Black and White Publishing - 2005)

Boulders at Hirti Geo – a 40-year Retrospective (self-published – 2007)

Down in the Glen Something Stirs – A Novel of the Scottish Independence Referendum (OTCEditions – 2014)